Also by Tony Parsons

Man and Boy
Man and Wife

one
for
my baby

one

for

my baby

A Novel

tony parsons

ATRIA BOOKS
New York London Toronto Sydney

ATRIA BOOKS
1230 Avenue of the Americas
New York, NY 10020

Originally published in Great Britain in 2001 by HarperCollins UK

ISBN: 0-7434-5664-5

First Atria Books hardcover edition March 2004

10 9 8 7 6 5 4 3 2 1

ATRIA BOOKS is a trademark of Simon & Schuster, Inc.

For information regarding special discounts for bulk purchases,
please contact Simon & Schuster Special Sales at 1-800-456-6798
or business@simonandschuster.com

Manufactured in the United States of America

For my son

Part One

I LIKE YOU, YOU'RE NICE

EAT THE COLD PORRIDGE

"You must eat the cold porridge," *he told me once.*

It's a Chinese expression. Cantonese, I guess, because although he carried an old-fashioned blue British passport and was happy to call himself an Englishman, he was born in Hong Kong and sometimes you could tell that all the important things he believed were formed long ago and far away. Like the importance of eating the cold porridge.

I stopped what I was doing and stared at him. What was he going on about now?

"Eat the cold porridge."

The way he explained it, eating the cold porridge means working at something for so long that when you get home there is nothing left to eat but cold porridge.

And I thought—who did he share a flat with out there? Goldilocks and the Three Bears?

That's how you get good at something, he told me. That's how you get good at anything. You eat the cold porridge.

You work at it when the others are playing. You work at it when the others are watching television. You work at it when the others are sleeping.

To become the master of something, you must eat the cold porridge, Grasshopper.

Actually he never called me Grasshopper.

But I always felt that he might.

And I tried hard to understand. He was my teacher as well as my friend and I always tried to be a good student. I am trying today. But I can't help it—somewhere along the line I took eating the cold porridge to mean something else. Something completely different from its Chinese meaning.

Somehow I got it into my thick head that eating the cold porridge means being in a time of suffering. Living through hard days, months and years because you have no choice.

I got the cold porridge of the East muddled up with the bitter pill of the West. Now I can't tell them apart.

That's not what he meant at all. He meant giving up comfort and pleasure for a greater good. He meant deferring gratification for some distant goal.

Eating cold porridge now so that you will have something better tomorrow. Or the day after tomorrow. Or the day after that. It's got nothing to do with Goldilocks and the Three Bears.

But I guess the concept of self-sacrifice is easier to grasp if you were born in one of the poorer parts of Kowloon. Where I come from, they don't really go in for that kind of stuff.

Eating the cold porridge—to me it means enduring something that has to be endured. More than that, it means missing someone. Really missing someone.

The way I miss her.

But she is gone and she is not coming back.

I know that now.

I will never kiss her again. I am never going to wake up beside her again. I am never going to watch her sleeping again.

That perfect moment when she opened her eyes and smiled her slightly goofy smile—a smile that seemed to reveal as much gum as teeth, and a smile that always made me feel as though something inside me was melting—I definitely won't see that again. There are ten thousand things that we are never going to do together again.

"You'll meet someone else," he tells me, with all the patience that my real father could never quite muster. "Give it time. There will be another woman. You'll get married again. You can have it all. Children and everything."

He is trying to be kind. He is a good man. Maybe this is what he really thinks.

But I don't believe a word of it.

I think that you can use up your love. I think you can blow it all on one person. You can love so much, so deeply, that there is nothing left for anyone else.

You could give it all the time in the world, and I would never find someone to fill the gap that she has left.

Because how do you find a substitute for the love of your life?

And why would you want to?

Rose is never coming home again.

Not to me.

Not to anyone.

And perhaps I could learn to live with it if I could resist this ridiculous urge to phone her. Things would be more bearable if I could remember, really remember, that she's gone and never forget it.

But I can't help it.

Once a day I go to call her. I have never actually dialed the number, but I have come pretty close. Do you think I need to look that number up? I don't even have to remember it with my head. My fingers remember.

And I am afraid that one day I will call her old number and somebody else will answer. Some stranger. Then what will happen? Then what will I do?

It can strike at any time, this urge to call her. If I'm happy or sad or worried, I suddenly get this need to talk to her about it. The way we always did when we were—I nearly said lovers, but it was that and much more.

Together. When we were together.

She's gone and I know she's gone.
It's just that sometimes I forget.
That's all.
So now I know what I must do.
I must eat the cold porridge, and fight this overwhelming urge to reach for the phone.

1

THERE'S SOMETHING WRONG WITH MY HEART.

It shouldn't be working like this. It should be doing something else. Something normal. More like everybody else's heart.

I don't understand it. I have only been running in the park for ten minutes and my brand-new sneakers have luminous swoosh signs on the side. But already my leg muscles are burning, my breath is coming in these wheezing little gasps and my heart—don't get me started on my heart. My heart is filling my chest like some giant undigested kebab.

My heart is stabbing me in the back.

My heart is ready to attack me.

It's Sunday morning, a big blue day in September, and the park is almost empty. Almost, but not quite.

In the patch of grass where they don't allow ball games, there is an old Chinese man with close-cropped silver hair and skin the color of burnished gold. He has to be around my dad's age, pushing sixty, but he seems fit and strangely youthful.

He's wearing a baggy black outfit that makes him look like he is still in his pajamas and he's very slowly moving his arms and legs to some silent song inside his head.

I used to see this stuff every day when I was living in Hong Kong. The old people in the park, doing their Tai Chi, moving like they had all the time in the world.

The old boy doesn't look at me as I huff and puff my way toward him. He just stares straight ahead, lost in his slow-motion dance. I feel a sudden jolt of recognition. I have seen that face before. Not his face, but ten thousand faces just like it.

When I lived in Hong Kong I saw that face working on the Star Ferry, saw it driving a cab in Kowloon, saw it looking forlorn at the Happy Valley racecourse. And I saw that face supervising some Bambi-eyed grandchild as she did her homework in the back of a little shop, saw it slurping noodles at a *daipaidong* food stall, saw it covered in dust, building spanking new skyscrapers on scraps of reclaimed land.

That face is very familiar to me. It's impassive, self-contained and completely indifferent to my existence. That face stares straight through me. That face doesn't care if I live or die.

I saw it all the time over there.

It used to drive me nuts.

As I struggle past the old boy, he catches my eye. Then he says something. One word. I don't know. It sounds like *Breed*.

And I get a pang of sadness as I think to myself—not much chance of that, pal.

I'm the last of the line.

Hong Kong made us feel special.

We looked down on the glittering heart of Central and we felt like the heirs to something epic and heroic and grand.

We stared at all those lights, all that money, all those people living in a little outpost of Britain set in the South China Sea, and we felt special in a way that we had never felt special in London and Liverpool and Edinburgh.

We had no right to feel special, of course. We hadn't built Hong Kong. Most of us hadn't even arrived until just before it was time to hand it back to the Chinese. But you couldn't help feeling special in that bright shining place.

There were expats who really were a bit special, hotshots in lightweight Armani suits working in Central who would one day go home covered in glory with a seven-figure bank balance. But I wasn't one of them. Nowhere near it.

I was teaching English at the Double Fortune Language School to rich, glossy Chinese ladies who wanted to be able to talk to round-eye waiters in their native tongue. *Waiter, there's a fly in my shark's fin soup. This is outrageous. These noodles are cold. Where is the manager? Do you take American Express?* We conjugated a lot of service-related verbs because by 1996, the year I arrived in Hong Kong, there were a lot of white boys waiting on tables.

I was a little different from my colleagues. It seemed like all the other teachers at the Double Fortune Language School—our motto: "English without tears in just two years"—had a reason to be in Hong Kong, a reason other than that special feeling.

There was a woman from Brighton who was a practicing Buddhist. There was a quiet young guy from Wilmslow who spent every spare moment studying Wing Chun Kung Fu. And there was a BBC—British-born Chinese—who wanted to see where his face came from before he settled down into the family business on Gerrard Street in London's Chinatown.

They all had a good reason to be there. So did the expats in the banks and the law firms of Central. So did the other kind of expats who were out on Lantau, building the new airport.

Everyone had a reason to be there. Except me.

I was in Hong Kong because I'd had my fill of London. I had taught English literature at an inner-city school for five years. It was pretty rough. You might even have heard of us. Does the Princess Diana Comprehensive School for Boys ring any bells? No? It was the one in north London where the woodwork teacher had his head put in his own vice. It was in all the papers.

If anything, the parents were more frightening than the children. Open evenings at the Princess Diana would find me confronted by all these burly bruisers with scowling faces and livid tattoos.

And that was just the mothers.

I was sick of it. Sick and tired. Sick of marking essays that began, "Some might say Mercutio was a bit of an asshole." Tired of teaching *Romeo and Juliet* to kids who laughed when one of the Shakespeareans at the back inflated a condom while we were doing the balcony scene. Sick and tired of trying to explain the glory and wonder of the English language to children who poured "fuck," "fucking" and "fucked" over their words like ketchup in a burger bar.

Then I heard that a Brit could still go to Hong Kong and automatically get a work permit for a year. But not for much longer.

It was around the time that one of my pupils' parents—one of the dads, funny enough, a man who was permanently dressed for the beach, even in the middle of winter—had a Great Britain tattoo on his arm *and it was spelled wrong*.

"Great Briten," it said, just below the image of a rabid bulldog wearing a Union Jack T-shirt that was either cut a bit snug or a few sizes too small.

Great Briten.

Sweet Jesus.

So I got out. Deciding to really do it was the hard part. After that, it was easy. After twelve hours, four movies, three meals and two bouts of cramp in the back row of a 747, I landed at Hong Kong's old Kai Tak Airport, the one where they came in for a heart-pumping landing between the forest of skyscrapers, close enough to see the washing lines drying on every balcony. And I stayed on because Hong Kong gave me that feeling—that special feeling.

It was a long way from "Great Briten." It was another world, when what I wanted most in my life was exactly that. Yet it was another world that made me love my country in a way that I never had before.

Hong Kong made me feel as though my country had once done something important and unique. Something magical and brave. And when I looked at all those lights, they made me feel as though there was just a little bit of all that in me.

But I didn't have a real reason to be there, not like the BBC guy who was looking for his roots and not like the people who were there because of Buddha or Bruce Lee.

Then I met Rose.

And she became my reason.

The old Chinese man is not the only sign of life. On the far side of the park there are some Saturday-night stragglers, a bunch of bleary teenagers who still haven't gone home.

The members of this little gang are every shade of the human rainbow, and although I am very much in favor of the multicultural society, something about the way these lads are casually spitting on the pigeons does not make you feel overly optimistic about mankind's ability to live in peace.

When they clock me struggling their way, they exchange knowing grins and I think: what are they laughing at?

I immediately know the answer.

They are laughing at a red-faced, panting, fat guy in brand-new running gear who clearly had nowhere to go on Saturday night and no one to go there with. Someone who gets a lot of early nights. Someone who is not special at all.

Or am I being too hard on myself?

"Check the cheddar," one of them says.

Check the cheddar? What does that mean? Does that mean me? Check the cheddar? Is that new?

"He so fat that he look like two bitches fighting under a blanket, innit?"

"He so fat he gets his passport photo taken by, you know, like, *satellite.*"

"He so fat he get fan letters from Captain Ahab."

As a former English teacher, I am impressed by this casual reference to *Moby-Dick*. These are not bad kids. Although they are roaring with laughter at me, I give them what I hope is a friendly smile. Showing them that the cheddar is a good sport and knows how to take a joke. But they just smirk at each other and then at me. Smirk, smirk, smirk, they go, radiating equal measures of youth and stupidity.

I look away quickly and when I am past them I remember that there's a Snickers bar in the pocket of my tracksuit in case of an emergency. Watched by a tatty gray squirrel, I eat my Snickers bar on a wet park bench.

Then for a long time I just sit twisting my wedding ring around the third finger of my left hand, feeling lonelier than ever.

I met her on the Star Ferry, the old green-and-white, double-decker boats that shuttle between Kowloon on the tip of the Chinese peninsula and Hong Kong Island.

Well, that's not strictly true—I didn't really meet her on the Star Ferry. We didn't exchange names or numbers. We made no plans to meet again. I was never much of a pick-up artist, and that didn't change with Rose. But the Star Ferry is where I first saw her, struggling through the turnstile with a huge cardboard box in her arms, balancing it on her hip as she stuffed a few coins into the slot.

She joined the throng waiting for the ferry, a Westerner surrounded by every kind of local—the smart young Cantonese businessmen heading to their offices in Central, the chic young office girls with their cell phones and miniskirts and swinging black hair, the shirt-sleeved street traders hawking up phlegm the size of a Hong Kong dollar, young mothers and their beautiful fat-faced babies with startling Elvis forelocks, the tiny old ladies with their gold teeth and scraped-back white hair, Filipina domestics heading for work and even the odd *gweilo* (white ghost) tourist quietly baking in the heat.

Her hair was black, as black as Chinese hair, but her skin was very pale, as though she had just arrived from some land where it never stopped raining. She was dressed in a simple two-piece business suit but the large cardboard box made her look as though she was going to work in one of the little side-street markets above Sheung Wan, west of Central. But I knew that was impossible.

The ramp clanged down and the crowd charged onto the Star Ferry in typical Cantonese style. I watched her wrestling with her cardboard box and noted that her face was round, serious, very young.

Her eyes were too far apart and her mouth was too small. But you would have believed that she was beautiful until she smiled. When she smiled—quick to apologize after smacking some Chinese businessman in the back with her box—the spell was immediately broken. She had this bucktoothed grin that stopped her from being any kind of conventional beauty. Yet something about that gummy smile tugged and pulled at my heart in a way that mere beauty never could. She was better than beautiful.

I found a seat. And seats were going fast. She stood next to me, smiling self-consciously to herself as she clutched her box and the ferry pitched and heaved beneath her, surrounded by the raven-haired crowds.

It is only a seven-minute journey between Kowloon and Hong Kong Island, the shortest sea voyage in the world, one brief kilometer spent weaving between junks, barges, cruise ships, tugs and sampans. But it must feel like a long time when you are carrying a box that is almost as big as you are.

I stood up.

"Excuse me? Do you want a seat?"

She just stared at me. I was really quite thin in those days. Not that I was Brad Pitt or anything, even during my lean period, but I wasn't the Elephant Man either. I wasn't expecting her to faint, with either desire or repulsion. But I expected her to do something. She just kept on staring.

I had assumed that she was British or American. Now I saw,

with that hair and those eyes and those cheekbones, she could conceivably be some kind of Mediterranean.

"You speak English?"

She nodded.

"Do you want to sit down?"

"Thanks," she said. "But it's only a little journey."

"But it's a big box."

"I've carried bigger."

That smile. Slow, though, and a bit reluctant. Who was this strange guy in a Frank Sinatra T-shirt (Frank grinning under a snap-brim fedora in an EMI publicity shot from 1958, one of the golden years) and ragged chinos? Who was this man of mystery? This thin boy who was, on balance, slightly more Brad Pitt than Elephant Man?

Her box was full of files, manila envelopes and documents with fancy red seals. So she was a lawyer. I felt a flash of resentment. She probably only talked to men in suits with six-figure salaries. And I was a man in a faded Sinatra T-shirt whose wage packet, when converted into pounds sterling, just about crawled into five figures.

"I don't think you're meant to offer your seat to a woman on the Star Ferry," she said. "Not these days."

"I don't think you're meant to offer your seat to a woman anywhere," I said. "Not these days."

"Thanks anyway."

"No problem."

I was about to sit down again when an old Chinese man with a nylon shirt and a racing paper shoved me out of the way and plonked himself down in my seat. He hawked noisily and spit right between my Timberland boots. I stared at him dumb-founded as he opened up his paper and began to study the runners at Happy Valley.

"There you go," she laughed. "If you've got a seat, you better hold on to it."

I watched her laughing her goofy laugh as we came into Hong Kong Island. The great buildings reared above us. The Bank of China. The Hong Kong and Shanghai Bank. The Mandarin Hotel. All the silver and gold and glass office blocks of Central, and beyond all of that, the lush greens of Victoria Peak, almost lost inside a shroud of tropical fog.

I was suddenly gripped by the fear that I would never see her again.

"Do you want a coffee?" I said, blushing furiously. I was angry with myself. I know women never say yes to anything if you can't ask them without going red.

"A coffee?"

"You know. Espresso. Cappuccino. Latte. A coffee."

"Come on," she said. "The seat was good. The coffee—I don't know. It's a bit predictable. And besides, I've got to drop this stuff off."

The Star Ferry churned against the dock. The ramp clanged down. The crowds got ready to bolt.

"I'm not trying to pick you up," I said.

"No?" Her face was serious and I couldn't tell if she was making fun of me or not. "That's too bad."

Then she was gone, swept off in a tide of Cantonese with her cardboard box full of legal documents to the wharf and, beyond that, the business district of Central.

I looked out for her on the Star Ferry the next day, and the day after that, and the day after that, expecting to suddenly find her smiling at someone she had struck with a large box of legal documents. Or—if I was very lucky—to strike me with her cardboard box. But she was never there.

Not that I had any slick new pick-up lines.

I just wanted to see that smile.

It was a Friday night and the penthouse bar of the Mandarin Hotel was crowded and loud.

I couldn't really afford to drink up there on what they paid me at the Double Fortune Language School. Yet once in a while I liked to get the lift to the top floor of the famous old hotel and watch the sun go down over an ice-cold Tsingtao beer—the best beer in China. It was a special treat.

But tonight, as I sipped my beer at the bar, some goon from back home started spoiling everything.

"As soon as the People's Liberation Army march in, you watch everyone in Central head for the airport," he said. "And it will serve the buggers right. Hong Kong was a fishing village when we arrived and it will be a fishing village when we leave."

He had a voice on him that cut right through me, full of private education and a lifetime of privilege and dumb words spoken with all the confidence in the world. His voice reminded me that not everything I hated about home had a bulldog tattoo.

"Give this place back to the great unwashed and just watch them kill the golden goose," he said. "But of course the great unwashed will eat anything."

I turned to look at him.

He was at a window table with some girl, trying to impress her. The girl had her back to me. I really didn't notice her at first. I saw only him—a beefy young man in a pinstripe suit, fair-haired and fit from a diet of red meat and rugby and Church of England hymns. A slab of pure British beef, with possibly just a touch of mad cow disease.

Beefy was making no attempt to keep his voice down. The young Cantonese bartender and I exchanged looks as he poured me a second beer. The bartender—just a kid—smiled sadly, not quite shaking his head, and something about the infinite gentleness of his gesture pushed me over the edge.

No, this is too much, I thought, putting down my Tsingtao. It wasn't just that Beefy was insulting the residents of Hong Kong. He was also doing the dirt on the special feeling that I got when I looked at all the lights. The barman's eyes told me to leave it.

Too late.

"Excuse me. Excuse me?"

Beefy looked up at me. So did the girl. It was her. And she shone.

I mean she really shone—the sunset, made spectacular by toxic fumes pouring from the factories of southern China, was throwing the last of its technicolor light across her face.

It lit her up.

Beefy was as blond as she was dark, they looked like some kind of couple, perhaps in the early days of an office romance. At least in Beefy's tiny mind.

"What?" he said. Rudely.

"Look at you," I said. "I mean, just look at you. They give you a company flat and a Filipina maid and you think you're some kind of empire builder. Who are you this week, pal? Stamford Raffles? Cecil Rhodes? Scott of the Antarctic?"

"I'm sorry—are you insane?" he said, uncertain if he should laugh out loud or punch my lights out. He stood up. A big bastard. Plenty of contact sports. Hairs on his chest. Probably.

"Calm down, Josh," she said, touching his arm.

You might have tagged him a chinless wonder but you would have been dead wrong. He was all chin. His kind always are, in my experience. All chin and nose. His noble snout and jutting chin seemed to compress his mouth into a thin, imperious, mean little line.

If anything, he was a lipless wonder.

"We're guests in this place," I said, my voice shaking with something that I couldn't quite identify. "Britannia no longer rules the waves. We should remember our manners."

His lipless mouth dropped open. And then he spoke.

"How would you like me to teach you some manners, you awful little man?"

"Why don't you try it?"

"Maybe I will."

"Maybe you should."

"Oh, shut up, the pair of you," she said. "You're both going home one day."

Going home one day? Going home? That had never occurred to me. I looked at her and I thought—*home*.

Then I looked at Josh. And after staring each other down for a bit, Josh and I felt like idiots and realized that we weren't going to beat each other up. Or, rather, that he wasn't going to beat me up. She finally shoved him into his chair. Then she smiled at me with that goofy grin.

"You're right," she said. "We should remember our manners." She held out her hand. "I'm Rose."

I took her hand.

"Alfie Budd," I said.

I even shook hands with old Josh. The three of us had a drink and, as Josh and I avoided eye contact, I told them about my job at the Double Fortune Language School. She told me about their law firm. Josh kept consulting his watch. Overdoing it a bit, I thought. Deliberately showing me—and her—that he was bored beyond belief.

But she smiled at me—that smile, those teeth, those baby-pink gums, effortlessly taking possession of my heart—and I felt it, I really felt it.

That somewhere in this world there really was a home for me to go to.

This is the way it starts. You look at someone you have never met before and you recognize them. That's all. You just recognize them. Then it begins.

Rose suddenly slapped the table.

"Oh, wait a minute," she laughed. "I remember *you*."

It shouldn't have worked. Her friends all thought she was too good for me and her friends were right. Rose was a Hong Kong Island girl. I was a Kowloon side guy.

She had a career. I had a job. She had dinner in the China Club surrounded by big shots. I had Tsingtao in Lan Kwai Fong surrounded by my fellow small fry. She came out to Hong Kong with a window seat in club class. I had an aisle seat in economy.

At twenty-five, Rose was already a success. Seven years older than her—and starting to look every day of it, what with the humidity and the Tsingtao—I was still waiting for my life to start.

She lived in a small but beautiful apartment on Conduit Road in the Upper Mid-Levels under the shadow of Victoria Peak—expat heaven. Security was a twenty-four-hour Gurkha. I had a room in a shared flat in Sai Ying Pun, rooming with a couple of my colleagues from the Double Fortune, the BBC guy from Gerrard Street and the Wing Chun man from Wilmslow.

Our place was one of those firetrap rabbit warrens with walls so thin you could hear the family down the hall watching Star TV. Security was a sleepy Sikh who came and went as the mood took him.

Rose hadn't drifted out to Hong Kong, not like me. She was a corporate lawyer who had been sent out for a year by her London firm—she called it *the shop*—to cash in on a market that, in the last year of British rule, was booming like never before.

While I was struggling to pay my rent, behind the closed doors of Central fortunes were being made. Hong Kong was screaming out for lawyers and every day more of them came through the fast track of Kai Tak Airport.

Rose was one of them.

"I would still be making the tea in London," she told me on that first night after Josh and I decided to have a drink instead of a fight. "Getting my bum pinched by some fat old man. Out here, I matter."

"What is it you do exactly, Rose?"

"It's corporate finance," she said. "I help firms raise money with share issues for Chinese companies. Initial public offerings. Fire fighting, they call it."

"Wow," I said. "Brilliant."

I had absolutely no idea what she was going on about. But I was genuinely impressed. She seemed like more of a grown-up than I would ever be.

Most of her colleagues—those loud boys and girls braying in the penthouse bar of the Mandarin every night, ignoring the sunset over the harbor—had an amused contempt for Hong Kong.

They saw a street sign for Wan King Road and howled about it for the duration of their stay, as though Hong Kong existed purely for their amusement. They collected and drooled over all the evidence of Hong Kong's madness. And there was plenty.

The local brand of toilet paper called My Fanny. The Causeway Bay department store—a Japanese store as it happened, but let that pass—where they sold truffles named Chocolate Negro Balls. The popular Hong Kong antifreeze spray known as My Piss.

And I laughed too when I first saw the ads for My Piss—I'm not saying that I didn't. But the lipless wonders never stopped. Sooner or later you should forget about My Fanny and go look at the sunset, go look at the lights. But somehow the lipless wonders never got around to that.

Rose wasn't like the rest of them. She loved the place.

I don't want to make her sound like Mother Teresa with a briefcase. The Cantonese can be an abrasive bunch, and confronted by a sulky taxi driver or a rude waiter or a pushy beggar, Rose was quite capable of feeling all the helpless frustration of any hot, tired expatriate. But the bad feelings never lasted for very long.

She loved Hong Kong. She loved the people and—unusual for a woman with her job, her salary, her skin color—she thought it was right that they were getting the place back.

"Oh, come *on,* Alfie," she said one night when I was going on about the special feeling, and how I didn't want it ever to end. "Hong Kong might be a British invention. But it has a Chinese heart."

She wanted to find the real Hong Kong. Left to my own devices, I would have nursed a Tsingtao in Lan Kwai Fong and looked at the lights. Left to myself, I would have vegetated quite happily in the unreal Hong Kong, convinced that the special feeling was all I needed to know.

Rose took me deeper. Rose took me beyond the lights. As she did so, she turned affection into something more. For Hong Kong. And for her.

She took me to a temple behind Central where everything was red and gold and the air was choked with incense as little old ladies burned fake money in huge stone drums. Through the perfumed mist you could just about make out two brass deer gleaming on the altar.

"For longevity," Rose said, and when I think about Rose talking about longevity now, it makes me want to weep.

Back in the days we thought would never end, she took me to places where I would never have gone without her. We had dim sum in a restaurant near my flat where we were the only *gweilo.* We walked the narrow streets between apartment blocks covered in TV aerials, potted plants and washing lines. She took my hand and led me down sunless alleys where toothless old men in flip-flops bet on two crickets fighting in a wooden box.

And I met her from work and we took the Star Ferry to Kowloon and a cinema where it seemed that every mobile phone in the audience never once stopped ringing. Everyone else I knew would have been maddened by the experience. Rose rocked in her seat with laughter.

"Now *this* is the real Hong Kong," she said. "You want to find Hong Kong, mister?" She raised her hand to the symphony of mobile phones. *"This is it."*

Yet she loved doing all the British things. Every Saturday afternoon, after she had finished work—the shop expected her to work half a day on Saturday—we had high tea at the Peninsula Hotel, looking out at Central on the other side of the harbor as we sipped our Earl Grey and tucked away our jam scones and noshed our little sandwiches with the crusts cut off. Once or twice we even watched Josh and his hairy-arsed friends playing rugby and cricket.

It was fun to do these typically British things not because they reminded us of home but because we had never done any of them at home.

Cricket, rugby, sandwiches with the crusts cut off—who knew about these things? Not me. And not Rose, whose non-partisan accent disguised the fact that she came from a pebble-walled duplex in a modest corner of the Home Counties. Nothing had been given to Rose. She had earned it all with education and hard work.

"So where exactly did you lose your Essex accent?" I asked her once. "University?"

"Liverpool Street Station," she said.

In Asia we found both the real Hong Kong and a Britain that we had never known.

Rose loved all of that.

And I loved her.

It wasn't difficult. The only difficult thing was working up the courage to call her after she gave me her business card in the bar of the Mandarin. It took me seven days. Right from the start, she mattered too much to me. Right from the start, I could not imagine my life without her.

Because she was beautiful, smart and kind. She was curious and brave. She had a bigger heart than anyone I have ever known. She was good at her job but her sense of worth didn't depend on that job. I loved her for all those reasons. And I loved her because she was on my side. She was on my side without conditions, without get-out clauses. It's very easy to love some-one when they are on your side.

Once, when we were all on the roof of the China Club, Josh said this interesting thing—probably a first for old Josh—after a few too many Tsingtao.

"If Rose met God, she would say: *why are you so nasty to Alfie, God?*"

He said it in this shrill, girlie voice and everyone laughed. I smiled, trying to be polite to the blockhead. But my heart beat a little faster. Because I knew it was true.

Rose was on my side in a way that nobody had ever been on my side. Apart from my parents. And my grandparents. But they were sort of obliged to be on my side. Rose was a volun-teer. She cared about me. Those kids in the park—the cheddar gang—would laugh at the idea of a woman like that caring about a man like me. But she really did. I'm not making it up.

And by loving me, she set me free. Free to be myself.

There was a dream I had once had in London—the dream of trying to be a writer—that I had never really had the guts to pursue. Rose made me believe that if I was prepared to put in the hours, I could do it. I could become a writer one day. She saw not only the man I was, but the man I could be. By loving me, she made me believe that my dreams could come true.

That's why it is all so difficult now.

That's why I have to force myself to carry on today.

Because for a little while back there, I had it perfect.

The old Chinese man has finished his slow-motion dance.

As I jog past him for the second time—well, by now it's actually more of a slow shuffle than a jog—he looks at me as though he has seen my face a thousand times. As though he rec-ognizes me too.

He speaks to me again and this time I understand exactly what he's saying. It's not *breed* at all.

"Breathe," he says.

"What?" I say, fighting to catch my breath.

"Not breathing properly."

"Who?"

"Who?" he snorts. "Who? You—that's who. Not breathing right. Too shallow, your breathing. No good. No breathe, no life."

I stare at him.

No breathe, no life? Who does he think he is? Yoda?

"What's that?" I say finally, not too friendly. "Some, like, wise old Chinese saying?"

"No," he says. "Not old saying. Not wise old Chinese saying. Just common sense."

Then he turns away, dismissing me.

So I try it as I run out of the park. Inhaling deep, filling my lungs, feeling them expand, letting the breath seep out. Doing it again. Inhaling, exhaling. Slow and steady.

Kicking through last year's leaves, making myself take another breath.

It's not easy.

You see, she was my reason.

2

WHERE DO DREAMS BEGIN? My dream of becoming a writer came from my childhood. That's where my dream began, and it didn't start to die until I was a young man. So that's not too bad. It lasted much longer than most dreams.

My father was a sportswriter on a national newspaper. His regular beat was horse racing, football and boxing, the sports he had grown up with in the East End. He also covered athletics during the Olympics, tennis during Wimbledon and pretty much anything else when he had to. Toward the end of his sportswriting career he even wrote a few pieces about the modern kind of wrestlers, those angry men in sparkling latex who look as though they have been taking steroids when what they really should be taking is acting lessons.

My old man wasn't a famous sportswriter. Most of the time he didn't even get his picture printed next to his byline. But he was always a glamorous figure to me. Other dads, the fathers of my friends, had to be in the same place at the same time every day. My dad traveled the country, interviewing people who were worshipped, and although sometimes my mum and I didn't see him all week, I always loved it that regular office hours meant nothing to him.

Even when I was a small child I knew that journalism wasn't the same as two weeks in Benidorm. I understood the tyranny of the deadline, and how subeditors can leave the last line off your piece, and how today's newspaper is the lining for tomorrow's cat litter. But my dad still seemed to be about as free as a man could be.

My dad was never very fond of the slog of reporting—sitting in the press box at Upton Park, phoning in copy from ringside in the NEC Birmingham—but when he was given space to write about the men and women behind the results and the statistics, when he told you about the brilliant young footballer whose career had suddenly been ended by an ankle injury, or the Olympic hopeful who had just discovered a lump in her breast, his stuff could break your heart. He was a cockle warmer, my dad. He could warm your cockles in just a twelve hundred-word, two-page spread. And when my old man warmed your cockles, your cockles stayed warm for quite a while.

My dad was never a great sportswriter because he was never that crazy about sports. He would have had a far happier, far more successful career if he had been writing for the front pages rather than the back pages.

But my father was my hero. And for years I wanted to go into the family business.

Then he wrote a book. You probably heard of it. You might even have *read* it. Because *Oranges for Christmas: A Childhood Memoir* was one of those books that start selling and then never seem to stop. And after that, my dreams of writing started to seem a little ridiculous. For how could I ever compete with my father now? As a modestly successful sportswriter he had been inspiring. As a wildly successful author, he was intimidating.

I was at teacher-training college by the time my dad's book came out, so I watched its ascent of the bestseller lists from a distance. It felt like one moment my father was what he had been forever—a journalist hanging around training grounds hoping for a few exclusive grunts from twenty-year-old footballers on thirty grand a week, and the next he was a bestselling author, cocooned by six-figure royalty checks, regularly appearing on the artier kind of talk shows, getting recognized in restaurants.

I know it wasn't that easy. *Oranges for Christmas* took years to write. But success always looks like it has come quickly, no matter how hard the rock it is carved from. And it felt like almost overnight my father went from being an unknown sports journalist to a respected writer, doing events in bookstores where he gave a reading, answered questions and signed copies of *Oranges for Christmas*. People actually place a value on his autograph these days, just like those fans at training camps who wait for the twenty-year-old footballers on thirty grand a week.

Oranges for Christmas: A Childhood Memoir was a good book. I liked it a lot. I wasn't bitter that it cast a massive shadow over my own half-baked dreams of writing for a living. It deserved its success.

The book was about my father's childhood in the East End, about how they were poor but happy, and how my dad and his army of brothers and sisters almost died of joy if they got an orange for Christmas.

Oranges for Christmas is full of dirty-faced urchins having a rare old time hunting for rats on bomb sites while their next-door neighbors are being blown up by the Luftwaffe. There is a lot of death, disease and rationing in *Oranges for Christmas* but the reason it sold so well is because it is ultimately as comforting as a cup of hot, sweet tea and a milk-chocolate cookie. For all the gritty anecdotes about polio, nits and the Nazis, my old man's book is endlessly sentimental about a kind of family that no longer seems to exist.

And that's ironic because *Oranges for Christmas* dropped like one of Hitler's buzz bombs among my father's family. His brothers and sisters were all happily settled into respectable middle age by the time *Oranges for Christmas* appeared. Suddenly their adventures of half a century ago were in the public domain.

My dad's eldest sister, my Auntie Janet, did not appreciate my dad telling the world about the time their own father had caught Janet jacking off a GI during a blackout. In the book the story was told as lovable, where-are-my-trousers farce, but the revelation caused a sensation at Auntie Janet's branch of the Women's Institute, where to this day she remains chief jam-maker.

My dad's brother Reg also hit the roof when he saw *Oranges for Christmas*. A bank manager in the Home Counties for many years, Uncle Reg felt my father had gone too far by revealing how one night during the Blitz, Reg, then four years old, had struggled into the Anderson air raid shelter in their back garden with his pants around his ankles and his tiny winkle quivering with fear. Uncle Reg felt that wasn't the image a bank manager should project to his customers in the current market.

Then there was Uncle Pete, a teenager in the book, whose exploits in the black market made many a young housewife with no nylons and a husband at the front willing to—as Pete called it—"put the kettle on." Uncle Pete—or Father Peter as he is known these days—had a lot of explaining to do to his congregation.

Auntie Janet giving executive relief to a young American soldier bound for the beaches of Normandy, Uncle Reg wetting his pants as the bombs dropped, Uncle Pete exchanging his virginity for a pair of nylons—the reading public loved this stuff. And thanks to *Oranges for Christmas*, everybody loves my old man. Apart from all his brothers and sisters and most of the people he grew up with in the old neighborhood.

They don't talk to him any more.

When you come back home after living abroad, you see your country with the eyes of a time traveler.

I was gone for just over two years, from the spring of 1996 to the summer of 1998. That's not very long at all, but now time seems somehow dislocated. A lot of that is to do with Rose, of course. When I left I didn't know she existed, and now that I am back I don't know how I can live without her.

But it's not just about Rose, this sense of displaced time.

It's there when I am driving my dad's car, looking at a newspaper, eating a meal with my parents. Everything is just a little bit out of whack.

There are refugees on the Euston Road for a start. That's new. I see them from my father's Mercedes-Benz SLK. And the refugees see me, because my old man's little red roadster is a car that is designed to attract attention, although probably not from people who have recently fled poverty and persecution.

There were no refugees on the Euston Road when I went away. You got the odd drunk with his hopeful bucket but nobody from the Balkans. Now these thin men and boys swarm around the stalled traffic in front of King's Cross Station, squirting windscreens and scraping away the grime, even when you ask them not to. The refugees point at their mouths, a gesture that looks vaguely obscene. But they are just saying that they are hungry.

That's all new.

And it's not just the refugees on the Euston Road.

Terry Wogan is playing REM on Radio 2. Princess Diana is rarely mentioned. And perhaps most shocking of all, my father has started going to a gym.

All these things seem incredible to me. I thought Wogan only played middle of the road music—but then perhaps REM became MOR while my back was turned. I believed that Diana would be as visible in death as she was in life. And I thought that my dad was the last person in the world who would ever start fretting about his love handles.

The old place looks pretty much the same—frighteningly

like its old self, in fact—but everywhere there are clues that things are secretly different.

Michael Stipe is suddenly whining among the easy listening. Diana is a part of history. And my old man has jacked in the takeout chicken tikka masala and is talking about the benefits of a full cardiovascular workout.

Sometimes it hardly feels like the same country.

I am currently living with my parents. Thirty-four and still at home—it's not great. But it's not the house where I grew up—that would be just too sad—so living with them doesn't feel as though I've completely regressed to childhood. At least, not until my mum hands me my pajamas, all neatly washed and ironed.

It's just a temporary thing. As soon as I get my life back together, as soon as I get a job, I'm going to find myself a flat. Somewhere close to work. I want it to look exactly like the apartment that Rose and I had in Hong Kong. We had a good place. I was happy there.

And I know I should be trying to move on. I know that I should be trying to put my time with Rose behind me. I know all of that.

But if you believe that you can recognize someone you have never met before, if you believe that there is just one person in the world for you, if you believe that there's only one other human being out there who you can love, truly love, for a lifetime—and I believe all of these things—then it follows that there's no point in pretending that tomorrow is another day and all that crap.

Because I've had my chance.

They've got this huge house now, my mum and dad. One of those tall white houses in Islington that looks big from the front and then goes on forever once you get inside. They've even got a swimming pool. It wasn't always this way.

When I was growing up and my old man was still a sports-writer, we lived in a tatty Victorian row house in a part of town that gentrification never quite reached. After *Oranges for Christmas* became a bestseller, everything changed.

The money is new too.

Now my dad is trying to write the follow-up to *Oranges for Christmas,* about how his family was horribly poor but deliri-ously happy in the immediate aftermath of World War II. It's going to be a heart-warming look at the good old days of bomb sites, banana rationing and teeming slums. I don't know how it's going. He seems to spend most of his time down at the gym.

I know my old man is worried about me. And so is my mum. That's why I've got to get out of their big, beautiful home. Soon.

My parents only want the best for me, but they are always having a go at me for not getting over Rose, for not getting her out of my system, for not getting on with my life.

I love my parents but they drive me crazy. They look exas-perated when I tell them that I am in no hurry to get on with what feels like a diminished life. Sometimes my dad says, "Suit yourself, chum," and slams the door when he goes out. Sometimes my mum cries and says, "Oh, Alfie."

My mum and dad act as though I am a nut job for not get-ting over Rose.

I feel like asking them—but what if I'm not a nut job at all? What if this is how you are meant to feel?

There's a strange man on our front doorstep.

He's wearing a pointy helmet like the one worn by the Imperial bikers in *Return of the Jedi.* Really going for that futur-istic look, he also has on black goggles, a bright yellow cycling top and black Lycra trousers that passionately embrace his but-tocks. Under his pointy helmet a Sony Discman is clamped to his head. He has dragged a bicycle up our garden path and now, as he crouches to look through the letter box, you can see the muscles tighten and stretch in the back of his legs.

He looks like a supremely fit insect.

"Dad?"

"Alfie," my father says. "Forgot my key again. Give me a hand with this bike, would you?"

As my old man pulls off his pointy helmet and the Discman, I catch a blast of music—a cry of brassy, wailing exuberance over a sinuous bass line that I recognize immediately as "Signed, Sealed, Delivered" by Stevie Wonder.

With his funky bike and buglike demeanor, my father might look as though he listens to all the latest sounds. In fact he still loves all the old sounds. Especially Tamla Motown. Stevie. Smokey. Marvin. Diana. The Four Tops and the Temptations. The "Sound of Young America," back in the days when both America and my dad were young.

I am more of a Sinatra man. I get it from my granddad. He's been dead for years, but when I was little he would sit me on his lap in the living room of his big project house in Dagenham, the house that became the setting for *Oranges for Christmas,* and I would smell his Old Holborn hand-rolled cigarettes and his Old Spice aftershave as we listened to Frank sing sweet nothings on the stereo. It was years before I realized that those songs are all about women. Loving women, wanting women, losing women.

I always thought they were about being with your granddad.

Sometimes my granddad and I would spot Sinatra in one of his old films when they showed them on television. *From Here to Eternity, Tony Rome, Some Came Running*—all those tough guys with broken hearts who seemed like a perfect complement to the music.

"Granddad!" I would say. "It's Frank!"

"You're right," my granddad would say, putting a tattooed arm around me as we peered at the black-and-white TV set. "It's Frank."

I grew up loving Sinatra but hearing him now doesn't make me dream of Las Vegas or Palm Springs or New York. When I hear Frank, I don't think of the Rat Pack and Ava Gardner and Dino and Sammy. All the things you are meant to remember.

Hearing Sinatra makes me remember sitting on my grandfather's lap in a project house in an East End banjo—that's what they called their cul-de-sac, because it was shaped like a banjo—hearing Sinatra makes me remember the smell of Old Holborn and Old Spice, and hearing Sinatra makes me remember being surrounded by an uncomplicated, unconditional love that I thought would be there forever.

My old man always tried to convert me to Motown. And I like all that *ooh-baby-baby* stuff—how could anyone dislike it? But as I grew up I felt that there was a big difference between the music my granddad liked and the music my dad liked.

The songs my father played me were about being young. The songs my grandfather played me were about being alive.

I open the door and help my dad get his bicycle into the hall. It is some kind of racing bike, with low-slung handles and a seat the size of a vegetable Samosa. I have never seen it before.

"New wheels, Dad?"

"Thought I'd cycle to the gym. Doesn't seem much point in driving there. It's good for me. Gets the old ticker going."

I shake my head and smile, amazed and touched yet again at this transformation in my father. When I was growing up he was a typical journalist, slowly growing more portly on a diet of irregular meals and regular alcohol. Now, in his late fifties, he's suddenly turned into Jean-Claude Van Damme.

"You're really into it, aren't you? This whole keep-fit routine."

"You should come with me some time. I mean it, Alfie. You've got to start watching that weight. You're really getting fat."

Sometimes I think my father has a touch of Tourette's syndrome.

I'm too embarrassed to tell Jean-Claude about my pathetic shuffle in the park. And I don't feel like arguing with him. I guess that's how you know you're not young any more—you don't feel the need to challenge your parents on every point of order. But as he wheels his bike down the hall and I catch a glimpse of myself in a mirror, I think: what does it matter anyway? I'm not going out on the make.

My dad and I go into the living room where my grandmother is sitting in her favorite chair with a copy of the *News of the World* on her lap. She appears to be studying a story with the headline TABLE DANCING TART STOLE MY TELLY STUD.

"Hello, Mum," says my dad, kissing her on the forehead. "Reading all the scandal, are you?"

"Hello, Nan," I say, doing the same. We kiss a lot in my family. My grandmother's skin is soft and dry, like paper that has been left out in the sun. She turns her watery blue eyes on me and slowly shakes her head.

I take her hand. I love my nan.

"No luck, Alfie," she says. "No luck again, love."

I see that she is holding a lottery ticket in her hands and checking it against last night's winning numbers. This is one of the rituals that I go through every week with my grandmother. She is always genuinely amazed that she has failed to win ten million pounds on the lottery. Every Sunday she comes around for lunch and expresses her total astonishment at failing to get six balls. Then I commiserate with her.

"No luck, Nan? Never mind."

"Work on Monday morning, Alfie." She smiles, although neither she nor I have to go to work tomorrow. She starts to rip up her lottery ticket. This seems to consume all her strength and she nods off after completing the task.

Through the tall window at the back of the room I can see my mother in the garden, raking up the fallen leaves. Although she has sometimes seemed out of place in the big new house that was bought with the money from my father's book, my mother has always loved this garden.

She looks up at me and smiles, jogging on the spot and puffing out her cheeks. It takes me a few seconds to realize that she is miming a run in the park. I give her the thumbs up and my mum goes back to raking the dead leaves in her garden, smiling quietly to herself. I know she was pleased to see me get out of the house for what she calls "a bit of fresh air."

The front door slams and a few seconds later a smiling young woman sticks her head around the door. She looks like God's second attempt at Cameron Diaz—an almost cartoon amalgamation of blond hair, blue eyes and ski-tanned skin. Lena is our Czech home help. She's really smart. It's only when she's listening to the radio that she seems a bit stupid because she sort of dances around to the music, even if she's sitting down and eating her bran flakes.

Lena's not stupid, though. She's just young. To be honest, I think she's got a soft spot for me. One of those irrational crushes that ambush the very young. I might have to tell her, as gently as possible, that I'm not looking for a new relationship. She's certainly a beautiful girl—she once inspired our paperboy to ride his bike right into a lamppost. There were free pull-outs and color supplements everywhere. How strange that I'm just not interested. Or perhaps it's not strange at all.

The slammed door has woken up my nan and she beams at Lena, who she perhaps believes is some kind of distant relation.

"Sorry I'm late," says Lena in English so good that she sounds like a native speaker. "The tube's awful on Sundays. I'll start getting lunch ready now."

"It doesn't MATTER," my nan says very slowly. My grandmother also seems to believe that Lena is either deaf, stupid, unable to speak a word of English or possibly all of the above. She points at me. "HIM NOT HUNGRY."

"So sweet," smiles Lena, who speaks five languages and who

is studying for an MBA at UCL. "I'll get started on lunch."

"I'll give you a hand," says my father.

"Oh, that's okay."

"But I want to."

They go out to the kitchen and my nan and I watch a new kind of program where some people are exchanging blows because one of them has discovered that his girlfriend is really a man. I haven't seen this kind of thing before. Even the rubbish is new.

From the kitchen I can hear the sound of laughter as my dad and Lena unload the dishwasher.

I have never in my life seen my father helping with the housework.

That's new too.

3

I WALK AROUND CHINATOWN.

Since coming back to London, that's what I do all day. I get
a tube to the West End and I head for that tiny patch of London
where the street names are in both English and Chinese. Then
I walk.

Entering Chinatown by one of its three gates—Wardour
Street on the west, Macclesfield Street on the north, Newport
Court on the east—I make my way down those loud, busy
streets until the place fills my senses, until it reminds me of that
other place on the far side of the world.

In minutes I am back in Hong Kong. There are no spectacular views of skyline and harbor and peak. But many of the
sights are the same as when I was in Kowloon or Wanchai.

Rows of laminated ducks in windows, good-looking girls
with glossy hair talking into brightly colored mobile phones, old
men with gold teeth pushing babies with eyes like brown jew-
els, young mothers with children dressed up to the nines, surly
teenage boys with slicked-back hair hanging around outside the
games arcade trying to look like gangsters, waitresses making
their way to work in their monochrome uniforms or mopping
the small square of pavement outside their restaurants, steam
pouring from a tiny kitchen behind misty plate glass, men in
filthy vests delivering boxes of iced fish.

Chinatown is the one place that I can be happy. It does more than remind me of Hong Kong. It reminds me of when Rose and I were still together.

There are shops, supermarkets and of course restaurants galore, but there are not really any places to stop and watch the world go by. Despite the proximity to the self-consciously Mediterranean street life of Soho, there are no little cafés or coffee shops or bars. If you want cappuccino and a quiet half-hour, then you are in the wrong place. That's not a Cantonese thing. Yet I don't care.

It means I keep moving—down the main artery of Gerrard Street, into Wardour Street where the western border of Chinatown shares space with pizza joints and nightclubs, then into dark, narrow Lisle Street, with its smell of roast duck and gas fumes, then maybe into Little Newport Street where you can see the huge head of a papier-mâché Chinese dragon in a martial arts shop called Shaolin Way, as if the dragon is guarding the punch bags and focus pads and cardboard boxes full of black Kung Fu trousers. Finally perhaps, after reaching the bookstores and theaters of Charing Cross Road, I'll double-back on myself into Newport Court where you can buy Chinese magazines, Chinese CDs, Chinese anything you like.

As I haphazardly patrol the streets of Chinatown, a poem keeps coming back to me, a poem by Kipling that we studied when I was teaching English literature at the Princess Diana Comprehensive School for Boys.

"Mandalay" is about a discharged British soldier wandering around London after serving "somewheres east of Suez," and as he roams the streets of Bank—is the ex-soldier now a messenger boy in the City? Does he make his living running errands for the ancestors of Josh?—he thinks of the wind in the palm trees and the elephants piling teak and the woman he left behind. Our ex-soldier should not be lonely—he tells us that, in the English drizzle, he steps out with fifty housemaids from

"Chelsea to the Strand." But he remembers when "dawn comes up like thunder outer China 'crost the Bay" and he remembers when she was by his side.

"So this is about his bitch, is it, sir?" one of my smarter, nastier students would enquire to guffaws of laughter from the back of the class. "Is it, like, a—what do you call it?—savage incitement of sexual tourism, sir? Not incitement, sir. What's the word? Indictment, sir? Is it an indictment? Sir?"

"Mandalay" didn't mean much to my pale thin charges with their Tommy gear and leering grins. It didn't, in truth, mean much to me at the time. But now that I am back in London it runs around my head and will not let me go and makes me sick for my lost home, my lost wife.

For the temple-bells are callin,' and it's there that I would be—
By the old Moulmein Pagoda, looking lazy at the sea.

I like to get to Chinatown early, before the sauntering tourist crowds with their cameras and their blank looks and their paranoid rucksacks strapped on back to front. I like to arrive while the trucks are still unloading their produce and the old ladies are setting out their stalls and there are groups of men standing around gossiping in Cantonese, men who will later go to work in the restaurants or disappear into the basement gambling joints to play mah-jongg.

That's when I like it best, when it is just the Chinese preparing for the day ahead. That's when it reminds me most of Hong Kong.

I always eat my lunch here. Sometimes I eat early, usually dim sum at the New World on Gerrard Place, one of those old-fashioned dim sum restaurants, dying out now, where they still have the girls pushing trolleys loaded with steamed buns and barbecued pork and fried eggplant, the trolleys going slowly round and round the huge red and gold restaurant, and they let you choose straight from the trolleys rather than just giving you a menu the way most dim sum joints do these days.

Sometimes I eat late, maybe a bowl of noodle soup at one of the smaller restaurants on Gerrard Street, where they don't mind if you ask for a table at four in the afternoon.

You can pretty much eat any time you like in Chinatown. That's what I have always liked about the Cantonese. They let you get on with your life. They don't make rules. They just don't care.

There's a lot to be said for not caring.

In my opinion, not caring is very underrated.

Ever since my time in Hong Kong, I have been a big fan of afternoon tea, that ritualized fix of sugar and caffeine just when your energy levels are starting to dip. Rose liked it too. She said that afternoon tea was the most indulgent of meals, because it was the one meal that happened when you were meant to be working.

Rose was always saying things like that—things that had a way of making your feelings understandable. I thought that I just liked stuffing my cake hole with scones and jam in the middle of the afternoon. Rose made me see that what I really liked was escaping from the Double Fortune Language School.

There's a swanky hotel near Bond Street where they serve afternoon tea. The clientele are all tourists who are seeking a slice of ye olde authentic England in a pot of Earl Grey. Apart from me.

The room is ringing with a dozen foreign tongues when I walk in with my *Evening Standard* under my arm. The waiter looks at me as if I have wandered into the wrong place.

"Tea, sir? How many?"

"Tea for one."

He brings me a pot of tea and a silver stand that looks like a wedding cake. The layers of the stand are loaded with chunky scones, pots of cream and ruby-red jam, and dainty little sand-wiches.

The waiter is friendly. The tourists are not too noisy. The scones are still warm. The salmon and cucumber sandwiches have all had their crusts cut off. The tea is brewed from leaves not bags.

Everything is exactly as it should be.

But it just doesn't taste the same over here.

The walk to the tube takes me through the shabby babble of Oxford Street.

Music that rattles my fillings pours from clothing stores, record shops, coffee bars. Once the cheap, vibrant glamour of this street seemed to be what London was all about. Now I feel out of place among the new music, the tired fashions, the acned mob. Now it just reminds me that I am getting old. Oxford Street has stayed the same while I have changed. I try to move quickly through the crowds but the rush hour has started and progress is slow.

Near the tube station there are a couple of young foreigners propped up against the wall like bored streetwalkers. They are the funky kind of foreigner, all moody looks and platform boots.

There's an Asian girl with dyed blond hair and a boy from some sunny corner of the Mediterranean with a pencil-thin moustache and razor-sharp sideburns.

They both have a stack of leaflets that they are listlessly offering to the crowds as they chat to each other in bad English. They give every impression of not giving a toss if they hand out their flyers or throw them in the nearest overflowing bin.

I take one.

Learn Good English
@ Churchill's International Language School
The First and Best
Start Any Monday

Low Low Prices
Near Virgin Megastore
Help with Visas, Work Permits, Accommodations
Ensuring Excellence!

The leaflet has a Union Jack border and inside that there's another border made up of flags from around the world. I see Italy, Japan, China, Brazil and plenty more that I don't recognize.

Next to the words "Churchill's International Language School" there's a black silhouette of a bald fat man who is either Alfred Hitchcock or possibly Winston Churchill. The man is flashing two fingers to indicate that you should get lost or possibly that victory is imminent. His mouth is stuffed with an enormous great sausage or possibly a cigar.

The silhouette has been drawn by someone with the artistic ability of a pigeon. I hate the glib modernity of the "@" symbol. I am stunned that an Oxford Street language school would stoop so low as to pilfer Winston Churchill's name to give it a touch of fake authority. There's something about all that cheap cynicism in one place that reminds me why I feel so lost on this street.

But I find that I can't throw the leaflet away. There's something about all those different flags and the generosity in the promises of help and the cheery exclamation mark after the assurance of excellence that lifts my spirits.

I don't know. It looks sort of hopeful.

We were never very far from the water in Hong Kong.

From the little café on Victoria Peak to the tea room of the Peninsula Hotel, every spectacular view that we ever held hands to featured the waterfront. We were always on the Star Ferry, shuttling between our apartments on opposite sides of the harbor. And Rose's firm had a company boat that they called the junk.

Calling it a junk conjured up images of one of those quaintly curved wooden ships with orange sails that bob in the Hong Kong harbor of a thousand tourist postcards. Which was probably the idea.

In fact this junk was a modern, motorized launch that gleamed with chrome and polished wood and was crewed by a smiling Cantonese husband-and-wife team in neat white uniforms. Even as late as the spring of 1997, out on the junk you could kid yourself that the changeover was never going to happen, that nothing was ever going to change, that life would always be this sweet.

The junk was meant to be for corporate hospitality, but if it wasn't being used for entertaining taipan clients from London or Shanghai or Tokyo, then the staff from Rose's shop could take it out and spend a day cruising around the hundreds of tiny islands that make up Hong Kong.

Usually it was taken out by parties of *gweilo* male lawyers courting Asian girls who worked as flight attendants for Cathay Pacific. Rose and I, already at the stage where you believe that the two of you need nobody else, always went out with just the crew.

The last time we took the junk out we sailed to a little island with no name where an old man in flip-flops served us cold beer and spicy prawns in a restaurant that was little more than a shack. I remember a wooden pier, half-wild dogs roaming the beach and a silence that was disturbed only by the murmur of our voices and the sound of the sea.

On our way back I nodded off on deck, my belly full of Tsingtao and what was surely the best seafood in the world.

I don't know how long I was sleeping but the sun had changed position by the time I awoke. It was very hot now. The deck was burning through the beach towel that I was lying on. I heard the distant caw of gulls, the soft hiss of waves on the shore, the boat creaking beneath me with the swell of the South China Sea.

And then suddenly Rose was standing directly above me, smiling, the features of her face hidden by the dazzle of the late-afternoon sun.

I squinted up at her, shading my eyes. The sun glared down and I couldn't really see her, just the dark shape of her, moving in and out of the blinding light. Still looking at her through scrunched-up eyes, I made a move to rise.

She held up her hand.

"Stay right where you are," she said.

Putting her feet either side of me, she carefully adjusted her stance so that her head completely blotted out the sun. It burned around her like the rim of a total eclipse. Her shadow fell across me, allowed me to see.

I uncovered my eyes, blinking away tears. Her face was clear now. She was smiling in the shade, this shade of her own making.

Rose filled the sky.

"Can you see me now?"

"Yes."

"Sure?"

"I'm sure."

"Good."

For a long moment we were motionless. It was as if she wanted to brand her face on my memory, as if she wanted me to keep this moment forever, as if she wanted to make sure that she would stay in my bones.

Then she moved away.

"You should put something on," she said. "You're going to get burned out here."

I walk past the doorway to Churchill's International Language School three times before I find it.

The entrance is between an ancient denim store and a brand-new coffee shop, at the part of Oxford Street where the milling crowds are at their thickest, so small that it is hardly there at all. I drink two heavily sugared cappuccinos and almost buy a pair of Levi's—unfortunately they don't have my size—before I finally see the open door.

It is being listlessly guarded by two more of Churchill's students. They are gabbing away and scratching their piercings—navel for her, nose and eyebrow for him—while offering flyers to the indifferent mob. They don't look at me as I go past them and up a steep flight of stairs.

Churchill's International Language School occupies one entire floor of a building that seems to open up the farther you go inside, like a secret cave or the magic wardrobe that led to Narnia. It echoes with foreign accents, distant laughter, the sound of a teacher patiently explaining the idiom, "to see the light."

Churchill's feels like a far happier place than either the Princess Diana or the Double Fortune. I can smell instant coffee and takeaway chicken teriyaki. The walls are yellow and peeling, but covered with notice boards and bright with posters. Someone is selling a rice cooker because they are going back home. There are messages in English, French, Italian and what looks like Japanese. Rooms to rent, household items for sale, classes offered and sought—all the bits and pieces of student life everywhere, conducted in every language under the sun.

This place doesn't have the menace of the Princess Diana or the earnestness of the Double Fortune. It's a young, bustling, friendly place. I feel so comfortable here that I ask at the reception desk if they have any teaching vacancies. After filling in an application form and waiting for twenty minutes, I am sitting opposite Lisa Smith, the principal. She has dyed red hair, combat boots and a pair of those chunky, vaguely ethnic earrings that look far too heavy for human ear lobes. Despite dressing like one of her students, she must be breathing down the neck of her sixtieth birthday. Her manner is business-like, unsmiling, only as polite as she needs to be. She studies my application form.

"The world needs English," she says. "Our students will go

on to look for jobs in tourism, business, information technology. Wherever they work, they can't do it without good English. English is the global language. The language of the next century."

"It's funny," I say. "I was in Hong Kong the night it was handed back to the Chinese. Everyone was saying that it was finally the end of empire, the end of colonial rule, the end of the Western century. All that. But the English language is stronger than ever."

A thin smile from Principal Smith.

"Oh, our students don't dream of becoming English, Mr. Budd. They harbor no ambitions to become British. They dream of becoming international."

Becoming international. That sounds good to me. When I went to Hong Kong, my dream was to become a part of something bigger than myself. And I did for a while. I made it. I was bigger than myself. Not because of the bright shining lights but because of a woman.

Rose transformed me. She swapped me for the person I had always wanted to be. Thanks to her, I was on the way to becoming myself. I had even started writing a few small things. Then suddenly it was all over, and everything slipped away from me.

I don't tell Lisa Smith that teaching has often sickened me. I don't tell her that I was bored and frustrated teaching the designer-clad old ladies at the Double Fortune, that I was overwhelmed and frightened teaching the designer-clad young thugs at the Princess Diana Comprehensive for Boys.

I am on my best behavior, asking some questions about pay and working conditions, because I feel that I must.

But I already know that I want to be a part of Churchill's International Language School, I want to be surrounded by people who still have their dreams intact, I long to be a part of all that distant laughter.

4

JOSH COMES OUT OF THE LIFT just after six o'clock, all blond and beefy inside his pinstripe suit, turning on the charm for some smitten secretary who is gazing up at him while he twinkles and smiles and pretends to be nice. Josh lets the young woman peel away into the home-going crowds before he approaches me, his smile fading.

"You look awful," he says. "Want a drink? How about a drop of Mother Murphy's Water?"

"Have they got Tsingtao?"

"No, they haven't got bloody Tsingtao. It's an Irish pub, Alfie. They don't sell Chinese beer in Irish pubs. God, it's pointless looking for the craic with you. You couldn't find the crack in your fat ass, could you?"

Josh is my best friend. I often think that he doesn't like me very much. Sometimes I believe he rues the day that I was born. When we go out for a drink, a large part of the evening is always spent with Josh insulting me, although he no doubt considers this mindless abuse constructive criticism.

As we walk to Mother Murphy's, Josh informs me that I have wasted my life. He tells me that no woman will ever want me. And when he hears my good news about Churchill's International Language School, he makes it clear that he disapproves of my new job, just as he disapproved of my old job.

47

Yet Josh is the closest thing I have to a real friend. We've stayed in touch since Hong Kong, when it would have been the easiest thing in the world to drift from each other's lives, what with him doing so well in the City and me spending most of my time wandering around Chinatown. But we are closer now than we were in Hong Kong.

There are people who have known me far longer and like me far more. People I knew at college, people I used to teach with at the Princess Diana. But none of them are real friends.

It's not their fault. It's mine. Somehow I have let them all wander off. I do not return their phone calls. I make lame excuses when I receive their invitations to dinner. I do not make the effort, the endless effort, that you need to keep a friendship alive. These are good people. But the truth is that I just don't care enough for the continual contact that friendship demands.

I have seen a few of them since coming back to London, for drinks or coffee, and it always seems quietly futile. The only person I really look forward to seeing is Josh. He is my last link to Hong Kong, my one way back to the life I shared with Rose. If I let Josh slip away, then it would really feel as though Hong Kong was over. And I don't want Hong Kong to be over.

"You were always a tourist," Josh tells me in an Irish bar full of Englishmen in business suits. "Sentimental about the locals. Gaping at the view. Treating the world like it's one big Disneyland. Buying little knick-knacks to put on the mantel-piece back home. You and Rose. What a pair of tourists."

Why did Josh call me up and ask me out for a drink? Why doesn't he spend his time with other hotshot young lawyers? Because it works both ways. Because I am Josh's last remaining link to his own happy past.

Josh is working in the City now. Making a lot of money, doing well, soon to be made a partner. He says he doesn't miss his life in Hong Kong. But I think he secretly yearns for the sense of endless possibility that every expatriate experiences, the feeling that your life has somehow opened up, that you are finally free to become exactly who you want to be. You lose all of that when you come back home. You discover that you are suddenly your old self again.

I think that Josh feels robbed. In Hong Kong he was considered to be what he presents himself as being—a cool, confident son of privilege, educated at schools that cost £15,000 a year, arrogant, to the manor born.

But that's not the truth. And back in London, some people see right through him.

There was a bit of money in Josh's distant past. His father was an underwriter at Lloyd's and for the first ten years of Josh's life there were private schools, tennis lessons and a big house in the suburbs. But that way of life started to recede when his father had a stroke.

From the age of twelve, Josh went to a comprehensive school in the Home Counties where he was tormented in the playground because he spoke like Prince Charles. His father lost his job. Josh lost his future. And all the insurance policies in the world can't give you back your future. By the time he became a teenager, all Josh had left was his name, his accent and his act. It's a good act. It fools me—even now—and many others.

But there are people in Josh's firm who really did go to Eton and Harrow and Westminster, pampered veterans of Barbados and Gstaad, who come from families where the money never ran out, where the father did not have a stroke at forty.

These people look at Josh and they smile. He doesn't fool them for a minute.

It's strange. Josh pretends that everything he has—the law degree, the fashionably empty loft in Clerkenwell, the brand-new BMW coupe—came easily to him. The truth is much more impressive. I know that none of it came easily and I think he resents that about me, I think that's why he never fails to abuse me. But there's something we will always have connecting us, something that other people will never understand.

"Hong Kong," he says. "How can you miss Hong Kong? All those weddings and funerals in a language you don't understand. The shore line changing every time you look at it. All those mobile phones going off at the movies. Checking your seafood for hepatitis B. Nobody smiling at you unless she's a Filipina. The obsessions with money, sex and shopping. In that order. And the other obsessions with typhoons, canto-pop and Louis Vuitton. Weather so humid that your shoes grow leaves. Air-conditioning so cold that you get hypothermia in the supermarket. People throwing their garbage from the eighteenth floor of their buildings. Including fridges."

"You miss it too, don't you?"

Josh nods. "Breaks my bloody heart," he says. "I remember the first time I ever had sex in Hong Kong. Think I've still got the receipt somewhere."

Josh likes me. He tries to hide it, but he does. Sometimes I think he envies me. It's true that I don't have a career, or money, or a flashy car, or any of the things that you are supposed to want. But I also don't have a boss, a suit and tie I have to wear, a position to protect. There's no lucrative partnership that I want. And there's nothing that anyone can take away from me. Not now.

Yet there has always been an edge to my relationship with Josh. His hostility is not just a cover because he likes me so much. I think Josh believes that I stole Rose away from him just when he was ready to make his move.

Personally I don't believe you can steal one human being from another. You can't steal people, despite what Josh thinks. People are funny.

They just slip away.

When we can't drink any more, we walk the entire length of the City Road and Upper Street looking for a black cab.

We get to the far side of Highbury Corner, where affluence and fashion abruptly give way to poverty and function, and we still haven't found a taxi. There's a dirty yellow light revolving among a tired row of shops.

"You get a minicab," I tell Josh. "I can walk home from here."

"Something to eat first," he says. "Got to line the old stomach."

Although we have left the bright lights behind, I know there are some really good places to eat around here. On one side of the Holloway Road there's Trevi, a little Anglo-Italian café, and on the other side there's Bu-San, one of the city's oldest Korean restaurants. But Trevi is closed and Bu-San is full.

"What about that place?" Josh says. "Looks like a dump but I'm desperate."

He's indicating a Chinese restaurant that is sandwiched between a dry cleaner's and a kebab shop. It's called the Shanghai Dragon and it is not much to look at. There's a line of smoked windows decorated with ancient takeout menus, curling reviews from local rags and listings mags, and some big red Chinese characters that are probably the name of the joint. There's a tiny sign in the window. NO DOGS, it says.

On the main door, a single rectangular slab of yet more smoked glass, there's a leering golden dragon who has seen better days. But beyond all the darkened windows and dog-eared menus, you can see heads moving about inside. The place is busy. A good sign. We go inside.

The Shanghai Dragon is nothing fancy. The interior has the shagged-out minimalism of a minicab firm at midnight. It's an L-shaped room with a large section for diners and a smaller area for takeout customers. In the restaurant section there are just a few courting couples left now, lingering over the coffee and mint chocolates. The takeout area is more crowded with people who have just come out of the local pubs. There are a few stray tables and chairs in this section but all of them are occupied. Suspended from the ceiling, there's a large television set showing some TV movie about Charles and Diana.

At the angle of the L-shaped room, an old Chinese lady is leaning on the counter of a bar the size of a telephone booth and taking orders, which she scratches on her pad in Chinese characters. There's a cup of green tea in front of her.

You can smell the kitchen beyond a tatty door at the end of the takeout section. Garlic and spring onion, frying beef and black bean sauce, noodles and rice. I look at Josh and I can tell he thinks it too. This smells like a good place. We study the menu.

"Next!" the old lady says.

A man with a shaven head and khaki shorts lumbers up to the counter. He is dressed like a young man although he is not young at all. He looks like a forty-year-old skinhead who is on his summer holiday, a style that is quite popular in these parts. His belly resembles a bucket of brewer's slop that is being poured into the gutter. He stinks of drink.

"Bag of chips," he says.

"Chips only with meal," says the old lady.

The man's face darkens.

"Just give us a fucking bag of chips, you monkey."

The old lady's bright brown eyes show no fear.

"No dirty words! Chips only with meal!" She taps a menu with her ballpoint. "Says so here. You want chips, you order meal. For goodness sake. I wasn't born tomorrow."

"I don't want a fucking meal," the man growls.

"No dirty words!"

"I just want a bag of chips."

"Chips only with meal," the old lady says in conclusion, and then looks over the man's shoulder. "Don't blame me if you got out of bed the wrong way. Next!"

The other customers are all waiting for their takeout. That means we are next. I step up to the counter and start to give our order. The man with the shaven head puts a meaty hand on my chest and propels me backward.

"Give us a bag of fucking chips, you old cow," he says.

"Who the *hell* do you think you are?" Josh says.

The middle-aged skinhead turns and brings his forehead smashing down onto Josh's nose. My friend reels backward with shock and pain. Already there's a Jackson Pollock–style splatter of blood across his white shirt and silk tie.

"And you can wait your turn, Lord Snooty."

The skinhead grabs a fistful of the old lady's jumper. She seems very small. For the first time she starts to look afraid.

I put a restraining hand on the old skinhead's shoulder. He turns and—very quickly, very hard—hits me three times in the ribs. As I clutch my sides, good for nothing, I think to myself that he has either done a bit of boxing or watched an awful lot of it on satellite television. I also think to myself—*ouch!* No, really—*ouch!*

"I don't want any greasy foreign muck," says the skinhead in a tone of voice that contrives to combine fury with extreme reasonableness. "I don't want any of your sweet and sour crap. Just . . . give . . . me . . . a . . . bag . . . of . . . fucking . . . chips."

"Chips only with meal!" the old lady cries, and the door to the kitchen opens as the skinhead pulls her toward him.

A cook is standing in the doorway. He is about sixty and wearing a white chef's apron that is stained and frayed. His head is also shaved. For a second I can't remember where I know him from.

And then I get it. He's the old man in the park who I saw doing his slow-motion dance. The one who told me to keep breathing. The Tai Chi guy.

The skinhead lets go of the old lady as the old man comes

toward him. The two men look at each other. The skinhead squares up for a fight, his fleshy fists half-raised, but the old man simply faces him, doing nothing, waiting.

The skinhead seems clenched with violence. But the old man is perfectly relaxed, his arms hanging loose by his side. He's clearly not afraid of the much larger man. The old lady barks something in Cantonese, gesturing at the skinhead.

"Chips only with meal," the old man says, very quietly.

Then he says nothing.

The two men stare at each other for a long moment. Then the skinhead looks away with a short, contemptuous laugh. Muttering to himself about Chinks and chips and greasy foreign muck, he leaves the Shanghai Dragon, slamming the door behind him. The relief in the place is tangible. We all watch the old man, wondering what has happened.

The kitchen door opens again and another Chinese man, this one much younger and plumper, comes out carrying a stack of silver containers in a plastic bag. He looks at me and Josh and his mouth drops open.

I am almost weeping with pain. Josh is sprawled in one of the plastic chairs, leaning his head back, a bloody handkerchief over his face.

The old lady says something else in Cantonese, not quite so angry now. The old man looks at us for the first time.

"Come," he tells us.

The old man takes us through a side door next to the steam and clatter of the Shanghai Dragon's tiny kitchen and up some stairs into a little self-contained flat where a number of Chinese people, big and small, are watching the TV movie about Charles and Diana.

They turn only mildly curious brown eyes our way as the old man leads us into a small bathroom and examines us with cold, expert fingers. My ribs are already turning purple but the old man tells me they are not cracked. But Josh's nose seems to be growing sideways.

"Broken nose," the old man says. "Have to go to hospital. But first push back in place."

"Push what back in place?" Josh says. "You don't mean my nose, do you?"

"Makes it better later," the old man says. "Easier to fix for doctors. At hospital."

Whimpering a bit and going oh-God-oh-God, Josh gingerly straightens his nose. Then the old lady is suddenly in the bathroom with us, almost crying with emotion, angrily ranting in English and Cantonese.

"What do they know?" the old lady says. "Drinking beer. Fighting. Saying dirty words. That's all they know. These English. For goodness sake. I am at the end of my feather. Eating sweet and sour pork. And chips. Chips and dirty words with everything."

"Not all English," the old man says.

The old lady looks at us, not remotely embarrassed.

"I'm talking about bad English, husband," she mutters. Then she smiles at us. "Want a cup of tea?" she says. "Cup of English tea?"

Her name is Joyce and his name is George. The Changs. He doesn't say much. She doesn't stop talking. Joyce is like a force of nature, wreaking havoc on any idiom that stands in her way, taking clichés and making them her very own.

"It's just a storm in a tea pot . . . pretending butter wouldn't melt in his trousers . . . dead as a yo-yo . . . I put my feet in it . . . don't mince your thoughts . . . you have hit the nail on the nose . . . don't be a silly willy!"

Joyce and George. They are the kind of English names that the Cantonese love to adopt—the names of kings and maiden aunts, the kind of English names that vanished from England decades ago. So far out of fashion that they are in danger of making a comeback.

George patches us up, rubbing Tiger Balm on my sore ribs and gently swabbing most of the dried blood from Josh's face. Then Joyce, talking all the while, serves us tea and biscuits in the living room.

The room is full of family. There's George and Joyce themselves and then their son Harold, the plump young man from the kitchen. There's also Harold's wife, Doris—another one of those Cantonese names that seems straight from some lost, ancient England—a young woman in glasses who avoids our eyes. And there are Doris and Harold's two children, a boy of five and a slightly older girl. We are not introduced to the children, although the old people make a continual fuss of them, George placing the girl on his lap and Joyce cuddling the boy as we all drink our tea—green for them, English for us—and we all watch the TV movie about Charles and Diana for a bit until the silence is broken by Joyce.

"What's wrong with you?" she suddenly demands, sizing me up over the green tea. "Cat got your mouth?"

She is a strange old lady. And yet this flat full of Cantonese seems oddly familiar to me. Is it the way the television dominates the room? The way that three generations seem perfectly at ease with each other? Or is it just the sweet tea and biscuits happily consumed on a crowded, worn-out old sofa?

There's something about this room that reminds me of a family from long ago, a family that I knew in my childhood, a family that somewhere along the way I have somehow got separated from.

5

WHAT I LIKE ABOUT TEACHING at Churchill's International Language School is that my students are definitely not children. They are young men and women, mostly in their late teens and early twenties, although there are quite a few who are older, mature students who only made it to London after the collapse of a bad marriage in Seoul or after too many boring years in an office job in Tokyo or after repeatedly having their visa application turned down by some spiteful little penpusher at the British Embassy in Beijing or Lagos or Warsaw.

I like their optimism, their youth, the way their lives are not yet set in stone. And I admire their nerve, coming halfway around the world to master another language.

So why do they dislike me so much?

Sometimes my students turn up late. Sometimes they do not turn up at all. And if they make it to class, they yawn and stretch and struggle to stay awake.

I finally snap when one of them, a Chinese boy in broken glasses called Zeng, loses his heroic battle against sleep and nods off in the middle of my interesting talk on the present perfect.

"What is it with you lot?" I demand. "You don't show up half the time. When you do show up you act as though you've been heavily sedated. Look at this guy. Dead to the world. Are my lessons really so boring? Come on. Let's have it."

They stare at me dumbfounded. One or two of them rub their eyes. Zeng begins to snore.

"Not at all," says a Japanese girl at the front of the class. She is one of the new kind of Japanese girls—dyed blond hair, heavy makeup and platform boots. She looks like one of the Glitter Band. "We *like* your lessons." She glances around at the rest of the class. There are a few nods of assent. "Present perfect? Present perfect continuous?" She smiles at me and I remember her name. Yumi. "Very nice indeed." She nods.

"Then why don't you turn up? Why is this guy out for the count? Why is everyone on the verge of total collapse?"

"Please," says a tall, thin Pole who has to be the same age as me. Witold. It took him about ten years before they ticked his card at the British Embassy in Warsaw. "Zeng is very—how to say?—knackered."

"He works every night," says the good-looking Pakistani kid sitting next to Zeng. Imran. He gives Zeng a shake. "Wake up. The teacher is talking to you."

Zeng grunts, opens his eyes, wonders what planet he is on.

"You work, don't you, Zeng?" says Yumi.

Zeng nods. "General Lee's Tasty Tennessee Kitchen. The one on Leicester Square. Very popular. Very busy."

"That's no excuse," I say. "I don't care if you've got some little part-time job. You should stay awake in my lessons. Falling asleep is rude."

"Not such a little job," says Imran.

"Work until three in morning," says Zeng. "*Do you want fries with that? Anything to drink? You want the General's Happy Meal special? Toilets only for customer use.*" He shakes his head. "Wah," he says.

"It's not insult for you," says Imran. "London so expensive. He has to work too hard. We all do."

"I don't work," says a young French woman. There are only a couple of French at Churchill's. She sniffs the air disdainfully. Vanessa. "But the rest of them have to, I suppose."

"I work in Pampas Steak Bar," says Witold. "A bad place. Many drunks. Call me bloody Argie. *What's it like to lose a war, Argie? Hands off the Falklands, Argie, okay? Hey, Argie—you like shagging sheep? You keep your filthy hands off those British sheep, Argie.'* I tell them I am Polish and they say they will smash my face in, wherever I come from."

"Very English, no?" Vanessa says and laughs. "Swear and fight and eat bad food. A good night out for the English."

"I work in Funky Sushi," says a Japanese boy called Gen. He's very shy and hasn't volunteered any information about himself until now. "You know Funky Sushi? No? Really? It's one of those—" He chats to Yumi in Japanese for a bit.

"Conveyor belt restaurant," says Yumi. She makes a circular motion with her hand. "Where the food goes round and round."

"Conveyor belt," says Gen. "Considered very low in Japan. Cheap place, for workmen. Driving trucks and so forth. Because sushi not fresh enough when it goes round and round and round. Too old. But here—very fashion. Funky Sushi always busy. Always the kitchen—what do you call it?—mental."

"We all work," says Yumi. "I work in bar. The Michael Collins."

"Irish pub," says Zeng. "Very good atmosphere. Guinness and The Corrs. I enjoy looking for my craic in an Irish pub."

Yumi shrugs. "Have to work. London too much money. Worse than Tokyo even. So we get tired from work. Apart from Vanessa."

"I get tired from my boyfriend," says Vanessa.

"But we like your lessons," Yumi says with conviction. She smiles at me, and I realize how pretty she is beyond all the war paint. "It's—what do you say?—nothing personal."

She looks down at her desk, then back at me, still smiling, until I am the one who is forced to look away.

•   •   •

When I get home I find Lena crying in the kitchen.

This shouldn't surprise me as much as it does. Since *Oranges for Christmas* went through the roof and my parents moved to this big white house, there have been a succession of au pairs and I have seen a few of them crying in this kitchen. There was the Sardinian who missed her mother's cooking. The Finn who missed her boyfriend. The German who discovered she didn't like getting out of bed before noon.

My parents treated all of these young women very well. Neither my mum nor my dad had grown up around any kind of hired help so they were far more than friendly to our au pairs. They were almost apologetic. Yet the au pairs still found a reason to cry all over their low-fat yogurt.

I thought Lena was different from the rest. She has that untouchable air about her that only the truly beautiful possess. For those of us who are merely average looking—or in my case, slightly below average—beauty seems like a magic shield. You can't imagine life ever wounding someone who has that magic shield around them.

But the ordinary looking always overestimate the power of beauty. Just look at Lena. A fat lot of good beauty did her. She has been crying her heart out.

Embarrassed to see me, she starts to dab away her tears with a piece of paper towel. And I'm embarrassed too, especially after I ask a stupid question.

"You all right, Lena?"

"I'm fine," she lies, wiping her perfect nose with the back of her hand.

"You want a coffee or something?"

She looks at me with wounded eyes.

"Just some milk. There's some organic left in the fridge. Thank you."

I bring Lena her glass of organic milk and sit across from her at the kitchen table. I don't want to get too close. In the presence of beauty, I always feel that I should keep my distance. Even at a time like this.

I watch her taking little bird sips from her milk, her lovely face red with spent emotion, her large blue eyes all puffy from crying. Strands of her blond angel's hair are damp with snot and tears. She twists the piece of paper towel in her fingers.

"What's wrong?" I ask, although I sort of know the answer already. An au pair doesn't cry these kind of desperate tears just because she misses Mutti's apple strudel.

This is man trouble.

Lena is silent for a while. Then she looks up at the ceiling, her mouth and chin trembling, her eyes suddenly full of tears.

"I just want someone who is going to love me forever," she says quietly, and I feel a surge of sadness and fear for her.

Forever? There's one thing wrong with forever. These days it seems to get shorter and shorter. That's the trouble with forever.

Blink and you miss it.

In the morning my mother waits until my father has gone to the gym and then she tells me that she wants us to give him a birthday party.

My mum is full of smiles and very pleased with this idea, even when I try to talk her out of it.

"He hates parties," I say. "Especially birthday parties. Especially his own."

"He's going to be fifty-eight," she says, as if that makes all the difference. "And he's got lots of friends, your dad."

Sometimes when I am talking to my mother I get the impression that we are having two different conversations. I tell her that he doesn't want to be reminded of his age. She tells me that he's going to be fifty-eight and that he has lots of friends. My mum often makes me feel like I've missed something.

"Mum, what's turning fifty-eight got to do with it?" I say.

"You think he wants to be reminded that he's fifty-eight? And he hasn't got lots of friends. Who are his friends?"

"You know," she says. "There are the journalists he worked with at the paper. All the sports people he knows. The book people."

"None of these people are his friends, Mum. They are just people he knows. He doesn't even like most of them."

She's not listening to me. She has made her mind up and she is busy getting ready for work. She already has her uniform on—a short-sleeved gingham dress made of nylon or some other man-made material with a kind of fake apron stitched on to the front. Later she will pull back her hair—still glossy and dark, although I think she might have been coloring it for a few years—and put on a little white pillbox hat.

My mum is a dinner lady at a local school. It's not the Princess Diana Comprehensive School for Boys, where I taught. She works at Nelson Mandela High, which is co-ed and even tougher. "The girls are as bad as the boys these days," my mum says. "Worse." But she refused to give up what she calls "my little job" even when the serious money started to pour in from my dad's book. That's why my parents need help with their big house. That's why Lena's here. Because my mum wouldn't give up her little job.

My mum loves Nelson Mandela. She really does. She likes having a laugh with the women she works with in the kitchen. She likes getting out of the house and giving some kind of shape to her day. But what my mum likes best about her job are the children.

I say children, although of course many of them are hulking great baritones who would sell their granny for the price of an ounce of pot. At least that's how I see them. My mother thinks that there's no such thing as a bad child.

"My kids," she calls them. She's sentimental about the children she feeds even though she has seen the worst of them, even though she has experienced them in all their surly, foul-mouthed violence, even though they are obviously not worth getting sentimental about. My mum still calls them "my kids."

She doesn't let her kids cheek her when they are lining up for their burgers and fries. She doesn't tolerate bad language in the school canteen. She doesn't even let the little bastards scrap with each other (better they beat the hell out of each other rather than their poor underpaid teachers, if you ask me).

My mother has been known to put down her ladle—or whatever it is she dishes out the gruel with—stride into the playground and break up a fight. I have told her dozens of times that she is barking mad, that she could get seriously hurt. She doesn't listen to me. She's only five foot two, my mum, but she's tough. And very stubborn.

She has worked at Nelson Mandela for almost twenty years, back in the days when it was still the Clement Attlee Grammar School. This means that there are men and women on the verge of middle age who remember her from their own years at the school. You might be walking down the street with my mother when some beer monster will suddenly come up to her and say, "Hello, Mrs. Budd, remember me?"

"Used to be one of my kids," my mum will say.

I don't understand how she can feel the way she does about these children. I guess it's because she has a lot of love to give. Far more than my father and myself ever really needed from her.

When I was growing up, my mother had a series of miscarriages. It's not something we talked about at the time. And it's not something we talked about later. But I clearly remember being a bystander to my parents' loss.

I don't know how many times it happened. More than once. I can remember that there were these times in my childhood when there was a lot of talk about me having a little sister or brother. Not from my parents—I guess after the first miscarriage you are too wary to count on anything—but I remember aunts and female neighbors smiling down at me, talking about how soon there was going to be someone that I would have to look after.

I didn't understand what they were talking about. I didn't understand the syrupy smiles or the coy allusions. I couldn't imagine anyone being so desperate that they needed me to look after them. I just didn't get it.

But later, when I saw my mother weeping without any apparent reason on the stairs of the little house where I grew up, when I saw her heart breaking while my father tried to comfort her, then I started to get it. The cute talk from the overconfident neighbors had abruptly stopped. I wasn't going to have a brother or sister. My parents were not going to have another child. Not this time. Not now. And, as it turned out, not ever.

I wondered where they were, my unborn little brothers and sisters. Were they in heaven? I tried my best to see them in my mind, my little brothers and sisters, but they were never real children to me, not like the other children at school or in the park, and not like the brothers and sisters of my friends.

These unborn siblings seemed more like an idea that someone had once had, an idea that had been thought about and then quietly put away. But I remember my mother weeping on the stairs, I remember watching her heart break, I remember her weeping as though those children were as real as me.

She loved me. She loved my father. She was very good at it. When we had hard times—when my dad was trying to write his book while still working full-time, when I lost Rose—my mum was our rock.

But no matter how much love she gave us, I always felt that she had more to give. I am not saying that's why she worked as a dinner lady at Nelson Mandela High. But all that unused love is why my mum can look at all those unlovely children and feel a genuine affection for them.

"We're giving him a birthday party," she says, putting on her coat. "Don't tell your nan. Or Lena. Or him."

"I don't know, Mum."

"It will do him good to celebrate his birthday," she says, and for just a second there I catch a glimpse of the woman who, at fifty-four years of age, still breaks up fights in the playground of Nelson Mandela High.

The work is not going well for my old man.

When the work was going well, the door to his basement study was shut but you could hear music blasting out of his stereo. It was always the old-school soul music he played, music that is full of profound melancholy and wild exuberance, music that was the sound of young America thirty years ago.

When the work went well, my dad played all the mating calls of his twenties—the Four Tops, Diana Ross and the Supremes, the Temptations, Smokey Robinson and the Miracles, Stevie Wonder—but now the work is going badly, or not going any-where at all, there is only silence in his basement room.

Sometimes I see him sitting at his desk, staring at his computer, a pile of fan letters by his side. People are always writing to his publishers to say how much they loved *Oranges for Christmas*, how they laughed and cried, how it reminded them so much of their own family. These letters, passed on by his publishers, should make my father feel good but all this appreciation seems to weigh heavily upon him, seems to make it even more difficult for him to get started on his new book.

My father is rarely at home these days. In the mornings he goes to the gym, pumping his pecs and crunching his abs and toning his buttocks until the sweat blinds him. At night he has endless chores and treats—there are drinks, dinners, launches, awards ceremonies and his wise, witty appearances at the artsy end of radio and television. Those long afternoons are the big problem for him. He stares at his computer screen for a while, Smokey and Stevie and Diana silent inside their CD cases and boxed sets, and then he calls a cab and slips off to the West End.

This is how my father fills his afternoons. He goes around the bookstores of Covent Garden and Charing Cross Road and Oxford Street, where he signs many copies of *Oranges for Christmas*. This makes his book easier to sell, so the stores are always pleased to see him, even though he is turning up unannounced and they have other things to do. The young staff fetch him a pile of books and a cup of coffee and my father sets to work.

I saw him once in one of those bookstores where they sell records, magazines and designer coffee, one of those new kind of bookstores where books are just one of the things they sell. He didn't see me and I didn't want to approach him. It would have felt like an intrusion into some private grief.

He looked so lonely.

It is possible that my father does other things in the West End when he escapes from his work and his family and his home. But that's how I see him, that's how he is fixed in my mind at this moment—sitting all by himself in the corner of a crowded bookstore, a cup of caffe latte growing cold by his side, passing the long, lonesome hours by writing his own name over and over again.

On Friday night some of my students want me to go to the pub with them.

I try to wriggle out of it, telling them that I don't really drink very much and I don't really go to pubs, but they seem hurt and disappointed and incredulous.

An Englishman who doesn't like pubs?

What's wrong with this guy?

So I tell them that I'll come along for just a quick one and they say that's fine, a quick one is good, because most of them have to go to work tonight in whatever bar or burger joint or sushi conveyor belt restaurant pays their rent.

Their local is an Irish pub off Tottenham Court Road called

the Eamon de Valera, and although it's not yet six, the place is already full of young men and women from all around the world and even a few locals knocking back the dark glasses of Guinness, Murphy's and Coca-Cola.

"Irish pub," Zeng tells me. "Very friendly atmosphere."

We find an empty corner of the Eamon de Valera and pull two tables together. My students start to get their money out but I tell them that their teacher will buy them a drink. I get in a round of stout and Coke.

There are five of us—me, Zeng, Wit, Gen and Astrud, a Cuban woman, married to a local. But Yumi and Imran are already in the pub, talking at the bar, and they come over to join us. Then Vanessa arrives with Churchill's other French girl and some young black guy with locks, and soon so many people are joining and leaving our party—Astrud thanks me for her Coke and goes, saying she has to meet her husband—that I can't tell where it begins and where it ends.

There is something touchingly democratic about our little group. Not just because they come from every corner of the globe, but because you couldn't imagine these people being friends or even sharing a drink in their home countries. Wit is pushing forty and Yumi is just out of her teens. Wit is permanently broke, sending every spare pound back home to his family, while Vanessa seems to have some kind of private income—all of her shopping bags are from Tiffany and Cartier. Then there is Imran, a handsome young man in Emporio Armani kit, and Zeng, who is wearing odd socks and spectacles mended with Scotch tape. They have nothing in common apart from Churchill's International Language School. But studying there has created a bond between them and I find myself doing something that I haven't done for a long time.

I find myself having a good time.

More drinks are ordered. Students shout at each other in fractured English over the sound of The Corrs asking what they can do to make you happy. Zeng is sitting next to me and I take the Guinness he is clutching away from him as he starts to nod off.

"Always sleeping," Yumi tuts.

"Wah," Zeng says, shaking himself awake. He smiles apologetically and reclaims his beer. "Sorry, sorry. Last night I did not sleep. My host family were arguing. Now I am very . . . I am very . . . fuck."

Gasps of astonishment around the table. A few snickers of laughter.

"No bad words!" Yumi says.

Zeng looks embarrassed. "Excuse me," he says, avoiding eye contact with his teacher.

"That's okay," I tell him. "These words are part of the language you're studying. A lot of great writers have used the vulgar vernacular. This is interesting. What are you trying to say? That you're very tired?"

Zeng sighs. "Yes. Last night my host family were arguing about some such thing. They were very drunk."

"He rents a room from a family who rent the room from someone else," Yumi says. "Illegal. And with very low people. Uneducated."

"They are not so bad," Zeng says. "But now I am very, very . . . fucking."

"No," Wit says. "You are fucked off."

"That means angry," I say.

"He is . . . perhaps . . . fucked up?" Wit suggests helpfully.

"He could say that. But that implies something other than tiredness. He could just say—I am fucked."

Zeng chuckles. "Yes, it's true. I *am* fucked."

"So many of these bad words in English," Wit says. "In German, there are many words for *you. Du, dich, dir, Sie, Ihnen, ihr* and *euch.* In English, there's only one word for *you.* But many bad words."

"Not so many bad words," I say. "But lots of different meanings to the bad words."

"Yes," Gen says. "Such as—*I do not give a fuck.*"

Yumi gasps. Vanessa titters. Wit stokes his chin in contemplation.

"Means—I do not care," Gen says loftily.

"Or you could call someone a useless fuck," I say.

"Means he is not very good at making love?" Yumi says.

"No, no," I say, blushing furiously. "It just means he's a useless person."

"Eskimos have fifty different words for snow," Wit observes. "The English have fifty different words for fuck."

"Fuck my old boots," I say.

Frowns around the table.

"What is this—fuck old boots?" Wit says.

"It's an expression of surprise," I explain. "Like fuck a duck."

"Sex with a . . . beast?" Zeng says. "Like in yellow films? Love with a duck?"

"We don't call them yellow films. That's a Chinese expression. Here we call pornography blue films."

"Wah!"

"No, fuck a duck's another exclamation of surprise."

"Like—fuck all?" Wit asks.

"No, that means—nothing."

"Fuck all means—nothing?"

"That's right. You're thinking of *fuck me.*"

"In the steakhouse where I work," Wit says, "there were these bad men. Very drunk."

"Mmm," Vanessa says. "Very English, no?"

"They were unhappy with their bill and called for the manager," Wit continues. "Then they threatened to kick the fuck out of him! And called him fuck face!"

"That's very bad," I say.

"What is this expression—to fuck someone's ass off?" Gen

says, as if he's enquiring about some arcane point of etymology. "Is it sex—how to say?—in the rear? Sex—how to say?—up the anal way? That you are a back door man?"

"No, it's got nothing to do with that. It just means sex that's done with a degree of enthusiasm. You see?" I tell them. "The great thing about English—the reason you are studying English rather than Chinese or Spanish or French—is that it's an endlessly flexible language."

"But English is a strange language," Wit insists. "What is this funny book—*Roger's Thesaurus?*"

"*Roget's Thesaurus,*" I say.

"Yes, yes. It's not a dictionary. It's a book of synonyms, yes? No book like that exists in my country."

"I think a book like *Roget's Thesaurus* is unique to English. That's why so many English words find their way into other languages. You can do what you like with it."

"Excuse me, please," Zeng says, getting up to go. "I must fuck off."

"He is leaving!" Gen says triumphantly. "Zeng has to leave for General Lee's Tasty Tennessee Kitchen."

"He must fuck off to work," Wit enunciates carefully, like a professor of phonetics concluding a particularly tricky tutorial. "Or the fuckers will give him the fucking sack."

And soon more of them are slipping away. Gen to the kitchen of a conveyor belt sushi restaurant on Brewer Street, Wit to that grim old-fashioned red-plush steakhouse on Shaftesbury Avenue where the bad men go, Vanessa to some smitten English boy at the bar who is going to take her dancing.

Soon there's only Yumi and me at our table in the Eamon de Valera and I'm finally speechless as I feel the effects of two pints of Guinness and her shining brown eyes.

"I like you, you're nice," she says.

Fucking hell.

6

MY GRANDMOTHER IS TELLING some big shot from the BBC that she is eighty-seven and still has all her own teeth. My mother looks wonderful in a long red dress, her hair piled on top of her head, and she seems very happy as she smiles and moves among the guests, checking that everyone is okay.

I am hovering on the edge of the evening, trying to overcome the quiet panic that I always feel at parties, fighting the fear that there will be no one for me to talk to. But after a while even I start to relax. It feels like a special night.

It's true that the guests are a very mixed bunch. The guffawing sports journalists with their Liverpool and Estuary and Irish accents seem to belong at a different gathering from the garrulous, well-spoken girls from television. The authors with their acres of corduroy and denim seem strangely subdued next to the leering late-night DJs with their big cigars. My nan, as frail as a sparrow in her floral party dress, seems to come from a different century from the man in Armani from the BBC.

But it is surprising how well people from different worlds can get on when there is goodwill in the air and expensive alcohol in their bloodstreams and good sushi being offered around. And there is real affection for my father in this room.

I told my mother that he had no real friends, but I was wrong. I feel that these people are all genuinely proud to know my dad. I sense that they admire and like him. They are honored to be here and excited about surprising him on his birthday. I feel proud of him, glad that he's my father.

They have come from the four corners of the city to celebrate my father's birthday. There are brash, beefy men who knew him from his years on the sports pages of national newspapers. There are youthful middle-aged men in colored spectacles, and loud girls in combat boots who know him from his appearances on their radio and television shows. There are people from his publishing house, sympathetic critics, important booksellers, talk show hosts, fellow writers, all these friends, colleagues and allies who have aided and abetted my dad's brilliant career.

The party is around our indoor swimming pool. We are in here because it is the only room in the house big enough to hide almost a hundred people. They are milling around the pool, taking drinks and satay and tamaki rolls from the waiters, making jokes about going for a dip. But this is a good place for a celebration.

The bright fluorescent lights make the party feel like it's being held in some kind of giant spotlight. The swimming pool shimmers turquoise and gold, the light catching the silver trays of the white-suited caterers as they move among guests holding twinkling flutes of champagne. A special night for a special man.

"He's coming!" my mother announces and the main lights go out. But the room is still not quite dark because there are spotlights in the swimming pool, shimmering under water like yellow ghosts. Someone hits another switch and the room is suddenly pitch black.

Guests giggle and murmur in the darkness as we listen to my father's Mercedes purring on the street. After a while the engine dies and soon there is the sound of his key in the door. There are another couple of self-conscious laughs which are urgently shushed. We wait for my father in complete darkness and total silence. Nothing happens. We wait some more. Still nothing happens. Nobody speaks. And then the door to the pool room finally opens.

There are shadows in the doorway, the soft ruffle of clothes, something like a sigh. We hear him step into the darkened room and wait for him to turn on the lights. But he doesn't. Instead there's the sound of creaking wood. He's on the diving board! He's going for a swim! All around me I can feel the laughter being stifled, the tension mounting.

Suddenly the lights come on and the room is full of grinning people and far too bright.

"Surprise!" someone shouts, and then the laughter abruptly dies in our throats.

My father is standing naked on the diving board, his disbelieving eyes slowly taking in the presence of everyone he knows. His eyes stop on my mother's face for a short horrible moment, and then he looks away in shame.

Lena is kneeling in front of him, fully clothed, her golden head bobbing up and down to some inner rhythm. She is making the diving board squeak.

But I'm the one she fancies, I think. *That should be me! It's not fair!* Then my father rests a hand on the back of her head. She stops moving, slowly opening her eyes, looking up at him.

The noise my mother makes is not a scream. It's not quite as formed as that, not so clear in its meaning. The noise my mother makes is more of a howl that somehow manages to contain disbelief, humiliation and a shame she doesn't deserve.

The party is paralyzed for a few seconds. Then my mother turns and barges her way through the guests, pushing aside a waiter, who loses his balance, seems to regain it for a second and then starts toppling toward the pool. A silver tray carrying half a dozen champagne flutes slips away from the palm of his hand and lands with a crash of metal and glass as he hits the water.

"Does this mean the party's over?" says my nan.

• • •

My parents were always Mike and Sandy. Never Sandy and Mike. Always Mike and Sandy. Always and forever, my father had top billing.

They seem like old-fashioned names to me, Mike and Sandy, names from an England that no longer exists, the England that was there when my parents and their friends and neighbors and my aunts and uncles were young.

It was an England of country pubs, dinner dances and trips to the seaside on Bank Holiday Monday. A land of small pleasures, quietly savored—card games (men and women) on Christmas night, football (men and boys) on Boxing Day, a trip to the local for a game of darts and a couple of pints (men only) when we had "guests."

That land was a cold, insular place with real winters, where every foreign holiday to Greece or Spain felt like the trip of a lifetime. The Beatles had come and gone and left behind a kingdom where suburban grown-ups smoked for the same reason that they wore paisley shirts and miniskirts, the same reason they nervously went to Italian and Indian restaurants— because they thought it made them look both young and sophisticated. The England of my childhood, that innocent place that yearned to be grown-up. Mike and Sandy's country.

Mike and Sandy. They are friendly names, approachable names, sociably abbreviated, the name of a respectable married couple who know how to have a laugh. Within reason.

Mike and Sandy. They are not their given names, of course. My father was Michael and my mother was Sandra. But somewhere in the sixties and seventies, when the clothes and the television sets and the expectations were going from black and white to color, when the austerity that had clung to the country like acne for twenty-odd years was finally clearing up, the names of the young—and the not quite so young, the new mothers and fathers—were becoming brighter and breezier too.

Mike and Sandy. The names of a married couple that was at home in a country where nobody ever left, nobody got divorced, nobody ever died and every family lasted forever.

He somehow gets his clothes on and escapes with Lena—or maybe he doesn't get his clothes on, maybe he just hops butt-naked into his flash car and drives away—but as the caterers fish the waiter from the pool we hear the Mercedes pulling away with a frightened shriek of rubber, as if he can't get out of our lives fast enough.

The next morning I wander through the silent house, looking at all the top-of-the-range detritus of his life, all those things he values so much, and I wonder why my mother doesn't trash the lot. It wouldn't settle the score. But it might make her feel better.

My mother could obliterate every trace of his rotten life. I wouldn't blame her. In fact I would be very happy to help her.

But she doesn't touch any of his things.

Instead, when she finally emerges from her bedroom the next morning, pale-faced and red-eyed, still wearing her beautiful party dress, insisting that she is all right, adamant that she doesn't want anything to eat or drink, my mother goes out to the garden she loves and sets about destroying it.

At the end of the garden there is a trellis where honeysuckle grows and smells sweet on summer mornings. My mother does her best to rip that down with her bare hands but she can't quite manage it, she can only pull down half of it and leaves the rest smashed but still attached to the wall.

There are terra-cotta pots containing new bulbs that she hurls against the garden wall, leaving behind shell bursts of exploded dirt. She hacks at her flower beds with rake and trowel and fingers, aborting all the spring bulbs that she recently planted with such endless care.

By the time I reach her she is tearing her hands to pieces by pulling up the rose bushes. I put my arm around her and hold her tight, determined not to let her go until she has stopped trembling. But she doesn't stop trembling. Her body shakes with shock and grief and rage and I can't do anything to stop it. She keeps shaking long after I have taken her back into the empty house and drawn all the blinds and tried to shut out the world.

And now I can sort of understand how it works, I can see how the world turns around and the child becomes the parent, the protected becomes the protector.

"Don't cry," I tell her, just as she told me after I had lost my first playground fight. "Don't cry now."

But I can't stop her. Because she's not just crying for herself. She's crying for Mike and Sandy.

You have to be a cold, hard man to walk out on a family and my father is not a cold, hard man.

Weak, perhaps. Selfish, definitely. Stupid, without question. But he is not cold and hard. At least, he is not cold and hard enough to do what he has just done—to amputate a family from his life—with ease. When I turn up at the doorstep of his rented flat, he looks torn. Torn between a life that is not quite over and another life that hasn't quite begun.

"How's your mother?"

"Take a wild guess. How do you think she is?"

"You're too young to understand," he tells me defensively, letting me inside.

Lena is not around. But there are the clothes of a young woman drying on a radiator.

"Understand what? That you felt the need for a bit on the side? That you thought you could play away and not get caught? That you're an old man who's desperate to recapture his youth? Understand what exactly?"

"To understand what can go wrong with a marriage. Even a

good marriage. The passion wears off. It just does, Alfie. And then you have to decide if you can live without it. Or not. Do you want a cup of tea? I think we've got a kettle here somewhere."

It's a good flat in a rich, leafy area. But it is very small and it belongs to someone else. The color of the paint was chosen by someone else. The pictures on the wall were bought to satisfy the taste of some stranger. I try hard but I can't imagine my father living here. In every way you can think of, this is just not his place. Everything feels rented, as though it could be repossessed at any moment, all snatched back by the rightful owner. The flat, the furniture, the girl. All just borrowed from someone else.

"How long is this going to last?" I ask him. He is still looking for a kettle. But he can't find one. "Dad? Can we forget the tea? You no longer own a kettle, okay? Start living with it. No kettle. Okay?"

"What are you talking about?"

"How long are you going to stay here with Lena?"

"Until we can find somewhere better."

"She's—what?—twenty-three?"

"Twenty-five," says my father. "Nearly."

"Younger than me."

"She's very mature for her age."

"I bet."

"What's that supposed to mean?"

I slump onto the leather sofa. My father hates leather sofas. Or he used to.

"Why couldn't you have just slept with her?" I ask, although I am very afraid that he is going to start giving me the details of their Olympian sex life. Please. Anything but that. "Isn't that what's meant to happen? I can understand why you're attracted to her. I can even sort of see why she would be attracted by you. An older, successful man. All that. But you're not meant to set up home together. This is madness, Dad."

My old man starts to pace up and down. The flat's living room is easily the biggest room in the place but it's still not very big. He takes a few steps and then he has to turn around. He is wringing his hands. I feel a jab of pity for the poor old bastard. He is not cut out for this game. He can't play it as ruthlessly as it needs to be played.

"These things have a momentum of their own. I tried to keep it under control, I really did. For a while there I felt like the luckiest man alive. I had the perfect wife and the perfect mistress."

"Your perfect wife wants to throttle you."

"But it doesn't last," he says, ignoring me. "That time doesn't last. It moves on. You can't have it all. And you have to decide." He turns to me, pleading for understanding. "Isn't that what every man wants? A wife and a lover? We want stability, support, a quiet life. But we also want romance, excitement, passion. Why should it be wrong to want the best of both worlds?"

"Because it's too much. You want too much. You ruin other people's lives by wanting too much."

"I can't help falling in love. I didn't plan for it to work out this way, Alfie."

"Love," I say. "Give me a break. Don't call it love."

"What else should I call it?" he says, suddenly angry. "Look, I'm sorry about your mother, Alfie. I really am. It's terrible the way she found out. But the heart wants what the heart wants."

"Dad," I say. "Listen to me. Lena is a great girl. But she dances when she eats. She still dances when she eats, okay? Haven't you noticed that? She bops around when she's listening to the radio, even if she's eating her breakfast. She's a child."

"She looks cute when she does that."

"Come on. She's young enough to be your daughter."

"Age has nothing to do with it."

"You'd love Lena if she was your age, would you? If she was almost sixty? I don't believe you. And she wouldn't want you if you were some kid of twenty-three living on a student loan and working in a burger joint."

"Twenty-five," he says. "Nearly."

"You can work it out with Mum. Apologize. Ask her to forgive you. We all make mistakes. You can't end a marriage because some au pair wags her tail at you."

"I can't do that. I've left your mother. And I've done it for love. Sorry, Alfie. But I have my principles."

I feel like hitting him.

"You've insulted love," I say, thinking of my mother's garden. "You've spat in its face, you ridiculous old man. You have someone in your life who has stuck by you for years, who supported you when you had nothing, and you do this to her. Don't talk to me about principles, okay? Don't paint yourself as some kind of romantic hero. You're not. And you didn't leave. You ran away."

He stops pacing.

"I'm sorry, Alfie. But I think I've done the right thing."

"Oh, you think you did the right thing, do you? You think that getting caught with your swimming trunks around your ankles in front of absolutely everyone you know was a smart move, do you? Well, Dad, that's open to debate."

"Leaving. I did the right thing by leaving." He gives me a strange look. "Did you know that your mother was expecting you when we got married?"

"I worked it out. It didn't take a mathematical genius. There's five months between your wedding and the day I was born."

"She was pregnant. That's why we got married. I loved her and everything. But we got married because—that's what you did back then. It's not like now. And do you know what they all told me? My family, my friends, my in-laws? They all told me:

you've had your fun. And I said nothing. But I always thought: *that was it? That was my fun?*"

"You think the party's just beginning, do you?"

"Look, I want to live with the person I want to sleep with. Is that so wrong? You're a man. You should try to understand. They say that if you want to stay with them you don't want to fuck them and if you want to fuck them then you don't want to stay with them. But I know now that's not true. Because I want it all from Lena."

"But it's not real. You've been listening to too many old records. This is not a Smokey Robinson song, Dad. This is real life."

My father looks at me with something approaching pity.

"Don't tell me about real life, Alfie," he says quietly, and I know exactly what he is about to say next so I get up to go. I try to leave quickly because I don't want to hear it, I am heading toward the door of his rented flat before he can even get the words out.

"You're still in love with someone who's dead," my father tells me.

Love didn't make me a better person. Just the opposite. Love made me indifferent to the rest of the world. Love narrowed my horizons down to a pair of blue eyes, to a goofy smile, to one young woman.

Shortly after Rose and I had begun, I was on a plane flying back to Hong Kong. I had just spent a week with my parents, my first trip home since leaving London, a trip that had been arranged long before I met Rose. It was too late to cancel so I went to see my mother and father and grandmother but there was no pleasure in it for me; my heart was somewhere else. I wanted to get it over with, to get out of London, to get back to Hong Kong, to get back to her, to get back to Rose.

But there was a problem on the plane. A serious problem. A

man—this middle-aged executive sitting across the aisle from me—suddenly became short of breath. He gasped for air, he made strange croaking noises, he looked like he was choking to death. At first I assumed that he had overdone the complimentary drinks. But then, as the stewardesses crouched by his side and the pilot asked if there was a doctor on board, it soon became clear that he was sick, very sick.

They laid him in the aisle, stretched out on the floor, right beside me, close enough to touch his terrified face, and two young doctors knelt by his side, pulling his shirt open, talking to him like priests beside a death bed.

We couldn't fly to Hong Kong. The man needed a hospital and so our flight diverted to Copenhagen where a medical crew was waiting to take him off the plane. And all the passengers were very understanding about the diversion, of course they were, even when they learned that we would have to wait for hours at Copenhagen Airport until we could get another crew. Our pilot explained that our crew could no longer take us to Hong Kong because, with the diversion, they would exceed their permitted hours in the air. So we had to wait. For hours.

Everybody was very understanding. Everybody except me.

I hated that sick man. I didn't want to divert to Copenhagen so that he could get medical treatment. I wanted the pilot to stick him in with the suitcases and let him take his chances. It was worse than indifference. I felt a rage toward him that I could hardly contain. I didn't care if he lived or died. It meant nothing to me. I just wanted him out of the way so that I could get back to Hong Kong, back to my girl, back to my life, back to the best thing that had ever happened to me.

That's what love did to me.

Love messed up my heart.

7

ROSE WAS BEAUTIFUL IN THE WATER. She had been diving for years, long before she came out to Hong Kong, and she had that still, weightless quality that separates good divers from the rest of us.

We looked like two different creatures when we were underwater. I was always a nervous wreck, struggling to maintain neutral buoyancy, constantly fiddling with the air in my BCD jacket, letting a little out as I started drifting to the surface, letting a little in as I began to sink, never getting it right for very long.

Rose just hung there, floating in space, doing it all with her breathing, doing it all with minor adjustments to the air in her lungs, remaining weightless with what seemed like little more than sighs.

I was never happy with my equipment, forever clearing my mask of water, nervously checking my air gauge to see exactly how much was left—I was a glutton for air, always having to return to the surface long before anyone else—and adjusting my tank as its heavy weight seemed to shift and slide on my back.

I just didn't look happy underwater. Like all good divers, Rose looked as though there was nowhere else she would rather be.

She had learned to dive at home. She had gotten her scuba

diving card in freezing dark waters off the south coast of England and in a flooded quarry in the Midlands. She had done it the hard way. So the dive sites of Asia—warm blue waters, endless coral reefs, so much marine life that sometimes the fish blotted out the sky—seemed like the next best thing to paradise.

I learned to dive because of Rose. I had a crash course on our honeymoon in Puerto Galera in the Philippines, getting used to breathing underwater in the hotel swimming pool with a local instructor and a couple of twelve-year-old Taiwanese, learning the theory in some little classroom behind the resort's dive shop and finally being taken out into open water for the real thing. Rose was as excited as me when I got my scuba diving card. Maybe more.

And we had some good times. Once, on a weekend trip to Cebu in the Philippines, I sucked up most of my air in a ridiculously short amount of time and got sent up by the dive master. I had to make a safety stop for three minutes at a depth of five meters to let the excess nitrogen seep out of my body. Although her tank still had plenty of air, Rose came up with me and those few minutes making that safety stop were the best diving that I ever had. We hung there together in the shallow waters where the light was dazzling, the coral reef shining like a treasure chest, watching a school of angel fish swarm around us as our bubbles of air mixed together and rose lazily to the surface.

But diving was just one of the many things that Rose did far more easily than me. She was comfortable at parties and meeting new people and floating weightless 15 meters below the surface of the South China Sea. But no matter how much I tried—and I tried hard because I wanted to please her more than anything in the world—I really couldn't be. It just wasn't in me. That was the difference between us underwater and, now I come to think of it, everywhere else.

I swam.

She flew.

• • •

It felt wrong from the start.

On Friday night the weather had been still and clear, typical of this part of the Philippines in late spring, but by the time we were walking down to the beach on Saturday morning, the blue skies were turning to gun-metal gray and the waves out at sea were showing flecks of white foam.

We were already in our wet suits. I was carrying a big yellow dive bag containing our masks, snorkels and fins. We would rent the rest of our kit from the.dive shop. I watched Rose squinting up at the sky.

"We could just chill out at the hotel," I said. "The weather doesn't look great."

"It'll be fine," she said. "Ramon won't take us out if there's any problem."

Ramon was the dive instructor of the resort, a stocky Filipino in his early forties, who watched over his dives with calm authority. A lot of dive sites in the Philippines have noto-riously unpredictable currents, which means you can see some beautiful coral growth. But tricky currents also mean you need an experienced guide to take you out. We had spent a few week-ends at this resort and Ramon had always led our dives and had taken good care of us. But when we arrived at the dive shop, Ramon wasn't there.

In his place there was a skinny kid, no older than twenty, unusually tall for a Filipino, his worn and ragged wet suit pulled off his brown, bony shoulders. He was laughing with a pair of European tourists, a couple of tall blonde girls in bathing suits who looked so healthy and milk-fed that they could only be Scandinavian.

"Where's Ramon?" I said.

"Ramon sick," he said, glancing at me for just a second before turning his attention back to the blondes. "I take the dive today."

I looked at Rose for a moment. She just shrugged and smiled. She really wanted to dive that day. So we joined the other divers next to a row of battered scuba tanks and started putting our equipment together as the little dive boat came into the bay and chugged toward the beach, its bow lifting and falling with the waves.

I selected a tank, BCD and regulator, strapped the BCD to the tank, made sure it was good and tight, then attached the regulator to the tank. The four black hoses of the regulator snaked around my feet like half an octopus.

Two of the regulator's hoses had mouthpieces—a black one for me and a bright yellow one for anyone who might need it— another hose ended with gauges monitoring air supply and depth, and the final hose had a metal clip that I attached to the BCD. There was a little hose on my BCD so that I could regulate my buoyancy by inflating or deflating it. Finally I turned on the tank's valve and, as it hissed into life, checked the air supply.

The gauge read 210 bar. A full tank. Everything was as it should be. Except somehow it wasn't as it should be at all.

What I liked about Ramon was that he was always there while we were putting our equipment together. He would advise us about the amount of weights we needed, he would check to see that our kit was up to scratch, he would make sure our checks were done properly. I needed all that.

Ramon always gave me the impression that nothing was more important to him than safety. But as the rising wind whipped off the sea, I thought that this skinny kid acted as though nothing were more important to him than large Norwegian breasts.

I stood at the stern of the boat, feeling it pitch and fall beneath my feet, taking a part of my stomach with it every time it fell. The fins that I was wearing made it easier for me to keep my balance but harder for me to move. I stood there staring at the heads bobbing up and down in the choppy sea. They looked so fragile.

Everyone else was in the water. The skinny dive master. The Norwegian girls. A young Japanese couple. A rubbery old German who looked as though he had spent his life under the tropical sun. And Rose, her face half-hidden behind her mask but lifted toward me. They were all waiting for me.

It was raining hard now. The coast wasn't far away—we had reached the dive site in less than twenty minutes—but it was completely hidden behind a mist that seemed to be growing thicker by the second. Black clouds rumbled and rolled above the dive boat. There was a clap of thunder overhead, a jagged slash of lightning on the horizon. The rain seemed to be coming in sideways. I placed one hand on my mask and another on my tank and stepped off the side of the boat.

I hit the water, went under for an instant and was suddenly on the surface. The waves were even rougher than they looked from the boat and I took in a mouthful of water, managing to gag most of it up.

My mask was already getting misty. I should have spat on the glass and cleaned it with sea water, as that always prevented it steaming up, but it felt like there hadn't been enough time. The skinny dive master had taken us all up to the bow to talk through the dive plan and next thing after that we were getting into the water. I pulled off my mask, hawked on the glass and dipped it under the water, rubbing hard.

Rose was finning to my side. "You okay?"

"I miss Ramon," I said, tasting the salt and bile.

"Me too. I think we're off."

I pulled on my mask and saw that the rest of them were already going down. I quickly stuffed in the mouthpiece of my regulator and faced Rose. She made a thumbs-down gesture, meaning *going down,* and I returned the signal. I released a few puffs of air from my jacket and exhaled, immediately starting to sink feet first below the waves.

I was aware of the hull of the boat, other divers nearby, the dive master floating weightless far below us. And that's when I felt the excruciating pain in the bridge of my nose. I was going down too fast, the pressure on the air space in my sinuses was causing a squeeze.

Rose was beside me, making a soothing gesture with her hands, slowly waving them in front of her chest—*take it easy, take it easy.* I nodded, went up a meter and the squeeze immediately cleared.

With one hand I made my thumb and index finger into a circle—*I'm okay*—and with the other I pinched my nose, gently blowing through it as I once more tried to go down. This time it worked and I slowly began to sink without my nose feeling as though it was in a vice.

Visibility was poor. I was used to seeing these waters flooded with sunlight and marine life, but today the sea was murky and dark, with only a few fish swimming through the gloom, bright splashes of color in the enveloping darkness. Then I realized that Rose and I were alone.

Rose was floating weightless by my side, looking all around. But there was no sign of the other divers. They had left us. Water began to seep into my mask. I tilted my head upward, pulled back my mask and roughly exhaled through my nose. My mask cleared. Rose was looking at me, her blue eyes wide behind glass, jerking her thumb from side to side.

Which direction?

I checked around, hoping for the reassuring sight of some human shapes finning through the darkness. There was nothing. And every direction looked the same. I gazed up at the hull of the boat, far above us now. It seemed to be drifting away from us. Or perhaps we were doing the drifting. Rose jerked her thumb to the right.

Go that way.

I shook my head. Was she crazy? She was indicating that we should swim out to sea. I stabbed my thumb in the opposite direction, toward the shore. Or to where I imagined the shore to be.

Go that way.

She shook her head, tapping the compass she had strapped to her wrist. My finger and thumb formed a reluctant circle.

Okay.

She led the way and we finned into the darkness. My mouth was dry with nerves. I looked at my air gauge. Still plenty left.

Then we were suddenly on top of it, emerging out of the twilight like some great abandoned city, the rotting gray and black metal encrusted with more than fifty years of coral.

A sunken Japanese troop ship from World War II.

We grinned at each other with shock and elation. This ship was the reason for our dive. There was still no sign of the others but they were probably on another part of the ship. You could only see a fraction of it in this light. By now we didn't care.

The ship was sitting in deep water but the upper deck and the bridge were just about within our limit. We finned across the deck and I felt something icy enter my heart. The gaping windows of the bridge were like empty eye sockets. The dead wood of the deck was like dried bones. Men had died in this place.

We were in a graveyard.

I knew that we shouldn't be here. Rose indicated the gaping hold, giving me the thumbs up as she pointed into the black abyss. I emphatically shook my head. Was she crazy? I tapped my air gauge. Time to think about going up.

Rose hovered weightless above the void, her arms crossed casually in front of her chest, her breathing regular. Then she reared backward as a giant turtle suddenly emerged from the darkness of the hold and almost collided with her. She looked at me, her eyes wide with wonder, and I had to smile.

The turtle had the head of a thousand-year-old man and yet it moved with an impossible grace. Below the crusty shell its legs were like magic paddles and it glided across the surface of the sunken ship as if it believed itself to be a thing of infinite beauty. And in a way, it was. So I was hardly surprised when Rose began to follow it into the colder waters where the bottom of the sea abruptly dropped away beneath us.

The turtle—it had to be a female, it was so large—turned its bald head to look at Rose, its large eyes blinking with what seemed more like shyness than alarm. Rose gently touched the scaly shell and spun on her back, shaking her head with a joy that was unconfined. Then the current hit us.

It was like being seized by a giant hand and thrown into a tunnel that went all the way to the end of the world.

Rose and the turtle and the ship were gone. I was going down into the freezing blackness and I couldn't stop myself. There was a sheer wall of coral by my side and I tried to fin toward it. I kept trying until my legs were heavy with exhaustion, but the down current was like being trapped in a broken lift, and I believed that this would be the last day of my life.

My face and body slapped hard against the coral, knocking my regulator out of my mouth and cracking my mask. I grabbed two fistfuls of razor-sharp coral and held on tight as it tore at my fingertips. Swallowing a gutful of sea water, I fumbled for my regulator through my broken vision and forced it into my mouth, gulping terrified mouthfuls of air. My mouth was dry. Completely dry. My wet suit was shredded on one side. There was a terrible pain in my hip.

I looked for Rose. I couldn't see her. I checked my gauges. Forty meters. And down to 30 bar of air. But I couldn't surface. Rose might be looking for me. Rose would definitely be looking for me.

Then I saw her, clinging to a clump of dead coral, her legs horizontal from her body in the current. She had lost her mask. Her eyes were half closed and almost blind. But she finned over to me, one bloody hand clinging to the coral, the other waving across her chest.

Calm down, calm down.

I nodded, sort of laughing and crying at the same time. I began to float upward. She gripped my BCD and pulled me down with a strength I never knew she possessed. If I came up too fast from this depth, I would certainly get decompression sickness and possibly die. But I couldn't stop myself from drifting upward. I just couldn't stop myself.

Rose pointed at my waist. I had lost my weight belt. Still holding on to me, she desperately tore a rock from the face of the coral and stuffed it into my hands to weigh me down. But my hands were ripped and torn, and I couldn't hold it. It slipped through my fingers.

I looked at my air gauge. It was all gone. Rose forced her spare mouthpiece between my lips. But there was next to nothing there. The short gasps of breath seemed to stutter and die. We were breathing borrowed air.

Rose touched the top of my head.

Then we let go of the coral.

I started to ascend to the gathering light while Rose, looking like an astronaut cut from her mooring in space, no longer trailing bubbles, drifted down into shadows that seemed to stretch to infinity.

I watched her drop away from me through the tears and bloody mucus that streaked the inside of my cracked mask. I tried to say her name but I couldn't make a sound.

She was my reason.

8

WHAT I NOTICE FIRST about her are the clothes.

Her black raincoat is unbuttoned and you can see her tube top, short skirt and these sort of furry high heels. Are they called kitten mules? She looks like she's on her way to a club. A bit too much makeup. Her skin is white and her tights are black and her hair is bottle blond. The roots need some attending to. Is that a gold ankle chain concealed beneath her tights? Probably. She doesn't look as though she's going to some funky, fashionable club in the middle of town. She looks like she's going to a club in the deepest suburbs.

She is pretty but exhausted looking, like a former beauty queen who is down on her luck.

She's in the staff room at Churchill's when I turn up for work. Usually the room is empty when I arrive, but today this tired, pretty woman is occupying our only armchair, her face in a battered paperback.

That's odd, I think to myself. You don't see many teachers dressed like that.

"Have you read this?" she says, looking up.

Her voice is pure, working-class London. She has to be from Essex. Nobody talks like that in London anymore.

"What is it?"

"The Heart Is a Lonely Hunter," she says. "By Carson

McCullers. She wrote it when she was twenty-three. It's about this young girl called Mick growing up in Georgia during the Second World War."

"I know what it's about. It's about loneliness. I used to teach it."

"Really?" she says, her painted eyes wide with wonder.

"Yes. To a bunch of fifteen-year-old boys who wouldn't know their heart from their elbow."

"You really taught this book?"

"That's right."

"But did you read it?"

"What do you mean?"

"I mean, did you love it? Did it mean anything to you?"

"Well, I thought that the plot was a little—"

"Because to me it's about the way life cheats you."

"Well, the central theme of the book—"

"Look at Mick. She starts out full of dreams, full of plans. She wants to travel the world. She wants to be a musician. She wants to bust out of her little town. Everything excites her. And then she gets cheated."

"Cheated?"

"Cheated. How old is she at the end of the book? Sixteen? Fifteen? She's got a job in Woolworth's because her family is so poor. And she already knows that none of her dreams are going to come true. Mick's been cheated." She smiles, shaking her head. "Wow! You taught *The Heart Is a Lonely Hunter*. Incredible."

"I'm Alfie, by the way."

She stands up. "Jackie Day," she says.

Then she does something that makes me realize that she is not a teacher at all.

She goes to the cupboard in the corner of the room, forages around for a minute and comes out wearing a pair of yellow gloves. Why is she wearing yellow gloves to teach English as a foreign language?

Next she pulls on a blue nylon work coat, a bit like the one my mum wears in the kitchens of Nelson Mandela. Then she is standing there with a bucket in one hand and a bottle of disinfectant in the other.

It's a bit like watching Clark Kent turn into Superman.

If Superman was a cleaning lady.

They pulled me from the sea and gave me oxygen on the deck of the dive boat.

I remember voices speaking in Tagalog, someone shouting into a radio, the boat's engine kicking into life. Someone said something to me about a recompression chamber in Cebu. They needed to get me to a recompression chamber. I had come up from too deep, too fast. There were bubbles of excess nitrogen in my flesh and in my blood, although I couldn't feel them yet. But I was definitely going to get the sickness. The decompression sickness.

I remember that I was flat on my back, the oxygen mask clamped across my mouth, the rain lashing my face. As I tried to sit up and tell them to wait for Rose, the bends began with a blinding pain in my back that made me gasp and weep. I had never known pain like it. My vision blurred with tears, and stayed blurred even when the tears were gone. With every second my eyesight was fading. I felt dizzy and sick, there was a tingling pain in all my joints, especially across my neck, shoulders and back, but what frightened me the most about the sickness was my fading vision. I was very quickly going blind. By the time we reached Cebu, I kept my eyes closed because the coming darkness terrified me, just terrified me.

Strapped to a stretcher, I was bundled on to the dock and into an ambulance. I couldn't move my legs by now. I couldn't even feel them. My head felt as though someone was hitting it with a hammer. A voice said something about an air embolism. They said it was a little bubble of air at the base of my brain, that was why I couldn't feel anything in my legs. An air embolism. Jesus. I remember I kept my eyes closed. I remember praying. Even though I had lost everything that ever mattered to me, I didn't want to die. I was very afraid.

The ambulance edged slowly through the thick Philippine traffic, its siren howling. At our destination there were excited voices in Tagalog and English as the stretcher was carried down crowded corridors. Finally we were in what seemed like some kind of cool, subterranean tomb. I remember there was the sound of a heavy metal door being opened and then, after I was carried inside, closing behind me. I remember I felt as though I had been deposited in a bank vault. This was the recompression chamber.

Someone was with me. A woman. A middle-aged Filipina. She held my hand and stroked my face and told me in good English that I was very sick but that everything was going to be all right. She promised to stay with me.

The chamber smelled damp and musty. It was all blackness. And I wondered how you know when you are dead, if it is possible to get it wrong, if you could mistake death for something else. I remember I kept thinking that perhaps I was dead already. Then after a stretch of time that couldn't be measured, there were shadows in the chamber and a numb sensation in my legs.

The woman holding my hand told me that I was doing fine but I needed a special injection to stop the bubble at the base of my brain from swelling. A steroid injection. The woman laughed nervously and told me that she had only ever injected oranges before. There were people looking through the little portholes of the recompression chamber, telling her what to do, excited voices speaking in Tagalog, although all Tagalog sounds excited to me.

Frankly, the needle in the hands of the woman who had only injected oranges seemed like the least of my problems. And after all the nerves and anticipation and excited voices, her injection was next to nothing, like a bee sting given to a man who had just had the living daylights kicked out of him.

I remember she stayed awake with me. She constantly reassured me, and I felt like crying at her kindness. My vision slowly began to clear, my eyes sticky and sore, and she was revealed to me as a small woman about my mother's age.

For the last ten hours in the chamber we were on special oxygen masks, and she squeezed my hand every time I had to take a breath. That's what she had to do, that woman who saved my life. She had to keep reminding me to take another breath.

We were in that recompression chamber for two days and two nights, the sickness slowly seeping out of me. But sometimes I feel they didn't get it all out. Sometimes I think sickness came into me that day. And it will be there for as long as I am.

It's strange the way the loss of one person can leave such a giant hole in the middle of your life. It's not as if the hole they leave behind feels like the size of another human being.

It feels more like the size of a world.

I should be going out more. I really should. Not all the time, of course. It's far too soon to be going out all the time. It will always be too soon for that. But I should be going out once in a while.

One thousand years from today, I will be ready to go clubbing. I'll put it in my diary. A man has his needs, you know. And a woman too no doubt.

But when I don't see Josh, and I don't see Josh all that often, I usually spend my nights in my room, listening to Sinatra on my mini stereo system, usually one of the great Capitol albums of the fifties, but sometimes a Reprise record from the sixties or seventies—not so good, of course, but not so familiar either.

What is it about this music? I like the upbeat stuff, songs like "Come Fly with Me" and "They Can't Take That Away from Me," albums like *A Swingin' Affair!* and *Songs for Swingin' Lovers!* But what I like best are the songs about love breaking down. "In the Wee Small Hours," "Angel Eyes," "One for My Baby," "Night and Day," "My Funny Valentine" and all the rest.

Listening to Sinatra makes me feel as though I am not the only person in the universe who ever woke up to find themselves in some place that they never imagined. Listening to Sinatra makes me feel that I am not so alone. Listening to Sinatra makes me feel more human.

Frank recorded entire albums—*Where Are You?, No One Cares, Only the Lonely*—about missing some woman. The hippies think they invented concept albums in the sixties, but Frank Sinatra was doing it in the fifties. Sinatra will talk to you about it all night long, if you need him to. And I need him to.

I need this music the way normal men need food and football. Sinatra seems to point a way forward, to encourage me to get on with my life. When Sinatra sings of love dissolving, there is always the consolation of love to come. Love is like a bus in these songs. There's always another one along in a minute.

But I know that's not how it was in Sinatra's heart. I have read all the classic texts, and I know that Sinatra never got over Ava Gardner. She was the woman who owned his heart. She was the one whose photograph he tore up, threw away and then stuck back together with Scotch tape. If Sinatra never got over Ava, then why should I get over Rose?

The music is an endless source of comfort, though. Sinatra makes missing someone sound noble, heroic, universal. He makes suffering sound as though it has some kind of point to it. And in the real world, it doesn't. It just hurts like hell.

And there's something else. As Sinatra mourns love, celebrates love, anticipates love, I can almost smell the manly cocktail of Old Holborn and Old Spice when my grandfather sat me on his lap, back when the world was young and everything was ahead and it felt as though everybody that I ever loved would live forever.

The way my mother deals with my father going away is to carry on as normal. She gets up in the morning, she goes to work in the kitchens of Nelson Mandela High, she comes home with an affectionate smile and stories of her kids. She even starts to take an interest in her garden—or at least she busies herself clearing up the mess she made when the old bastard walked out. This is how my mum reacts to a crisis.

It's not that she ignores it. She just refuses to look it in the eye.

I go to work, wander the streets of Chinatown, listen to Sinatra in my room. And all the while I fantasize that one day my father will be there, bearing flowers and full of apologies, on his knees before my mother, begging for forgiveness. It doesn't happen.

I don't see how he can build a life with Lena on such flimsy foundations. I can't imagine how they can form a lasting union when they don't even own a kettle. I am convinced that one morning he will see her dancing in her chair as she eats her high-bran breakfast, and it will drive him nuts.

But I start to realize that even if their love nest does get repossessed, that doesn't mean that my old man is ever coming back home.

There are phone calls between my parents. I make no attempt to listen because there are things that happen between your mother and father that you want to keep your distance from. The pattern is always the same. He calls her. There are long silences while he—I don't know. Pleads for understanding? Asks when he can pick up his Stevie Wonder records? Asks if he can borrow a kettle? I don't know what she tells him, but I can hear that she tries to keep the bitterness and hurt and anger out of her voice.

It's impossible.

She likes to act as though nothing that my father does surprises her, that she knows him so well, that all this upheaval is only what she would expect from the man she has been married to for half a lifetime. It's not true.

His new life in some other part of the city is beyond her

imagination. She doesn't understand how he got there, why this happened, when the world-sized hole in her life started to form.

When she comes off the phone she is smiling—a smile that is there for her protection, a smile as rigid as a bulletproof vest.

My mother and I have an early dinner at the Shanghai Dragon.

This is not a normal night out for us. Apart from the summer holidays of my childhood—bed-and-breakfasts in the seaside towns of southern England when I was small, the tourist canteens in the hotels of Greece and Spain when I was bit bigger—we have not spent a lot of time together in restaurants. Surprisingly for a woman who gets so much pleasure from feeding one thousand brats every day of the school year, my mother prefers "my own cooking, in my own house."

But since my father went away, she is not eating very much and that frightens me. Always slim—where my dad's life as a working journalist meant his waist size increased with every passing year, one extra pound per annum being the general rule—she is starting to look hollow-eyed and gaunt. I know that part of that is a lack of sleep because I hear her wandering around downstairs in the middle of the night as I toss and turn in my own bed, my own solitude. It is also because there are no more real family meals to prepare, because there is no more real family.

But my mum seems happy when she gets her first look at the Shanghai Dragon.

"Very nice, dear," she says, admiring a grotesquely deformed root swimming in a jar like the outcome of some abominable scientific experiment. I now see that the dark nooks and crannies of the Shanghai Dragon are full of these roots. "Very nice indeed."

Joyce emerges from the kitchen. She looks at my mother admiring the things in jars.

"You like?"

"Lovely!"

"You know?"

My mother squints at the jars. "It's ginseng, isn't it? The real thing. Not the capsules and pills that you buy in a drugstore."

Joyce smiles, pleased with my mother. "Ginseng," she says. "I can't pull the sheep over your eyes. Yes, ginseng. Good for stress. When your body tired. When your body sad."

"I could do with some of that," my mum laughs, and I feel like hugging her.

"Please," Joyce says, indicating the empty restaurant with an expansive gesture, asking us to choose a table.

The atmosphere in the Shanghai Dragon at six is very different from the mood at midnight. There are no drunks. Apart from my mother and me, there are not even any customers.

While we eat our Peking duck, my mum doing better with the chopsticks than I expected as we load our pancakes with spring onions, cucumber, plum sauce and duck, the Chang family are also eating their dinner at one of the tables in the takeout section. All the tables in the Shanghai Dragon have a white tablecloth apart from one. This is where the Changs eat their meals.

The entire family is there. George is spooning soup noodles from a huge bowl into six smaller bowls. He has his grandchildren next to him, the small boy on one side and the girl on the other side, both of them expertly wielding chopsticks that look far too big for them. The children's dad, plump Harold, is noisily slurping noodles as though he has to do it within a certain time limit. His wife Doris is eating more slowly, but with her face so close to her bowl that her glasses are steaming up. Joyce barks instructions in Cantonese—at her husband, her son and his wife, and especially her two grandchildren—between checks to ensure that my mother and I are all right.

I realize how much I envy the Changs. I envy their closeness, their sense of belonging, the unbroken quality of their lives. Their completeness. Looking at them together makes me feel sad. But not really sad. It's a kind of longing. Because I was once part of a family like that.

The Changs have dispersed by the time we pay the bill—George and Harold into the kitchen, the children and Doris to the flat upstairs. Only Joyce remains to welcome the first of the evening rush.

When we leave she pushes a brown paper bag into my mother's hands that I know contains something to help my mum with all the things that are wrong in her broken world.

"My gift to you," Joyce says.

What did Rose see in me? She could have had the pick of any lipless wonder in her firm's office. Why did she choose me?

Because I'm a nice guy. That doesn't sound like much—it sounds like the kind of thing that women say they want, just before they go off with the spunky hunk in his Maserati. But Rose wanted a nice guy. And she picked me.

It's true. I *was* a nice guy. I always fell in love with the women I slept with, even when love was neither requested nor appropriate. I could never fuck around without feeling. A lot of the things that young men do without thinking were beyond me. Because I had listened to too many Sinatra records. Because I always wanted a trip to the moon on gossamer wings rather than a quick lay. Because I was looking for the one.

She saw something in me. Something that was worthy of love.

But niceness is finite. It's like money and youth. It ebbs away when you are not looking. It leaks out of you. Look at me now. I'm nowhere near as nice as I used to be.

I don't want to give up on life and love and all the rest of it, but I can't help myself. It's because life and love and all the rest of it have given me a good hiding. Life has made me feel like death warmed over.

I've lost my faith and I don't know how I can ever get it back. Because I still miss someone. And because I will always miss her.

Is that okay, Rose? Is it okay to miss you?

9

IT IS THE DEAD PART OF THE AFTERNOON but the private members' club is still full of soft-looking men and hard-looking women lingering over their drinks and talking about projects that will probably never happen.

Just like my father.

If you ask me, my dad's new love is a project that will never get the green light. My old man and his girlfriend—something tells me they are going to be languishing in development hell. Just a hunch.

"You'll come to the wedding, I hope," he says.

I look at him, hiding behind a still mineral water in his Soho club, nervously hunting in the free bowl of Twiglets. I can't quite tell if he is trying to provoke me or if he is completely insane.

"Whose wedding is that?"

"My wedding. My wedding to Lena."

"Oh, did you get a divorce?"

"Not yet."

"Did you even get a divorce lawyer?"

"Not yet."

"Then maybe it's a little premature to start playing 'Here Comes the Bride' and chucking around confetti, don't you think? Maybe it's a little early to start sending out the embossed invitations and ordering the cake."

He leans forward, trying to keep this between the two of us.

"I'm just attempting to make you see that this is serious," he says. "You act as though it's laughable."

"You're mutton dressed up as ram, Dad. That's not funny?"

"What would be funny would be if I wanted a woman my own age. But why would I want someone that looks like me?"

"Like your wife, you mean?"

"I love your mother, Alfie. Always did, always will. And I intend to take care of her."

"All heart, aren't you?"

"But passion dies. It does. You don't believe me because you never got the chance to find out."

"That's right."

"And I'm sorry about that, Alfie, I truly am. I loved Rose. You know that."

It's true. My dad loved Rose. He broke down at the funeral. Right at the end. He just fell to pieces.

"Passion fades away, Alfie. It turns into something else. Friendship. Affection. Habit. That's enough for some people. And for other people, it will never be enough."

I call for the bill, sick of talking to him, but he insists on paying. What a big shot.

When we are out on the street he puts a conciliatory hand on my shoulder and, although I make no move to touch him in return, I can't help but love him. He will always be my father. I can't imagine ever replacing him with a better model. I am stuck with him.

"I just want one more chance for happiness," he says. "Is that so wrong?"

I watch him move off through the narrow streets of Soho, a good thirty years older than most of the people here, all sipping their designer coffee and eyeing each other up and letting the afternoon drift by, all these youngish people with time to waste, and I feel a surge of enormous pity for my father.

One more chance, I think.

Doesn't he know? Doesn't he get it? Doesn't my father understand anything?

You get one shot at happiness.

The funeral was all wrong.

I had been to funerals before, but they were not like this, nothing like it. The funerals of my three dead grandparents were nothing like the day we buried Rose.

Too young. Not just her. The mourners were too young. In their twenties, most of them, friends from school and the old neighborhood, mates from university and the shop. Many of them looked as though they were going to a funeral for the first time. They had probably never even buried a grandparent. One or two of them might have lost a goldfish or a hamster. And they were in shock. They didn't even own black ties—that's how absurdly young they were. They didn't know what to wear, how to act, what to say. It was all too soon. Too soon. I knew how they felt.

I was in the front car with Rose's mother and father and I couldn't find the words to comfort them because there were no words. It was worse than that. There was no bond. We were already strangers, we were already slipping from each other's lives. The bond between us was in the car ahead of us, in a pine coffin covered with three wreaths of red roses. One from Rose's parents, one from me, one from my mum and dad. Separate wreaths for separate grief.

The cortege reached the small church on top of a little hill. Below us the fields of rural Essex were covered in yellow. Fields of rape. A terrible name. Why can't they call it something else? Because I still can't look at those yellow fields of April without thinking of the day we buried Rose.

A vicar who had never known Rose talked about her qualities. He had tried his best, this vicar, he had talked to friends and family and me, so he spoke of her humor and her warmth and her love of life. But it was only when Josh climbed the steps to the plinth that I felt as if it meant anything.

"The words of Canon Henry Scott Holland," he said. " 'Death is nothing at all. I have only slipped away into the next room. I am I and you are you. Whatever we were to each other, that we are still.' "

I held myself together because it was worse for Rose's parents, this quiet man and his kind wife who had been so proud of their lawyer daughter, this decent man and woman who I had spent Christmases with and who I would probably never see again. I held myself together because it would have been shaming to place my loss above their loss. They were doing the worst thing in the world. They were burying a child.

" 'Call me by my old familiar name,' " Josh said. " 'Speak to me in the easy way which you always used. Put no difference into your tone, wear no forced air of solemnity or sorrow. Laugh as we always laughed at the little jokes we enjoyed together. Play, smile, think of me. Pray for me.' "

There was none of the comfort that you clutch at when you bury someone at the end of their life. Josh did his best. But this black day had arrived fifty years too soon. Nature had been violated. And although I tried to make sense of the words I was hearing, although I tried to tell myself that it was worse for her parents, all I could think was one selfish thought—*I want my wife.*

" 'Let my name be ever the household word it always was. Let it be spoken without effect, without the ghost of a shadow on it. Life means all that it ever meant. It is the same as it ever was—there is absolutely unbroken continuity. What is this death but a negligible accident? Why should I be out of mind because I am out of sight? I am but waiting for you, for an interval, somewhere very near, just around the corner. All is well.' "

It was a bad moment following the coffin out of the church,

feeling all those eyes on me, feeling all that pity that I didn't want. But I held it together while we were walking behind the coffin. And it was a bad moment when Rose's parents were holding each other by the graveside and her oldest friends were starting to come apart. But I held it together at the graveside.

It was only when the funeral director—there are no more undertakers—took me aside and softly asked me if the wreaths were to be buried with the coffin or kept for the graveside that I began to unravel.

"All with her," I said, "bury it all with her," suddenly overflowing with helpless tears.

Not for myself or for her parents or even for Rose, no, but crying for the children who would never be born.

I always get a jolt of surprise when I enter my nan's tiny flat. One little box in a block of sheltered accommodation, it's as fashionably minimalist as any local restaurant or art gallery, all white walls and creamy blankness, a study in trendy emptiness. Damien Hirst would be right at home in my nan's flat. One look at this place, and Damien would want to chop my nan in half and stick her in a jar of preservative.

Not that my nan is trying to keep up with the cutting edge of interior design. A few years ago the stairs got too much for her in the home she had lived in for over fifty years, the *Oranges for Christmas* house in that East End banjo, and this white flat is where the council put her. She refused to move in with my parents.

"I value my freedom, love," she told me.

The TV has the sound turned down and Sinatra is playing. It's *Sinatra at the Sands with Count Basie and the Orchestra,* Frank's finest live album, in my opinion. My nan is a habitual player of Sinatra records. She is not really all that interested in music, but I know Frank reminds her of my granddad. No, it's more than a reminder, hearing Sinatra swagger through "You Make Me

Feel So Young" or "Fly Me to the Moon" or "The Shadow of Your Smile." It's a kind of communion.

Among all the souvenirs from other people's holidays—my nan is keen on grinning Spanish donkeys and leering leprechauns—there are lots of family pictures on the mantel-piece. Rose and I on our wedding day. Me as a child. Me as a baby. My parents on their wedding day. Her own wedding day—she is black-haired and smiling, a beautiful young woman, a woman who shines—on the arm of her husband, my granddad. But the white flat remains stubbornly indifferent to these signs of life. My nan just hasn't had the endless years to impose her personality here the way she did in the old place. As I watch her shuffling around the kitchen, laboriously making us some tea—she forbids me from making it as I am her guest—I wonder if she ever will.

"He was here," my nan says. "Yesterday. With his fancy woman."

For some reason I am dumbfounded.

"My dad?"

She nods, smiling grimly. "With her. His fancy woman."

"He brought Lena? Here?"

"His fancy woman. His bit on the side. Bit of crumpet. Bit of skirt. His tart."

I am glad that my nan is not siding with her son in the dismantling of our little family. She still comes around to our house for lunch on Sundays. Either my mum or I deliver a bag of shopping once a week. We talk on the phone every day, even when we have nothing much to say. We are all pretending that our family is still intact, and I am comforted by that pretence. But something stops me from smiling and nodding at these slanders on Lena.

"You really liked her a little while ago," I say. "Lena, I mean. You thought she was okay."

She snorts. "Young enough to be his daughter. What are they

going to do? Have a baby?" Another snort. "He won't be able to pick it up. The old goat. Do you want a biscuit?"

"No thanks, Nan."

"Chocolate digestive or custard cream?"

"Not for me, Nan."

"I'll just bring some in case you change your mind," she says. "That marriage hasn't been right since her last loss. You know. Miscarriage. If you dip them in your tea, they go all soft. Do you have sugar? I can't remember." She laughs with delight, shaking her head. "Sorry, Alfie. It's my old timer's disease."

"What did he want?" I say, helping her to cart the tea and biscuits to the low table that faces the television. She doesn't mind me helping with this bit. "I mean, of course he wanted to see you. You're his mum. But what did he want?"

"To explain. To explain everything, he said. And he brought her with him. Bold as brass. Sitting there holding hands, they were. Like some kind of courting couple. I said—I'll have none of that in my house. None of your holding hands business. They brought me a box of Quality Street. And then she went and had the strawberry. Bloody cheek. He knows I like the strawberry. I can only eat the soft ones."

I can believe that my nan has given her son and his girlfriend a hard time. My grandmother was endlessly tolerant when she was visiting my parents. She contemplated all manner of strange phenomena that she has never had any truck with in her life—au pairs, exercise equipment, foreign food, bestselling books—with a benign smile.

But in her own home she makes all the rules and expects you to obey them.

"He says he loves her."

"Men say a lot of things. You can't listen to what men say. Men will say anything to get what they want."

"He says he's not coming back."

"I wouldn't have him back. I'd kick him out. If he came

back. I would. If I was your mum, I'd be hoping he came back so I could kick him out. I mean it. I knew something was going on. It's ridiculous."

Ridiculous is one of my nan's favorite words.

"I'm worried about my mum," I say.

"He's disgusting."

Disgusting is another one. She gets a lot of mileage out of ridiculous and disgusting.

"She's lost without him. She pretends she's not, but she doesn't know what to do with herself. She put so much into him."

But my nan is no longer listening to me. She turns off Sinatra and Count Basie and hits the mute button on the TV's remote control, really pushing it as hard as she can, as if she has never got used to remote controls. Then she produces her lottery ticket from an old biscuit tin with a kilted Highland piper on the front and stares with rapt concentration at the chortling game-show host who is presenting this week's live draw.

My nan is happy to debate adultery, miscarriages and fancy women with me.

But only if they don't clash with the National Lottery.

10

I SAW THEM EVERY DAY, the old Chinese people moving through the morning mist of Kowloon Park, Victoria Park and Chater Gardens. But I never really noticed them. I saw no beauty and no meaning in their unhurried ballet. They were old and I was young and I believed that there was nothing they could ever teach me.

I saw them doing their slow-motion exercises—saw it most mornings for over two years—but it was never more than a little background color to me. The Tai Chi I saw in Hong Kong registered on the same shallow level as the stalls selling their nameless herbs on Ko Shing Street, the incense smoldering in a temple's stone cauldrons on Hollywood Road, the skyline full of countless potted plants on the balconies of apartments ten, twenty, thirty stories high, the occasional talk of good and bad feng shui among the Cantonese staff of the Double Fortune Language School, the fake money burned in the streets every August for the Festival of Hungry Ghosts.

I saw all these things but they never even began to have meaning for me, they meant nothing beyond reminding me that I was a thrillingly long way from home. These images were all postcards with nothing written on the back.

But now, when I huff and puff my way around Highbury Fields, looking for a way to live inside my own skin, I see

George Chang doing his Tai Chi and somehow this ancient dance finally starts to make sense.

Sometimes he is not alone. Sometimes he has a student or two with him, if you can call them students, these long-haired hippy chicks and those guys with nonaggressive shaved heads and John Lennon spectacles. Alternative types, I think to myself, everything in their lives organic. But they never seem to stick at it for very long, and I am sort of glad about that.

I like to watch him best when he is alone.

It is always very early, that fleeting moment of the day when the whole city seems to be sleeping. All the night people—the drinkers, the ravers, the screamers—have finally gone home to bed but the day people—the joggers, the go-getters, the early worms earning six figures a year—have yet to stir. The only sound is a distant truck barreling down the Holloway Road. This pause never lasts long. But George Chang moves as though he has all the time in the world.

He moves as though he is at once both rooted to the earth and weightless. His arms and hands have the supple grace of wings, slowly pushing and pulling and rising and falling without ever seeming to make any effort at all. As his weight shifts from one foot to the other, his back remains poker straight and his head stays up, an unbroken line running from the base of his spine to the back of his skull.

There's an air about him that I can't quite name. At first I think of it as tranquillity but it's more than that. It is more than serenity. It's a feeling that combines both peace and strength.

His face is calm, concentrated, composed. His upper body seems impossibly relaxed. It stays relaxed. Perhaps this is what holds my attention so completely. I have never seen anyone so at ease with himself. When he is finished I walk up to him.

"Thanks for the other night," I say.

He looks at me for a second, placing me.

"How is friend's nose?"

"Covered in bandages. But you were right. About pushing it back in shape straight away, I mean. Apparently it made it a lot easier to set."

"Ah. Good."

"I don't think I told you. I lived in Hong Kong. I haven't been back in London for very long."

He looks up again. I realize he is waiting.

"For two years. I was a teacher. At a language school. I got married out there."

He nods with what I take to be approval. "Hong Kong lady?"

"English lady."

I don't tell him anything else about Rose. I don't talk about it all the time. I just don't want to. Historically, the British are meant to be too shy for this sort of thing, for talking about their deepest, darkest feelings to strangers. But I find that's something else that has changed while I was away, just like Terry Wogan playing REM and my father acting like Rod Stewart. These days the British can't stop talking about their feelings.

Perhaps Diana had something to do with it, perhaps she persuaded us to exchange our stoic, stiff upper lips for emotional, wobbly bottom lips. Perhaps it's because the hole in the sky is making not only the weather more Continental but also our temperaments. But our national character has certainly changed.

The problem these days is not getting the British to talk about their feelings. The problem these days is getting them to shut the fuck up.

"I saw a lot of Tai Chi in Hong Kong. In the parks."

"Very popular in Hong Kong. More than UK."

"That's right. But I could never really understand what they got out of it. I mean, it looks great," I say quickly. "Especially when you do it. I just didn't get it."

"Tai Chi for many things. For health. For stress. For stopping your body being attacked."

"You mean for self-defense?"

"Many kinds of self-defense. You know? Many kinds. You can be attacked inside and outside. There's the cheeky man who broke your friend's nose."

"The cheeky man?"

"The cheeky man. There's also disease. Tai Chi good for internal organs. For sickness. You know what Chinese word *chi* means?"

"Well, I know it's supposed to mean your body's internal energy. The life force."

"Yes."

"But I don't think I've got any. At least, I've never been aware of it."

"Got any blood in your veins?"

"What?"

"Do you got any blood in your veins?"

"Sure."

"You aware of that?" He nods with satisfaction. " 'Course not. Same as *chi*. It's there. If you know it or not. *Chi* means air. It also means energy. The spirit leads the mind. The mind leads the *chi*. The *chi* leads the blood. Tai Chi is about controlling your *chi* for better life. We say—every journey of a thousand miles begins with one step. The first step—that's Tai Chi."

I nod, sort of getting it, but suddenly feeling a bit hungry. I can feel my life force rumbling, so I pull out a Snickers bar from my tracksuit pocket. George Chang narrows his eyes.

"You want half of this?"

"Okay."

I unwrap the Snickers bar, break it in half and hand him his share. We munch in silence for a few seconds.

"Prefer Mars bar," he says through a mouthful of chocolate, peanuts and tasty nougat. He examines the Snickers bar like a wine connoisseur considering the bouquet of a particularly fine Burgundy. Then he closes his eyes, reaching for the memory.

"A Mars a day . . . helps you work, rest and play."

"What's that?" I say. "Some old Chinese saying?"

George Chang just smiles at me.

For a week the ginseng sits in our kitchen like a piece of modern sculpture. My mother and I spend a long time staring at it, like baffled art lovers searching for meaning in a work we don't quite understand.

The ginseng looks like a vegetable from another planet. It is pale yellow and white, horribly misshapen, dangling a tangle of thin roots like tentacles. Those trailing membranes make it look vaguely squidlike.

"And I thought you bought it in Boots," I say. "In convenient handy-to-swallow capsules."

"Perhaps you're meant to boil it," my mother says thoughtfully. "You know. Like a carrot."

"Like a carrot. Right. That sounds possible."

"Or maybe you chop it up and fry it. Like an onion."

"Like an onion. So you could even eat it raw."

We study the ginseng. It is the only plant I have ever seen that reminds me of the Elephant Man.

"I wouldn't fancy that very much, dear," says my mother.

"No. Me neither. Look, why don't we just ask Joyce what you're meant to do with it?"

"Now?"

"Why not? It's only six o'clock. The restaurant's not open yet. You want to use it, don't you?"

"Oh yes, dear," my mother says. "It's meant to be very good for stress."

There's a voice being raised inside the Shanghai Dragon. A woman's voice. My mother and I hesitate for a moment and then go inside.

It is cool and dark in the restaurant. We are expecting to find the entire family clustered around the dining table, happily eating their soup and noodles. But tonight there is only Joyce and her small grandson. She seems very angry with him, and barks at him in a mixture of English and Cantonese.

"You think you're English?" she asks him. A blast of Cantonese. "Look at your face in the mirror!" Some more Cantonese. "Look at your face! You're not English!"

Although he can't be more than five years old, the boy is bent over some homework. He is writing in his little exercise book, his big beautiful moon face all damp with tears.

"You are Chinese! You have Chinese face! You will always have Chinese face!" Some Cantonese. "You have to be smarter than English!"

Joyce notices us hovering in the doorway. She looks at us without embarrassment. I realize that I can't imagine Joyce ever feeling embarrassed about anything.

"Hello!" she seems to shout. She is still very excited. "Didn't see you. I don't have eyes in the back of my face."

"Is this a bad time?" I say.

"What? Bad time? No. Just teaching cheeky grandson that he has to work hard."

"He seems very young to be doing homework," my mother says.

"Father sets homework. Not school. School just let them do anything. Relax. Watch television. Watch video games. Just relax. Like millionaires. Like playboys. As though the world owes them a loving."

"I know, I know." My mother sighs, staring sympathetically at the child. "What's your name, darling?"

He says nothing.

"Answer lady!" Joyce roars like a sergeant major faced with a dopey private.

"William," he says. A tiny voice, full of tears.

"Like Prince William," Joyce says. She ruffles his thick mop of shiny black hair, pinches his smooth round cheek. "Sister called Diana. Like Princess Diana."

"What lovely names," my mother says.

"We were wondering how you prepare the ginseng," I say. I want to get out of here. "How you are meant to take it."

"Take it? Many ways. Can drink it. Like tea. In a nice cup of tea. Can put it in soup. Like Korean people. Easiest way—just chop up ginseng. Put it in saucepan with water. Boil it. Let it simmer for ten minutes. Strain it off. Use one pint of water for every ounce of ginseng."

"That sounds easy enough," my mother says, smiling at William.

He stares up at her with blank wet eyes.

"You tried ginseng yet?" demands Joyce.

"Not yet. That's what we—"

"Good for you." Her fierce brown eyes blaze at my mother. "Especially women. Older ladies. But not just older ladies." She looks at me. "Good for when you not sleep. Tired all the time. Feeling—how to say?—a bit run over."

"Run down."

"Yes. Run over." She pushes her face close to mine. "You looking a bit run over, mister."

"Just what I need!" says my mum, clapping her hands with delight.

Joyce offers us tea—English tea, she calls it—but we make our excuses and leave. Before we are out of the door, Joyce is shouting at William about having a Chinese face.

And for the first time I get a sense of how hard it is when you want to become international.

"I can't stay long," Josh tells me when we meet for lunch in a crowded City pub where I am the only man not wearing a suit.

"Got to reach somebody in Hong Kong before they leave the office?" His firm still does a lot of business with Hong Kong and

I like hearing about it. It makes me feel as though I still have some connection with the place. Something more than memories.

"No. Got a client coming in. A woman. You should see her, Alfie. Top-of-the-range pussy, mate. Looks like Claudia Schiffer but talks like Lady Helen Windsor or somebody. A real plums-in-the-mouth job. Not so much tits and arse as tits and class. Quite fancy my chances, I do."

"A bit of posh? Just right for you, Josh. Knock off your rough edges. Show you which fork to use. Teach you when to say lavatory and when to say sofa. Stop you wiping your nose on your sleeve. Keeping coal in the bath. All that."

He flushes, not liking it very much when you suggest that he is not quite the Duke of Westminster. Usually you can say what you like to Josh. He has the sensitivity of a brick. But you are not allowed to suggest that he wasn't born with a silver spoon in his mouth, or up his butt.

"She's coming into the office at two," he says, looking at his watch. "Can't stay long."

I am not offended. Our meetings often begin with Josh telling me that he has to be somewhere else very soon. I'm used to it.

We order curry at the bar and I notice that the damage to his face is fading. The bandages are long gone and there's no sign that his broken nose has been reset. There are black and yellow bruises under his eyes, but they look as though they are the result of a night without sleep rather than a head butt from a drunken middle-aged skinhead. We collect our curries and find a glass-strewn table in a smoky corner of the pub.

"You ever think about that night?" I ask him.

"What night?"

"You know. That night in the Shanghai Dragon. The night you got your nose broken. The night I got my ribs smacked."

"I try not to."

"I think about it all the time. I can't quite work out what happened."

"Surprise attack. Caught me off guard. Pearl Harbor and all that. Fat bastard. Should have called the police."

"I don't mean what happened to us. I mean the old man. What happened to him."

"Nothing happened to him. It was all over by the time he showed up."

I shake my head.

"That guy—that fat skinhead—was ready to fight anyone. Then the old man turned up. And the skinhead backed down. I didn't understand it then. I still don't."

"There's no great mystery," Josh says through a mouthful of curry. "The skinhead probably thought that Charlie Chan had fifty of his relations out the back, all armed with machetes. Come on. I can't hang about. Eat your curry before it gets cold."

"That's not it. At least, I don't think that's it. It was just that he was—I don't know. Perfectly relaxed. You could see it in him. He wasn't afraid. He wasn't afraid of a much younger, much bigger man who was ready to fight anyone. He just wasn't scared of him. And the skinhead could sense it. There was no fear in him."

Josh snorts.

"Did you feel a tremor in the Force, Alfie? Did you sense that the Force was strong in the old cook? Were you once more privy to the mysteries of the East?"

"I'm just saying that he wasn't afraid. That's all. And he should have been afraid."

Josh is not listening to me. He is quickly shoveling in his curry and thinking about the blonde, upper-class client who is coming into his office at two. He is thinking about his chances with her. But I still feel the need to explain something to him.

"It just made me think how great that must be—to go through your life without fear. Imagine how liberating that must be, Josh. Imagine how free that must make you feel. If you're not afraid of anything, then you can't be hurt, can you?"

"Only if they've got a baseball bat," says Josh. "How's your old man? Still shacked up with Miss Sweden?"

"Miss Czech Republic. He's gone for good. I'm pretty sure of it."

Josh shakes his head. "You've got to take your hat off to him. Still getting the shaven haven at his age. It's not to be sniffed at."

"I don't want some old swinger for a father. Nobody does. Everybody admires Hugh Hefner. Everybody likes the old boy who plays around. But nobody wants him for their dad."

"Not much of a role model, I suppose. Shagging the hired help."

"He doesn't have to be a role model. I just want a bit of sta-bility. A bit of peace and quiet. That's all anybody wants from their parents, isn't it? That's the best thing they can give you—a little less embarrassment. I don't want my dad to be out there chasing young Czech women and trying to pump up his biceps and all the rest of it. I want him to think about other things. He's had his time. He should understand that. He's had his time for being young. Nobody wants to get old any more, do they?"

"Not if they can help it."

"Nobody wants to get out of the way and let the next gen-eration come through. Everybody wants one more chance."

"What's so bad about that?"

"It makes a mockery of the past. Every time you start again, it diminishes what you've had before. Can't you see that? It chops your life up into these little bite-sized morsels. If you have endless goes at getting it right, then you will never get it right. Not even once. Because constantly starting again turns the best thing in the world into just another takeout. Fast love. Junk love. Love to go."

"Don't you want one more chance, Alfie?"

"I've had my chance."

11

JACKIE DAY IS IN THE STAFF ROOM when I arrive. She has her bucket in one hand and her copy of *The Heart Is a Lonely Hunter* in the other. She has all her kit on—the yellow gloves, the blue nylon coat, the flat shoes she cleans in—but she is making no move to go to work. It's nearly nine o'clock but she still has her face buried in that old paperback.

"How's Mick?" I ask her. "Still got her dreams?"

"Hello," she says, not looking up.

Lenny the Lech walks in. Lenny is one of those short, fat men who swaggers around as though he is some kind of tall, thin catch. Like me, Lenny is a former teacher who went out to sell English by the pound in Asia—Manila and Bangkok in Lenny's case. Something about him spoiled out there. He has that soft, bloated look that Europeans often get when they stay too long in the tropics—or when they stay too long in tropical bars. Lenny got laid a lot more in Asia then he ever did at home and now he looks at women the way that a farmer sizes up his cows. At Churchill's his lechery is legendary.

"Have you seen that new little Polish number in the Advanced Beginners?" he asks me, rolling his eyes. "I wouldn't mind showing her a bit of solidarity. What do you reckon, Alfie? I wouldn't mind letting that comrade get her hot little hands on my means of production."

"I don't think the Poles are Communists anymore, Lenny."

"She's a little red minx, that's what she is," says Lenny the Lech. Then he notices Jackie. "Ah, our resident Essex girl. Top of the morning to you, my girl." He goes over to her and puts a proprietorial arm around her shoulders. "Stop me if you've heard this one, darling. Why do Essex girls hate vibrators? Give up? Because—"

Suddenly Jackie is on her feet, her eyes blazing, accidentally kicking her bucket.

"Because they chip our teeth," she says. "Heard that one already, Lenny. Bit obvious, that one. What else would an Essex girl do with a vibrator but suck on it—right, Lenny? You're going to have to do better than that."

"Steady on," says Lenny. "It's just a joke."

"And I've heard them all," she says. "Why does an Essex girl wash her hair in the kitchen sink? Because that's where you wash vegetables. What do Essex girls and beer bottles have in common? Come on, Lenny, come on."

"I don't know," says Lenny, practically scratching his fat head.

"Both empty from the neck up."

"Now *that's* funny," chuckles Lenny.

But Jackie is not smiling. "Think so? Then you'll like this one. What do a blonde Essex girl and a plane have in common?"

"They both have a black box," says Lenny. "I know that one."

"You do? But I bet you don't know as many as me. I've heard the lot, Lenny. What's the difference between an Essex girl and a mosquito? A mosquito stops sucking if you hit it on the head. Why do Essex girls wear pants? To keep their ankles warm. How do you make an Essex girl's eyes sparkle? Shine a torch in her ear."

Lenny smiles, but it is starting to look a little strained. Jackie is standing in front of him, holding her copy of *The Heart Is a*

Lonely Hunter in one of her yellow-gloved hands, trying to stop her voice from shaking.

"I know all the jokes. And you know what, Lenny? I'm not laughing."

"Keep your hair on, darling," Lenny says, quite offended. "It's nothing personal."

"I know it's nothing personal, Lenny. And I even know it's nothing to do with Essex girls. I know that a man like you thinks all women are stupid whores."

"I love women!" protests Lenny. He turns to me. "If I can say that without sounding like Julio Iglesias."

"I don't think you can," I say.

"From what I hear around this place," says Jackie Day, "only one person in this room is a dumb tart. But do you know what, Lenny? It's certainly not me."

She slips her book inside her nylon coat and picks up her bucket. Then she walks out without saying another word.

"Some people just can't take a joke," says Lenny the Lech.

Lena is waiting at the end of our street.

There's an old spit-and-sawdust pub on the corner and grinning men with pints in their fists are looking out of the stained windows at her, leering and evaluating and scratching bellies that are displayed like prize gourds.

"Alfie."

I walk straight past her.

"You used to like me."

I look at her, this young woman who has bewitched my father, made him move to a rented flat, encouraged him to search for his youth on a rowing machine, made him drop his swimming trunks in a public place, and I try hard to find her ridiculous. It's difficult. She has got the blonde hair and legs that go on like a river, but I know she is no bimbo. I know that she is smart. Although how smart can she be if she has shacked up with my old man?

Lena is not ridiculous. It's the situation that's ridiculous. It's my father who is absurd.

"I still like you," I say.

"You just don't like the thought of anyone having sex with your father. Except your mother."

"Not even my mother, now you come to mention it."

We smile at each other.

"I don't know what to say to you, Lena. It's hard to think of you as a friend of the family. My family is in pieces."

I look at her, trying to imagine how my father sees her. I can understand how he could fall for the face, the legs, the body. I can understand how exciting she must be after half a lifetime of marriage. But surely he can see that wanting her is being greedy?

"You should understand, Alfie. If you love someone, you want to be with them."

"My father doesn't know the first thing about love."

"Why are you like this? I know you feel sorry for your mother. But it's more than that."

"Because he wants too much. Too much life. He's had his life. He should accept that."

"You can't want too much life."

"You can, Lena. You can be a glutton for life, just like you can be a glutton for food or drink or drugs. If this thing with you is more than just a fling, if my dad really wants to start again, if it's serious, then he wants more than he deserves."

She asks me if I want a coffee and I agree to go across the road with her to the little Italian café called Trevi, just to get her off the street. It's not the grinning fat men in the old spit-and-sawdust pub that bother me. It's the thought that my mother might come around the corner at any moment.

"I just don't understand what's in it for you," I say when we have ordered our cappuccino. "You haven't got any visa problems, have you? There are no problems staying in the country, are there?"

"That's not fair."

"Why not? I don't get it. Even if you want an older man, you don't have to go for my dad. I mean, there's old and there's ready for the knacker's yard. There's old and there's *Jurassic Park.*"

"He's the best thing that ever happened to me. He's wise. He's kind. He's lived."

"I'll say."

"He knows things. He's seen life. And I love his book. *Oranges for Christmas.* It's just like him. Full of tenderness and heart."

"What about my mother? What happens to her? Is she just meant to crawl into the corner? Where's the tenderness and heart for her?"

"I'm sorry for your mother. I really am. She was always very good to me. But these things happen. You know that. When two people fall in love, someone else often gets hurt."

"It can never work. He's an old man. You're a student."

"Not anymore."

"He's not an old man anymore?"

"I'm not a student anymore. I'm not going to do my MBA. What's the point?"

"What happened?"

"I dropped out of college. I'm going to be Mike's personal assistant."

"Mike doesn't need a personal assistant."

"He does, Alfie. There are always people calling him up and asking him to write things. To do events. To appear on TV or radio."

"What he needs is an answer machine."

"He needs someone to protect him from the outside world. He can't concentrate. I can help him. He can take care of the writing. I'll deal with everything else. That's more worthwhile than any degree. And it will give us a chance to be together all the time."

"Sounds like a nightmare."

"You should be happy for us, Alfie. He needs me. And I need him."

"You both need your heads examined. Especially you."

"Older people can be amazing, Alfie. We saw your grandmother. We took her some of those chocolates she likes. With the old-fashioned soldiers and the ladies on the box. Something street."

"Quality Street. She said that you ate all the soft ones."

"I don't blame you for being angry at me."

"I'm not angry at you. I feel sorry for you. I'm angry at my father. You're silly. He's a cruel, stupid coward."

"Oh, Alfie. He's a wonderful man."

I shake my head. "He's only doing this—setting up home with you—because he was forced into it."

"It would have happened anyway."

"That's not what married men do. Married men stay. They stay in their homes for as long as they can." Under the table, I touch the ring I still wear. "They stay until they are forced out."

I get a complaint about Lenny the Lech from one of my students. Yumi, the Japanese girl with all the blond hair, stays behind after class and tells me he has been pestering her.

"In the corridor he tries to touch me. He always says— 'Come for a drink, baby. Let me give you extra lessons, baby. Oral lessons, baby. Ha ha ha.'" She shakes her head. "I don't want those kind of lessons from Lenny the Lech. He's not even my teacher. You are."

"Can't you tell him you're not interested?"

"He doesn't listen."

Her eyes well up with tears and I pat her arm.

"I'll have a word with him, okay?"

During morning break I find Lenny in the staff room. He is drinking instant coffee with Hamish, a fit-looking thirty-year-old down from Glasgow who is far too good-looking to be heterosexual.

"So basically you came to London because you're a bum bandit?" Lenny is saying.

"You could put it like that," says Hamish. "I came here because it's the best place to pursue a discreetly gay lifestyle."

"And does a discreetly gay lifestyle mean you have a committed relationship with one partner? Or that you get jerked off on Hampstead Heath every night by a succession of anonymous strangers?"

"Can I have a word, Lenny?" I say.

I take him to one side. He puts his arm around me. Lenny is a very tactile man. But it's more than that. I think he actually likes me. Because I have also taught in Asia, he is under the illusion that we are the same kind of guy.

"What is it, my old mate?"

"It's a bit embarrassing, Lenny. One of my students has had a word with me. About you. Yumi."

"The little Jap model? Miss Toyota, 1998? Not very big but you can bet she really burns your rubber."

"Yumi. The girl with all the hair. The thing is, Lenny, she says you're misreading the signals."

"Misreading the signals?"

"How can I put it? She's not interested in you, Lenny." Lenny's monstrous sweating head is corrugated with a frown. "God knows why not, Len, but there you go. Women, eh? It's just not going to happen, mate."

"I'm sorry, mate," Lenny says. "I really am. I had no idea little Yumi was spoken for."

"No, it's not—"

"There's plenty more fish in the sea." He chortles in that Lenny the Lech way. "I'll cast my enormous hook elsewhere." He slaps me on the back. "No problemo."

I turn to leave.

"And Alfie?"

"What?"

"Give her one for the Lech."

Yumi is sitting by herself in the Eamon de Valera, nursing a mineral water at a corner table.

"He's not going to bother you anymore," I tell her.

"Thank you. I buy you drink."

"That's okay, Yumi."

"But I want to." She goes to the bar and spends half the night counting out her money in loose change. Usually I feel a kind of envy for my students but right now I feel sorry for Yumi. Coming halfway round the world to improve your English and then getting some fat old Englishman like Lenny the Lech offering you oral lessons. She returns with a pint of Guinness clutched in both hands and sets it before me.

"He's a very bad man," she says. "All the girls at Churchill's say so. He wants rub-rub with just anyone. Any student with nice face. And even some ugly ones. If they are large breasted."

Then she stares at me with these eyes, these moist brown eyes, that make me realize just how lonely I have been.

"Incredible," I say. "What kind of teacher does a thing like that?"

12

YUMI'S ROOM IS AT THE END of a dark corridor in a large, crumbling town house that has spent the last fifty years being chopped up into smaller and smaller flats. As we make our way down the hall you can hear music, voices, laughter, doors slamming, telephones ringing. The cacophony of too many people in too small a space. And having the time of their life. We take off our shoes at her door and go inside.

It's not much to look at. A bay window dominates the tiny flat, but it overlooks some kind of junkyard piled high with trashed cars. The room's exhausted carpet looks as though it has been trodden on by an itinerant army of students. The only heating comes from a two-bar electric heater.

It's a dump. Yet it doesn't feel like a dump because all over her modest apartment Yumi has decorated the peeling wallpaper with photographs from home. Everywhere you look there are all these Polaroids, snapshots and photo-booth pictures of smiling Japanese girls making V signs. One round-faced, shyly grinning girl seems to feature in many of them.

"Younger sister," Yumi says.

There is something deeply affecting about Yumi's attempts to turn this cold, rented little box into some kind of home. Armed with just her memories and a stack of photographs, she has tried to make it her own.

Yumi lights a perfumed candle, turns on the radio to jazz FM and unrolls a futon. The unfurled mattress takes up most of the floor. We stand facing each other for a moment and I realize how nervous I am.

"I haven't got anything," I say.

"That's not true," she says. "You have good heart. Lovely smile. Nice sense of humor."

"No, I mean I haven't, you know, got any condoms."

"Ah. Okay. I have some. I think."

"And I haven't been with anyone," I say. "Not since my wife, I mean."

She touches my face.

"That's okay," she says. "Whatever happens, everything's okay."

It's what I need to hear. I take it as slowly as I can, and although at first I am overwhelmed by how different she seems to Rose, it is much better than I could ever have hoped. Her body is shockingly young and lithe, and she is a sweet and tender lover, smiling at my excitement, but in a way that doesn't make me feel bad. Yumi makes me feel nothing but good.

Afterward she hides her face in my chest and laughs, calling me her favorite teacher—her favorite *sensei*—and hugging me with a strength that surprises me. I laugh too, relieved and pleased, dumbfounded by my good fortune.

Later she sleeps in my arms while I watch the candle burn down until the only light in the little room comes from the glow of the two-bar electric heater. And then, feeling happier than I have in a long time, I start to drift away too.

Just before I slip into sleep I notice the large red suitcase in the corner of the room, as if Yumi has just arrived, or is just about to leave.

I wake up as the first light is creeping into the room. Yumi is sleeping wrapped up around me, that incredible mass of blond hair almost completely covering her face so that only the tip of her nose is visible. I smile to myself. I can't believe that she's with me.

I gently disentangle our limbs, slip off of the futon and pull on my Calvins. Quietly letting myself out of the room, I pad down the hallway, looking for the bathroom.

Suddenly he is on top of me. A naked man. The metal studs and rings that pierce his stubbled face glinting with menace in the darkness. His head is shaved. His mouth is above me and wide open, a great black maw that seems about to take a chunk out of my throat.

"Sweet Jesus!" I mutter, leaping backward.

But the man is only yawning. When his mouth has completed the yawn, he smacks his lips, scratches his exposed scrotum for a bit and then blinks at me a couple of times.

"Mind if I use it first, man?" he says in an Australian accent. "Bit of a heavy night."

Trembling, I lean against the flaking plaster of the hall, trying to stop the pounding of my heart. A toilet flushes and the man emerges from the bathroom, soon disappearing once more into the darkness.

Back inside on the futon, Yumi stirs, warm as toast and smooth as ice cream, as I try to explain the terrible vision I have seen.

"Oh," she says sleepily. "Roommate."

We have a perfect weekend. It's the kind of time that I like best. It seems ordinary and special all at once.

We wake up late and Yumi says she will make us breakfast. But someone—probably the pierced roommate, if you ask me—has stolen her bread from the communal kitchen and the milk that she thought was still okay has gone bad. So after taking a shower together—it seems like a good idea, but we are surprisingly shy with each other—we go to a little café at the end of her street and order full English breakfasts. It takes Yumi ages to work her way through all that fried food.

We spend the afternoon wandering around Camden market.

Yumi loves looking at all the second-hand clothes, and seeing her happy makes me happy too.

We hold hands and she gives me little kisses when I am not expecting them. I realize things about her that never really registered at Churchill's. Her clothes are a little off-beat—today she is wearing some kind of antique dress that looks like it once belonged to Zelda Fitzgerald—and an Asian girl with a mop of dyed blond hair gets a lot of stares. But I am proud to be seen with her. She's a great girl, funny and smart, and we drink latte in a little café while she tells me about her family back in Osaka.

Her old man was a hotshot salary man at a big corporation who lost his job in the recession. Her mother was a typical Japanese housewife who suddenly found she had to support a family with her secretarial work. Her sister is a brilliant violin player who her parents always preferred because she never dyed her hair or went out with boys who had dyed hair. Yumi says she came to London because life in Japan felt like it was a play, and everybody knew their role. Except her.

And I tell her my story. I want to. I tell her about teaching in London, moving to Hong Kong, meeting Rose. I tell her about losing Rose, about the accident, all of that, and she holds my hand, tears in her brown eyes. I even tell her about my father and his girlfriend.

Then I remember that I have to do some shopping for my nan. I expect Yumi to go home or to go off somewhere, but she tells me she will do the shopping with me. So we find a supermarket and I get my nan's usual Saturday shop—white bread, I Can't Believe It's Not Butter, baked beans, corned beef, spam, bacon, sugar, milk, tea bags, custard creams, chocolate cookies, ginger nuts and a single banana. That single banana always tugs at my heart. It seems to me like more than an old person's shopping list. It feels like a shopping list from long ago.

My nan, always delighted to see new faces, welcomes Yumi with open arms. With Sinatra's *A Swingin' Affair!* in the background—for me, Frank's finest album, although of course traditionalists would always nominate *Songs for Swingin' Lovers!*—they sit chatting while I unpack the shopping.

Yumi tells my nan that she really has to see the temples of Kyoto and the snow on Mount Fuji and the cherry blossoms of a Japanese spring. My nan agrees that all these things will go straight to the top of her agenda.

"Lovely teeth," says my nan when Yumi goes to the bathroom. "Must be all that rice. Where did you say she's from again, dear? Is it China?"

"Japan, Nan."

"Everybody speaks English these days," says my grandmother.

Yumi is a gracious guest, gamely eating the ginger nuts she is plied with by my nan and tapping her foot along to *A Swingin' Affair!*

"Ah," she says. "Old music."

"Like a bit of Sinatra, do you, sweetheart?" asks my nan.

These casual endearments are one of the loveliest things about my grandmother. Even total strangers get called the sweetest names under the sun. Sweetheart and dear, darling and love. My nan says these words to everyone she meets.

In Yumi's case, it feels like only what she deserves.

As the year starts to run out, my mother goes back into her garden.

I would have thought that the garden was dead in November, but my mother happily tells me that there's lots to do.

"You don't know a thing about gardens, do you?" she laughs. "At this time of year you have to finish planting your tulips and all your other spring bulbs. You have to clean and store all your flower pots and seed trays. And you have to get ready for your roses. Remove the weeds, add lots of compost and fertilizer, plant your roses." My mother smiles at me. "Do you know how much work that is, getting ready for your roses?"

Sometimes I come home and find she's not alone out there. I can hear smatterings of Cantonese mixed up with the English and I know that Joyce Chang and her grandchildren are in the garden with my mother, Joyce and my mum side by side on their hands and knees, laughing about something as they sink their fingers into the dirt while William and Diana solemnly sweep up the last of the dead leaves with brooms that are bigger than they are.

"Good time to make ground for new vegetable plot," Joyce tells me. "How's the job?"

"What?"

"How's new teaching job? Good money? Teachers treated very badly in this country. No respect for teachers here. In China, teacher equal to father."

I look at my mother accusingly but she is busy with her soil. How much is she telling this woman?

"It's going okay, thanks."

"Teaching not well paid but steady," Joyce informs me. "World always need teachers. Hard work, though. Teaching not money for old string." She digs her gnarled hands into the dirt. "Have to help mother."

Is she talking about me or her or both of us?

"November," Joyce says. "Best month for vegetable plot."

"Joyce is going to help me make a vegetable garden," my mum says. "Isn't that wonderful, darling?"

My mother does something that I would have bet was impossible with my old man gone. She carries on getting ready for the roses. And I know she wants the same for me.

"I'm glad to see you getting out a bit more, darling," my mum tells me.

Joyce nods agreement, fixing me with her shrewd, beady stare. "Need to put your hair down. Not too old in the tooth."

I shake my head. "You mean *let* my hair down. And I'm not too *long* in the tooth."

"You know exactly what I mean, mister."

That's true enough.

13

SATURDAY NIGHT WE GO DANCING. I try to get out of it, but Yumi insists that Saturday night is for dancing, so we go to this little club in Soho where the music is not as bad as I expect it to be and where the atmosphere is not as fashionable as I fear it will be. And it's great. It's not like when I was twenty. Nobody is trying to look cool or tough. Nobody cares what you dress like or dance like. So we just leap about and bounce around and have a laugh, and soon Yumi is trying to sit down and rehydrate with a little bottle of Evian while I want to keep on dancing.

Late at night we go to a conveyor belt sushi restaurant on Brewer Street. You sit at a long round bar, small plates of sushi trundle past your eyes and you help yourself to whatever takes your fancy. It turns out to be the place where Gen works and he comes over to say hello. For some reason he doesn't seem surprised to see Yumi with me.

Then Gen goes back to work and Yumi tells me that Japanese people do not usually like these kinds of places because the fish is not as fresh as when it's made to order. But it tastes pretty good to me, and we demolish a pile of different-colored plates bearing two pieces of tuna, salmon, eel, egg or prawn.

Back at her flat we make love—slowly, sleepily, relaxed with each other now—and when we wake up around noon the next day, we take a walk to the very top of Primrose Hill where it's one of those shining winter days and we can see the whole of London spread out before us.

"So beautiful," Yumi says.

"Yes," I say, looking at her face. "So beautiful."

Monday morning, after my mother has gone off to dish up the burgers, beans and tacos at Nelson Mandela High, my father comes to the house.

I am sort of glad to see him. I miss him. Just miss having him around. Miss the way it used to be. But I can see that his timing is an act of supreme cowardice and that makes me despise him. I sit on the stairs as he fills a couple of suitcases. Files, books, clothes. Videos, documents, stacks of CDs.

Taking them, leaving us.

The CD on top of a pile waiting to be packed is called *Dancing in the Street—43 Motown Dance Classics,* a window to a world of youth and optimism and perfect grooves that seems out of place and out of time.

"So how's the new book coming along?" I ask him. "Getting it done, are you?"

He doesn't look at me, just carries on trying to close a Samsonite that is far too full. He's going to struggle to get that into the SLK's boot. I don't offer to help him.

"The book will be fine."

"Good stuff."

"You think this is easy for me. But it's not. I miss my home. You can't imagine how much I miss it."

"What about us?"

"What do you think? Of course I miss you. Both of you."

"What I don't understand is how you explain it to yourself."

"What are you talking about?"

"Leaving, I mean. You inflict all this pain on Mum, and I don't understand how you live with it. You must justify it to yourself. But I don't know how."

"Lena's a special girl. Hardly a girl. A special young woman."

"But what if she's not, Dad? What if she's just another girl who happens to be really pretty? Does that mean you got it wrong? That all of this was a mistake? Will it still be worth it?"

"She's far more than a pretty face. Do you really think that I would turn my world upside down for a pretty face?"

"Absolutely."

"Anyway," he says, getting the Samsonite to shut at last. "It was a relief to finally get it out in the open."

"Your nasty little knob?"

"My relationship with Lena. I was sick of sneaking around. It couldn't have gone on like that forever."

"So Lena is—what?—your mistress?"

"God. No. Lena is certainly not my mistress."

"But you must give her money? You slip her a few quid, don't you?"

"Well, yes. Not that it's got anything to do with you."

"For exclusive rights."

"That's not the reason."

"You slip her money for exclusive rights. If that's not a mistress, then what is? And you see her when you can, right?"

"Not anymore." He looks at me for the first time with a bit of defiance. "Now I see her all the time. When I want."

My old man has nearly finished packing. There are lots more of his possessions here. Wardrobes full of suits. A study full of books. Enough sports equipment to stock a small gym. But this is just a quick raid to grab the bare essentials. Today is not the final reckoning. Right now he just wants clean underwear and his Diana Ross compilations.

"How did it work?" I ask him. "How did you get away with it? You must have lied through your teeth. You must have been pretending to do one thing when what you were really doing was Lena."

"Would you like to watch your mouth?"

"Didn't that make you feel a bit grubby? Lying like that?"

"I didn't enjoy it."

"But you didn't hate it so much that you stopped doing it."

"I guess not."

"And she never knew. Mum, I mean. Never even suspected. Ignorance is certainly bliss, isn't it? Or at least it's very under-rated."

"I really must go."

"Mum trusted you, you bastard. That's why you got away with it for so long. Not because you're clever. Because she trusted you. Because she's kind and good. And you probably think that you're a decent guy, don't you? Is Mum just supposed to crawl away and die now? Is that what she's supposed to do?"

"Christ! You're making more of a fuss than her."

He tries to leave. I step in front of him.

"Look, I'm not a kid, okay?"

"Then stop acting like one."

"I can understand how you would want to go to bed with Lena. I can even understand how you might want to do it more than once."

"Thank you so much for your understanding."

"What I don't understand is how you could be so cruel."

"I'm not trying to be cruel. I'm just trying to get on with my life. Didn't you ever feel like that, Alfie? Like just getting on with your life?" He shakes his head. "No. Probably not."

And there's something else that I don't understand. What happens to all the old photographs? All the old photographs in their albums and the shoe boxes and drawers—where do they go now?

My father is not going to take them with him. He's not going

to sit around in his rented love nest looking at all the old photographs with Lena. She doesn't want to see pictures of me and my
mum and my dad at the seaside, in the garden of the house where
I grew up, grinning in our party hats at all those lost Christmases.

Lena's not interested in all that stuff. And neither is my
father. Not anymore. He doesn't want reminders of his old life.
He wants to get on with his new life.

And the old photographs are not much good to my mother.
She doesn't want to see them anymore. That's what I resent
most. My father's actions haven't just contaminated the present.
They have reached back across the years, making our happiness
seem misplaced, our innocence seem foolish, all that was good
seem second-rate.

Our party hats at Christmas, our smiling faces in the back
garden, looking happy and proud in our best clothes at some
cousin's wedding—how wrong it all seems now. The old photographs are all ruined.

My father hasn't just messed up the present. He has messed
up the past.

I buy her some flowers on the way to work. Nothing too flashy.
I don't want to overdo it. Just a bunch of yellow tulips for when
we get a moment.

But it's strange. Yumi doesn't act differently. That is, she is
just the same as she always was—making jokes and cheeky comments in her Advanced Beginners class, but always working hard,
getting the job done, being a good, conscientious student. Same
as always. As if nothing has happened. As if the world hasn't been
changed. At lunchtime she picks up her books to leave.

"Can we talk?" I ask her, producing the tulips from under
my desk.

"Later," she says, not looking at the flowers.

My heart sinks, but she kisses me quickly on the cheek,
slightly crushing my tulips. And my heart soars.

But at the end of the day I take my flowers to the Eamon de Valera and as I stand in the doorway I see that Yumi is at the bar with Imran. I move toward them but then I stop, because Imran has one hand wrapped around her tiny waist while his other hand is giving her small tush a familiar pat.

She kisses him on the mouth, and then rubs her head against his shoulder, like a little cat that hasn't gotten the cream, but expects to get it some time soon. Like she did with me. I quickly turn and walk out of the pub, holding the flowers so tight that I can feel the stems breaking in my fist.

Then Gen is by my side, looking at me with concern.

"She likes him," he says simply.

"I don't care."

Gen shrugs. "She likes him long time. Since he began at this college." He stares at me, searching for something else to say. "Sorry."

"Thanks, Gen."

"You okay?"

"I'm fine."

"Come back inside, *sensei*. Have Guinness. Listen to The Corrs."

"Some other night."

"Good night then, *sensei*."

"Good night, Gen."

You're so stupid, I tell myself, stuffing the flowers in the nearest trash bin. But for a few sweet moments there—dancing in that little club, Sunday morning on Primrose Hill, making love while her red suitcase stood guard—I honestly thought that I heard tomorrow calling.

Whoops, wrong number.

I see her. Rose, I mean. See her on a London street, see her in a place where she could never possibly be.

I am in a cab coming back from the West End. And suddenly there's Rose—not a woman who looks like Rose. But Rose herself—the same face, the same patient expression she always wore when she was waiting for something. The clothes are different but she is the same girl. And although I know it could not possibly be her, for a long, dizzy minute, I cannot help believing.

She is waiting at a bus stop. I have to restrain myself from shouting at the taxi driver to stop and rushing to her side. I know that if I approach this woman, Rose will disappear to be replaced by some imperfect stranger. It isn't Rose. She has gone and I will never see her again. At least not in this world.

Me get in touch with the dead?

That's a joke.

I can't even get in touch with the living.

14

It's Monday morning and my students are driving me nuts.

Zeng is nodding off at the back of the class. Imran is staring blankly at a text message on his mobile phone. Astrud and Vanessa are gabbing. Witold is trying to stop crying while Yumi tries to comfort him. Only Gen is looking up at me, waiting for something to happen.

I stand in front of them, waiting for my physical presence to register. Zeng starts snoring.

I clear my throat.

Imran taps a text message into his phone. Astrud and Vanessa burst out laughing. Witold starts weeping, burying his face in his hands. Yumi puts her arm around him. Gen looks away, as if embarrassed for me.

"Right, who's got that homework for me?" I ask them. "Homework? Anybody?"

By the way they all shift in their seats and avoid eye contact, I can tell that none of them have done it.

Usually I would let it go. But today the lack of homework makes me wonder what I am doing here. And also what they are doing here.

"Can anyone remember what the homework was?"

140

"Discursive composition," Yumi says, handing Witold a tissue. "Giving information and your own opinions on something." We stare at each other. "Very formal style," she says.

Very formal style? Well, that's right. But I don't know if she's talking about discursive composition. Or us.

"What's wrong with you, Witold?"

He shakes his wizened Polish head.

"Nothing."

"Nothing's wrong?"

"No."

"Then why are you crying?"

Yumi puts a protective arm around him. "He misses his family."

Witold starts sobbing harder, his shoulders shaking and his nose all snotty.

"My wife. My children. My mother. So far away. This place is so . . . hard. Oh, this is a hard place. The Pampas Steak Bar is a hard place. *'Hands off the Falklands, Argie. Tell Maradona we are going to chop his hands off, Argie.'*"

"You spend ten years trying to get a visa to this place and then you miss your family?"

"Yes."

"Well, in future be careful what you wish for, Wit. Because you might get it."

Yumi glares at me. "He has a right to miss his family."

I glare back at her. "And as your teacher I have a right to be treated with a little respect. That means no nervous breakdowns in class. It means no mobile phones in class. Thank you, Imran. It means you treat this place as somewhere to study rather than a place to get forty winks."

"Forty winks?" someone says.

"New idiom," says someone else.

Zeng is still fast asleep. I crouch next to him. His skin is soft and smooth with just a few wispy black hairs on his upper lip.

He doesn't look as though he shaves more than once a month. I put my face close to his ear.

"Would you like fries with that?" I hiss and he awakes with a jolt. Vanessa and Astrud laugh, but stop when they see my face.

"Why did you come to this country, Zeng?"

"A better life," he gasps, blinking furiously.

"If you want a better life, then try staying awake in class." I give him a cold smile. "A little less effort in General Lee's Tasty Tennessee Kitchen. And a bit more effort at Churchill's International Language School. Okay?"

"Okay."

Then I get the little bastards to write a discursive composition. The subject is developments in science and technology and whether these will affect mankind positively or negatively. As they scribble away I wander among them.

"I want to hear both sides of the argument," I say. "For and against. Negative and positive. Link your points with expressions such as, *some might say . . . others might argue that . . . there are, however, some risks such as . . .*"

Usually they would ask for advice and kid around with me but today they are all too frightened or too angry to ask for my help. And it makes me feel blue to think that they don't like me anymore.

When the bell rings they all get out of there as fast as they can. Apart from Yumi. I am packing my things away when I feel her standing by my desk.

"Don't take it out on them," she says.

I don't look at her.

"I'm sorry, Alfie."

"Sorry for what? There's nothing to be sorry about."

"I had a good time with you," she says. "But you frightened me."

"How did I frighten you?"

"The flowers. The flowers frightened me. They made me feel you want—I don't know. Too much."

I finish stuffing my books in my bag and zip it closed.

"Don't worry about it," I tell her. "That's the last of the flowers."

Josh and his new girlfriend are at that stage of their relationship where they want to share their happiness with the rest of the world. I don't understand why happy couples can't be happy in private. Why do they need the rest of us to validate their happiness? Is it that they don't really believe in what they have found? That they suspect it might be a mirage? Why can't they just fuck off and leave us alone?

Josh and Tamsin—the new girlfriend, who happens to be the client he was so keen to rush back to the last time we met—are having supper at her place. It's their coming-out ball as an official couple, so I can't get out of this dinner party, although God knows I have tried. I came up with a couple of really good excuses but Josh kept giving me alternative dates, the cunning bastard. The only way to get out of it would have been to say to him, *oh, just fuck off and die, Josh—I never liked you anyway.* Which does cross my mind. But I can't say that because Josh is my best friend, the only link to the past that I have left, and I am afraid of losing him.

So that's how I come to find myself outside a big white terraced house in Notting Hill, holding a bottle of something dry and white, and getting buzzed up to the third floor. I am a little spooked because I saw someone on the tube reading the paperback of *Oranges for Christmas*. That always feels strange to me. Especially when they start laughing at one of my father's hilarious anecdotes about all that adorable East End poverty and deprivation.

Josh opens the door and lets me into an expensive little box. There are highly polished wooden boards on the floor and black-framed Japanese prints of bony peasants struggling through rainy landscapes on the wall. A rectangular glass table set for six people. The place is as spartan as a morgue.

Josh is not wearing a tie, the sure sign that he is off duty. He slaps me on the back, a grin splitting his face, very pleased with himself. He has that glow about him that everybody gets when they get it bad.

I can smell some kind of lemony fish being grilled. The aroma of food cooking gives the place its only sign of human life. Then a smiling blonde in bare feet comes out of the kitchen, drying her hands and walking toward me.

"Something smells good," I tell her. "And it's not me."

"Alfie," Tamsin says, kissing me on either cheek. "I know it's a cliché, but I really have heard so much about you."

I can understand why Josh is dead keen. There's an ease about her that I really like, and while Josh is fussing with the dessert that he's making—doing his enlightened man bit, which is the joke of the century—Tamsin and I sit on the sofa and I tell her about my train journey here, and how strange I felt seeing someone reading my father's book.

"Oh, I love that book!" she says. "It's so warm and funny and real!"

"But the interesting thing," I tell her, "is that my dad is none of those things. Warm. Funny. Real. He's not like that at all. He's more cold, unfunny and fake. In fact, he's a right—"

Josh sticks a bowl of chips under my nose.

"Pringle?" he says. "Cheese and onion or barbecue flavor?"

Josh opens a bottle of champagne and Tamsin tells me about her job. As far as I can understand, she does something important for a merchant bank and came to see Josh for advice about a company flotation.

"Our shop has one of the largest corporate finance practices in Europe," Josh boasts. Tamsin stares up at him adoringly. *My hero.* But I can understand why they are happy, and we have a good time until the other guests turn up.

Then the evening starts to go horribly wrong.

First, another couple arrives. It's one of Josh's rugby-playing mates from his company and his snooty, stick-thin wife. Dan and India. They breeze in, and as Josh keeps the champagne flowing, they are soon acting as if they own the place.

"And what do you do?" India asks me.

"I teach," I say, and they both look at me as if I said, "I clean the sewers of the city with a second-hand toothbrush." Or maybe that's just my imagination. Or the champagne. But they don't say anything after I tell them what I do, so while Tamsin and India talk about the celebrity chef who invented tonight's fish and while Josh and Dan bellow at each other about various areas of commercial law, I sit silently on the sofa, slowly getting completely and utterly stewed. Just when I think I am so drunk that I might curl up and have a little nap, Josh looks at me with a secret smile.

"Guess what I've got for you," he says. He goes to the kitchen, gets something out of the fridge and comes back pouring a foaming, yellow beer into a tall glass. I immediately recognize the silver and green can he is holding.

"Tsingtao," I say.

"Your favorite," Josh says.

I am touched. I know this means Josh has gone to great lengths to make me feel comfortable tonight. But the beer on top of the champagne turns out to be not exactly the best idea in the world. In fact, it's a rotten idea. Soon my eyes start crossing if I don't make every effort to keep them in focus.

"Alfie's father wrote that wonderful book," Tamsin tells India, trying to include me in the evening. "*Oranges for Christmas.*"

"Really?" India says, interested in me for the first time. "*Oranges for Christmas?* God, it's such a classic, isn't it? I bought it ages ago. Keep meaning to read it."

"He's getting more famous," I tell them. "My father, I mean.

There was a picture of him and his girlfriend at some party the other day. In the *Standard*. They were grinning and trying to pretend they didn't know their picture was being taken." I have a swig of my Tsingtao. "He's getting more famous but, the funny thing is, he doesn't deserve it. Because he's not even writing anything. And—I ask you—how's that meant to make me feel?"

They all stare at me, dumbfounded.

"I wanted to be a writer. I really did. First of all, I was going to write about Hong Kong. About why it's important. About why it's touched with magic. Now—well, I don't know what I would write now. I sort of lost the urge."

"Why don't you write about some stupid dickhead who can't hold his drink and who is not fit to be in civilized company?" says Josh. "You've got to write about what you know."

Then the buzzer goes again and the final guest arrives. A pretty, rather overweight young woman called Jane from Josh's firm. Mid-thirties. Very friendly. A bit nervous. We are seated next to each other at dinner. I'm not meant to get off with her, am I? Plates are put in front of us containing some kind of fancy salad.

"Warm salad of radicchio, gem and pancetta," Tamsin says.

"She's such a genius," Josh says, and they exchange a little sweet kissy-kiss that provokes an involuntary sneer on my flushed face. Some distant part of me realizes I am not being the perfect guest.

"Delicious," India declares.

"Radicchio, gem and pancetta?" Dan says. "Sounds like a firm of Italian lawyers."

Everybody roars apart from me. I can feel Jane looking at me, trying to think of something to say.

"Josh told me you were in Hong Kong," she says pleasantly.

"That's right."

"I was in Singapore for two years. I really fell in love with Asia. The food, the people, the culture."

"Not the same thing," I tell her.

"Excuse me?"

"Not the same thing. Hong Kong and Singapore. It's the difference between a rain forest and a golf course. Singapore being the golf course."

"You don't like Singapore?" she says, her face crumpling.

"Too sanitized," I say firmly. "Singapore is nothing like Hong Kong. Didn't somebody once say that Singapore is Disneyland with the death penalty?"

Jane sadly turns her face to the fancy salad before her.

"When were you ever in Singapore, Alfie?" Josh demands.

"What?" I say, playing for time.

"I said—when exactly were you in Singapore?" He is not smiling at me any more. "I don't recall you ever going to Singapore. But suddenly you're the big expert."

"I've never been to Singapore," I say with an infuriating smugness.

"Then you don't really know what you're talking about, do you?" Josh says.

"I know I wouldn't like it."

"How do you know that?"

"I wouldn't like anywhere that they say is like Disneyland with the death penalty."

"Singapore Sling," India says. We all look at her as if she is mental. "Fine cocktail," she adds, spearing a piece of gem lettuce. Then they are all yakking about their favorite cocktails, even poor old Jane perking up a bit as she weighs in with her thoughts on the humble Piña Colada.

"I like a Long, Slow Screw Up Against the Wall," Dan says, predictably enough, and they all hee-haw their stupid laughter.

"I bet you do, mate, I bet you do!" cackles Josh.

"How about you, Alfie?" Tamsin asks me pleasantly, still trying to include me in the evening, acting as though she knows it's a meaningless question but it's just a bit of harmless fun.

How did Josh ever get a woman like her? Isn't she much too good for him? "What's your favorite cocktail?"

"Not much of a cocktail man," I say lightly, as if this conversation is beneath me, draining my beer. "Not much of a drinker really."

"Clearly," Josh says.

I examine the empty glass in my hand as if I am secretly some kind of expert.

"But I do like a Tsingtao. Reminds me of home."

"Home?" Jane says. "Do you mean Hong Kong?"

But India has a question of her own.

"Why are you wearing a wedding ring?" she says, looking at the hand that holds my Tsingtao, and everything around the table seems to get all silent.

"What?"

"Why are you wearing a wedding ring?" she asks again. "You're not married, are you?"

I set down my glass and look at the ring around the third finger of my left hand as if I am seeing it for the first time.

"Used to be," I say.

"And you still wear your ring? Ah. That's sweet."

"Lot of divorce about these days," Dan says philosophically. "Rotten for the kids. Still, probably better than if the parents stay together and, you know, don't get along."

"I didn't get divorced," I say.

"No," Josh says. "He didn't get divorced. His wife died, didn't she, Alfie? She was a beautiful girl and then she died. While scuba diving. And that means we all have to feel sorry for you, doesn't it? Poor little Alfie and his dead wife. The rest of us are meant to apologize for going on living."

"Josh," says Tamsin.

"Well, I'm sick of it."

Suddenly Josh and I are standing up. If there wasn't a glass table and half a dozen fancy salads between us, I swear we would be exchanging punches.

"I don't want you to feel sorry for me, Josh. That's not necessary. But it would be nice if you would leave me alone."

"Perhaps I will in the future."

"Perhaps you should."

I bow stiffly to Tamsin and leave the table. Josh follows me, getting more angry by the second. He's not going to let me go that easily.

"Your wife's dead and that's your excuse for coming in here and acting like a complete asshole, is it? Is that your excuse, Alfie?"

But I don't answer him as I make my way to the door. I think to myself—no, that's not my excuse.

That's my reason.

15

THERE IS NOTHING CASUAL ABOUT JACKIE.

Every morning she arrives for work dressed for a date with Rod Stewart. Her heels are high and her skirts are short, but there is a curious formality about her. She looks as though she has spent a long time deciding what to wear. She looks as though putting on her makeup took about as long as minor heart surgery. But her provocative clothes are like a uniform, or a shield, or a glossy shell. It's a very self-conscious sexiness. As if she looks that way not to advertise something, but to protect it.

Even when she has changed into her cleaning kit, Jackie is still as formal as a flight attendant or a policewoman. It's got something to do with the highlights in her hair, the mascara that is just a touch too heavy. She spends far too long trying to make herself look good. She looks good already.

Sometimes I see her in the staff room, or the corridor, or a class that is empty of students. Bumping around with her bucket, polishing something in her yellow gloves. For some reason I don't understand, I never ask Jackie about herself. I always ask her about the young girl in *The Heart Is a Lonely Hunter*.

It makes me feel good to ask Jackie about the book. It's like a secret we share.

"How's Mick?" I say.

"Still dreaming." She smiles.

• • •

My students are not like Jackie. My students dress down. Depending on their personal circumstances, and their country of origin, they are either expensively scruffy or poverty stricken scruffy. Vanessa, for example, wears white or black Versace jeans every day, while Witold always wears the same pair of counterfeit Polish denims with "Levy's" misspelled on the back. But unless they have a hot date after class, they stick with T-shirts and sneakers, combat trousers or jeans. Except for Hiroko.

Hiroko was an office lady in Tokyo and she still wears the classic OL uniform—pale, neat little matching jacket-and-skirt suits, black high heels and even those flesh-colored tights that OLs seem to favor. I have seen those flesh-colored tights on young female Japanese tourists buying their designer tea bags at Fortnum & Mason—I couldn't help noticing—but I have never seen them on any of my students.

Apart from Hiroko.

Hiroko is not like Yumi. Hiroko is twenty-three going on fifty. With her dyed blond hair and funky fashion sense, Yumi looks like the maverick, but in fact she is far more typical of the Japanese girls at Churchill's than Hiroko.

It's not just Hiroko's clothes. She is diligent in her work, deferential to her teachers, never speaking unless she is spoken to, and then only in bashful, monosyllabic sentences. She doesn't actually bow, but when you are speaking to her she gives all these suppliant, encouraging little nods of her head that strike me as pure Japanese, far more so than the legendary bowing. Sometimes I think Hiroko has never really left that office in Tokyo.

Hiroko is having problems with her course. She is one of my Proficiency students and her written work is faultless. But she is having trouble with her spoken English. Hiroko doesn't like talking. Hiroko hates talking. At first I thought it was because she is cripplingly shy. But it's far more than shyness.

Hiroko has that very Japanese terror of doing something imperfectly. She would much rather not do it at all.

So she sits in my Proficiency class, silent as a mute, hiding her sweet, bespectacled round face behind a long black curtain of hair. It gets so bad that I have to ask her to stay behind after class and she nods her assent, her eyes blinking nervously behind her glasses.

I start off with the good news—she is one of my best students, I can see how hard she works—and then I tell her that she has to start talking more in class or she will flunk her exam on the oral section. In her strained, faltering English—she visibly flinches at every minor mistake she makes—Hiroko asks me if she should drop down a level or two. I tell her that the problem would be exactly the same even if she was with the Advanced Beginners.

"Listen, you just have to get over your hang-up about speaking English," I say. "Don't let it become too important, okay? Even native speakers make mistakes. It doesn't matter if it comes out sounding different from the textbooks. Just open your mouth and give it a go."

Hiroko looks at me with wide, frightened eyes, furiously nodding in agreement. Where does it come from, this myth that all Asian eyes are mean little slits?

She stares at me with a kind of touching trust, waiting for something else to happen, and so very soon the pair of us are sitting in the Eamon de Valera with Hiroko nursing a spritzer and me sipping a stout. That's where she tells me all about her broken heart.

"It's no good if it's too important," I said to her on the way to the pub. "That's what I've learned. If you make it too important, then it ruins everything."

Hiroko of the broken heart.

There was a man back in Tokyo. A man from Hiroko's

office. An older man. Hiroko lived with her parents and the man lived with his wife. Their work brought Hiroko and the man together. He was friendly and charming. She was young and lonely. She liked him a lot. And so they began.

Hiroko and the man had to go to love hotels, those briefly rented rooms in buildings shaped like ocean liners and castles and space ships. She knew he wasn't free but she also knew that they really cared for each other. He was funny and kind and he told her that she was beautiful. He made her feel good about herself, as though she could really be the person she had always wanted to be. And he told her that he loved her, he told her that he loved her so very much in one of their two-hour stays in a love hotel. Then he went home to his wife.

Something happened. Something momentous that makes her eyes fill with tears, something that she will not talk about.

"You got pregnant, didn't you?"

A quick bob of the head. Heartbroken assent.

"But you didn't have the baby."

A small shake of the head, her hair falling over her face.

"And pencil dick stayed with his wife."

Her voice is not much more than a whisper, but I am struck by how little accent she has. When she doesn't think about it too much, her spoken English is actually pretty good.

"Of course."

I reach out and touch her hand.

"Don't worry about him, Hiroko. He's going to have a really unhappy life."

She looks at me gratefully and smiles for the first time.

"Promise me that in the future you will steer clear of pencil dicks like that," I say.

"Okay," she says, laughing and crying all at the same time. "I promise."

"No more pencil dicks?"

"No more—no more pencil dicks."

Two drinks and a £10 black cab ride later, Hiroko and I are outside the house of her host family in Hampstead. It's a hell of a house—a big, detached mansion on one of those wide, tree-lined avenues that they have up there—but not much of a family—just one rich old lady who rents out a room to female students because she gets lonely. Hiroko makes sure that the old lady is tucked up in bed with Tiddles the cat and Radio 4 and then she sneaks me up the stairs to a converted loft where a shaft of moonlight pours through the skylight and onto her single bed.

And as she showers—they are so clean, these Japanese girls, always jumping in the shower and wearing their pants in bed—I think to myself that there's another way that Hiroko is different from my other students.

Most of them are in London looking for fun. Hiroko is here looking for love. Or perhaps she is just escaping from it.

I know she will never feel the same desperate passion for me that she felt for that second-rate salary man back in Tokyo. And I know that she will never own my heart in the way that my wife owned my heart. Yet that's okay. It doesn't seem sad tonight. In fact, in some way that I can't quite understand, it feels sort of perfect.

"I'm very exciting," she says.

She means: *I'm very excited.*

It is, apparently, an easy mistake to make. I have had a number of students say to me, "I'm very boring," when what they really mean is, "I'm very bored." There's some glitch in the translation from Japanese to English that causes the mistake. But I like it. I like that mistake.

I'm very exciting too.

A panic attack on the train.

At first, when I get a twinge in my chest and feel the cold, creeping fear dripping down my back, I think that it's just another one of my phony heart attacks.

But it's much worse than that.

I am bumping south on the Northern Line, escaping from Hampstead before Hiroko's nice old cat lady stirs, before Tiddles alerts her to my presence. I am strap-hanging in a crowded carriage because the rush hour starts just after dawn these days, when without warning my breath starts coming in these short, fast gasps, like a diver who finds himself a long way down and suddenly sucking on the last drops of air in a broken tank.

Panic.

Real, terrified, sweating panic. I can't breathe. It's not my imagination. I literally can't breathe. I am horribly and desperately aware of the crush of people around me, the sick yellow light of the carriage, the dead air of the tunnel, the entire weight of the city pressing down on us.

Trapped. I feel like weeping, screaming, running, but I can do none of these things. I need to be out of this place immediately and there is nowhere to go, there is no end in sight.

Pure, howling terror. My eyes sting with perspiration and tears. I feel like I am choking, falling, watched. Passengers—all the other calm, unforgiving passengers—glance my way and seem to stare right into my cracked soul. My face crumples and I close my eyes, my legs gone to jelly, the roar of the train deafening, gripping the worn leather strap until my knuckles are white.

Somehow I make it to the next station. I stumble from the train, up the escalators, burst into the light, the air. Filling my lungs. When I have stopped trembling I start to walk home. It takes a long time. I am miles from home. The streets are crowded with commuters on their way to work and school. I seem to be going in a different direction from everyone else.

My walk home takes me through Highbury Fields where George Chang is standing in his patch of grass.

His face seems young and old all at the same time. His head

is erect, his back poker straight. He doesn't see me. He gives no indication of seeing anything. I stand perfectly still watching his slow-motion dance. His hands move like punches, and yet there is no violence in them. His legs and feet move like kicks and sweeps, but there is no force in them. Every move he makes looks like the softest thing in the world.

And I realize that I have never in my life seen anyone who looks so totally at peace inside his own skin.

"I want you to teach me," I tell George. "I want to learn Tai Chi."

We are in the new General Lee's Tasty Tennessee Kitchen on the Holloway Road. George is eating his breakfast. Chicken wings and fries. You would think that a man like George Chang would avoid fast-food joints like General Lee's, that he would be squatting somewhere with a bowl of steamed rice, but you would be wrong. George says the food in General Lee's is "very simple." He's a big fan.

"Teach you Tai Chi," he says. The way he says it, it's neither a question nor an agreement.

"I need to do something, George. I mean it. I feel like everything's falling to bits." I don't say what I really feel. That I want to be comfortable inside my own body. That I want to be like him. That I am sick and tired of being like myself, so sick and tired that you wouldn't believe it. "I need to be calmer," is what I say. "Much calmer. Right now I can't relax. I can't sleep. Sometimes I can't even breathe."

He sort of shrugs.

"Tai Chi good for relaxation. Stress control. All the problem of modern world. Life very busy."

"That's right," I say. "Life's very busy, isn't it? And sometimes I feel so old. Everything aches, George. I've got no energy. I feel frightened—really frightened—but I can't even say what's wrong. Everything seems to overwhelm me."

"Still miss wife."

"That's right, George. But every little thing that goes wrong feels like a major trauma. Do you know what I mean? I lose my temper. I feel like crying." I attempt a little laugh. "I'm going crazy here, George. Help me. Please."

"Tai Chi good for all that. For tension. For tired."

"That's exactly what I need."

"But I can't teach you."

My heart lurches with disappointment. Once I had worked up the nerve to ask him, it had never even crossed my mind that he would turn me down. I stare at him munching his chicken wings for a while, waiting for him to offer some further explanation. But the silence just grows. He has apparently said it all.

"Why not?"

"Take too long time."

"But I see you teaching people all the time. There's often someone with you."

He smiles down at his chicken wings.

"Always someone *different*. Different man, different woman. Come for a few mornings. Maybe a little bit longer. Then stop coming. Because Western people don't have patience for Tai Chi." He looks at me over a chicken wing. "It's not pill. It's not drug. Not magic. To be any good for you, for anyone, take a long time. A *long* time. Western people don't have time."

I almost tell him that I've got all the time in the world, but I don't bother.

Because suddenly I see myself with George in the park, both of us in our black pajamas, doing a graceful slow-motion waltz as the packed tube trains rumble 100 meters below our slippered feet, and the image just seems ridiculous.

George is right. There are some dances you never learn. That stillness, that peace, that grace. Who am I kidding?

I just don't have it in me.

16

HIROKO IS GOING BACK TO JAPAN for Christmas.
I meet her at Paddington, under a huge fir tree decorated with
brightly colored boxes that are meant to look like presents, and
we catch the Heathrow Express to the airport.

Saying good-bye to her feels strange. I am sad to see her go.
At the same time, I am glad to feel something, anything. But—
and this is the important bit—not too much.

We embrace at the departure gate and Hiroko waves to me
right up until the time she disappears behind the screen before
passport control. Then I wander around Terminal 3, reluctant
to go home. The airport is awash with real emotion today.
Lovers are saying good-bye and being reunited. Families are
separating and coming back together. There are lots of hugs and
laughter and tears. The departure gate is pretty interesting but
the arrivals hall is even better, because you can't do it in your
own time at arrivals. You can't decide when it's time to say hello
in quite the same way that you can decide it's time to say good-
bye. Hello just happens. The people anxiously waiting for
someone don't know when that face is suddenly going to appear
before them, slowly pushing a luggage trolley, smiling through
the jet lag, ready for a kiss and a cuddle, ready to begin again.

There's something else that I notice about the arrivals hall.
It is full of young women arriving in the UK to study English.

Everywhere you look there is shining black hair, bright brown eyes and Louis Vuitton luggage. They don't stop coming.

It's a kind of miracle.

Behind the barrier there are bored drivers and chirpy representatives of two dozen language schools standing with their little signs and placards and notice boards, waiting for the next Jumbo from Osaka or Beijing or Seoul or somewhere else where Christmas doesn't really matter.

And as I stand among the men and women with their placards—MISS SUZUKI, KIM LEE, GREEN GABLES LANGUAGE SCHOOL, TAE-SOON LEE, MIWAKO HONDA AND HIROMI TAKESHI, OXFORD SCHOOL OF ENGLISH, MISS WANG AND MISS WANG—I suddenly realize that this city is full of young women learning English.

The Terminal 3 brigade is Asian. At the other terminals, you would no doubt find the Scandinavian regiments, or the Mediterranean battalions. But there are thousands of them, an entire army of them, with fresh reinforcements arriving daily.

For the first time I understand that there's no reason for me ever to be lonely again.

Some of these young women—laughing, confident, looking forward to their new life—find their drivers or their schools' representatives immediately. Others struggle to make the connection. They wander in front of the barrier, looking for their name on one of the little hand-held placards. Hopeful but a touch worried. And my heart aches for them.

I watch them for the longest time, these beautiful stragglers in this magnificent brown-eyed invasion, fresh off the plane and looking for a sign.

And somewhere high above me, in the Muzak that is pumped around the airport, "Silent Night" segues into "O Come All Ye Faithful."

As soon as my nan has her front door open, I can smell the gas.

I brush past her and quickly go into the kitchen where the smell is even stronger.

"Alfie?"

One of the gas burners on her cooker is turned up to full and unlit. The gas feels so thick it's like you could reach out and touch it. Coughing like a madman, I turn it off and open up all the windows.

"Nan," I say, sick and eyes streaming, "you've got to be more careful."

"I don't know how that happened," she says, all flustered. "I was making—I don't remember." She blinks at me with her watery blue eyes. "Don't tell your mum, Alfie. Or your dad."

I look at her. She has her makeup on. Her eyebrows are two shaky black lines and her lipstick is very slightly off, like a double exposure on a photograph. The sight of her worried face and erratic cosmetics makes me put my arm around her shoulders. Inside her cardigan she feels as small and fragile as a child.

"I promise I won't tell anybody," I say, knowing she is worried that my parents already think she is unable to live alone, knowing that her great terror in this world is that she will one day be taken from this place and put in a home. "But please don't do it again, okay, Nan?"

She beams with relief and I watch her make a cup of tea for the pair of us, muttering to herself, elaborately turning the gas off after the kettle has boiled. I feel for the poor old thing, constantly being assessed for signs that her warm, intelligent, curious mind has finally turned to mush. At the same time the gas has frightened me. I am afraid that one day I will stand outside her flat with the fumes seeping under the door and nobody answering the bell. Then I remember why I am here. Jesus. I'm getting a touch of old timer's disease myself.

"Where's your tree, Nan?"

"In the little room, love. In the box with Christmas written on it."

My nan loves Christmas. She would put her tree up in mid-August if we didn't physically restrain her. Although she always spends Christmas Day with my family—and this year she will spend it with my mother and me, which is all that's left of my family—she still likes to have her own tree, alleging that it's "nice for Alfie when he comes round," as if I am just coming up to my fourth birthday.

I can remember the Christmas Days we had with my nan when I was small. She was still in her old house in the East End, the house where my father grew up, the house in *Oranges for Christmas*, the house with a chicken run in the back garden and a stand-up piano in the living room. The place always seemed to be full of my uncles and aunts and cousins, the children playing with their new toys while the adults got merry—big glasses of dark beer for the men, small glasses of something red and sweet for the women—and played brag and poker, or bet on the horses that were racing on television. The old house was constantly filled with people and music, cigarette smoke and laughter. There was a huge tree that looked as though it had come straight from some Norwegian wood.

Now the old house has gone and so has my grandfather and so has my father and my nan lives alone in this small white flat, the belongings of a lifetime shrunk to fit a few bare rooms. The uncles and the aunts are scattered, spending Christmases with their own children and grandchildren, and the real tree has been replaced by a fake silver one that comes in three parts—top half, bottom half and base, like a fake Santa half-heartedly going *ho ho ho*. I find the tree and a collection of fairy lights and assorted decorations in a torn cardboard box marked "Xmass." My nan watches me with excited eyes as I screw the thing together.

"Lovely," she says. "That silver looks smashing, doesn't it, Alfie?"

"It does, Nan."

As I stretch to put the angel on top of the tree I feel something bad happen to my back. Some muscle seems to go at the base of my spine and I am suddenly hunched up with pain, the angel still in my fist.

And as I sit on the sofa waiting for the pain to pass, and my nan goes off to make another cup of tea, I think I finally understand her passion for her fake tree.

Christmas trees are a bit like relationships. The real thing is certainly more beautiful, but it's just too much fuss, too much mess.

You can say what you like about fake ones.

But you can't deny that they are a lot less trouble.

The way I come to sleep with Vanessa is that I find her standing outside the college with Witold handing out new leaflets for the school.

The massed ranks of late Christmas shoppers are not paying them any attention so Vanessa is folding the flyers into little paper planes and throwing them into the crowd. Witold is watching her with an embarrassed grin.

"Study with the best!" she cries, launching a leaflet at a middle-aged businessman. *"Estudia en Churchill's! Studia alla Churchill's! Studieren in Churchill's!"*

"What are you doing, Vanessa?" I ask her, rubbing my back.

"Getting new students!" she laughs. *"Nauka w Churchill's! Etudiez à Churchill's!"*

"Well, knock it off," I smile.

"But nobody's *interested*," she says, stamping her foot and giving me one of her sulky pouts. She puts her hands on her hips. "It's Christmas."

"Just give them out normally," I tell her. "Please."

"What will you do for me? Give me an exam paper in advance?"

"I'll buy you a drink." Vanessa is the kind of woman who

makes you think that banter is compulsory. "As it's Christmas. You know. A glass of German wine or something."

"Anything but German wine."

"I like German wine," Witold says.

And so later I find myself in the Eamon de Valera having a drink with Vanessa. She is not herself. She doesn't dance, or flirt, or shout across the pub to someone. She tells me that she is not going back to France for the holiday—it's difficult to know where she should go now that her parents are divorced—but staying in London is even worse.

"Why's that?"

She looks at me for a second.

"Because I will not see my boyfriend," she says. "He will be with his family."

Later still I see pictures of the boyfriend in Vanessa's flat.

It is a good flat in an affluent part of town, nothing like the tiny bedsit that Yumi lives in, or the room in a shared house that Hiroko occupies. Vanessa has her own small but beautiful one-bedroom flat in one of the swankier parts of north London. It must cost well over £1,000 a month and judging by the number of photographs of Vanessa and her boyfriend—this gym-fit forty-year-old, his arm casually circled around Vanessa's waist, a platinum wedding ring glinting on the third finger of his left hand, a wide white smile on his face—I guess that he is the one paying the bills.

"Difficult time of year for him," Vanessa says, picking up a photograph of the pair of them sitting outside some country pub. "He has to be with his family." She replaces the picture. "His children. And her. But he doesn't sleep with her anymore. He really doesn't."

I go to bed with Vanessa and that cheers her up. Not because of my dazzling sexual technique but because she seems to find it mildly amusing being in bed with me. She's physically very different from Yumi or Hiroko. Just everything. Her hair, her breasts, her hips, her skin. I find the novelty exciting—I'm very exciting—and I'm about to say rash things, but luckily Vanessa's small smile stops me from saying anything stupid. I know that she takes tonight very lightly because somebody already owns her heart.

And I understand completely. I'm not offended.

Later she has a little cry into the pillow and I can hold her without saying, "What's wrong, darling, what's wrong?" because I know for certain that it has absolutely nothing to do with me.

I lie awake in the darkness of a strange bed and I think about Yumi. About Hiroko. About Vanessa. About waiting in the arrivals hall at Heathrow. About how I have realized that I need never be lonely again.

And I know why I am attracted to the girls in the arrivals hall. It's not because, as a nut doctor might suggest, a permanent attachment is unlikely.

It's because they are all a long way from home.

Even if they have many friends here, even if they are happy in this city, they have their lonely hours. They don't have someone who is always there. They don't have to rush home to anyone.

They are all ultimately alone.

It's funny. They sort of remind me of me.

17

I AM TRUE TO MY WIFE. Even in these other beds, with these women who sometimes talk in their sleep in a language I do not understand, I am always true to my wife.

Because nobody else touches me. Nobody even comes close.

And I come to see that as a kind of blessing. To love without loving—it's not so bad once you get used to it. To be that far beyond harm, where nothing can hurt you and nothing can be taken away from you—is that really such a bad place to be? There's a lot to be said for the meaningless relationship. The meaningless relationship is hugely underrated.

There are no little lies told in these trysts, these transactions. The rented rooms we meet in are not cold places. Far from it. There's no contempt, no boredom, no constant searching for an exit sign. We are there because we want to be there. The death by a thousand cuts that you get in most marriages—there's none of that.

And who is to say that these relationships are meaningless?

I like you—you're nice.

Is that really so meaningless?

Or is that all the meaning you need?

Things start to go wrong when Vanessa gives me an apple.

There's a knock on the staff room door and Hamish gets it.

When he turns to look at me—his impressively plucked eye-brows lifting wryly above his handsome face—I see Vanessa's smiling blond head over his shoulder. She has a shiny red apple in her fist. Bringing me an apple is a very Vanessa thing to do.

Both genuinely affectionate and mildly mocking.

"An apple for my teacher."

"Sweet."

Then she softly places a kiss on my lips—still acting as if it's all a joke, which it is to her—and just at that moment Lisa Smith comes up the stairs and sees us. Vanessa turns away laughing, oblivious of the principal's dirty looks. Or perhaps she just doesn't care. But Lisa glares at me for a few long seconds as if she wishes I were dead by the side of the road. She goes into her office on the other side of the corridor.

Back in the staff room Hamish and Lenny are both looking at me. Hamish mumbles something to me but I am not quite sure if it's, "You should watch that, mate"—meaning Vanessa—or "You should wash that, mate"—meaning the apple.

Lenny, once he gets over his initial shock, is more forthright.

"Vanessa? You haven't got a multiple-entry visa there, have you, mate? You're not going full speed up the newly opened Euro tunnel, are you?"

Before I can lie to him the phone rings and Lisa Smith tells Hamish that she wants to see me in her office. Now.

"Jesus," says Lenny. "She's going to have your bollocks for ethnic earrings, mate."

Lenny lifts his eyebrows and smirks. There is a hideous admiration in his eyes.

I'm not like Lenny the Lech, I tell myself. *I'm not.*

"I don't understand, Lenny. You get away with murder. And I get lifted. Why haven't you ever been busted?"

"Why? Because I've never screwed any of the students, mate."

"What?"

"It's all talk with me, mate. Dirty talk, I'll grant you. Filthy talk, even. But I wouldn't actually put my barnacle-encrusted old todger anywhere near this lot. Are you kidding? In the current climate, it's more than my knob's worth."

"Never?"

"Not once. Well, there was a cute little Croat who let me put my hand inside her Wonderbra at last year's Christmas party. But that modest handful is the only penetration there has ever been."

"I can't believe it."

"It's true, mate. Besides, what would all these hot young things want with a fat old cunt like me? Go on, off you go."

So it's true. I'm nothing like Lenny the Lech. I'm much worse.

As I leave the staff room, I hear the clank of a bucket at the other end of the corridor. There she is, going about her work— a thin, blond figure in a blue nylon coat, her copy of *The Heart Is a Lonely Hunter* stuffed in a torn pocket, mopping the floor in a pair of mules that were designed for dancing. No flat shoes this morning for Jackie Day.

And I can't tell if she is staring into space or looking right through me.

"It's sexual imperialism," Lisa Smith says. "That's what it is. That's all it is."

"I don't know what you're talking about," I say, my face burning, my back aching.

"Oh, I think you do," she retorts. "Yumi. Hiroko. Now Vanessa. I saw her give you that golden delicious."

I'm shocked. I was caught red-handed with Vanessa. But how does she know about Yumi? How does she know about Hiroko?

"Do you think our students don't talk?" she says, answering my question, and I think: Vanessa. Vanessa and her big, mocking mouth. "And don't pretend you don't know what I'm talk-ing about. You've insulted this college. Please don't insult my intelligence."

"Okay," I say. "But I honestly don't feel that I've done any-thing wrong."

Lisa Smith is dumbfounded.

"You don't think you've done anything wrong?"

"No."

"Can't you see that we are in a position of trust?" she asks me, crossing her legs and impatiently tapping a combat boot against the side of her desk. "Can't you see that you're exploit-ing your position?"

I never saw it as exploitation. I felt that we were always sort of equal. I know I'm their teacher and they are my students, but it's not as though they are children. They are grown women. Most of them are more mature than me. And yet they are young. They are gloriously young, with all their lives stretching out before them. True, I'm the guy with the piece of chalk, but they have time on their side, they have years to burn. I always felt that gave us parity, that their youth leveled it up. Youth has its own kind of power, its own special status. But I can't say any of this to the principal.

"They're all old enough to know what they're doing," is what I say. "I'm not cradle snatching."

"You're their teacher. You're in a position of responsibility. And you have abused that position in the worst possible way."

At first I think that she is going to sack me then and there. But her face softens.

"I know you think that I'm some kind of old battle-ax who can't stand to see anyone having a good time," she says.

"Not at all, not at all."

That's exactly what I think.

"I understand the temptations of the flesh. I was at the Isle of Wight for Dylan. I spent a weekend at Greenham Common.

I know what happens when people get thrown together. But I can't condone sexual relations between my staff and my students. Do it again and you're out. Is that understood?"

"Absolutely."

Even as I am nodding, I am thinking to myself: you can't stop me. This city is full of young women looking for friendship, romance and a little help with the native tongue. Even as I am being given my final warning, I am telling myself that it is going to be all right, that I need never be lonely, that I am doing nothing wrong.

I like you, you're nice.

Where's the harm in that?

When the pain in my back gets so bad that the painkillers no longer have any effect, I go to see my doctor. At first he looks at me as though it's another psychosomatic thing, like my heart feeling as if it's an undigested kebab, but when I tell him about the angel on top of my nan's Christmas tree, he gets me to take my shirt off and gives me a full examination.

Then he tells me there's nothing that he can do.

"Tricky thing, the lower back," he says.

I bump into George Chang on my way home. He is coming out of General Lee's with takeout, on his way back to the Shanghai Dragon to help with the lunch trade. He looks at my face and asks me what's wrong.

"Done my back in," I tell him. "Putting up my nan's Christmas tree."

He tells me to come to the restaurant with him. I say that I've got to get back to work, but he does this thing that I've noticed his wife does all the time. He just acts as though I haven't spoken. When we are inside the Shanghai Dragon, he tells me to stand perfectly still. He places his hands at the base of my spine. He is not quite touching me, but—and this is strange—I can definitely feel the warmth of his palms. He is not touching me, but I can feel the heat of his hands. It's like stand-ing next to a quiet fire. How do you explain that?

Then he tells me to lean slightly forward and very gently pummel my lower back with the back of my hands. I do what he tells me. And then I look at him. Because something inex-plicable has happened.

The pain in my back is going away.

"What happened there?"

He just smiles.

"How did you do that?"

"Keep doing that exercise." He leans forward and lightly paddles his back. "Do it every day for a few minutes. Not too hard, okay?"

"What—what was that? George?"

"Very simple Chi Kung exercise."

"What's Chi Kung? You mean chi as in Tai Chi? Is it the same thing?"

"Any kind of exercise with the chi is Chi Kung. Okay? For keeping healthy. For curing sickness. For martial arts. For enlightenment."

"Enlightenment?"

"That's all Chi Kung. You remember chi. You told me you don't got any chi. Remember?"

I feel foolish. "I remember."

"Does it feel bit better?"

"It feels a lot better."

"You think maybe you got some chi after all?"

He is laughing at me.

"I guess I have."

"Then maybe you should come to the park on Sunday morning."

"You're going to teach me?"

He sort of grunts. "I'll teach you."

"What made you change your mind?"

"Sunday morning. Don't be late."

This year my family teaches me the true meaning of Christmas—surviving the thing.

But the long hours between the Christmas pudding and the blockbuster movies and my old man's sheepish arrival with his last-minute booty from Body Shop give me a chance to do some thinking.

With the sex police patroling the corridors of Churchill's International Language School, I figure that it is going to be difficult to meet new faces at work.

So I decide to go private. I place an ad in the back of a listings magazine, in the Personal Services section, which comes just after Introduction Agencies and just before Lonely Hearts.

Need Good English?
Fully qualified English teacher seeks private students.
We can help each other.

Then I put on Sinatra singing "My Funny Valentine" and I wait.

18

IT FEELS GOOD to be starting something new on such a beautiful day.

There's a light frost glinting on the park's stubby grass, but above our heads the usual flat gray shroud has been replaced by an endless blue sky and sunlight that is more dazzling than high noon in August. Although our breath is coming out as chilled steam, George and I are squinting our eyes in the light. We face each other.

"Tai Chi Chuan," he says. "Means—the supreme ultimate fist."

"Sounds violent," I say.

He ignores me.

"Everything relaxed. All moves soft. All things relaxed. But all moves have martial application. Understand?"

"Not really."

"Western people think—Tai Chi Chuan very beautiful. Very gentle. Yes?"

"Right."

"But Tai Chi Chuan is self-defense system. Every move has a reason. Not just for show." His hands glide through the air. "Block. Punch. Strike. Hold. Kick. But flowing. Always flowing. And always very soft. Understand?"

I nod.

"Tai Chi Chuan good for health. Stress. Circulation.

Modern world. But Tai Chi Chuan not the weakest martial art in the world." His dark eyes gleam. "Strongest."

"Okay."

"This Chen style."

"What style?"

"Chen style. Many style from different family. Yang style. Wu style. This Chen style."

I am not quite following every word of this. How can something so soft also be hard? How can something so gentle be a kind of boxing?

George steps away from me. He is wearing his usual black Mandarin suit and soft, flat-bottomed shoes. I am in a tracksuit with the helpful reminder of JUST DO IT inscribed down one leg. He moves his feet about shoulder-width apart, standing with his weight evenly distributed and his arms hanging by his side. His breathing is deep and even. His weight seems to sink into the ground. He looks both completely relaxed and yet somehow immovable.

"Stand like a mountain between heaven and earth," he says.

Stand like a mountain between heaven and earth? No problem, Yoda. This kind of talk should embarrass me. But I find that if I make a big effort, it doesn't. I try to stand like George. I close my eyes, seriously thinking about my breathing for the first time in my life.

"Open your joints," George tells me. "Let your body relax. Sink your weight to the center of the earth. And keep breathing. Always keep breathing."

Like diving, I think to myself. That's the first thing they teach you when you learn to scuba dive. You must always keep breathing.

Then I hear the laughter behind us.

"Look at this pair of buttheads. Fuck me. It's *Come Dancing* for fags."

There are three of them. Saturday-night stragglers, foaming

brown bottles in their fists, their faces as pale as curdled milk. Although they can't be older than about twenty, they already have the telltale swelling stomachs of committed boozers. Yet they are all wearing vaguely sporty clothes—sneakers, hooded running tops, baseball caps. Sort of funny, when you think about it.

But I feel a sudden rage inside me. These morons—dressed for sports day, built for happy hour—remind me of all the morons just like them that I taught at the Princess Diana Comprehensive School for Boys. Maybe that's why, when I open my mouth, I sound just like a teacher on the verge of a nervous breakdown.

"Haven't you lot got somewhere to go? Go on, piss off out of it. And take those stupid expressions off your faces."

Those faces darken, tighten, harden. They glance at each other and then all at once they are coming toward me, the bottles in their hands, their teeth bared like nicotine-stained fangs.

George steps in front of them.

"Please," he says. "No trouble."

The biggest one, his podgy face scarred by the livid souvenirs of acne, stops and smiles at his mates.

"No trouble at all."

Then he goes to put his meaty hands on George's chest, but as Zit-face attempts to grab George, the older man sort of goes with him, transferring his weight to his back foot as he intercepts Zit-face's hands by simply lifting his arms. Those meaty paws do not touch George. And suddenly Zit-face is pitching forward, grasping nothing, completely off balance. Lightly holding Zit-face's arms, George seems to twist his waist and casually tosses the youth to the ground. It is far too gentle to be called a throw. It is more as if Zit-face is a big insect with rather bad skin and George is gently swatting him aside.

"Jesus," I murmur.

George tries to help him up but Zit-face angrily shakes him off, although he appears to be more humiliated than hurt. I can see that George has used only the minimum of force on Zit-face, although I don't quite understand how that can be. I mean, I don't understand why George and I are not being given a good hiding right at this moment.

There's a second where I think it is going to get worse for us, but then the three of them skulk away, their faces twisted with shock and loathing beneath their baseball caps, Zit-face still clutching his shoulder, telling us to watch our fucking backs if we know what's fucking good for us. But he doesn't sound very frightening any more.

And I stare at George, realizing for the first time that I am not in dance class. We look at each other.

"How long before I can do that?"

"Practicing hard?"

"Yes."

"Very hard?"

"Very hard."

"About ten years."

"Ten years? You're kidding me."

"Okay. Maybe not ten. Maybe more like twenty. But remember—Tai Chi Chuan not about external strength. About internal strength. Not strength in muscles." He gently slaps his chest three times. "Strength inside."

Then he gives me a patient smile.

"Lots to learn," he says. "Better get started."

I am expecting the girl from Ipanema. What I get is the girl from Ilford.

Jackie Day is standing on my doorstep.

"Alfie? Hi. We spoke on the phone? About the ad? To learn English?"

I am thrown. It's true that we have spoken on the phone. Unfortunately there have only been a handful of callers, perhaps because we are in that dead period between Christmas and the New Year, or perhaps because they can smell an Alfie-sized rat.

But Jackie called. She was shocked and delighted to discover that it was her old pal from Oxford Street who was offering English lessons. And I naturally assumed that the cleaning woman from Churchill's was enquiring on behalf of somebody else.

I don't know who. I didn't even think about it.

Some hot Hungarian fresh off the jumbo who Jackie met while cleaning at another language school? Some leggy Brazilian who Jackie bumped into doing the lambada in a suburban nightclub? But there's no hot Hungarian, no Brazilian beauty.

Jackie brushes past me as she comes into the hall and I see that the roots of her blond hair need some attending to. As usual, she's all dressed up, as if she has somewhere to go. For some reason she is acting as though this is the place.

Our telephone conversation was short and sweet. Was that really me? Yes, it was really me. Small world! What were my rates like? How flexible were the lessons? I told her that my rates were reasonable, and my flexibility was endless. She thanked me and said she would think about it. But I swear to God I thought she was thinking about it for some foreign friend.

And now we look at each other. Jackie smiles eagerly. If I were a cartoon, a question mark would be hovering above my head.

"I'm so glad it's you," she laughs. "What a coincidence. I can't believe my luck."

I show her through to the living room, thinking that eventually all this will be worth the trouble. Be patient, Alfie. Somewhere out in the night the drums are calling and they are doing the lambada.

But it's still the middle of the afternoon. I've only got the run of the house because my mum has taken my nan to the sales in the West End. So I sit on the sofa with Jackie, note her tight little sweater, strappy shoes, the skirt the size of a face towel. I don't know how she can walk around like that. She dresses for seventies night even when she's trying to look respectable. She crosses her legs demurely.

"And who would the lessons be for?" I ask her.

She looks a little surprised.

"Sorry, I thought that was clear." A pause. "They're for me."

"But—why would you want to learn English?"

"You told me once you taught English Literature? Before you taught English as a foreign language?"

I nod cautiously. It's true that Jackie knows the details of my glorious teaching career. But I thought she understood that my ad had nothing to do with the subject I taught at the Princess Diana Comprehensive School for Boys. I thought she was just getting a few details before she introduced me to her Brazilian pal.

So that I could teach English as a foreign language.

"Well, that's what I want," she says brightly. "Lessons in English Lit. See, I need to get an A level in English Literature. I mean, I really need it. So that I can go back to college. So that I can restart my education."

"There's been some mistake," I say. "My advertisement was for students who want to learn English as a foreign language. Wasn't that clear? I'm not looking for students who want an A level in English Literature. Sorry. I honestly thought you were calling for somebody else. Some—I don't know—Brazilian, possibly."

"Some . . . Brazilian?"

"I don't even know why I said that."

Her smile fades away.

"You're not qualified to teach English to A level standard?"

"Well, I am. But that's not—"

"I'm thirty-one years old. I was thirty-one on Christmas Day."

"Well—happy birthday."

"Thank you. Twelve years ago I was doing really well at school. Top of the class. Straight A student. All that. Then I had to drop out."

This is more than I need to know. I stand up. She remains sitting.

"I've got two A levels. French and Media Studies. Very good

grades." She looks at me a little defiantly. "I'm not stupid, if that's what you're thinking. And I've got money. What I need is an English A level so that I can go back to school."

"Well, that's great, but—"

"I know the course I want, I know the college I want. If I get that English A level, I can study for my BA at the University of Greenwich."

I stare at her.

"Go to night school," I tell her.

"I can't."

"Why not?"

"I need a private tutor. I need to be more flexible than night school would let me be."

"And why's that?"

Her pale, pretty face darkens, as though a cloud has suddenly passed over it.

"Personal reasons."

I let my voice go all firm and commanding. Playing the teacher. Which is sort of ironic, when you think about it.

"I'm sorry to disappoint you, Jackie. I really am. But I'm not teaching anyone A level English. Not you or anyone else. I'm teaching English as a foreign language. And you don't need that. Do you?"

She makes no move to get up. I can see how disappointed she is, and I feel a stab of compassion for this overdressed, undereducated young woman.

I like her. I have always liked her. I just don't want her for a student.

"If you take an old man's advice, Jackie, qualifications are just meaningless pieces of paper." Trying to make my voice all jaunty and friendly. "They do you no good in the end. Believe me, I know."

"That's easy for you to say. Because you've got them. They're not meaningless bits of paper to me. They're a way out."

Vanessa's sleepy voice drifts down from the top of the stairs. "Alfie? Come back to bed. I have to go soon."

I don't usually entertain at home. I'm lucky that the sales are on.

Jackie Day stands up. She seems to see me for the first time.

"What kind of a teacher are you anyway?"

Sometimes I wonder that myself.

On the first day of the new year my father comes around to pick up the last of his stuff. This is it. He is taking the final traces of his existence from this house. It should feel more traumatic than it does.

But with the shabby white van he has hired sitting outside the house, it feels anticlimactic, like this has all been dragging on for much too long and everybody wants it to be over.

My mother doesn't even bother disappearing. She doesn't come into the house while my old man is here, she stays out in the garden with Joyce and her grandchildren. But she doesn't run away either. She stays in her garden with her friend.

As my father lugs boxes down the stairs I stand in the living room watching my mum and Joyce and Diana and William through the window. I am afraid that Joyce is going to barge into the house and corner my father with one of her impromptu interrogations.

Who is this young woman you live with? How old? Will you marry? Do you want children? Do you think you are a wise man or an old fool? Is this girl just a gold digger? Is it about more than getting your end far away?

But she doesn't. Joyce just stays out in the back garden with my mother, planting lilies in patio pots, moving shrubs that have outgrown their space, preparing for the new season as the two children gently brush the morning's fall of snow from ever-green shrubs and conifers.

"January," Joyce had barked at me. "Busy time of year for

garden. Time to get smacking. The early bird is always on time."

"Catches the worm, Joyce."

"You know what I mean, mister."

According to Joyce, it is always a busy time of year for the garden. And I can hear her voice now, surprisingly gentle as she murmurs to my mother, and although I can't hear her words, I am certain that they are not talking about my father. That feels like some kind of victory.

I turn to watch my dad coming down the stairs with the last of his things. It is a box of old vinyl albums. I can see *Four Tops Live!* and Stevie Wonder's *I Was Made to Love Her* and Gladys Knight and the Pips' *Feelin' Bluesy*.

"Aren't you getting a little old for all that baby, baby, baby stuff?" I say, nodding at the box of Motown records in his arms, wanting to hurt him.

"I don't think you're ever too old for a little bit of joy," he says. "You believe in a little bit of joy, don't you, Alfie?"

And I hate him so much not because I can't understand him, but because I understand him so well. He is my father, he will always be my father, and I am afraid that there is much of him in me.

Our lives feel closer than I care to admit. All those nights in rented rooms with women who keep a suitcase by their bed and talk in their sleep in a language you can't understand. All that sneaking around, all those little lies, all that settling for something that you know in your heart is only second best.

Yes, I believe in a bit of joy. These days that's pretty much all I believe in. But I have this fear that, for me and my old man, those rented rooms are the only home we will ever know now, the only home we will ever deserve.

Then he is gone, bumping awkwardly out of the front door, while in the back garden I can hear the laughter of the women.

Part Two

CHIPS ONLY WITH MEAL

19

JACKIE TURNS UP ON OUR DOORSTEP when I am in the park with George. My mum lets her in, gives her a cup of tea and biscuits, tries to make her feel at home. My mother will let anyone into our house. It's a wonder she hasn't been murdered by now.

"She's in the living room," my mum says. "Nice young girl. Dressed a bit—well—tarty, perhaps."

"Oh, *Mum*," I say, sounding as though I have just broken my Action Man.

"Well, she said she had an essay for you," my mother says breezily. "I thought she was one of your students."

"My students are all foreigners, Mum."

I peer through the crack in the living room door. There she is on the sofa, still dressed for dancing or double pneumonia. Strapless top, minimal skirt, heels that could take someone's eye out. Sipping her tea, looking at the pictures on the wall, all these arty black-and-white photographs of working men that my old man collected when he started making some money.

I think about making a run for it. But she might start stalking me. Best to get it over with.

"Hi," I say, coming into the living room.

"Oh, hello." She smiles, trying to get up, and then deciding against it with the tea and biscuits on her lap. "Look, I'm really sorry to bother you but—"

"It's okay. But I thought I made it clear that I'm not an English teacher."

"Oh, you made it clear that you *are* an English teacher," she says and laughs, making a little joke of it. "You just don't want to teach me." She places her tea and biscuits on the coffee table and picks up a manila envelope by her side. She hands it to me.

"What's this?"

"An essay. About *Othello.*"

"*Othello?*"

"It's the one about sexual jealousy. *One that loved not wisely, but too well.* Desdemona, Iago and all that lot."

"I know the play."

"Of course. Sorry."

An essay about *Othello?* Just what I need in my life.

"Will you read it?"

"Look—"

"Please," she says. "I'm desperate to go back to school. And I'm serious about this subject."

"But I don't—"

"And I was good at it! I was so good at it! Because I loved it! Books made me feel as though—I don't know—as though I was connected to the world. Magic, it was. Just give me a chance, okay? Before you decide you don't want to teach me—read my essay."

I look at her, wondering what an Essex dancing queen could know about loving not wisely but too well.

"I'm really sorry to bother you. Really sorry to come barging in like this. But if you read my essay and decide you still don't want to teach me, then I promise I'll leave you alone."

So I promise to read her essay just to get rid of her. And as I lead her to the door and she says good-bye to my mother, I feel a pang of sympathy for Jackie Day. She just doesn't understand. Teaching has got nothing to do with it.

"What a nice girl," my mother says when Jackie has left. "Bit on the thin side. I've seen more meat on a butcher's apron. But she speaks English already, doesn't she? What does she need you for?"

"She doesn't."

There's a new barmaid at the Eamon de Valera. Russian. Short red hair. Starting at Churchill's when the new term begins, Yumi tells me. I watch the young Russian struggling with pints of Paddy McGinty's Water and packets of pork scratchings before I introduce myself. She's going to be one of my Advanced Beginners.

By now these conversations have developed their own internal rhythm. Where you from? How you finding London? Any trouble getting a visa (not applicable to students from the EU or Japan)? Do you miss your mum's apple strudel/prawn tempura/chicken kiev?

Olga tells me what they all tell me. London is more crowded than she imagined, more expensive than she bargained for. Even the kids with rich parents flinch when they see the price of a room in this town. How much harder must it be for a young woman from a former Communist hell?

I can't help Olga with her accommodation problem. I'm looking for my own place right now, and I'm also struggling to find somewhere I can afford, although I don't tell Olga any of that. But this standard complaint about the price tag of everything in London gives me my favorite opening gambit.

"This city's not cheap," I say, leaning on the bar. "But there's lots of great stuff that you can get for free."

"Really?"

"God, yes. You've just got to know where to look. For a start there are the parks. The view of London from the top of

Primrose Hill. The royal deer in Richmond Park. Holland Park is full of all these sculptures that you suddenly come across. Walking by the Serpentine—"

"The Serpentine?"

"That's a lake—in Hyde Park, where there are these wide, sandy paths where people ride horses. Next door to Kensington Gardens."

"Where Diana lived?"

"That's the one. She lived in Kensington Palace. That's a fantastic building. People still put flowers on the gates. Then there's Saint James's Park by Buckingham Palace—beautiful. And Kenwood House by Hampstead Heath. It's this gorgeous house full of Rembrandts and Turners and in the summer they have these classical concerts. Mozart drifting across the lake as the sun goes down over Hampstead Heath . . ."

"Two pints, love," calls a voice from down the other end of the bar. "When Mozart gives you a moment."

I change the tempo when she comes back.

"You shouldn't miss the Columbia Road flower market. Or the piazzas at the British Library."

"I love pizza."

"You can watch a trial at the Old Bailey. You should see Prime Minister's question time at the Houses of Parliament. The markets at Brick Lane and Portobello Road. The meat market at Smithfield. The Picassos and Van Goghs at the National Gallery . . ."

I make it sound wonderful. And it is wonderful. That's the beauty of it. I'm not lying to her. It's all true. You can get anything you like in this city. And you can get it for free. You just have to know where to look.

She goes off to pull a few pints of O'Grady's bathwater and when she comes back I tell her about the Harrods food hall and how there are always people giving away top-of-the-range nosh. She gets very animated, and at first I think she must really have been on a rotten diet back home, but it turns out she's just excited about the prospect of bumping into Dodi Fayed's dad. I tell her about the music at the Notting Hill carnival, the fountains at Somerset House, the way the Embankment of the Thames looks at night.

It's all going great. It's only when they ring for last orders that I realize I was meant to have gone to the airport hours ago, to meet Hiroko's flight from Japan.

The arrival gate is deserted now, but Hiroko is still waiting for me at the meeting point.

It seems very Japanese the way she has stuck it out, a combination of stoicism and optimism. And here I come, ridiculously late, running across the empty hall to hug her, full of shame and relief, wishing she had someone to meet her who was much nicer than me.

She is exhausted after the flight from Narita, but we decide to go into town and have something to eat. We jump on the Heathrow Express and soon we are in a little noodle restaurant in Little Newport Street.

Hiroko is really starting to fade now. Behind her glasses her eyes are puffy from lack of sleep. But she has some presents she wants to give me. Two pairs of chopsticks, one large pair for a man and one smaller pair for a woman, thirty years of feminism apparently not yet reaching the Japanese chopsticks industry. Then she gives me a sake set—two small cups and a pot. And a bottle of Calvin Klein's Escape from duty free.

"Thank you for these lovely gifts," I say. There is something about Hiroko's formality that encourages me to be formal too. "I will always treasure them."

She smiles with delight. "Welcome," she says, with a little nod of her head. And I feel bad that I haven't even missed her.

We drag her suitcase down to the Bar Italia on Frith Street for a nightcap. And that's where we see my father.

At first I think I must be hallucinating. My old man is dressed exactly like John Travolta in *Saturday Night Fever*.

White three-piece suit, heavily flared trousers, dark shirt, no tie, stack-heel shoes. In any other part of the country the way he looks would get him arrested. In the middle of Soho he hardly attracts a second glance.

He comes into the Bar Italia, scanning the faces drinking espresso and latte, sweating heavily inside his white disco suit despite the hour and the season. Then he sees me.

"Alfie," he says.

"This is Hiroko," I say.

He shakes her hand.

"I'm looking for Lena," he says. "We've been to a club in Covent Garden."

"Some kind of seventies night?"

"How did you know? Oh, of course. The clothes."

I feel that I can't be too hostile to my father in Hiroko's presence.

"She's not here," I tell him. "Get separated, did you?"

"We had an argument." He runs a hand through his hair. He's still a good-looking old bastard. "Nothing really. It was stupid."

"What happened?"

"It was the music. It was all over the place. The DJ was playing stuff from the sixties, stuff from the eighties. As though it was all the same. Then he put on 'You Can't Hurry Love.' " He looks at Hiroko. "By the Supremes."

Hiroko smiles and nods.

"And Lena said, *'Oh, I love Phil Collins.'* " My old man shakes his head at the memory of this sacrilege. "And I said, 'Phil Collins? Phil pigging Collins? This isn't Phil Collins, sweetheart. This is the original. This is Diana Ross and the girls. This is one of the greatest records ever made.' And she said she had only heard Phil pigging Collins's version, and who cares anyway? It's only a bit of pop music. It's just a bit of fun. Then I wanted to go home. But she wanted to stay." He looks at us like a man in shock. "Then she left. Just like that. But she's not there. She's not at home." My old man scans the Bar Italia. "And I don't know where she is."

"Do you want a cup of coffee or something?"

"No, no. Thank you. Better keep searching."

My father says good-bye to Hiroko and me and goes back out into the Soho night, looking like the ghost of discos past.

After that first day, George and I do not get hassled in the park. It's strange. We are out there very early on Sunday mornings when the place still belongs to the creatures of the night. But they leave us alone. They watch for a few minutes. Then they move on.

And it's because of George. The way he moves, there's nothing limpid or weak or namby-pamby about Tai Chi. His movements radiate internal strength. The drunks just walk on by.

"Why did you change your mind about teaching me?"

"I saw how much you want to learn."

I read Jackie's essay. It's depressingly predictable stuff—talking you through Iago's scheming, Othello's rage and Desdemona's innocence as though she is telling you the plot to *Lethal Weapon 4*. A tale of sexual jealousy, betrayal and revenge. Starring Mel Gibson. Up against the wall, Iago. This time it's personal.

Just what you would expect from a high school dropout. She even produces Rymer's hoary old quote about one of the morals of the play being "a warning to all good wives that they look well to their linen." Whatever that means.

I feel sorry for Jackie, but it gives me a warm feeling to know that I don't have to teach this stuff anymore.

• • •

There's no cover note with her essay, nowhere to send it back to. Just a business card—DREAM MACHINE: CLEANING THE OLD-FASHIONED WAY—and a mobile phone number. I could wait until I see her at Churchill's but I don't want to leave it that long. I want to get rid of Jackie Day as soon as I can.

I call the mobile and get a recorded message that she is working at the Connell Gallery on Cork Street. That's not far from Churchill's. I decide to return the essay in person so that I don't have to come home and find her camping out in our front garden.

Although it's only a ten-minute walk, Cork Street feels like another city compared to where I work. You can smell the money in the air. I find the Connell Gallery, thinking I will drop her essay off at the reception desk. Then I see her.

She is not dressed for dancing. Her fair hair is pulled back and tied with an elastic band. She is wearing her blue nylon overalls. And she is cleaning the plate-glass window. When she sees me she stares at me for a moment and then steps into the street.

"What are you doing here?"

"Returning your essay. I didn't have an address."

"I would have picked it up. At Churchill's. Or your mum's house. Why are you looking at me like that?"

"Like what?"

"I've got my own company," she says. "Dream Machine. We work all over the West End."

"Who's we?"

"Me. And sometimes I bring in another girl. If the work's there." A pause. "What's wrong?"

What is wrong with me? I don't know. It just feels like all at once I understand why she wants to go back to college. Why it means so much to her. This is the first time I have really understood that she is not some student doing a little part-time job. This is how she makes a living. This is what the next thirty years or so will be like for her. This is her future.

"There's nothing wrong with cleaning for a living," I say, as if I'm thinking aloud. "Nothing at all."

"No. It's not a bad job. But I want a better one. And I can get it if I go back to school."

"Somebody has to do it. Cleaning, I mean."

"Would you?"

People are staring at us. All these art lovers and their well-spoken flunkies squinting at the cleaner and the bum standing on the pavement of Cork Street.

"Listen, your essay was okay."

"Just okay?"

"That's right. It's full of some teacher's opinions. Or some critic's opinion. Not enough of you."

She smiles at me. "You're good."

"What?"

"You're a good teacher."

"You don't know me."

"I can feel it. You're a great teacher. You're so right—there has to be more of me in there. So you'll do it? You'll teach me?"

I want to get away from here, away from Cork Street and Dream Machine, away from Desdemona and her dirty laundry.

But I think of George Chang, and how patient he is with me, how he encourages me, how he helps me learn because he thinks it's the right thing to do.

I don't know what comes over me.

"When can you start?" I find myself saying.

20

I RING MY NAN'S DOOR BELL but she doesn't answer. That's strange. I know she's in there. At least, it sounds like she's in there because I can hear the TV audience elaborately ooh-ing and ahh-ing as the numbers are drawn for the midweek National Lottery. Is the prospect of ten million pounds why she's not answering? Or is it something else?

I keep waiting to hear the soft shuffle of slippers on carpet coming slowly toward the door, followed by the scrape of the safety catch and then her smiling face peering around the door, her eyes bright with welcome, happy for some company. It doesn't happen. There's no answer to my nan's door bell.

There's also no smell of gas, no sign of smoke seeping under the door, no cries for help. But she is eighty-seven, almost eighty-eight, and I feel the panic rising inside me as I put down her shopping and fumble with the key that I hold for emergencies.

This is the way it happens, I think.

Everybody dies. Everybody leaves you. You turn your back for a moment and they are gone forever.

I burst into the little white flat. The TV is on much too loud. There's no sign of my nan but I immediately see the unknown man by the mantelpiece, holding a silver-framed photograph in his hand, calculating its worth.

As he half turns, the frame still in his thieving paw, I see that he is more of an overgrown boy than a man. Sixteen, maybe seventeen, but way over six foot tall, a baby face flecked with wisps of facial hair.

I come quickly across the room and throw myself at him, cursing him, knocking him backward against the mantelpiece, my voice and my body shaking with anger and fear. He drops the silver frame—his booty, the thieving bastard—but he is still on his feet, suddenly over the moment of shock at my surprise attack, and as we grapple with each other I can feel his superior strength, and his own rage and terror.

He swings me sideways, smashing me into the sideboard cabinet with all the holiday souvenirs, making leering leprechauns and smiling Spanish donkeys jiggle and jump behind the dusty glass.

And then my nan comes out of her tiny kitchen carrying a tray containing tea and biscuits.

"Oh, have you two met?" she says.

The young man and I are suddenly apart, boxers told to break by the referee, panting at each other on opposite sides of the coffee table. My nan gently places the tea and custard creams between us.

"I ran out of breath at the bus stop," my nan says. "I was coming back from having a little look round the shops and it was just suddenly gone. Do you ever get that feeling, Alfie? That breathlessness?" She smiles affectionately at the young man I have just assaulted. "Ken helped me get home."

"Ben," he says.

"Len," she says. "I felt quite peculiar. But Len carried my bag. Helped me get inside. Wasn't that nice of him, Alfie?"

"Thank you," I say.

The young man looks at me with total, all-consuming hatred.

"Don't mention it," he says. A quick smile at my nan. He is trembling. "I have to go now."

"Ken," I say. "Ben. Please stay and have some tea."

"I really must run." He is not looking at me any more. "I do hope you feel better," he says to my nan.

I follow him to the door but he refuses to meet my eyes.

"I didn't realize," I say as he lets himself out. "I thought—"

"Dickhead," he mutters.

It's true. I am a dickhead. I can't quite believe that kindness and goodness still exist in this world. I think it's all a thing of the past. And I can't even see what's right in front of my dickhead face.

I go back into the living room where my nan is asleep in her armchair, a lottery ticket in one hand and a custard cream in the other. She has been falling asleep without warning a lot recently. Sometimes she pitches forward and I have to catch her before she does herself some damage.

"I fall asleep all the time," she is always telling me. "Just tired, I suppose, love."

But now I realize that she is not falling asleep at all.

She is blacking out.

"Soong yi-dien!" George tells me, time and time again. *"Soong yi-dien!"*

Soong yi-dien. It's one of the few Cantonese expressions I know. In Hong Kong you would hear it all the time in the little tailor's shop next to the Double Fortune Language School when customers were complaining that the suit they were being fitted for was too tight.

"Soong yi-dien!" they would shout in the face of Mr. Wu the tailor. "Loosen it up!"

George wants me to loosen it up. He believes that I try too hard. He's right. My Tai Chi strains for effect. Everything is an effort for me. I make Tai Chi look like manual labor. But George moves the way Sinatra sang, radiating that kind of effortless power, as if all this craft and art is the most natural thing in the world.

"Soong yi-dien," he says. "Very important for when we play Tai Chi."

Play Tai Chi? Surely he means *do* or *practice* or *learn* Tai Chi? Surely he doesn't mean *play?*

Although thick with a Cantonese accent, George's English is very good. He has none of the linguistic tics that his wife has. Sometimes his tenses get a little confused, and he has this habit of dropping the definite article. But you never have trouble understanding him. So I am surprised that he could get his choice of verb so wrong.

"You don't mean play Tai Chi, do you, George? I think you mean study Tai Chi or something. Not play."

He looks at me.

"No," he says. "We play Tai Chi. We *play.* Always, always. Tai Chi not the gym. Not about sweating and getting six-pack on belly. Not about *working out.* When you understand that, then you start to learn. Then you *soong yi-dien.* Why do Westerners always want to strain? Okay, try again."

So I do.

I spread my feet shoulder width apart, sinking into my horse stance, bending my knees but making sure they don't extend farther than my toes. Neck erect but relaxed. Chin tucked slightly in. Spine straight and lengthened, although without standing to attention. Butt tucked in. Trying to slow and soften my breathing, trying to make it deep but unforced. Relaxing my wrists. Throwing open all my joints. Trying to feel my *dan tien,* my energy center, which I have learned is located two inches down from my navel and two inches inside my body.

It doesn't feel much like play.

"You know that saying—no pain, no gain?" George says.

"Sure."

"It's rubbish."

"I'm not early, am I?" says Jackie Day. "If I'm early I can—"

"It's okay," I tell her. "Come in."

She comes into my new flat, staring at all the unpacked boxes.

I have finally found a place of my own. A one-bedroom flat in a Victorian house full of music students. You can distantly hear them scratching away at cellos and violins, but because they are so good it is more calming than annoying. It is a nice place. But with my nan going into hospital for tests and the new term starting at Churchill's, I haven't had time to unpack yet. Apart from a few essentials.

Pictures of Rose.

Some classic Sinatra.

Electric kettle.

I go into the photo-booth-sized kitchen to make instant coffee while Jackie wanders around looking for somewhere to sit down.

"I love this old-fashioned music," she calls to me, as Frank finishes "Wrap Your Troubles in Dreams" and begins his timeless rendition of "Taking a Chance on Love." "What CD is this?"

"It's *Swing Easy,* which actually incorporates the vinyl album of that name with the entire contents of the LP that was originally released as *Songs for Young Lovers.*" I listen for a bit. "I like it too. It's one of my favorites."

"And is it Harry Connick Junior?"

I almost drop the kettle.

"Harry Connick Junior? Is this Harry Connick Junior? This is Sinatra. Frank Sinatra."

"Oh. He sounds a bit like Harry Connick Junior, doesn't he?"

I say nothing. When I come out of the kitchen she is looking at all the pictures of Rose.

Rose on her firm's junk in Hong Kong. On our wedding day. At a New Year's Eve party on Victoria Peak. On Changeover Day.

And—it's my favorite picture of her—a blowup of her passport photograph, Rose looking straight at the camera, impossibly young and serious and beautiful, her hair longer than I ever saw it, although the picture was taken shortly before we met.

I always thought Rose was the only person in the world who ever looked good in a passport photo.

"Your girlfriend?" Jackie Day says with a little smile. "This is not the girl I saw at your parents' place."

It takes me a second to realize she's talking about Vanessa.

"That was just a friend. This is my wife. Her name is Rose."

"Oh."

I can almost hear her brain ticking over. And I think: why do I always have to have this conversation? Why can't they just leave us alone?

"Are you divorced?"

"My wife died," I say, taking the photograph from her and giving her a cup of instant coffee in exchange. I carefully place the picture back on top of a packing case. "She died in a diving accident."

"A driving accident?"

"A diving accident. When we were living in Hong Kong."

"God." She stares at Rose's picture. "I'm so sorry."

"Thanks."

"How terrible for you." She looks at all the photographs—I suppose it's a sort of shrine—with real pain on her face. "And for her. How old was she? How old was Rose?"

"She was twenty-six. Almost twenty-seven."

"You poor man. That poor woman. That poor girl. Oh, I am so, so sorry."

There are tears shining in her eyes and I look at her, really wishing that I could feel some genuine gratitude for this sympathy.

But it's difficult to take her show of compassion seriously when under her leather coat she is dressed for another night picking up strange men at the Basildon Mecca. French Connection T-shirt, pastel-colored miniskirt, high heels that leave little dents in the wooden floor of my new flat. I wonder what we are doing here. Then I remember.

"You want to study A Level English Literature."

Her pretty, painted face brightens.

"If I can just get this one subject, I can go back to school. Put it with the two I've got already. French and Media Studies. I told you. Go to the University of Greenwich. Get my BA. Get a good job. Stop cleaning the floors of art galleries in Cork Street and language schools on Oxford Street."

"Why does it have to be the University of Greenwich? It's not exactly Oxford or Cambridge, is it?"

"Because that's my plan," she says. "You've got to have a plan. I've got an acceptance letter and everything. I was doing so well at school. I really was. But then I had to give it all up."

"For personal reasons. You told me that too."

"Now I'm going to have another go."

"Okay. Sit down, will you?"

She looks around. There's nowhere to sit. I pull up a couple of chairs either side of a large packing case.

"The core of English Literature works from a very concrete base. The subject is very specific about the basis of study." I tick them off my fingers. "One prose work. One work of poetry. One work of drama. And one Shakespeare play. In the end, you need to learn two things to pass this subject. To read and to write."

"To read and to write. Okay. Fine. Good. Yes."

"That is, you need to understand the text and then demonstrate your understanding of the text. That's the essence of this subject."

I know my lines.

This is a speech that I remember from the dark days at the Princess Diana Comprehensive School for Boys, although by the time that A Levels came around, most of my students had graduated to the technical college of life.

My door bell rings.

"Excuse me," I say.

"Oh, that'll be for me," says Jackie Day.

"What?"

"I think it's my daughter."

Daughter? What daughter?

Together Jackie and I go out of the flat and down to the front door of the house. An enormous great lump of a girl is standing outside. It's difficult to judge her age. She hides her face behind a curtain of greasy brown hair. Her clothes are as dark and shapeless as Jackie's are tight and bright.

"Say hello to Mr. Budd," says Jackie Day.

The lump says nothing. Behind the unwashed veil of her fringe, a pair of bright-blue eyes swivel briefly toward me and then turn away with shyness or contempt or something.

She has a fistful of magazines in her hand. They feature men in masks and spandex grimacing and grunting and climbing on top of each other. At first I think this awful child has hard-core pornography in her possession. But then I see that the magazines are about some grotesque new kind of wrestling. In a daze, I return to my flat, Jackie and the lump following behind me, Jackie all happy chatter and questions as they come up the stairs, the lump replying with monosyllabic grunts. Although there is no physical resemblance between them, there is no doubt that they are mother and adolescent child.

The lump walks into my new apartment and looks around, clearly unimpressed.

"This is my girl," says Jackie. "I hope you don't mind if she sits quietly in a corner while we work."

I stare at this woman dressed like she should be standing in an Amsterdam window lit by a single red light, and wonder why I ever allowed her into my life.

"Why do you think I gave up studying?" says Jackie, suddenly all defiant.

And I look at her surly, nameless lump of a daughter leafing through a wrestling magazine and think to myself: why do you think I gave up teaching?

21

WHEN I SEE HIROKO waiting for me outside Churchill's, I remember this thing I once read in an advice-to-the-lovelorn column about the person who holds the power in any relationship.

The sob sister reckoned that the person with the power is always the one who cares less. And as Hiroko looks up at me with her open, hopeful smile, I see the wisdom of that sob sister.

There's no reason why I should have any power over Hiroko. She is younger than me, smarter than me, prettier than me. She's also a lot nicer than me. Whichever way you slice it, Hiroko is a far better bet than me.

But Hiroko cares more than I do. So in the end everything else—her looks, her youth, her niceness—doesn't matter.

"I haven't seen much of you, Alfie."

"I've been really busy."

"How's your grandmother?"

"Still in the hospital. They're doing tests on her while they drain some fluid off her lungs. But she's made friends with all the other old girls on her ward."

"She's always so cheerful."

"I think she'll be okay."

"Good. Well. Do you want to get some lunch later?"

"Lunch? Well, I've got to see Hamish about something at lunch."

"Dinner?"

See, it was okay for her to suggest lunch. That was perfectly reasonable. But going for dinner too made her seem desperate and made me feel cornered. Dinner pushed me to the point of no return.

"Hiroko, I really think we need to give each other a bit of space right now."

"A bit of space?"

She starts crying. Not the kind of tears that are meant to blackmail you. Not the kind of tears that are meant to make you back down, change your mind or offer concessions. Not the kind of tears that are meant to make you give in about dinner. Just tears.

"You're a great girl, Hiroko."

And it's true. She is a great girl. She has never treated me with anything but sweetness. What's gone wrong with me? Why can't I be happy with this woman?

There's never an agony uncle around when you need one.

The bad news at Churchill's is that there has been a bit of a sex scandal involving one of the teachers. Lisa Smith has got smoke coming out of her ears, the students are all talking about it and we have even had a couple of uniformed cops on the premises, sniffing around and asking questions, as if the incident is just the tip of a very dirty iceberg.

The good news is that it has absolutely nothing to do with me.

Hamish has been arrested for his conduct in a public lavatory on Highbury Fields. I actually know the place, funnily enough—it's one of those public toilets where, if you go in for a quick pee, all the guys in there think that you are some kind of sick pervert.

Anyway, Hamish has been arrested for lewd and indecent

behavior because late one night he reached for what he imagined was some willing, perfect stranger and it turned out to be a policeman's nightstick. Now the poor bastard is watching his world unravel. I take him for a drink at the Eamon de Valera.

"I feel like I'm in danger of losing everything," he says. "My family, my flat, my sanity. Just for a quick jerk-off. It hardly seems fair. It hardly seems like justice."

"How's old Smith taking it?"

"She says she will have to see if the police are going to press charges. I'm not so worried about her. I can always get another job as badly paid as this one. I'm more worried about my parents. And my partner. It's his flat we live in. If he gets rough . . . I don't know what will happen."

"Wait a minute. Your partner knows you don't go over to Highbury Fields at midnight for a game of tennis. Or what?"

"I told him I'd given it up. The cruising thing. It upsets him."

"Ah."

"My mum and dad will be even worse. They'll go crazy. Especially my father. Christ. He was in the Govan shipyards for forty years. When he finds out I'm what he calls 'bent,' he'll never speak to me again."

"Hold on. Your parents don't know you're gay? Your parents don't know? Jesus, Hamish."

"I come from the East End of Glasgow. We haven't quite caught up with London. Not that there's much difference between Glasgow and London, in the final analysis. You come to this city thinking it's going to be so totally free and easy. Then you find out that in its own sweet way, this place is as repressed as anywhere."

I feel sorry for Hamish, so I don't tell him what I'm thinking. Which is: how can you have a private life when you take it into a public toilet?

And he's wrong about London. There are some bad things about my city, but the best thing is that you can be anything you like here, anything at all. As long as you keep it away from the policeman's flashlight, of course.

But you are free to invent your own life, I think to myself, watching Olga struggling to pull a pint at the other end of the bar.

You just have to be a bit discreet.

Sometimes I think that love is a case of mistaken identity.

It's like Hiroko and me. She sees someone else when she looks at me—someone decent and good, someone she wants me to be. An English gentleman. David Niven. Alec Guinness. Hugh Grant. Someone I'm not and could never be.

Or it's like Hamish and his partner. Hamish's boyfriend probably likes to believe that Hamish really wants a serious, monogamous relationship. That he wants to go shopping in Habitat on Saturdays and give small, stylish dinner parties and sit around listening to Broadway musicals on CD and be faithful to only one partner. But that's just another case of mistaken identity.

What Hamish wants is to go to public places and have sex with people whose names he will never know. That means more to him than anything. His partner just can't see it. His partner doesn't want to see it.

Does that still count? Is that still real? When you don't know the other person at all?

For as long as I can remember, my nan has had a profound loathing of doctors. She always seemed to believe that she was locked in a never-ending battle for her freedom with the medical profession. My nan wanted to stay in her home. The doctors—"the quacks," my nan called them, even the ones she liked—wanted to steal her away and lock her up in a hospital where she would be left to die.

But now she is actually in a hospital bed, my nan is showing signs of going over to the other side. She thinks her doctors deserve a raise, believes her nurses should be on television.

"They're as pretty as weather girls," says my nan. High praise indeed.

As my mother, Joyce Chang and I sit around her bed, my nan regales us with stories about the characters she has met in here. The nurse who "should be a model, she's that lovely." The old woman—younger than her—in the next bed who (this whispered) is "not right in the head, the poor old thing." The Indian doctor who has told her that she will soon be "fit as a fiddle." The orderly who is a flirt, the nurse who is a miserable cow, the elderly patient in the bed opposite who is her friend, who she has a right laugh with, who she will see for tea when they are finally set free. My nan doesn't stop talking. She seems almost giddy with exuberance. Are they slipping something into her cream of tomato soup?

She seems happier than she has been for a long time, despite the squat, ugly machine on the floor by her bed that has a long thin tube rising out of it, slipping under the white gown that makes her look like an ancient angel, the tube piercing her side under that white gown, burrowing deep into her body, slowly draining the buildup of fluid from her clogged, breathless lungs.

One of her lungs showed up completely white on the X-ray, it was so full of fluids that should not have been there. The doctors gathered around, staring at it with awe. They were amazed she had kept breathing with all that stuff inside her.

But she seems happy, despite the humming of that ugly machine on the floor, despite the fluid being sucked out of her, despite the pain she must be in with that tube in her side. Night and day, the tube stays inside her. It will stay inside her until the fluid has all been drained. But my nan doesn't stop smiling. How does she do it?

I know that my nan is a brave and tough old woman. But her sunny mood is more than courage, although she has plenty of that. Perhaps being in a hospital bed is not quite as bad as she thought it was going to be. Because she knows that, unlike her husband, my grandfather, she is not going to die in here. Not this time. Not yet.

She suddenly stops talking and we all turn to look at my dad standing awkwardly at the foot of the bed. He is carrying flowers and a box of Maltesers.

"Hello, Ma," he says, coming forward to kiss her cheek.

"Mike," she says. "My Mike."

I am afraid that Joyce is going to start grilling my father about his sex life with Lena, but she remains stereotypically inscrutable, possibly for the first time in her life. She just takes my nan's hand and tells her that she will soon be "as right as raindrops."

My mother and my father seem more like brother and sister than husband and wife. They seem like two people who have a history together, but that's all. There appears to be no hatred between them, and no overwhelming affection either. They are polite, businesslike, discussing doctors' opinions and what my nan will need while she is in here. Only their avoidance of eye contact gives any clue that they both have a divorce lawyer.

And for the first time I feel sorry for my father. He hasn't shaved today. His hair needs cutting. He has lost some weight, but not in any gym.

He has everything he wanted, but he doesn't seem happy. Suddenly he seems to be getting old.

And he looks—what do you call it?

Only human.

Jackie Day's first homework assignment was to write a critical appreciation of two poems: W. B. Yeats's "When You Are Old and Grey and Full of Sleep" and Colonel Lovelace's "To Lucasta, on Going to the Wars."

I read her essay—neat, spidery handwriting—while she sits

on the other side of the table, biting her painted fingernails.

Over by the window, the lump—does she have a name? have I already been told it?—is taking up most of the sofa and reading one of her disgusting magazines. The glossy cover features two sweaty, fat men rolling around on top of one another in spandex underpants. I wonder why her mother allows her to read this trash. I say nothing. Somewhere in the house, a cello is practicing scales. Outside the rain is falling.

"This is okay," I say, placing the essay on the table.

Jackie looks disappointed.

"Only okay?"

"Well, you weren't asked to review them. You're not Frank Rich. You were asked to write a critical appreciation."

"That's what I did."

"No, you didn't. You stated a preference. You clearly liked the Yeats poem. And disliked the other one. The Lovelace."

"I thought I had to put myself into my writing. That's what you said. *Put yourself into your writing.*"

"Well, you do have to put yourself in there. But you weren't asked to state a preference. Nobody cares which one you prefer. It's not a beauty contest."

"But the Yeats is so good. Isn't it? It's about growing old with someone. It's about loving someone for a lifetime and still loving them even when they are old and worn out."

"I know what it's about."

She closes her eyes. " '*How many loved your moments of glad grace, / And loved your beauty with love false or true: / But one man loved the pilgrim soul in you, / And loved the sorrows of your changing face.*' " She opens her eyes. They shine with excitement. "That's so great. '*One man loved the pilgrim soul in you.*' I love that."

"You write very well about it. But you're too dismissive of the Lovelace. In an exam, that will cost you marks."

"This Lovelace bloke—what does he know about it? 'To Lucasta, on Going to the Wars' is all about putting things before

love. Above love. Honor. Country. All that stuff." She snorts
contemptuously and puts on a ridiculous, high-pitched upper-
class voice. *'I could not love thee, Dear, so much, Loved I not Honour
more.'* What a load of old guff. What a tosspot."

"It's one of the most famous love poems in the English language. I think you'd probably lose marks for calling Lovelace a
tosspot."

"Mum?"

It's the lump.

The lump has spoken.

It lives.

"What is it, darling?"

"There's a lady outside. Standing in the rain. She's been
there ever since we came in."

Jackie and I go over to the window.

A young woman is standing under a lamppost on the other
side of the street. The hood of her parka is pulled up and she is
hiding under a Burberry umbrella that looks on the verge of
collapse. Although I can't see her face, I recognize the beige tar-
tan of the umbrella, recognize the parka, recognize the waves of
shiny black hair pouring out from the hood.

Hiroko.

She is holding a bunch of flowers. Perhaps they are for my
nan. That's just the kind of thing that she would do. That small,
thoughtful gesture is typical Hiroko. She has a good heart.

"Why do you live like this?" Jackie asks me.

For a moment I can't speak.

"Live like what? Jesus. I can't believe I'm hearing this. What
did you say?"

"Why do you hurt these girls?"

Jackie Day and her fat daughter are staring at me. My cheeks
are burning.

"I don't hurt anyone."

"Oh, but you do," Jackie Day tells me. "You do."

22

THE FACES ARE ALWAYS CHANGING at Churchill's.

New students are constantly arriving at the school, eager and bewildered, no matter if the part of the world they come from is dirt poor and developing, or affluent and overdeveloped, while the old students all eventually go back home, transfer to some other college, get married to some love-struck local, get deported for working without a permit or simply disappear into the life of the city.

But many faces remain the same.

I have all of my Advanced Beginners in class today.

There's Hiroko and Gen, both of them peering up at me through their shimmering, iridescent hair. Imran, looking sleek and quietly studious next to Yumi, her face of delicate Japanese beauty framed by what looks like a cheap blonde halo: Kyoto goes to Hollywood.

There's Zeng and Witold, both fighting off the exhaustion of long hours slaving in General Lee's Tasty Tennessee Kitchen and the Pampas Steak Bar. Astrud, who is either piling on the pounds or in the early stages of pregnancy. Olga, sitting right up front, chewing her pen, struggling to keep up with the rest of the class. And finally Vanessa, inspecting her immaculate fingernails as I ramble on about past perfect forms.

Vanessa has her back to the door so she doesn't see the man

whose face suddenly appears in its little window, scanning the room. He is a good-looking forty-year-old, but seems a bit battered, as though something very bad has happened to him quite recently.

There's a red mark on his cheek and one arm of his glasses is missing. There's something wrong with the way his shirt is buttoned. He has made a quick escape from somewhere.

His eyes light up behind those broken spectacles when he sees the back of Vanessa's golden head and I know immediately who he is, even before he begins to tap on the door's little window. She turns around, gasps—really gasps—and then stands up, staring at our visitor in wonder.

"We often use the past perfect when we mention two past situations," I am saying, "and we want to show that one happened before the other. For example—*when he saw the woman, he knew he had been waiting for her all his life.* Get it? *He had been waiting.*"

Nobody is listening to teacher. They are all watching the face at the window.

When the man opens the door, we see that he is carrying a stuffed traveling bag. He comes slowly into the classroom. We all stare at him, waiting to see what happens next.

"I've done it," he tells Vanessa. "I've left her."

Then they embrace, their mouths stuck together, their foreheads bumping awkwardly, his traveling bag hitting the ground with a soft thud, the broken spectacles rising from his face in protest.

I look at my class—Hiroko and Gen, Yumi and Imran, Zeng and Witold, Astrud and Olga—and we exchange self-conscious grins.

We know that we are watching two lives—three lives—no, even more than that, because doesn't this man have children he has left behind?—being turned upside down and inside out before our eyes. All those lives that will never be the same again after today.

So we smile nervously, a little embarrassed, wanting to look away but unable to quite manage it, uncertain what our reaction should be, undecided if what we are seeing is gloriously romantic or totally ludicrous.

But something about the man's broken glasses touches my heart—*he had been waiting for her all his life*—and makes me feel like giving them the benefit of the doubt.

June 30, 1997. Changeover night. The night that the British gave Hong Kong back to the Chinese when the clock struck midnight. The night that the skies above Victoria Peak opened and it rained as it had never rained before, as if the heavens were heartbroken because this glittering place was being given up.

The nobs were down in the harbor. Prince Charles and the last governor. The soldiers and the politicians. Watching the bands march and lowering the flag. But we were in Lockhart Road, Wanchai, with what felt like the rest of the expat population.

Rose in a Mao suit. Josh in black tie. Me in a Mandarin number looking like a particularly pasty member of the old Imperial Court. And a crew of boys and girls from Josh and Rose's shop, all of them either in formal dinner gear or Chinese drag.

We splish-splashed and bar hopped through the flooded streets of Wanchai, once upon a time the old red-light district, now more of a drinking trough for big-nosed pinkies like us.

And we wondered how we should feel.

Were we celebrating or in mourning? Were we meant to be happy or sad? Was this a party or a wake?

There wasn't much joy in the air. We started drinking early and didn't know when to stop. We were not the only ones.

Fights were breaking out all over the Wanch. Outside an expat bar called the Fruity Ferret we saw a man in a rain-sodden tuxedo being head butted by a youth in a torn soccer shirt. They were both British. The Chinese were not fighting in the streets of Wanchai. The Chinese had better things to do.

We ducked inside the Fruity Ferret. Josh and I pushed our way to the bar. He had been in a mean mood all evening, muttering about the ingratitude of the People's Republic of China, getting steadily stewed on shooters and Tsingtao. But as we waited for the Australian rugby player behind the bar to notice us, he seemed suddenly sober.

"Not long to your wedding," he said.

"Next month."

"Didn't fancy getting married back home?"

"Hong Kong is our home."

"Your folks coming over?"

"That's right."

He sighed.

"Before you get married to Rose, there's something I want to tell you."

I looked at him to see if he was joking. But he wasn't. I turned away, shouting at the bartender for service. The big Aussie was busy up at the other end of the bar.

"I mean it. There's something you should know, Alfie."

"I'm not interested."

"What?"

"I don't care. Whatever you're going to say, I'm not interested. Save it."

"It's about Rose."

"Fuck off, Josh."

"You need to hear this."

I shoved him away and although the Fruity Ferret was packed to the rafters, he still went flying. Glass smashed and someone cursed in a London accent, but I was already gone, pushing my way through the mob, past a bewildered-looking Rose and the crew from the shop, all of them in their rain-soaked fancy dress.

"Alfie?"

But I was out of the bar and into the street, a red-and-white cab swerving to miss me as I walked into the middle of Lockhart Road and all the beautiful fireworks suddenly started to explode over the harbor.

Midnight. The night that everything was supposed to change forever. The night when they expected us to believe that the dream was finally over. As if it's so easy to stop dreaming.

Then Josh was standing by my side, pulling my arm, the rain flattening and darkening his nice yellow hair, his dinner jacket sopping wet, his bow tie askew.

"You stupid bastard," he said. "She's just another girl. Are you such a soft head that you can't see that? Rose is just another girl."

I shook him off and went back inside the Fruity Ferret. Somebody from the shop had got a round in. Rose handed me a Tsingtao and I kissed her face. I loved her so much.

"What was all that about?"

"Nothing. He's had a few too many. Come on. Dance with me."

She laughed. "But there's no dance floor. And no music."

"Dance with me anyway."

And she did.

A couple of months later my father gave us a video of our wedding day. And, as is the nature of all wedding videos, my dad wasn't quite sure who was important to the happy bride and groom and who was more of a casual acquaintance. So he tried to film everyone.

The image that sticks in my mind from that wedding video is the slow, panning shot of the guests outside the Happy Valley church as Rose and I posed for our wedding photographs.

In the middle of all those aunts and uncles, those college friends and work colleagues, there is old Josh, a big handsome fellow in his morning suit, his arms folded across his chest.

He is watching the bride and groom.

And he is very slowly shaking his head.

I'm waiting for Jackie Day when she comes out of the Connell Gallery in Cork Street.

There's some kind of launch party going on in there tonight. A mob of casually well-dressed people are all talking at once. Glasses of wine in their hands, ignoring the paintings behind them.

I say her name and she sees me, nowhere near as surprised as I thought she would be. I hand her the envelope.

"What's this?" she says.

"That's your money back. I'm sorry, Jackie, I really am. But I can't teach you anymore."

She looks at the envelope. Then at me.

"Why did you change your mind?"

"It's just not going to work out. I've already got too much on my plate. You'd be better off at night school. I'm sorry."

"I told you. I need to be flexible. For personal reasons."

"I understand. I know it must be difficult. Working, bringing up a child alone."

"You probably think I'm stupid. The Essex girl who wants to go to university. Sounds like a joke, doesn't it? It really does. It is a joke. Oh, I've heard all the jokes. And not just from your friend Lenny the Lech."

"He's not exactly—"

"There are a million like him out there. And you're one of them. That's fine. It's okay if you think it's a joke. It's okay if you think I'm stupid."

"Jackie, I don't think you're stupid."

"People have been telling me I'm stupid all my life."

"I don't—"

"My parents. My teachers. My ex-husband. That bastard. But I thought you were going to be different." She looks at me carefully. "I don't know why. I thought I saw something in you. Some spark of decency. Or something."

I find myself hoping that she's right. "Jackie—"

"You don't like the way I dress."

"The way you dress has got nothing to do with me."

"I've seen you looking at me. Down your nose. The Essex girl. I know."

"I couldn't care less how you dress."

"Well, I'll tell you something, mister." Her voice is shaking now. "I think the way I dress is *pretty*. I think the way I dress is *nice*. What's so great about the way you dress? Like some old tramp, you are."

"I've never been much of a snappy dresser."

"No kidding. You look like you should be sleeping in a doorway. You know what your problem is, Alfie? You think you're the only person that anything bad ever happened to."

"That's not true."

"I'm sorry your wife died. Rose. I really am. But don't blame me."

"I don't blame you. I don't blame anybody."

"You blame the world. I know all about your hard life. You want to hear about my hard life? You want to hear about a man who got me pregnant when I was doing really well at school? The same man who knocked me around every time he got pissed for the next ten rotten years? You want to hear about any of that?"

I don't say a word. There's nothing I can say. There are tears of defiance in her eyes.

"I'm going to get this exam, mate. With or without you. I'm going to put it with the two I've got already and I'm going to the University of Greenwich to get my BA. It's not Oxford or Cambridge, you're right. But that's my dream. You can sneer at it if you want. It's still my dream."

"I'm not sneering."

"And when I've got my degree, my daughter and I are going to have a better life than the one we've got at the moment. That's my plan. If you can't help me—if going around breaking some poor foreign girl's heart is more important than that—then I don't know what you are, but you're certainly not much of a teacher. And not much of a man."

We stare at each other for a long time. Behind her, the launch party is in full swing. All those overpaid, overeducated people talking too loudly. And I realize that what she thinks matters to me.

"I wish I could help, Jackie. I really do."

"But you *can*. You *can* make a difference. You don't believe it, do you? You think the world is out of your control. You can't imagine the changes you can make in someone's life. It's not too late for you, Alfie. You can still be one of the good guys."

I don't know what comes over me.

"I'll see you Tuesday night then," I say.

Now how did that happen?

23

GEORGE TEACHES ME TAI CHI in three stages.

First I learn the movement, carefully attempting to replicate his unhurried grace, although I often feel I must look like a drunk mimicking a ballet dancer. But I am starting to see that every single move has its purpose.

Next I learn to put the breathing to the movement, inhaling and exhaling as instructed, slowly filling my lungs and just as slowly emptying them. It is like learning to breathe again.

And finally and most important I learn—what? To relax? To do something without making excessive effort? To be in the moment and only in the moment? I don't know.

As I try to clear my mind and calm my heart, to forget about the world that is waiting for me beyond this little patch of grass, I am not even sure what he is teaching me.

But it feels as if it has got something to do with letting go.

It is near midnight now and the hospital ward is as dark and silent as it gets, for this place is never completely dark and never totally silent. There is always a kind of twilight because of the lights blazing through the night in the nurses' office at the entrance to the ward and there are always the sounds of distant voices, the creak of trolleys being wheeled across polished floors, the murmur of disturbed sleep, the soft sighs of pain.

When my nan is sleeping, I watch her face for a while and then leave the ward to find my father. He is in the hospital canteen, a half-eaten sandwich and a cold cup of coffee in front of him.

My old man comes to the hospital every day, but he is not good at sitting by his mother's bedside. He likes to feel that he is doing something useful, so he jumps up and talks to the doctors about my nan's progress, asking how she is doing, working out when she will be able to go home, or he runs endless errands to the hospital shop to get her the little things she suddenly discovers she needs.

He would rather be off buying her another bottle of orange cordial—she refuses to drink plain water, even when I tell her that it has been filtered through the glacial sands of the French Alps—than sitting by her bed. He can't just be with her. He doesn't feel as if he is doing enough.

"Is your grandmother asleep?"

I nod. "I think she's still getting a lot of pain from that tube in her side. But she doesn't complain."

"That generation never does. They don't know how to whine. That began with my lot."

"Anyway. They've nearly got all the fluid off her lungs. So she'll be home soon."

"Yes."

"And how are you?"

He looks surprised at the question. "I'm all right. A bit tired. You know."

"You don't have to come here every day. Mum and I can take care of her. If you're busy. If you've got a lot of work to do."

He sort of laughs and I know that he is still not writing. "Work's not the problem it once was. But thanks for the offer, Alfie."

I am thinking of the night I saw him in the Bar Italia, dressed in his John Travolta drag.

"How's Lena?"

"I haven't seen her for a while."

"You haven't seen her?"

"She walked out."

"I thought she was going to be your PA. I thought she was going to be your wife."

"It didn't work out as planned."

"What happened?"

"It wasn't the same. It can't be the same, can it? Not the same as when you are stealing the odd hour here and there." He looks up at me. "The odd night in hotels. Away for the weekend."

Business trips, I think. All those business trips.

"It's exciting," he says. "It's romantic. But it's not the same when you're living together and the boiler is on the blink. When one of you has to put the rubbish out. I couldn't quite get used to the idea that the girl in those hotel rooms was the same girl who told me that we needed a plumber."

"But sooner or later we all have trouble with our pipes. And you knew it wouldn't be the same. Come on. You must have known that."

"I guess so. I'm old enough to know better, aren't I?"

"What do you think?"

"It was more of a disappointment for her. She thought she had landed this—I don't know—this older man. Mature. Sophisticated. A couple of bob in his pocket."

"The author of *Oranges for Christmas*. Mr. Sensitive Bollocks."

"And then he's sitting around the house all day staring at his computer screen, and he doesn't like the same music as her—in fact, he thinks the music she likes sounds like a burglar alarm—and he doesn't want to go dancing in the kind of clubs where people wear their rings in their belly buttons. Then you don't seem like an older man. You just seem like an old man."

"Is she still in the flat?"

He shakes his head. "She moved in with some guy from Wimbledon she met at Towering Inferno. On the night I saw you. Christ, she was all over him."

"What's Towering Inferno?"

"It's the seventies night they have at Club Bongo Bongo. You don't keep up, do you?"

"I'm trying."

"Don't bother. It's exhausting. She says she's not having sex with this guy. She says he is just giving her a futon in his living room until she gets settled. Until she can find a place of her own."

"You don't believe her."

"There's no such thing as a free futon."

For a moment I glimpse the world restored. I see Lena finding true love on that futon in Wimbledon. I imagine my father begging my mother to take him back, and her eventually relenting. And I glimpse a future where my mother is happy in her garden, my father is writing his brilliant, bestselling follow-up to *Oranges for Christmas* in his study and my nan never has to go back into hospital to have her lungs drained.

Then my old man spoils everything.

"I'll get her back," he says, and it takes me a few seconds to realize that the mad bastard is not talking about his wife or his mother. "I mean, I ask you—a futon in Wimbledon. She'll see sense in the end. I know she will. And I just can't live without her. Does that sound stupid, Alfie?"

No, I think.

That sounds like trouble.

If I have a Tai Chi lesson after work I eat an early dinner with the Changs at the Shanghai Dragon.

The Changs eat around six, after Diana and William have had their daily lesson and before the restaurant is open for business. These children study something almost every day, violin for Diana, piano for William, Wing Chun Kung Fu and Cantonese for both of them. It feels like they are either eating or being educated.

The food the family eats bears little resemblance to the menu of the Shanghai Dragon. It is plainer, fresher, fiercer.

Nothing is drowned in sweet and sour sauce, nothing is wasted. Tonight we are eating steamed fish, served whole, the head and tail intact, the fish eyes glistening blankly, with plain boiled rice and lots of vegetables—bean curd, baby corn, bean sprouts, Chinese cabbage and mushrooms.

Our plastic chopsticks clatter and clack as we decimate the fish, our heads dipping to greet the bowls of rice, which is shoveled into our mouths with noisy abandon. The Changs wash down their meal with tea or tap water, although they insist that I drink mineral water, fetched from the Shanghai Dragon's tiny bar.

"It soon New Year," Joyce tells me.

"New Year?" We are near the end of January.

"Chinese New Year. Very important for Chinese people. Like Christmas and Easter for Westerners. When I little children size, we don't even think of Christmas. We don't care for toys. We don't care about Ken and Barbie going to the disco. Only Chinese New Year."

"It's based on the lunar calendar, right? When is it this year?"

Joyce confers with her family in Cantonese.

"New Year's Eve, February fifteenth," she says.

"It's going to be the Year of the Rabbit," William tells me in his pure London accent, his mouth full of noodles.

"We have party," Joyce says. "Here. Shanghai Dragon. You come."

"Can I bring someone?"

"Bring someone? Of course. Bring everyone. Bring your family."

My family? That's easy for Joyce to say.

This simple certainty about family is the thing that I envy most about the Changs. Joyce and George and Harold and Doris and Diana and William all know exactly what their family looks like.

But I am finding it increasingly hard to know where my little broken family begins, and where it ends.

24

ON THE DAY THAT MY NAN is discharged from the hospital, I am meant to be giving Jackie Day an English lesson.

When I arrive home from doing my nan's shopping, a fistful of supermarket bags in my hands, Jackie is already waiting for me on the doorstep, her daughter by her side. The lump silently contemplates me from behind her greasy brown fringe.

"Jackie—sorry I'm late, I tried to call you."

"My battery's flat."

"I had to do some shopping for my grandmother. There's nothing in her flat. She just got out of hospital a few hours ago."

"Well, that's good."

"But now I've got to take this stuff round to her." I apologetically lift the heavy supermarket bags. A packet of jam tarts falls out and Jackie retrieves them for me. "I've got my mum's car. So I can't give you a lesson."

"I'll take her shopping round for you."

The lump has spoken. Her voice is surprisingly high-pitched and girlish.

"What?"

"I'll take it. If you tell me where she lives. I'll get the bus."

I think about it for a moment. Why not? She wouldn't do in my grandmother for her jam tarts. Would she?

"Would you?" I say.

"Sure. Haven't got anything better to do, have I? And you don't exactly need me here, do you?"

"That's really sweet of you, darling," says Jackie.

"It's not far," I say. "I'll give you the address and get you a taxi."

"I can get the bus."

"I'll get you a cab."

I realize, to my shame, that I do not even know this child's name. Jackie saves me.

"Thanks, Plum," she says.

Plum?

"Yes," I say. "Thank you, Plum."

She shuffles her feet, stares at the ground through her protective fringe, doesn't know what to do with her hands.

"No problemo," mutters Plum.

When we have called a taxi and Plum has been packed off with my nan's address and provisions, I make a cup of tea.

"So," I say. "You named your daughter after a fruit?"

"Don't make fun of her." But she doesn't say it angrily. She says it almost gently, as if I am too stupid to know any better. "She gets enough of that at school. People making fun of her, I mean."

"She gets bullied?"

"What do you think?"

"I don't know." I manage to stop myself saying—she's a big girl, I wouldn't fancy meeting her up a dark alley. But I rephrase the statement in my head. "She looks like she can stand up for herself."

"She's a lamb," Jackie says, and I am touched by the undisguised and unembarrassed affection in her words. "I know she's a bit overweight, but she's as soft as they come. And kids can be cruel, can't they?"

"They certainly can."

"They pick on anyone that's a bit different."

"They certainly do."

"And for your information, I didn't name my daughter after a fruit."

"No?"

"No. I was in my doctor's waiting room when I was pregnant and I picked up this glossy magazine. You know the kind of thing. Full of glamorous parties and famous people inviting you into their lovely homes."

I know the kind of thing.

"And there was this sort of society page. Full of beautiful people having a rare old time. Not that all of them were beautiful. Under their suntans, you could tell that some of them were—what's the word?"

"Ugly?"

"Yes, ugly. Especially the men, who tended to be a lot older than the women. But even though they weren't all beautiful, they all looked happy. You know what I mean?"

"I guess so."

"And there were these two girls. Now they really were beautiful. Models, they must have been. Or actresses or something. Or the daughters of rich men. They looked like sisters, but they weren't. Blond, tall, tanned. Wearing dresses that were like little slips. The kind of dress that looks like you could sleep in it. They were smiling. White teeth. Leggy. What do you call those special glasses for champagne? The long, thin ones?"

"Flutes."

"Flutes. They both had these flutes of champagne in their hands. I mean, I guess it wasn't Spanish cava or Asti Spumante, right? They had their arms around each other. These long, thin, brown arms. And what I thought about them was—they looked as though nothing bad had ever happened to them in their lives. Nothing bad. Ever. And the funny thing is, they were both called Plum."

Jackie sips her tea.

"It's a pretty name for a girl."

"Do you think so?"

"I do."

"My husband—although he wasn't my husband then—always thought it was . . . stupid. No, not stupid. Pretentious. They don't like that where I come from. They don't like you getting above yourself. My husband was typical. *'You're too clever by half, Jack. Too clever for your own good, Jack.'* I mean, as though being stupid was something to be proud of. But I went ahead and called her Plum anyway, went to the registrar of births, marriages and deaths by myself and had Plum put on the certificate. Stuff him, I thought. Stuff Jamie. If it wasn't for Jamie, I wouldn't have been in that doctor's waiting room in the first place. And I would never have seen that magazine with the Plum girls."

"You mean you were seeing the doctor because you were pregnant?"

"No," says Jackie. "I was seeing the doctor because Jamie had just broken two of my ribs."

When we have finished our lesson, we drive around to my nan's place. Plum answers the door. She is smiling.

"We're watching the wrestling," she says.

Inside her white flat, my nan is propped up on the sofa. There are pillows behind her back and a blanket over her legs. She is staring with enchanted delight at the television where two fat men in luridly colored latex are screaming at each other. One of the men has a shaven head, the other has Pre-Raphaelite locks that tumble to his meaty shoulders.

"Oh, it's The Slab," says Jackie, as the screen fills with the image of a bald madman. "Your favorite, darling." She turns to me. "The Slab is Plum's favorite."

"The Slab rocks," says Plum. "The Slab kicks butt. Big time." She sort of snarls at me through her fringe. "Your ass belongs to The Slab. He will bring you down. He will nail your worthless hide to the Tree of Woe, mother."

"Language, darling," says Jackie.

"Hasn't she got lovely eyes?" says my nan.

We all stare at her. She's talking about Plum.

"Me?" says Plum, blushing with disbelief. "Lovely eyes?"

"Have you ever seen this program, Alfie?" my nan asks me, as if I have been deliberately keeping its existence from her. "They're having a right old punch-up."

"But it's all fake, isn't it?" I sniff.

"It's *not*," says my nan. "Go on, mate—give him one in the cake hole."

"Nice Greco-Roman style counter!" says Plum, shaking her fist. "Elbow strike to the face. Knee to the gut. Headlock take-down."

"But it's not *sport*, is it?" I say. "Not real sport."

"It's sports-entertainment," says Plum, not taking her eyes from the screen. "Sports-entertainment, they call it."

"Who's The Slab fighting, darling?" Jackie asks. Thirty minutes ago she had been asking me about the dialogue of Carson McCullers in the same quietly inquisitive tone.

"Billy Cowboy. He sucks. Big time. His ass belongs to The Slab."

For several minutes we watch the ludicrous waltz being played out on what I assume is some godforsaken satellite station. In normal circumstances I might have taken control of the situation and turned over to *Newsnight*. But I am grateful to Plum for bringing my nan her shopping, and I am glad to see my nan looking so happy after her ordeal in hospital. So we watch the pumped-up, buck-naked brutes beating each other up for our entertainment—or pretending to.

The bald wrestler—Plum's hero, The Slab—appears to have the upper hand. He advances across the ring beating back the longhair—Billy Cowboy, apparently—with a series of forearm smashes that may or may not have connected. Billy Cowboy is soon flat on his back, his overdeveloped body glistening with sweat and baby oil.

"Your cold, candy ass is mine, he-bitch!" The Slab howls at the prostrate Billy Cowboy. "Your giblets belong to the buzzards!" He jabs a furious finger at his rival's lifeless body. "Know your damn place and zip your damn lip! He-bitch!"

The Slab turns his back on Billy Cowboy to climb the ropes and lecture the crowd, who all appear to be grotesquely overweight children dressed for their yearly trip to the gym.

The referee turns away to consult with a judge at the ringside, and that's when Billy Cowboy leaps to his feet, the fringes on his boots dancing with excitement, as one of his henchmen pushes a large silver trash can under the ropes.

"Oh yeah," I say. "As if they would just happen to have a trash can in their corner. For those moments when what you really need is a trash can."

"Ssshhh!" says my nan.

"Bow down before your master, he-bitch!" The Slab is shouting. "Smell the fear and pass the beer! For The Slab is back in town! Come with me to the Tree of Woe!"

Despite the ten thousand voices bawling at The Slab to turn around, Billy Cowboy manages to creep up behind him and brings the large silver trash can crashing down on his back. The Slab falls from the ropes like a dead bird and for the first time I believe that someone could get slightly hurt out there.

"What's wrong with the referee?" I demand. "How did he miss that?"

"Come on," says Plum. "If the referee saw everything, that wouldn't be true to life, would it?"

Plum and my nan stare at me, amazed that I still don't get it.

Then the pair of them turn back to the TV screen, as if what is being played out before them is neither sport nor entertainment, but all the injustice of the world.

25

"ARE YOU SLEEPING WITH OLGA?" Lisa Smith asks me.

"Olga?" I say.

"Olga Simonov. One of your Advanced Beginners."

Lisa Smith squints at me over the top of her reading glasses. On the other side of her wafer-thin office door, we can hear the laughter of the students, the scuffle of their work boots, the rhythmic chatter of Japanese.

"I know her."

"I know you do. But how well?"

The heat is on again at Churchill's. Lisa Smith is watching me like a short-sighted, bilious old hawk. I am the focus of her attention once more because the police are not going to press charges against Hamish for what he did in that public toilet on Highbury Fields. My colleague was so relieved to be off the hook that he immediately walked down to Leicester Square and offered oral sex to an undercover policeman.

I really admire Hamish. There are plenty of cute young boys he could be chasing at Churchill's—smooth-skinned East Asians, brooding Indians, tactile Italians—but he never goes anywhere near them. Hamish has that enviable ability to separate work and pleasure which I so painfully lack.

"I haven't slept with Olga. On my life."

"Is that the truth?"

It's the truth. I have walked to the top of Primrose Hill with Olga on a Sunday morning—the one time of the week when she is free from the demands of both Churchill's International Language School and the Eamon de Valera public house. We have held hands as we looked down at the city, and then walked to Camden Town where she let me chastely kiss her on the lips over a full English breakfast.

Olga and I have walked by the canals of north London, looking at the house boats as I slipped my arm around her waist and marveled at the springiness of youth. That's what you lose as you get older—that springiness. We have wandered the wilder parts of Hampstead Heath on Sunday afternoon, eaten ice cream in the grounds of Kenwood House, and she has told me about her home, her dreams, the boyfriend she left behind. But I haven't slept with her. Not yet. I'm still waiting for the green light.

Why not? What possible harm could it do?

When I come out of Lisa Smith's office, I see that Hiroko is waiting for me down the hall. She is pretending to read the notice board—rooms to let, rice cookers for sale, bicycles wanted—but she slowly turns to face me as I approach her, her black hair swinging across her glasses, and I am afraid that she is also going to ask me if I am sleeping with the Advanced Beginner known as Olga Simonov. But she doesn't.

"I want to apologize," she says.

"You haven't done anything wrong."

"For standing outside your house that night. I just thought— I don't know. I thought we were good. You and me."

"We were good."

"I don't know what happened."

I don't know how to explain it. You cared too much for me, I think. And if you knew me—really knew me—you would understand that I am really not worth it.

You are kind and sweet and generous and true and decent, and I am none of these things, haven't been for quite a while. You got me wrong. So wrong that it scared me off. Never give someone that power over you, I want to tell her. Don't do it, Hiroko.

"You'll meet somebody else," I say. "There are a lot of nice people in the world. You could feel something for any one of them."

"But I met you," she says.

Then she smiles, and there's something about that smile that makes me doubt myself. There's something about that smile that makes me think Hiroko knows more about all this than I ever will.

The window of the Shanghai Dragon is full of flowers and light. Displays of peach, orange and narcissus blossoms are aglow with the warm light coming from dozens of red candlelit lanterns. The restaurant is a riot of scent and color among the drab grays and traffic fumes of the Holloway Road. There is a CLOSED sign on the door, but the old place has never looked more alive than it does tonight.

We stand on the street looking at this small miracle on this busy north London road. My mother, my nan, Olga and me, basking in the warm glow of all the red lanterns.

"So beautiful," says my mother.

Pasted to the door of the Shanghai Dragon are two red posters with gold Chinese characters, signifying happiness, long life and prosperity. There are also two smiling, bowing figures on the door, a girl in traditional Chinese dress and a boy also in traditional Chinese dress, mirror images of each other, their hands clasped, open hand on closed fist, in salutation to the New Year. They both look absurdly cute, happy and fat. And, above all, prosperous. We ring the bell.

William suddenly appears behind the plate-glass door, his

round face grinning as he fiddles with the catch, swiftly followed by his sister Diana. Then there are the parents, plump Harold and shy Doris, followed by Joyce and George. They are all smiling with pleasure. I have never seen them so happy.

"*Kung hay fat choi!*" the Changs tell us, as we go inside.

"Happy New Year to you too!" My mum smiles, although *kung hay fat choi* means "wishing you prosperity" more than anything to do with the passing of another year. Or perhaps the Chinese believe that prosperity is necessary for happiness. I reflect that sometimes this family seems completely British to me—when George is diving into his fried chicken wings at General Lee's Tasty Tennessee Kitchen, or when I see Joyce drinking "English tea" with my mum, or when Doris is watching *Coronation Street,* or when I hear the undiluted London accents of Diana and William, or when Harold goes off to play golf on Sunday morning. But tonight the Changs are Chinese.

Inside the restaurant we can hear the sound of fireworks.

"It's only a tape," William tells me, rolling his eyes with all the world-weariness a six-year-old can muster. "It's not real fireworks."

"Chinese people invent firework!" Joyce tells him.

"I know, Gran, I know." Trying to placate her.

"But authority don't like people having real firework," she says, calming down a little. "They get all in a dizzy. So now everybody use tape to scare away devil spirits. Works just as well."

I introduce the Changs to Olga, who Joyce immediately sizes up with an expert eye.

"Alfie not getting any younger," Joyce tells her. "Can't live like playboy forever. Need a wife pretty quick."

Everybody laughs, apart from Joyce, who I know to be perfectly serious.

In any other gathering, Olga, as the youngest, hottest woman on the premises, would be the belle of the ball, the center of attention and the first to be offered drinks. But in the

Shanghai Dragon tonight, and in Chinese homes around the world, it is age that takes precedence. My nan is the star guest here.

She is seated at the head of a table covered with plates of what looks like uncooked dumplings, or triangular ravioli, which she eyes dubiously, as if hoping to spot something she recognizes, such as a fish finger or a custard cream. William and Diana both bring her green tea, which she tastes carefully, before giving a jaunty thumbs up.

"Tastes a bit like Lemsip," she says.

We have chicken for dinner. Chicken and steamed rice and some dishes that I can't even look at—silkworms, blackened in the pan, full of their white mushy meat—and food that I love, like little sausages that look as though they should be on the end of a cocktail stick.

I sit next to Joyce and she keeps dropping bits of chicken into my rice bowl, making me feel like a baby bird having worms dropped into its nest. Olga says she is not so hungry because she had something to eat at the Eamon de Valera, although I think that she is just a bit embarrassed by her chopstick technique. There is really no need for her to feel bad, because the Changs assume that every *gweilo* needs Western cutlery. My nan can't use chopsticks either, so she saws away at her tiny piece of chicken with a knife and fork.

"My husband was fond of red meat," she tells Joyce. "Bloody, he liked it. *Just wipe the cow's arse and bring it to the table,'* he used to say. He was a bit of a joker."

After dinner we make more dumplings to eat at midnight. They look like what Yumi and Hiroko call *gyoza,* but Joyce tells us they are called *jiaozi.* We clear the table and make plates and plates of *jiaozi* dumplings, hand rolling the flour, stuffing in the pork filling, sealing it up and handing it to Joyce and Harold to fry.

Olga can't quite get the hang of making *jiaozi,* so she sits in a corner, smoking a cigarette, smiling at our efforts. George tells us that three of the dumplings are very special. One contains sugar, one contains a coin and one contains vegetable.

"For love, for fortune, for intelligence," he says.

We eat the *jiaozi* as the clock chimes midnight and the Year of the Tiger makes way for the Year of the Rabbit.

Diana gets the *jiaozi* that will bring her love.

Her father Harold gets the *jiaozi* that will bring him fortune.

And I get the *jiaozi* that will bring me intelligence.

So everything works out perfectly.

"Like putting a sixpence in a Christmas pudding," says my nan. "They don't do that any more, do they?"

Then it is time to go.

"Kung hay fat choi," I tell George as we are leaving, sticking out my hand. He takes it, although he is not a great hand shaker, and I am surprised, as always, to feel the infinite softness of his grip. Behind us we can hear my nan and my mum and Olga saying good-bye to the rest of the Changs. Outside it is past midnight, a freezing February in London. The red lanterns in the Shanghai Dragon burn like fire.

"Kung hay fat choi," George says. "How is back?"

"My back's fine now."

"No painkiller, okay?"

"Okay, George."

"Not so good, the painkiller. Sometimes best to just feel the pain. Sometimes the healthiest way. The way to get better."

I can't explain why, but I realize that George is not really talking about my back.

He is talking about Olga.

And I suddenly see that bringing her tonight was not the best idea that I ever had. Olga has been made welcome by the Changs, and she has made every effort to enjoy the food and be enchanted by the rituals of Spring Festival, but it was all a bit forced, all a bit of a strain.

I know that in all honesty she would probably have had a better time in the bar of the Eamon de Valera with some disco hunk with a pierced knob and the complete works of Robbie Williams.

She didn't enjoy Chinese New Year at the Shanghai Dragon the way that, say, Hiroko would have enjoyed it.

I see for the first time that—despite her endless legs, her lovely face and her enviable youth—Olga is not the girl for me and I am not the man for her.

And armed with that knowledge, we go straight back to my place and make our baby.

26

THEY HAVE HAD SOME KIND OF ARGUMENT.

Jackie and Plum come into my flat and the silence between them crackles with resentment. Jackie goes straight over to the table where we work, moving surprisingly fast in those leopard-print boots, unbuttoning her raincoat with barely contained fury. Plum lingers in the middle of the room, staring morosely at her scuffed sneakers, her fringe dangling in front of her face, hiding her from the wicked world.

And then I say something stupid.

"What's wrong?"

Jackie whirls on me.

"What's wrong? What's wrong? Madam here gave her dinner money away, didn't you? And her bus money. *And* her bus money, if you please."

Plum peers up through her greasy brown veil, her face collapsing with agony.

"I *didn't*."

"Don't *lie* to me." Jackie takes a step toward her daughter, and for a second I am afraid that she is going to hit her. The girl fearfully retreats a couple of paces. "She lets them walk all over her. Those bloody kids at her school."

"I *didn't*. I *lost* it. I *told* you."

"Do you know how long it took me to earn that money? Do

you have any idea how many floors I had to clean to get that money? That money you gave away? Do you?"

Plum starts to cry. These terrible, bitter tears running down her pudgy young face.

"I lost it. I did. Really I did."

"She lets them walk all over her. If they tried it with me, I would have killed them."

"But I'm not you, am I?" Plum says, and it sounds exactly like something I might say to my father. I feel a stirring of sympathy for this awkward child. "And I *lost* it."

This feels like it could go on forever. I step between them, like a UN representative mediating between the Israelis and the Palestinians.

"Jackie, what were we doing last week?"

"Studying emotions in a dramatic extract," she hisses, still staring angrily at her daughter. "From *The Heart Is a Lonely* pigging *Hunter.*"

"Okay. Well, can you get on with that while I take Plum round to my grandmother's place?"

They both look at me.

"Your grandmother's place?"

"My nan would be glad of the company. She's going back to the hospital next week."

"What's wrong with her?" says Plum.

"She's getting the results of the biopsy they took to find out what caused all that fluid on her lungs. She's a bit nervous."

"Okay," says Plum.

"Fine," says Jackie.

So while Jackie takes out her copy of *The Heart Is a Lonely Hunter* and studies emotions in a dramatic extract, I take Plum round to my nan's. We drive in silence for a while, as Plum flicks through the radio stations looking for something that interests her. Eventually she switches it off with a sigh.

"Who's bullying you at school?"

She shoots me a look. "Nobody."

"Nobody?"

She stares out of the window as the shabby end of north London drifts by. Rental agents and shabby pubs, kebab shops and junk stores.

"You don't know them."

"I probably know the type. Want to talk about it?"

"What good would it do?"

"Are they boys or girls?"

A moment's silence. "Both."

"What are their names?"

She smiles at me. It's not friendly. "You going to come to my school and give them a detention?"

"Sometimes it helps talking about things. That's all."

She takes a breath.

"The girl's called Sadie. The boy's called Mick. They're big. The way some kids are big, you know?"

"I know."

"He shaves. She's got tits. They're only my age. And they've got this little gang. All the cool kids. The hard kids. The kids that have been having sex since the first year. And they hate me. They fucking hate me, don't they? I can't walk down a corridor without someone saying something. 'Fatty Day.' 'Fat Slag.' 'Who ate all the pies?' Every single day for two years. Since the very first day of the very first year. They think it's funny."

We pull up outside my nan's block of flats. A small white block containing all those little old ladies living on their own. I can't imagine Plum at that age. It feels like her teenage years are going to drag on forever.

"How much did they take?"

"I told you—I *lost* it."

"How much?"

"Sixty pounds."

"Jesus. You must eat a lot of school dinners." I immediately regret it.

"Yeah, that's right. That's why I'm so fat. Didn't you know?"

"Come on. That's not what I meant."

"I've got a problem with my glands, okay?"

"Okay. Why did you have so much money on you?"

"Dinner money for the week. Bus money for the month. And my savings."

"Your savings?"

"I was going to buy a book."

"A book?"

"A book called *Smell the Fear, He-bitch.* It's a hardback. They don't come cheap, mate."

"*Smell the Fear, He-bitch?* Is it the new Salman Rushdie?"

"Who's Salmon Rushdie?"

"Never mind."

"*Smell the Fear, He-bitch* is the new book by The Slab. He's a wrestler."

"I remember. Sports-entertainment. So you lost all this money. How did you manage that?"

"I thought it might make them like me but—" She stops, laughs, shakes her head. "Tricked me, didn't you? Typical teacher."

"It takes your mum a long time to earn sixty pounds."

"Don't you start." She is staring down at her hands. Her fingernails are chewed to the quick and there it is again—a surge of sympathy for this sad, lonely child. "I realize it takes her a long time to earn that money. I do know that. I'm not a complete idiot."

I take out my wallet and pull out three £20 notes. "In fact, it takes anyone a long time to earn that kind of money." I hold out the notes. "Be more careful next time, okay?"

She looks at the money, not taking it. "What's this for?"

"You've been good with my nan. I appreciate that. So—just take it, okay?"

"I don't need paying. I like her."

"I know you do. And she likes you. I just don't want you and your mum to fall out over a couple of creeps like Mick and Sadie."

"How do you know they're creeps?"

"I've met them."

"That's a lie. You never met them."

"Their kind. I met their kind. Lots of times. When I was a teacher. And when I was a kid."

She looks at the money. Then she takes it. "Thanks, Alfie."

"Don't mention it. And don't tell your mother. Shall we go up and see the old girl?"

"Okay."

After ringing my nan's bell we wait patiently as her carpet slippers shuffle slowly toward the door. I turn to face Plum. She is still hiding behind her fringe, but looking a little happier.

"What is it with you and The Slab anyway?"

"The Slab?"

"Yeah. I don't get it."

"What do you think I should be into? Some dopey girl singer with long hair and an acoustic guitar going '*boo-hoo-hoo, nobody understands me'?*"

"Something like that. Why does The Slab mean so much to you?"

"Isn't it obvious? The Slab doesn't take shit from anyone."

Olga calls me just before midnight and says she has to see me.

I am just about to clean my teeth and go to bed, so I suggest tomorrow at morning break, in the coffee shop across from Churchill's. She says it has to be now, and something about her voice—how quiet it is, how full of an emotion that I can't quite place—stops me from arguing with her. I get dressed and take a cab down to the Eamon de Valera.

We sit at a corner table surrounded by the dregs of a dozen glasses, and I expect her to tell me that she has had a conversation with Lisa Smith about me, or that she has some kind of visa problem, or that her boyfriend is coming to London. But it is worse than all of that.

"I'm late."

"Late?"

"My period hasn't come."

"Maybe it's—I don't know—can't it be different every month?"

"I took a test," she says, and it occurs to me how much of the language of procreation resembles the lexicon of student life. Being late with something, taking tests, getting your results. But what's a pass and what's a failure? That's the question. "One of those tests that you buy in a drugstore."

I say nothing. I am waiting, unable to really believe that this thing is happening at this time, with this girl. This woman. And not my wife.

Rose and I tried for this moment and it never happened. We really tried. It was never ending. I remember the constant cycle of disappointment and her crippling period pains, I remember being asked to produce an erection every time the ovulation arrived. We laughed about it—"You're performing tonight, Alfie, so no mucking about with yourself in the shower"—but it was slowly breaking our hearts, this longing for a baby, a baby who would complete our world.

Is it that the people who want a baby don't get it, and the ones who don't want a baby do? Is that the way it works? Rose and I tried for almost a year. It didn't happen for us. It will never happen for us now.

"I'm pregnant," Olga says, this woman who is not Rose, with a little laugh that signals that she feels the same disbelief as me. "I'm going to have a baby."

We let the weight of it sink in. They are clearing the glasses all around us. Someone is shouting for last orders.

"A baby. God, Olga."

"I know. I know."

On Chinese New Year Olga and I returned to my flat and discovered that the Hong Kong souvenir sugar bowl where I kept my supply of Gossamer Wings condoms was empty. And we decided to take a risk. No, that's not true. It wasn't as rational as that. We just didn't think about it. We did not think.

She starts to cry a bit and I reach out and take her hands. They are sticky with beer, because she has been working tonight. She works every night.

"I'll stick by you," I say, unable to come up with anything better than the cliché. "We're in this together, okay? This is our baby."

She pulls her hands away from me.

"Are you crazy? I'm not having a baby with you. I'm twenty. You're nearly forty. You're just a teacher in some little language school. I've got my life ahead of me. My boyfriend would kill me."

So after that we do not discuss the baby.

We only talk about the abortion.

Later I take her back to the flat she shares with three other Russians in a part of south London that gentrification passed by, a neighborhood of burned-out cars and distant cries and sprawling projects.

When I try to kiss her cheek, she turns her face away. After deciding what we are going to do, or rather what we are not going to do—we are not going to have this baby—every gesture of affection or support seems inadequate, laughable, pathetic.

She disappears into her block of flats. We have not even said goodnight.

At the moment of this small miracle, this baby she has growing inside her, we have never seemed more like total strangers.

First Rose, now this baby. I am tired of thinking about it all, too ashamed for words, sick to my stomach with guilt.

I feel like I am getting away with murder.

27

I CAN SEE WHY she doesn't want to have a baby with me. I am not so stupid that I can't see that. But as we make the arrangements for the termination, which seems as cold and clinical as arranging to have a car taken in for its annual service, I can't shake the feeling that we have somehow contrived to turn a blessing into a curse.

It's not a baby, I keep telling myself. Not a real baby. Not yet. It never will be. But the problem is, I don't believe it. I don't believe it for a second.

It would be a baby, if there was any space for a baby in our selfish, stupid, fucked-up lives. It would be a baby if we just left it alone. That's not much to ask for, is it? Just to be left alone. Then it would be a little boy or a little girl. If we weren't making these arrangements to get rid of it.

But that's what we are doing. Getting rid of it. I can't believe—I just can't believe, although I wish I could—that what we are about to do is just another kind of contraception. That what we are going to do is no different from buying a packet of Gossamer Wings condoms. This is not contraception. It's too late for all that.

We have brought a life into being that nobody wants. Olga doesn't want it. I try to want it, I really do. I try to want our baby, but it is too much for me when I contemplate bringing up the baby by myself.

I see myself feeding the baby its bottle, taking it for a walk in the park, giving it a go on the swings. Is that what you do with babies? Or does that come a bit later? The truth is I would not know where to start. Bring up a child? I can hardly look after myself.

We have an appointment at the clinic. Olga has to talk to a doctor to explain why this baby's existence is impossible. It doesn't take long. What was I expecting? Tears, anger, emotional pleas on behalf of the unborn baby? I would have liked some of that. I would have liked to have heard someone standing up for the baby. I would have appreciated hearing someone say—don't do it. Don't get rid of this baby.

But the forms are signed, a bill is presented and I put it on my credit card. It's that casual, that cruel, that simple.

Killing your unborn baby?

That'll do nicely, sir.

I know it's the only way. Isn't it? Don't I? But it still feels like we are stealing something from someone. Stealing a life. I try to support Olga at this difficult and painful time, I really do. I assure her that everything is going to be all right, yet it's suddenly as if we have never met.

Maybe she feels it too. Maybe she also believes that we are stealing something sacred. Or perhaps she is just sick of the sight of me. That's another possibility. I know we have to do this thing because our fragile little relationship was already collapsing by the time we made the baby. I can see that. I don't for a moment think Olga wants to spend her life with me. To be honest, I don't think she wants to spend an evening with me. I think she would be happy to never see my face again.

It would never have worked out between us.

The baby should thank us.

Yeah, sure.

•   •   •

Josh once told me, "No relationship can survive an abortion." The line was delivered with such world-weary certainty, such manly conviction, that I thought it must surely be true. He had got a girl into trouble—on this subject, I always find myself reverting to my mother's vocabulary—in Singapore on some drunken rugby tour.

She was a lawyer, BBC—British-born Chinese—expensively educated, very well spoken, which always got his attention, and Josh was keen. But when he told me about it over Tsingtao at the top of the Mandarin Hotel, he said that there was no real future for them after the termination. "Something about this thing messes with nature," he said, "just messes it all up forever," and I thought how much older and wiser he seemed than me.

Yet when I pick Olga up at the clinic, I find that I like her more than I ever did.

She looks so young and so pale and so drained, as though she has been through something that will stay with her for the rest of her life, something that will change the way she looks at the world, and I don't want to split up with her. I really want to make a go of it. To try. This feeling lasts until the moment I put my arm around her and she gives me a flat, dead look.

"I'm okay."

"Come back to my place."

"What?"

"Don't go back to your flat. Come back to mine. You can have your own room. I'll sleep on the sofa. Just until you—you know." What are the words? "Feel better."

I can tell she doesn't like the idea much. But the idea of returning to the damp south London apartment she shares with three other Russians appeals to her even less. So we get a taxi and—silently, not touching me, huddled inside her cheap black coat—she comes back to my apartment, where she moves very slowly, as if in great pain or afraid of breaking something, and she spends a long time in the bathroom before going to bed.

I look in on her after a while and see her sleeping, her face almost as pale as the pillow she rests on. Later she gets up and asks me if she can make a phone call, and I say of course you can, you don't even have to ask me, and she spends a long time talking in Russian to someone I guess is her boyfriend, the glottal stops of the language made even harsher by her crying.

I have no idea how much she tells him. But she politely thanks me for the use of the phone, as if we have just been introduced and I have just passed the salt, and then she shuffles off to bed, soon falling asleep as the winter day quickly dies and darkness creeps into my flat. I don't turn the lights on.

What makes me laugh—no, what makes me sit with my face in my hands in the living room, sit alone in the gathering darkness with Olga sleeping in my bed, sometimes muttering in her sleep, sometimes crying out what could be a name—is that Rose and I wanted a baby so much.

It would have been the best thing in the world. For us.

My wife and I. We tried. We had been trying since our wedding day. She even had all the equipment. By her bedside there was this little white and pink box the size of a glasses case with a thermometer to take her temperature when she woke up. She also had this stick thing that she took into the bathroom every morning to tell her when her ovulation was on the way and we should think about getting started. Pencil the date into our diaries.

Trying tonight.

Oh, she had all the kit.

After almost a year of disappointment, we were about to take the tests. Me making love to a little plastic jar, Rose having her plumbing checked out—whatever it is you have to do. We tried to make a joke of it, the way we tried to make a joke of everything.

"And how would you like your eggs, madam?"

"Fertilized!"

We ran out of time. It never happened for us. Our baby never came. And then Rose was gone.

She really wanted a child with me. You might find that hard to believe. It's true. She thought I would be a good father. That's not a joke. "You'll be such a wonderful dad, Alfie," she said to me. Rose really wanted to have a baby with me, although of course that was back in the years when I was really alive and, I realize, a far better man than I am today.

The next morning I leave Olga asleep and go to my local book shop to buy a gift for Plum.

"I'm looking for a book," I tell the young man behind the counter. "It's called, ah . . ."

"Title? Author?"

"It's . . . ah . . . *Smell the Fear . . . something-something.*"

"*Smell the Fear, He-bitch?* Yeah, it's the new one by The Slab. The wrestling person. You'll find it by the door."

Right by the double doors at the front of the store, I find a huge display of *Smell the Fear, He-bitch*. I pick up a copy and look at a massive, seminaked bald man grinding his teeth on the cover. He looks like a bodybuilder modeling underpants.

I flip through the picture-packed pages. Most of the images are of The Slab beating up other big men in skin-tight Lycra— or at least pretending to. But there's one section toward the back of the book where The Slab is seen posing with small children of every race and color. In the large print surrounding the photos, The Slab speaks of his philosophy. The importance of charity work, the need to combat racism, the moral imperative of being good to each other when the day's bloody mayhem is done.

He calls it doing the human thing.

And I find that, no matter how hard I try, I just can't raise a sneer today.

"The Slab says do the human thing—or I will whip your candy ass all the way to the Tree of Woe."

Do the human thing?

It feels like the best advice I have heard for years.

When I get back home I discover that Olga has gone. No note, no good-bye, just a few stray red hairs in the bathroom sink. I decide we can't end it this way and call her flat. I am anxious to do the human thing. One of her roommates answers and goes to get her. Then she comes back to tell me that Olga doesn't want to talk to me.

Sometimes you can leave it too late to do the human thing.

And I think about Chinese New Year, Spring Festival, and how much I love what I think of as the symmetry of the Changs.

George and Joyce, Harold and Doris, little Diana and William—there is a balance and harmony about their family that makes me ache with envy.

My own family feels like all broken bits and jagged edges and half-forgotten leftovers compared to the Changs.

My nan with her husband long dead, my mum with her husband run away, and me and Olga, who must have looked like something approaching a normal couple on Chinese New Year, but who, out of all my shattered family tree, have turned out to be the most defective branch of all.

But I had a family once, and we had a plan. We were going to have children and everything.

That's what we wanted, Rose and I, that was what we wished hard for, that was our plan. Children and everything.

28

I KNOW THAT HIROKO WILL TALK TO ME. I know that Hiroko still gets the soft look in her eyes when she sees me. Hiroko will do the human thing. Especially if she can sneak me past her landlady. Then we will do the human thing from midnight to dawn. Well, at least until about five past twelve.

I meet her at the little fake French café where we used to have our full English breakfasts and cappuccino-flavored kisses. I wonder why I let that time end and feel a huge wave of relief when she walks into the place, her shiny hair swinging just as it always did, her eyes still shy and gleaming behind her black-framed glasses. She is such a wonderful young woman. Why did I ever let her get away? Was it something to do with her liking me more than I like myself?

It's early evening and the place is full of couples. We have come to the right place. I put my arm around her and try to place my mouth on top of her mouth.

"No," she says, laughing and turning her face away.

I find myself pecking the side of her head, tasting a cocktail of hair, ear and spectacles.

"No?"

She holds my hands by my side. It seems partly an act of affection and partly a self-defence technique.

"I still care about you," she says.

"That's great. Because I still care about you too."

"But differently."

"That doesn't sound so great."

"You said I would meet someone else."

"Yes, but there's no need to rush things."

"I've been spending a lot of time with Gen."

"Gen?" I see the quiet, funky Japanese boy in the front row of my Advanced Beginners, peering up at me through a haystack of dyed brown hair. "But Gen's just a kid."

"He's the same age as me."

"Is he? Wow. I thought he was younger."

"We're going traveling. After the exam. Maybe Spain. Maybe Thailand. Up north. Chiang Mai. Neither of us have really seen Asia." She laughs, reaching out to squeeze my hand. "And it's true what you say. There are a lot of nice people in the world. What's the idiom? *So many fish in the sea.*"

And all of them so slippery.

It was always simple with Vanessa.

Fun and easy. The way it should be. Never a pain, never a strain. Never a *what are you thinking?* Or *why are you crying?* As I recall, there were no arguments, no recriminations. That's a French woman for you. Sophisticated enough to keep it uncomplicated. Suddenly I miss Vanessa like crazy.

When I call her flat, a man answers. I guess I imagined that the man would have faded from the scene by now, the way people so casually and quickly fade from my own life. What did I expect? I expected him to go back to his wife. To go back to his life.

"Hello?"

"Is Vanessa there?"

A pause on his end. "Who's calling?"

A pause on my end. "Her teacher."

"Hold on a second."

The receiver is placed down with a clatter. I can hear voices in the background. The man's suspicious baritone, Vanessa's singsong, slightly defensive response.

" 'Ello?"

I smile to myself. There's no contest, is there? This really is the greatest accent in the world.

"Vanessa, it's Alfie."

"Alfie?" She puts her hand over the phone for a second, does a bit of explaining to her married man. As if she owes him any kind of explanation. "What do you want?"

"I was wondering if you would like to come out for a drink or something."

"With you?"

"Of course with me."

"But that's not possible. I'm not living alone anymore. I thought you knew that."

"Just a drink, Vanessa," I say, trying to keep the rising panic out of my voice. "I'm not asking you to pick out curtains."

"But what's the point?"

"The point? Why does there need to be a point? That's what I always liked about us. There was never any point. Why does everybody always need a point?"

"Sorry, I can't."

"It doesn't have to be this minute. I'm not talking about *now*. How about Friday? How's the weekend looking for you? Pick a night. Go ahead. Any night. I'm free all weekend."

"I've got to go, Alfie."

"Hold on. I thought we got on well together."

"We had—what do you people call it?—a laugh. Okay? We had a laugh. But that's all it ever was, Alfie. Just a laugh. Now I want something more than just a laugh."

I have a few Tsingtao by myself in a pub in Chinatown and find myself in the Eamon de Valera just before closing time. It is packed with foreign language students from Churchill's. Yumi and Imran are sitting by the door.

"Let me get you a drink," I tell them.

"No thanks," Imran says.

"Why don't you go home, Alfie?" Yumi says. "You look tired."

"What you drinking, Imran? Get you a pint of Paddy McGinty's stout?"

"I don't drink alcohol."

"Don't you? Don't you? I never knew that." I look at Yumi. That beautiful face surrounded by the mass of fake yellow hair. "I never knew that Imran doesn't drink alcohol. Is that a religious thing?"

"Yes. It's a religious thing." Not looking at me, the handsome bastard.

I put my arm around him, press my face close, watching him recoil from the fumes of a few Tsingtao. "But your religion doesn't stop you from stealing someone else's girl, does it, you hypocrite?"

They get up to leave.

"Nobody stole me," Yumi says. "You can't steal a woman. You can only drive her away."

Then they go.

I see Olga behind the bar and push my way through the crowd. Laughter, smoke, the sound of breaking glass. Zeng and Witold are at the bar.

"You okay?" Zeng says.

"You look all funny," Witold says.

I ignore them.

"Olga," I say. "Olga. I want to talk to you. It's important."

She moves to the other end of the bar. A guy with an Australian accent tries to serve me. I tell him I want to be served by Olga. He shrugs, walks away. Zeng is pulling at my arm. I shake him off.

"This is not so good," Witold says. Olga is still at the other end of the bar. She is laughing with someone.

"Olga!"

Someone taps me on the shoulder.

I turn round and have just enough time to watch the fist coming toward me but not enough time to get out of its way.

The fist—all bony knuckles, plus the sharp sliver of a ring—smacks into the side of my mouth and I feel the warmth of split lips on the tip of my tongue. My legs have gone, and I find that I am only on my feet because of the elbow that I have resting on the bar. A pale, thin boy in cheap clothes is facing me, blood on his fist and something like hatred on his face.

He is being held back by Zeng and Witold but he is clearly ready for more. All around us the conversation has stopped and the patrons of the Eamon de Valera are looking forward to the floor show. Why are people so nasty? Why can't they do the human thing? Why don't they listen to The Slab when he's talking to them?

"Who are you?" I say.

"I'm Olga's boyfriend."

"Really? That's incredible. Me too."

"No," he says. "You're nobody."

Then they throw me out. The two bouncers. The big black guy who is built like a fridge and the big white guy who is built like a dishwasher. They pin my arms to my side and march me to the door, where they eject me into the street with more force than is strictly necessary.

There's a beggar and his dog sitting on the pavement outside and I sort of stumble over them, lose my balance and pitch head first in the gutter.

I lie there for a while looking up at the stars faintly shining beyond the sick yellow of the streetlamps. My skull aches. My mouth hurts. There's blood smeared down the front of my shirt. The dog comes over to me and starts licking my face but the beggar calls his name—"Mister," which I have to say is a pretty good name for a dog—and finally even the beggar's dog decides to have nothing to do with me.

And suddenly I know what I have to do now.

I have to sleep with Jackie Day.

29

I CATCH THE LAST TRAIN OUT TO ESSEX.

My carriage is full of young men who dress in suits and young women who dress like Jackie Day. It is like the rush hour for overdressed drunks. Everyone is loud and happy. There's no trouble. The carriage smells of kebabs, lager and Calvin Klein.

Near midnight the train slowly rattles out of the great metal barn of Liverpool Street Station. It is difficult to know where the city ends and where the suburbs begin, where the underground stations give way to small towns, what is London and what is Essex.

Drifting by in the darkness I can see the rotting hulks of sixties tower blocks, endless railway yards, lots crammed with second-hand cars, and then a track for dog racing, pubs, drive-through burger bars, Chinese and Indian restaurants, more pubs, ratty strings of shops, projects that seem to go on and on for ever. A world of cars, public housing and small pleasures. Essex looks like London with the big money gone.

The stops clatter by—Stratford, Ilford, Seven Kings, Chadwell Heath, Romford, Harold Wood, Billericay. The urban sprawl stretches deep into the night, the city never seems to come to an end. And then, after almost an hour, with most of the overdressed drunks sleeping or gone, it suddenly does.

The city's overspill is abruptly replaced by flat green fields, black and silent beyond the lights of railway and road, and the next stop is Bansted. Out where the city finally starts trying to pass itself off as the countryside.

Bansted. Their home town.

The minicab drives slowly down a narrow street of modest houses. Some of the houses have pretty little gardens, full of terra-cotta pots and flower beds. Others have their front lawns brutally bricked over, a car or a van parked where the grass should be. Almost as if you have to choose between the flowers or the cars. And maybe you do.

Jackie's house has grass out front, but that's all. No border for flowers, no space for plants. Just a plain grass lawn. I pay the minicab driver and walk up the drive she shares with her next-door neighbors. The house is in darkness. I ring the bell.

She answers the door in—what's it called? the silky Japanese robe?—a kimono. And I smile to myself because that is just so typical of Jackie. She couldn't have an ordinary dressing gown like everyone else. It has to be a kimono.

"What happened to you?" she says.

"You're never knowingly underdressed, are you?"

"Have you been beaten up?"

My face. She is looking at my face. I touch it and feel the dried flakes of blood by the side of my swollen mouth. I shrug bravely and she lets me into the house, turning on a few lights, offering me tea or coffee. The house is small and tidy, nothing fancy, with little red flowers on the wallpaper.

There's a photo by the door of Plum as a little girl, smiling in the sunshine of what looks like the English seaside. A lovely little kid. Not overweight, not hiding behind her fringe, not sad at all. What happened?

I look at Jackie. This is the first time I have seen her without makeup. Liberated from all the usual war paint, her face is quite shockingly pretty. We go into the living room. There's a huge TV set, a terrible orange carpet, more pictures of Plum, some of them with Jackie, young and laughing, and a lot of the kind of mementos that my nan loves—Celtic crosses, Spanish bulls, Mickey Mouse waving a white-gloved paw, a souvenir from Disneyworld.

"What are you doing here?"

"I just wanted to say—it's great."

"Are you drunk? You're drunk, aren't you? I can smell it on you."

Plum's voice from the top of the stairs. "Mum, who is it?"

"Go back to sleep," Jackie calls up to her.

"I think it's great that you want to go to college," I tell her. "I mean it. Get an education. Change your world. I admire your determination. I really do. I wish I could change my world. My world is just about ready for a change."

"That's it?"

"What?"

"That's what you want to tell me?"

"And—I like you."

She laughs, shakes her head, pulls the kimono a little tighter.

"Oh, you like me, do you?"

I collapse on the sofa. The leather creaks with protest beneath me. I suddenly feel very tired.

"Yes."

I realize that it's true. I like her a lot. The way she is bringing up her daughter alone, the way she works hard at her crappy job, doing things for all the phonies in Cork Street and Churchill's that they can't do themselves, dreaming of going back to college. No, she's not dreaming. She is making it happen. Cleaning floors and toilets in Cork Street and then writing essays about *The Heart Is a Lonely Hunter* in her spare time. It's impressive. She has more fight in her than anyone I know. I admire her. The way I haven't admired anyone since Rose.

So I go to put my arms around her, feeling a great undigested chunk of affection mixed with all that Tsingtao welling up inside me. But she pushes me away.

"Oh, I don't think so," she says, taking a step backward, tightening the kimono a bit more. "I don't think that would be the greatest idea in the world. Jesus Christ. Do you have to go to bed with all your students? Can't you just—I don't know— *teach* them or something?"

"Jackie, I didn't mean—"

"You've got a lot of nerve. I mean it. This is not funny. What made you think you could come here and have sex with me?"

"I don't know," I say. "The way you dress?"

"I should give you a slap. You bloody bastard. You make me so angry."

"I don't want you to be angry with me. I just wanted to see you. I'm sorry. I really am. I'll go."

"Where? You're not in Islington now. You think you can just step into the street and flag down a black cab? There are no taxis, no trains. Not at this time. You're in the sticks now, mate." She shakes her head, the anger subsiding in the face of my total ignorance. "Don't you know anything at all?"

So she lets me sleep on her sofa. She says the first train to London isn't until the morning, and although she thinks I deserve to be curled up in the photo booth on Bansted station, she is going to take pity on me.

She goes upstairs and I hear voices. Two women. No—a woman and a girl. Then Jackie comes back down with a pillow and a single comforter. She throws them at me, still shaking her head, but smiling at the same time, as though, now that she comes to think about it for five minutes, I am funny-pathetic more than offensive-pathetic. She leaves me to it, still adjusting her kimono.

I make up my little bed on the leather sofa, take off my trousers and climb under the comforter. The only sound I can hear is Jackie cleaning her teeth in the bathroom. It is very quiet out here, there's none of the city's constant background noise of sirens, faraway voices and the roaring traffic's boom.

I find myself nodding off, only waking up with a start when I feel someone looking down at me.

It's Plum in her stripy pajamas.

"Please don't hurt her," she says.

Then she is gone.

In the morning I wake up when I hear the front door close. It's still dark, but there's the sound of a bicycle being wheeled down the little drive. I push back the comforter and go to the window. And there's Plum, wrapped up inside one of those big down jackets, a woollen hat jammed down on her head, an orange bag slung around her shoulders, pushing her bike. She sees me, grins and waves. I watch her cycle off down the silent street.

"She's got a paper route." Jackie is in the doorway, already dressed. "I hope she didn't wake you."

"A paper route? You Day girls work really hard, don't you?"

"We have to," she says, and her smile makes her words softer than they really are. "There's nobody else to do it, is there? Want a cup of coffee?"

I put on my trousers and follow her into the kitchen. My mouth feels dry and sour. Now that the night and the Tsingtao have gone, I am embarrassed to be here.

"How do you feel?" she asks me. "As bad as you look? Surely not quite as bad as that?"

"Sorry. It was a dumb idea to come here. But I didn't come all the way out here just to sleep with you. I wouldn't do that."

"You're a smooth talker, aren't you?"

"I just felt like talking to someone. Something happened. Something bad."

She hands me a cup of coffee. "Want to talk about it now?"

"I don't know how."

"Want to give me a clue?"

"It was a girl. At my college."

"Ah, one of your students. Of course."

"She had an abortion."

Then she is not laughing anymore. "That must have been a hard thing to go through."

"It was the worst. The worst thing."

"How old is she?"

"Not very old. Early twenties."

"I was seventeen. When I fell with Plum." Fell with. Sometimes she uses the expressions of my mother and my grandmother. "Not that I thought about an abortion."

"You didn't even think about it?"

"I'm a Catholic. I believe that all life is sacred."

"That's a good thing to believe. If you're going to believe in anything."

"But having a baby changed my life. I left school. Didn't go to university. Didn't get my degree. Couldn't get a good job. Stayed in Bansted. Not that Bansted is such a bad place."

"You kept your baby. And it—she—messed up everything."

She shakes her head. "No, it didn't. Not really. It just put things on hold for a while. I'm going back to college, aren't I? Thanks to you."

"You never regretted it? Having the baby?"

"I can't imagine a world without my girl in it."

"She's lucky to have a mum like you."

"And she's unlucky to have a dad like her dad. So I guess it all evens out in the end."

"What's wrong with her dad?"

"Jamie? There's not a lot wrong with him when he's sober. When he's had a few, things happen. Usually to me. But he started on Plum, so we left. Two years ago. Got this place. I didn't recognize him by then."

"You must have liked him once."

"You kidding? I was nuts about him. My Jamie. Tall, dark, built like a brick house. He was a good little footballer. Midfield. A good engine, as they say. Very fit. Had a chance of turning professional. Trials with West Ham. Then he did his knee in. The left one. So now he works as a security guard. And gets pissed. And knocks around his new partner. But not me. Not anymore. And not my daughter."

"Why did you leave it for so long? I don't mean leaving your husband, leaving Jamie. The education thing. Why wait? If it was so important to you, why didn't you do it years ago?"

"Jamie didn't want me to. I think he was a bit jealous. He didn't want my dream to come true when his dream didn't. Men are very competitive, aren't they? Another word for simple. My ex-husband wants the world to have a bad knee."

"Well, we'll get you through your exam." I raise my coffee cup in salute. "And I hope it makes you happy."

She raises her own cup. "You think it won't. You think I'm expecting some student paradise that doesn't really exist. Beautiful young people sitting around talking about *The Heart Is a Lonely Hunter*. And you don't think it's like that. You think it's all a waste of time. Qualifications. Education. Getting my exams, as my old mum would have said. But it wasn't a waste of time for Rose, was it?"

"Rose?"

"She came from out here, didn't she?"

"Not far away."

"If she hadn't got an education, you would never have met her. If she hadn't gone to university and become a lawyer and gone to Hong Kong, you would never have known her. If she had had a baby at eighteen with someone else—don't look at me like that—then what would your life have been like?"

"I don't know. I can't imagine. I can't imagine what my life would have been like without knowing her."

"You were mad about her, weren't you?"

"I still am. But what can you do? I loved and lost. I've had my turn."

"Your turn?"

"My turn at—come on, you know. Love. Romance. Relationships. All that stuff."

She shakes her head. "Well, I don't think I've had my turn. Not after Jamie. Are you kidding? I reckon I deserve a second turn after that lot. I reckon everyone deserves a second go at being happy. Even you, Alfie. You should have a little more faith."

"A little more faith?"

"That's right. A little more faith. Don't be like my ex-husband. Don't sit around wishing that everyone had a bad knee."

"I just think you get one chance—one real chance—then it's gone forever. I don't think that you can go around starting over again and again. That's not the real thing, is it? How can it be the real thing if it comes along every few years or so? That makes a mockery of the real thing."

"Maybe. But come on. What else are you going to do with the rest of your life? You don't have to stick with your students just because you know they're going home one day. You don't have to stick with young women who can't really hurt you."

"Is that what you think I do?"

"Don't you?"

"I don't know."

"You don't know? You're not very smart for a teacher, are you?"

"I'm one of the stupid teachers."

"Yeah, it shows."

I watch Jackie washing up our cups in the sink and I think: perhaps she's right. I don't want to be like someone's bitter ex-husband.

I should have a little more faith.

30

A BABY IS LOOKING AT ME.

The baby is as bald and round as a billiard ball, a half-pint-sized Winston Churchill in a pink bodysuit, a thin stream of drool coming from the corner of its pouty little mouth. The baby looks brand new. Everything about it—her? How do you tell? Just by the color of the bodysuit?—looks freshly minted.

The baby is the most beautiful thing I have ever seen in my life. And it is watching me. Because it knows. The baby can tell.

Those huge blue eyes follow me as I move slowly toward the hospital's reception desk. I stop and stare back at the beautiful baby, overwhelmed by its perception.

The baby can see into my heart. The baby can read my mind. The baby knows the terrible thing I have done, the unspeakable act I put on my credit card.

The baby can't believe it.

I can't believe it myself.

The baby is surrounded by happy, laughing adults, parents and siblings and grandparents by the look of them, people happy to see the baby, meet it for the first time perhaps, but the baby ignores them all and just kicks its limbs as if it is testing them for the first time; the baby does nothing but lie there and flex its new little arms and legs and watch me, watch me with this terrible accusation.

"You all right, love?"

I nod uncertainly, tearing myself away from the baby, taking my nan's arm.

"I've got a bad feeling about today," she says.

I reassure her that this is just a checkup, that she has been through the worst, that the fluid is off her lungs and this appointment will soon be over and she will be free. And I truly believe it. But it doesn't work out like that.

First we are directed to a small waiting area that is so crowded we have to stand. Most of the people here are old and frail, but not all of them; there are young people with no luck who have ended up here fifty years before their time, and it is one of these unlucky young people, a dangerously overweight woman, who gets up to offer my nan her seat.

What everyone waiting here shares is a kind of gentle cynicism. They deal with the indignity and anxiety of this place with little jokes, knowing smiles and endless patience. We are in this thing together, they seem to say, and I feel a rush of love for these people. It is no surprise that my nan acts as though she knows them. They remind me of everyone I grew up with.

Eventually we see the specialist, a doctor whose name my nan has difficulty with, so she always calls him "that nice Indian gentleman," although I have no idea if he is really an Indian; his name could just as easily be from some other part of the world, and he is a good man, I like him a lot too, so we don't even complain or roll our eyes or sigh when he immediately tells my nan that he would like her to go and have an X-ray and get a blood test and then come back to him later.

More waiting. More standing room only. Another little ticket that you hold on to until your number appears after a wait that seems never ending.

The blood test is easy enough. I go into the little room with my nan, watch her roll up the sleeve of her blue Marks &

Spencer sweater and stare at the needle with a childlike curiosity as the nurse slips it into her pale, papery skin. The nurse sticks a Band-Aid on top of the bubbling pinprick of blood and we are out of there.

I can't accompany my nan into the X-ray department. People have to get undressed in there, my nan has to get undressed, and so of course I stay in the waiting room while she goes inside to get changed. But the terrible thing is she gets a little confused after she undresses for the X-ray, and I can see her standing in the middle of the corridor of the X-ray department in her hospital smock, and what really does me in is that she hasn't fastened her smock at the back, she has left it open, so the world can see her poor old back and legs, those bones so delicate they always remind me of a baby bird, and I want to protect her, I want to do up her smock and find out where she needs to go, but I can't, I am not allowed in there, and she wouldn't want me in there, wouldn't want me to see her not coping, with half her clothes off, so she just stands there half-naked in the X-ray department, looking around, her face frowning with confusion, when all she wants is to be at home with Frank Sinatra and the National Lottery and a nice cup of tea, not much to ask for, until a friendly nurse with a loud, cheerful voice sees her and points her in the right direction.

Then we go to see the nice Indian doctor that my nan likes so much, and he tells her—so matter of fact that I will remember it forever—that she is dying.

"We've had a look at the result of your biopsy, Mrs. Budd, and I have to tell you that we have found a tumor in the lining of your lung. And, as I would expect in someone of your age, the tumor is malignant."

They have known this for how long? Hours? Days? Weeks? Certainly before we arrived today, before the hearty good mornings and my nan wandering the X-ray department with her hospital smock undone.

But it is news to us.

Tumor. Malignant. Nobody says the word. And I feel ashamed that nobody in my family—not me, not my mother, not my father—has had the courage to say the word since all this began. We assumed—we were so sure—that the word would go away if we never said it. And here it is, still not being said out loud, but growing in the lining of my grandmother's lung.

They didn't know, the doctor says, absolving my family of cowardice at not saying the word. They couldn't know until the fluid was drained from her lungs and the biopsy had been performed. And he really is a good man, but he does not burst into tears or allow his voice to tremble with emotion when he tells my nan that there is nothing that can be done, no chemo, no surgery, no miracle cure, and that the tumor in the lining of her lung is secondary, meaning that the source of this thing, this terrible thing, is somewhere else, could be anywhere else in her poor old body, and they just don't know.

It is not the first time that the doctor has given this speech. Perhaps not even the first time today.

More undressing, more examination. When the doctor and I are alone, and my nan is chatting happily to the young nurse on the other side of the screen, I ask him the obvious question.

"How long has she got?"

"In a patient of your grandmother's age—probably a few months. Perhaps even until the summer."

He talks about the medical term for what my nan has, the technical word for this pleural tumor—it's called mesothelioma—and I get him to write it down, mesothelioma, thinking how you should know how to spell the thing that is going to kill you.

• • •

When my nan is examined and dressed, she thanks the doctor. She really likes him. She is a woman of courage and manners, and I feel ashamed again, wondering how I will carry myself when this day comes for me.

Outside the hospital her mouth is set in a firm line. I notice how crooked her eyebrows are drawn on today. The gap between her desire to look nice and her inability to do it as well as she once did shreds my heart.

She rubs her side, the side where they drained her lungs, and I remember that we thought it was where the tube had been stuck into her side that was hurting, a wound that wouldn't heal, but we now know it was always more than that, this pain that comes in great waves and doesn't let her sleep and takes her from her bed in the middle of the night.

"I'm going to beat this thing," she declares, and I don't know what to say, because I know it can't be beaten—can it?—and so anything I say will sound either like surrender or a lie.

We go back to her little white flat and she slips into her old routine. Kettle on, music on, Sinatra singing "I've Got the World on a String," the *Mirror* on the coffee table, turned to the TV page, circles in blue ballpoint around the programs she wants to watch while the rest of us are off doing something else when we should be with her, making the most of every day, every moment, and these shaky circles around her favorite TV programs make me feel like crying.

She is singing. I am shaking, scared of what I have to do. I have to call my father, I have to call my mother. But that can wait. Now we sit on the sofa, drinking our hot, sweet tea, listening to Sinatra sing "Someone to Watch over Me," and my nan holds my hand like she will never let it go.

When I go to the park for the first time in ages, the morning is cold and frosty, the scrubby grass covered in a mist that the weak winter sunlight can't burn away. He is there, of course, as I knew he would be, and I watch him for a while as he moves under the bare trees with that unhurried power, making what he is doing look like everything—meditation, martial art, physical exercise, breathing lesson and slow, lonely dance. Making every movement special, making every second sacred.

But today George Chang is not alone.

There's a bunch of young business types in their dry-cleaned running gear politely watching him. There must be ten of them, mostly young men, their soft office bodies pumped up from weight training and contact sports, but there are also a couple of thin women with dyed blonde hair, good-looking but hard as nails. Modern boys and girls. They all look as though they should be going for the burn in a gym, or whatever it is they do in there.

"Alfie?"

It's Josh. He looks a little heavier than I remember. And I am accustomed to seeing him in a suit from Hugo Boss or Giorgio Armani or Paul Smith, not a tracksuit from Nike. But it is definitely old Josh.

"What are you doing here?" I ask him.

He indicates George.

"Our company sent us to him."

"What for?"

"Tai Chi is part of our new corporate strategy for stress management. Our firm loses too many person-hours to stress."

"Person-hours?"

"Yes, too many person-hours. Tai Chi is said to reduce stress levels. And it's also to help us think outside the box."

"Think outside the box? What's that supposed to mean?"

"Change the way we use our imagination. Help us think creatively. Stop us using the same old tired business techniques. Think outside the box, Alfie. At first I thought it was just a load of New Age business bollocks, this year's half-baked corporate philosophy. But I've changed my mind after watching Master Chang."

Master Chang? George never calls himself Master Chang. Who are these posers and what are they doing in our park?

George demonstrates the opening moves of the form. Then he gets them to do it. Or to try. It's very basic stuff. He doesn't even get them to put the breathing with the movement. As Josh and his friends wave their arms about, I take George to one side.

"You're not really teaching these idiots, are you?"

He shrugs. "New students."

"I don't understand how they got here. I don't understand how our park is suddenly full of suits talking about thinking outside the box and person-hours. All these suits talking about Tai Chi saving money for some rich company that has probably got too much money in the first place. This is our park."

"Their boss comes to Shanghai Dragon. Good client of mine. Lives not far. Big-shot lawyer. Says, 'George—I want you to teach Tai Chi to some of my people. Hear it good for stress. Will you do it, George?' I say, sure, why not?"

"Why not? Because they're not going to stick at it, that's why not. You think they're going to stick at it? They'll last five minutes. Next week it will be something else. Yoga. Muay Thai. Morris Dancing. Anything."

"How long did you last?"

"That's not fair. I've had a lot on my plate lately."

He turns and faces me. "Everybody always has a lot on plate. Everybody. Always. Lot on plate. You talk, talk, talk. Talk as though this is part of rat race. One more thing you have to do in busy life. It's not. Tai Chi is get away from rat race. Understand?"

"But I liked it when it was just you and me, George."

"Things change."

"But I don't like change."

"Change part of life."

"But I can't stand it. I like it when things stay the same."

He shakes his head impatiently. "Tai Chi all about change. About coping with change. Don't you know that yet?"

When Josh and the other off-duty suits have finished waving their arms around, George announces that he is going to show us some pushing hands. I've never done pushing hands before, I have never even heard of it, but I try to look like I know what I'm doing when George asks me to help him demonstrate.

"Pushing hands," he says. "Called *toi sau* in China. Not about strength. About feeling. For two peoples. Can be improvise. Can be set moves. About anticipate."

That's the introduction. George is not much of a talker. He prefers to show you rather than tell you.

I copy George. We face each other in a left bow-and-arrow stance—left leg forward and bent, representing a bow, right leg behind and straight, representing an arrow—and, following his example, I lightly place the back of my left wrist against the back of his left wrist. We are hardly touching.

He closes his eyes and slowly starts pushing his hand toward me. Somehow I know what to do. Staying in contact with his wrist, I turn my waist, rolling the back of my hand over his hand, letting him fully extend his arm, then I slowly push back toward him. He receives my force, goes with it, slowly brushes it aside. Our hands never lose contact.

It goes on. We push and yield and neutralize, push and yield and neutralize, and soon I trust myself enough to close my eyes too, letting go of everything around me, to forget about the suits and Josh and person-hours and thinking outside the box, to forget that we haven't spoken since I disgraced myself at his dinner party, to forget about hospital waiting rooms where they tell you there's nothing that can be done, to forget the mist on the bare trees and my swollen lips and my chipped tooth, to just feel the light touch of skin against skin, to embrace the giving and taking, relaxing into the ebb and flow, just feeling what I need to do, and becoming what I need to become.

Part Three

Oranges for Christmas

31

SUDDENLY THE LITTLE WHITE FLAT is too much for my nan. Suddenly it is full of traps to remind you that it's not the getting old that kills you. It's the getting sick.

The stairs to her first-floor flat are all at once too steep. She needs to pause to catch her breath on the little half-landing, gasping for air as if she is drowning, her face raised to the ceiling. The bath is suddenly too high to get into without somebody supporting her, so my mother or Plum or one of my nan's female neighbors—and all of her neighbors are female—has to be there to help her in and out of the water. And the well-meaning bureaucrats of terminal illness are suddenly all knocking at her front door.

There is a cheerful district nurse who organizes a social worker, meals on wheels once a day and a scarred metal air tank that stands guard by my nan's favorite chair.

My nan wants to please the district nurse, just as she always wants to please everyone, but the little white flat is her home and although she knows these people are just trying to be helpful, she does not approve of the commode provided by the social worker ("I'm not doing my business in that, dear, thanks all the same"), the fetid meals on wheels are left untouched ("I'll just have a bit of toast, sweetheart") and the air tank makes no difference at all to her fits of terrible breathlessness ("I think it's empty, love").

But she carries on. She meets her old female friends for coffee and cake and talk, and the talk, the human connection, the human thing, is the point of those meetings. She comes to my mother's house for lunch on Sunday, she makes her daily trips to the local shops for the tiny supplies of white bread and "a nice bit of ham" that she seems to live on, plus the river of tea and the biscuit mountain.

When she starts to feel uncertain on her feet, the social worker kindly produces a walking stick. My nan rolls her eyes that it has come to this, and brandishes her walking stick in imitation of a doddery old pensioner, which is pretty funny coming from her at this time.

"Ooh, I remember the good old days," she jeers, waving her walking stick, and we all laugh, even the social worker.

My nan faces cancer in exactly the same way that she has faced life—with good grace, with endless stoicism, with quiet humor.

As she would say herself, she doesn't like to make a fuss.

Despite the nagging pain in her side from the tumor and despite the desperate battles for breath, for a while life seems to go on in the same old way. There are trips to the shops in the morning, some gentle housework in the afternoon and nights spent watching television, her favored programs circled in shaky blue ballpoint in the newspaper's TV guide, forever tugging at my heart.

But in the middle of all this ordinary life, I become aware that something extraordinary is happening. The people who love my nan show that they are ready to walk though fire for her.

My mother and my father are there, of course, there every day, although rarely at the same time, and there are countless visits from elderly ladies who live in the nearby flats or who know my nan from the old neighborhood, the old house where my dad grew up, the *Oranges for Christmas* house, friends from the old life before children grew and husbands died and busy specialists said there was nothing that they could do.

Then there is Plum. Among my parents and the elderly friends, there is this awkward girl who has somehow formed a real bond with my grandmother. Enduring endless hours on trains to and from Bansted, night after night Plum sits with my nan watching the programs that have been circled in the TV guide and selections from her personal collection of wrestling videos featuring The Slab in all his large-breasted glory.

Plum holds my nan's hand, strokes her forehead and brushes her thin, silver hair, as if this old woman is the most precious thing on the planet.

The district nurse and the social worker look in once a week, but I do not know how we would cope if my nan didn't inspire so much affection in the people whose lives she has touched. If we had to rely on the kindness of the local council, everything would be lost.

Because someone has to be with my nan all the time now. It's just too dangerous for her to be alone. We realize that she can lose consciousness at any moment. My nan still calls it "falling asleep," but the doctor who comes around says these fainting spells are blackouts caused by a lack of oxygen to the brain.

One night I watch as my nan's eyes close while she is staring at the news, without her usual running commentary of "ridiculous" and "disgusting."

Her head suddenly drops, her mouth falls open and she pitches forward toward the little fireplace. Before I can move, Plum catches my nan, as Plum has caught her before, and very gently eases her back into her chair.

And after a while it becomes what we think of as normal, an unremarked-upon part of our lives, these blackouts that my nan waves away as nothing that a good night's sleep couldn't cure.

The staff room of Churchill's International Language School is empty. It's still early. There are a couple of students sneaking a joint down on Oxford Street but nobody is upstairs yet. I dump my shoulder bag on top of the coffee table, and a yellow flyer is lifted up by a gust of wind. The flyer is not one of ours. I pick it up and read it.

Dream Machine.
Cleaning your work place the old-fashioned way—
on hands and knees

There's a line drawing of what looks like a fifties housewife with a feather duster, both sexy and domestic, like Samantha in *Bewitched,* and below that there are two telephone numbers. One is an out-of-town number, the other for a mobile. I recognize both of them.

I can hear the sound of her vacuum cleaner across the corridor in Lisa Smith's room. She's in there, giving the tatty green carpet what she would call a good going over.

"What's this meant to be?" I say, waving the flyer.

Jackie smiles brightly. "Didn't I tell you? Business is booming. I've been putting flyers all over West One. I thought I'd drop a few around here. Even though I've got the job already."

She seems very happy. God knows why.

"Dream Machine," I snort. "You mean *you.* Dream machine— that's you."

Her face falls. "What's the problem? Even if I get some extra work, it's not going to interfere with our class. You don't mind, do you?"

"Why should I mind?"

"I don't know. But you do mind. I can tell. What's wrong?"

What's wrong? I can't say what's wrong.

I know I don't like her working in Churchill's, cleaning our rooms the old-fashioned way, on her hands and knees. I don't want the teachers and the students staring straight through her, as though she is nothing. And yet I don't want her working for the stuck-up snobs in Cork Street or—now that I come to think about it—anybody anywhere else. I don't know what I want. Something more worthy of her than this. I know I don't want her here. Not anymore.

"The whole cleaning thing. I don't know. It's getting me down."

She has a laugh at that. "Getting *you* down? What's it got to do with you? And if it doesn't get me down, why should it bother you? I thought there was nothing wrong with cleaning."

"There's not."

"I thought there was dignity in labor."

"I didn't say that. Come on. I didn't say anything about dignity in labor."

"You told me there was nothing to be ashamed of in doing what I do."

"That's right."

"And yet you are ashamed."

"I'm not. I just want something better for you. Better than cleaning a toilet that Lenny the Lech has recently taken a leak in. Why should I be ashamed?"

"I don't know. But you are."

"That's ridiculous. I just don't see why you have to do it here. The place where I work."

"I have to do it wherever I can. I have to make a living. To pay my bills. Dead simple. I can't rely on any man to keep me, can I?"

"Is that you, Alfie?"

Vanessa is in the doorway. She stares at Jackie. Jackie stares back. I don't know if they recognize each other from that first day at my mother's house. I can't tell.

"*Pardon,*" Vanessa says.

"Come in," Jackie says. "You're not disturbing us."

There's only a few years' difference in their age but they seem like different generations, Jackie in her blue nylon coat,

Vanessa in some little red-and-black number from Agnès B. They look as though they come from different worlds, different lives. And I guess they do.

"I'm looking for Hamish," Vanessa says. "He has some notes for me."

"Hamish is not in yet."

"Okay."

She looks back at Jackie, as if trying to place her.

"Je crois qu'on se connaît?" Jackie says, and I am dumbfounded until I remember that her two A Levels are in Media Studies and French.

"Non," Vanessa says. "I don't think we have met."

Jackie smiles. But she looks as though she wants to argue about something. *"Pourquoi pas?"*

Vanessa hovers uncertainly in the doorway. "I go now, Alfie."

"See you later, Vanessa."

"C'était sympa de faire ta connaissance," Jackie laughs. *"Ne m'oublie pas!"*

"Leave her alone," I tell Jackie when Vanessa has gone. "She hasn't done anything to you."

"Want a bet? She was looking down her nose at me."

"Why would she do that?"

"Because I'm cleaning up after her and all the little snot-nosed bitches like her."

"I'm so glad you're not bitter."

"I'm entitled to be a little bitter. So would you be if you saw the world from down on your hands and knees."

"I thought you boasted about that. In your stupid flyer."

She shakes her head. "It's funny how dirt seems to stick to the people who clean it up. Rather than the people who make it."

She picks up her light little modern vacuum cleaner and heads for the door.

"But I'll tell you something for nothing. I'm not ashamed of myself. I don't feel the need to apologize for making a living any way I can. I thought you'd be pleased about the flyers. I thought you'd be happy that I'm trying to drum up a little extra work to pay my way through college. How naive of me."

"Sorry."

"Forget it."

"The flyer caught me off guard. I don't know. You'll be an undergraduate soon. That's how I think of you."

This is meant to placate her. It doesn't.

"No problem. I'll try to be gone by the time you arrive in the morning. You and all your hot little students. Then you can all pretend that the place was cleaned by magic."

"Don't be so angry."

She turns on me, nearly catching my face with one of the vacuum cleaner's furry attachments.

"Why not? You're the worst kind of snob. You can't clean up by yourself, but you despise the people who do it for you."

"I don't despise you."

"But I embarrass you. Jackie the cleaning lady. Who wants to be a student, as though it's the greatest thing in the world. When it's nothing at all."

"You don't embarrass me, Jackie."

"You don't want to be around me. You don't like the way I talk, the way I dress, the job I do."

"That's not true."

"You felt like sleeping with me the other night. But only because you were drunk."

"I like you. I respect you. I admire you."

I realize that all of this is true. She doesn't believe me.

"Sure you do."

"Come out with me on Saturday night."

"What? Come where?"

"My friend Josh is getting engaged. An old friend. We lost touch for a while but he's invited me to the party. And I'm inviting you."

"I don't know. Plum—I don't know."

"You can't have it both ways, Jackie. You can't hate the world for shutting you out and then hate the world when you're invited in. Stop feeling like a martyr, will you? Do you want to come out with me or not?"

She thinks about it for a moment.

"But what should I wear?" she says.

"Wear what you usually wear," I tell her. "Wear something pretty."

The day comes when my nan can't carry on as normal. The pain is too bad, the breathlessness is too fierce. She is afraid of falling asleep in public, afraid of pitching into the road with no Plum to catch her and ease her back into her favorite chair.

So she stays at home. And then increasingly she stays in bed. There will be no more trips to the shops, no more coffee and cake and talk with her friends. Not now. Perhaps not ever.

I sit with her thinking that she is the one person in the world whose love for me was uncomplicated and unconditional. Everybody else's love was mixed up with other things—what they wanted me to be, what they hoped I could become, their dreams for me.

But my nan just loved me.

Knowing that I am losing her, I take her hand, the bones and veins more visible than they should be, and I stare anxiously at her face, the face that I have loved for a lifetime. Her eyebrows are drawn on all wrong and crooked, and those uncertain pencil marks chew me up inside.

"Are you okay?" I say, asking her the most stupid question in the world, desperate for reassurance.

"I'm lovely," she tells me. "And you're lovely too."

My nan still thinks I'm lovely. And I wonder if she knows me better than everyone else, or not at all.

32

HE LOOKS LIKE THE KIND OF GARDENER who should have his own TV show.

He is tanned and fit, casually funky, his sun-bleached hair pulled back in a ponytail and tied with a yellow elastic band. Inside his New Zealand rugby shirt, his body is lean and hardened by all that pruning, or whatever it is he does.

The funky gardener is wearing well. What is he? Fifty? At the very least, despite those space-age sneakers and a pair of combat shorts with an impressive number of pockets. But he is well preserved and has that kind of genial openness that you find in Aussies and Kiwis, or at least the ones who come over here and enjoy showing off about how easy-going they are compared to all us sour-puss Brits.

My mother and Joyce watch him snip quickly and expertly at the rose bushes.

"Spring's almost here," says the gardener. "Time to get rid of all your unproductive old stems and clear the way for your lovely new shoots." He turns and flashes them a wide, white smile, snipping all the while. "Bish, bash, bosh."

I expect them to set about him with their gardening tools for daring to touch my mum's roses without permission. But they both seem charmed by the handsome gardener.

"What your age?" Joyce asks him.

"Ha ha!" he says. "Ha ha ha!"

"Good money as gardener?" she demands. "You marry?"

Under that tan he is blushing, which makes me think that beyond the slick charm offensive he must be a decent guy. Bastards don't blush, do they? My old man isn't the biggest blusher in the world.

"I notice you're pruning just above the bud," my mother says, restoring some order.

"This young lady's got sharp eyes," he says, and now it's my mum who is laughing and going red. The gardener gets serious. "You always prune just above to control the shape of the bush, Mrs. Budd."

"Not Mrs. Budd," Joyce informs him. "She not married anymore. Divorce come through. Decree absolute. All finish."

"Joyce!"

"She single."

"Well, she's too good-looking to be single for very long," the gardener says.

My mother throws her head back and laughs, having the time of her life.

"Yes," she says, "and too clever to ever get married again."

"Never say never, Mrs. Budd."

"Sandy," says my mother.

"Sandy," says the gardener, savoring it in his mouth. "Sandy."

It shouldn't have worked out like this, but it is my mother who looks as though she has been released from some kind of open prison, with time off for good behavior. And it is my father, the one who made the break for freedom, who looks like the partner who got left, dumped, elbowed.

Now how did that happen?

While my mother has lost weight, done something to her hair and slowly put the pieces of her life back together, finding herself in her garden and in her friendship with Joyce

Chang, my father seems to have unraveled before my eyes. My mother helps Joyce in her garden, watches what she eats, works in her own garden. My father drinks too much, eats rubbish, doesn't work enough. There's a sad bloated look about him. For the first time that I can remember, he looks much older than his years.

Living alone in his tiny rented flat, he seems lost between two lives, the old one with my mother as a family man and the new one with Lena as a born-again mister lover-lover. With both my mother and Lena out of his life, he is neither a family man nor mister lover-lover. He is in a twilight zone of takeout pizzas and rented rooms, living the life of a student although he is almost sixty.

I see him every day at my nan's flat. I watch him talking to my mum about what they should do. The situation seems to change daily. Phrases that meant nothing to us a while ago— words like "housebound" and "bedridden"—are now charged with meaning, coming home to us in all their awful reality.

Can she live here? Should she be moved? What does the doctor think? When will the doctor see her again?

My parents are polite to each other. My father treats my mother with an almost painful formality, as though he is well aware that the manner of his leaving inflicted a terrible wound that will take years to heal. She is far more natural with him, allowing herself to feel frustration or exasperation when they can't decide if it is too soon to start calling hospices or homes, and then blowing her top—in her own sweet-natured, moderate way—because she feels guilty for even thinking about putting my nan into care.

My old man never lets his guard down that far. It's only with me that he allows himself to be irritable.

When my mother has gone I put *The Point of No Return* on the stereo, knowing my nan likes to fall asleep to a bit of music. It's one of the great underrated Sinatra albums, the last thing

Frank recorded for Capitol in September 1961. A lot of Sinatra fans think that *The Point of No Return* was a bit of a throwaway, just a fulfilment of contractual obligations, but there's some timeless stuff on there. "I'll Be Seeing You," "As Time Goes By," "There Will Never Be Another You."

All those songs that, when Sinatra sings, somehow make you feel a little less lonely.

"Does it always have to be Frank bloody Sinatra?" my father says. "Christ. I had eighteen years of this stuff when I was growing up."

"She likes it," I say.

"I know she likes it. I'm just saying that maybe we could put on something else once in a while. Some soul music or something."

"She's eighty-seven," I tell him, ashamed that we are bickering about music while the woman who is my grandmother and his mother is in the next room being eaten up by cancer. "She hasn't got any Bee Gees records. Sorry."

"The Bee Gees are not soul music," says my old man.

"What are they then?"

"A bunch of buck-toothed disco assholes."

"I can tell you're a writer. You've got a real way with words, haven't you?"

"I'm off duty."

"You're always off duty."

When Plum arrives he drives me home in the SLK and I find myself wishing that I could hate him more than I really do. His life is unhappy, and while I believe that he deserves to be punished for walking out on my mother, I wonder if the sad, undergraduate life he is living is not too much.

Does he really deserve all this? The nights alone in rented rooms, the takeout pizzas, the collapsing body, the abiding contempt in my heart?

Just for wanting one more go at getting it right?

• • •

"Did they know Rose?" Jackie asks me as we are leaving my flat.

I turn to look at her. She is wearing some Western designer's idea of a cheongsam. It's midnight blue with red piping, very tight fitting, cut short with a small slit up the side, but she doesn't look anywhere near as tarty as she usually does. In fact, she looks great.

"Did who know Rose?"

"These people we're seeing tonight. The people at the party. Did they know your wife?"

"Josh knew her. He worked with her in Hong Kong. He's another lawyer. Nobody else. Why do you ask?"

"I just want to know if I'm going to be compared to her. To Rose. I want to know if they are all going to be looking at me and saying—oh, she's no Rose, is she? She's not like our Rose."

"Nobody's going to compare you to Rose, okay?"

"Honest?"

"Honest. She was never their Rose. They never knew her. Only Josh. And he's not—he doesn't—oh God. Jackie, shall we just go?"

"How do I look?"

She smoothes the sides of her dress with her hands, and something about the small, insecure gesture tugs at my heart.

"You look—incredible."

"Really?"

"Really. Incredible is exactly the word. Believe me. I know words. I'm an English teacher. Incredible, adjective. Hard to believe, amazing. You really do."

Her smile just beams.

"Thanks."

"Don't mention it."

"I just feel that Rose is this perfect woman and nobody can ever compete with her and nobody can ever be as good as her."

"Jackie—"

"This perfect woman who never said the wrong thing and always knew exactly what to wear and who always looked beautiful."

"How do you know what she looked like? How do you know how she dressed?"

"I've seen enough pictures of her. In your shrine. Sorry, I mean—your flat."

"Look, you don't have to compete with Rose. And nobody's going to compare you to her."

"Really?"

"Really."

Apart from me, I think.

But that's nothing personal.

I've done it to every woman I've met since Rose died.

I just can't stop myself.

I look at them all—Yumi, Hiroko, Vanessa, Olga, Jackie, all of them, even the smart ones, even the beautiful ones, even the incredible ones—and I always think the same thing to myself.

That's not her.

33

SOMEONE BUZZES US UP to the third-floor flat of the house in Notting Hill. We can hear the roar of the party behind the closed front door. Laughter, glasses clinking, everyone speaking at once. I go to knock. Jackie stops me.

"Wait, wait."

"What's wrong?"

"I don't know, Alfie. I mean, I really don't know. What am I doing here? Why am I here? What's the point? Really?"

"To meet my friends," I say. "To have a good time. Okay?"

She shakes her head uncertainly but I go ahead and knock. Nobody answers. I knock louder, longer, and Tamsin opens the door, pretty and friendly, blonde and barefoot, smiling at me as though I have never disgraced myself in this flat, as though I didn't act like a prize dickhead after one Tsingtao too many, as though I am her best friend in the whole wide world. I do like her. There's a generosity of spirit about her that disarms me. We kiss cheeks, squeeze arms, and she turns on Jackie with wonder.

"I *love* your dress," Tamsin says. "Where did you get it? Tian Art? Shanghai Tang?"

"No," Jackie says. "Basildon."

There's a second of silence. Then Tamsin throws back her head and laughs. She thinks Jackie is joking.

"I'll give you the address if you like," Jackie says, smiling uncertainly. "It's near the market. A shop called Suzie Wong. They say Posh Spice went there once. But I don't believe it."

"Come in and meet everyone," Tamsin says, ushering us inside.

The place is packed. Everyone seems to know each other. Champagne flutes are put in our hands, then someone—a woman—gasps with shock at the sight of Tamsin's engagement ring and she is whisked away to display it. There is something overstated about these people. Every twist and turn in a conversation—about property prices, private schools and, above all, work—is greeted with something approaching awe.

Josh is in the middle of the room braying about Tai Chi.

"Taught by this marvelous little Chinaman. Really knows his onions. Damn good for stress. Encourages you to think outside the box, Tai Chi."

Josh begins waving his arms around, champagne sloshing from his flute.

"Oh, I know Tai Chi," says a woman I vaguely recognize. India. From the dinner party. "It's the exercise tape by that big black man."

"That's Tae Bo, darling," somebody says, and they all have a good chuckle about her adorable mistake.

"Tai Chi, Tae Bo, tie-dyed—it's all the same to me!" India chortles, her thin little face creasing with laughter.

"They're so confident," Jackie whispers. "Even when they say something really, really stupid."

I recognize Dan, India's husband, and Jane, the fat, pretty girl from the dinner party, who seems to have lost some weight and gained a man. She nods at me with some coolness. I can't blame her. Dan stares right through me. It's not hostility. I think he probably has the memory banks of a tropical fish.

"Old Josh getting married," says Dan. "How does a woman know when her husband's dead?"

"The sex is the same but you get to use the remote control," says Jackie.

"What's the difference between a girlfriend and a wife?" says Josh.

"Forty-five pounds," says Jackie.

"What's the difference between a boyfriend and a husband?" says Josh.

"Forty-five minutes," says Jackie.

"Bloody funny," says Dan.

We are having a good time, Jackie and I, knocking back our champagne and sort of holding on to each other. The party swirls around us. There is something in the English middle class that reminds me of the Cantonese. It is a kind of glorious indifference. They truly don't care about you. It's not hostility. They just don't give a monkey's. And if that doesn't bother you, it can be quite relaxing to be around them.

Then somebody asks Jackie the standard metropolitan middle-class question, and it all goes out of key.

"And what do you do?"

It's Jane. The fat girl who has started working out, and who looks pretty good now, and who must be feeling pretty good too with her quiet boyfriend in the glasses behind her, his arms around her newly slim waist as if he is afraid of her getting away. And although I know that it is only the standard question on London nights such as this, it still feels as if the question to Jackie has a certain edge, as if Jane is getting her own back on me for not falling for her over the warm, fancy salad.

"What do I do?" Jackie says, and my heart sinks, because we were having such a good time tonight, and I love to see her trading dumb jokes with Josh and Dan and whispering little comments to me on the proceedings and the people and just quietly enjoying herself. Now Jane has gone and spoiled everything. And I once thought she was nice.

"Yes. What do you do—I'm sorry, I've forgotten your name."

"Jackie."

"Jackie," Jane says, as though Jackie is an impossibly exotic name that she has never heard before. Which is a distinct possibility, I suppose.

"I've got my own company," Jackie says.

They are impressed. They all want to be a credit to capitalism. They look at Jackie with new eyes. They are thinking—a dot-com start-up? Or a go-getting little PR company working out of one room in Soho? Or possibly something in the fashion game? The dress *is* rather striking.

"Dream Machine," Jackie says. "That's the name of my company."

"Dream Machine," says Jane, with a grudging respect. "What kind of line are you in?"

"Well," says Jackie. "It's a cleaning service."

I want to stop her while she is ahead, get her to cash in her chips and leave the table, but the champagne and the polite, interested expressions on all the flushed, well-fed faces around her are encouraging her to go further.

"Dream Machine cleans offices all over the West End of London. We've got this line: *cleaning the old-fashioned way—on our hands and knees.*"

"Money in that," Josh says. "Good money, I'll warrant. Get the old bog holes sparkling, mate. Can't beat it, can you? Key to the executive washroom and all that."

"Fab!" India says, as though nobody has ever thought of cleaning offices before in the history of the world.

Jackie smiles her happy, beaming smile, very pleased with herself, and I think she's gotten away with it.

But she hasn't. Jane is still watching her.

"So you've got this—what?—army of Mrs. Mops who go around scrubbing and scouring all over London?"

And I think to myself—I'm so glad I gave you the cold shoulder, you cruel bitch. You were never nice at all. Just overweight and lonely, which is not quite the same as being nice.

"No," Jackie says. "There's just me. Sometimes I get a friend in. If there's extra work. But usually it's just me."

"Oh," Jane says. *"You're* Mrs. Mop."

Then they are all laughing at Jackie, and she can't do what they all do, she can't laugh at herself and make it nothing, defuse the lonely moment, take the sting out of the words with the magic trick of just not caring; her life is too hard for her not to take it seriously, to take everything seriously, so she has to stand there going red while Jane and India and Josh and Dan and Jane's four-eyed boyfriend all cackle with glee.

But then it passes, because I know there is no real harm in these people, except possibly Jane, and soon they are talking about the politics of housework and chore wars and feminism's response to the fact that somebody has to clean toilets, all these half-chewed scraps of public debate that they have picked up from some Sunday tabloid that they skimmed through a red-wine hangover. From here they glide effortlessly into a conversation about how difficult it is to hire someone you can trust to clean your home, but by now Jackie is pulling on my sleeve, her lovely face still burning.

"I want to leave."

"You can't leave."

"Why not?"

"Because then they win."

"They win anyway. They always win."

We stay. But the night has gone flat for both of us. She makes half-hearted conversation only with people who approach her first. I retreat with her to a corner and make small talk about the prints on the wall, Tamsin's ring, any rubbish that comes into my head. Just before we leave, when she goes off to the toilet, Josh pulls me to one side.

"I like her," he says. "She's nice."

"I like her too."

"But, my dear old Alfie, when are you going to get yourself a proper woman?"

"What does that mean? A proper woman?"

"It's always—I don't know—someone *inappropriate*. Your little harem of foreign girls. Very nice and all that. A different flavor for every day of the week. I'm not knocking it, mate. I've been in my fair share of foreign parts too, as you well know. But you cannot be serious, man. Not if you think you can make the hot and spicy stuff last a lifetime. It's *inappropriate*. And now Mrs. Mop and her tickling stick."

"Don't call her that."

"Sorry. But, come on, Alfie. When are you going to get real? She's no Rose, is she?"

"I think Rose would have liked her. I think Rose would have thought she was funny and bright."

"Oh, she's horny enough, in an obvious sort of way. She is definitely wise to the rise in your Levis."

"I wouldn't know."

"But what's so admirable about cleaning floors for a living? I mean, just because you're poor, it doesn't make you a good person, does it?"

"She's bringing up a kid alone. A girl. Twelve years old. I think anyone who does that has got some guts."

"She's got a child? Then I think you're the one with guts, Alfie. I wouldn't go out with someone who was dragging around a reminder of the man that came before me. If you'll pardon the expression." He raises his champagne glass in mock salute. "You're a better man than me."

"I never doubted it, Josh."

We laugh, but there is no warmth or humor in our laughter, and I wonder what I am doing in this place, with these people. Is it because I don't have anywhere else to go? Or do I secretly want to join them, to be able to laugh that easily and chat that mindlessly and care so little about everything under the sun?

Perhaps I shouldn't be so scared of caring. Perhaps that has been my problem.

"What do you call it when a woman is paralyzed from the waist down?" says Dan.

"Marriage," says Josh, and the room roars as Jackie and I leave the apartment.

She is silent in the back of the black cab on the way to Liverpool Street.

"I thought you were the best-looking woman there," I say. "And the smartest."

"Me too. So why do I feel so bad?"

I can't answer that.

And I watch her back as she walks down the platform and gets on the train for the long ride out into Essex. She doesn't turn around. But just as I am about to walk away, she sticks her head out of the window and waves, smiling, as if to say: don't worry, they can't hurt me for long, it's going to be okay in the end.

She's brave. She is. That's exactly the word. Jackie is a brave woman.

Ah, I think to myself.

That could be her.

34

SOMETIMES I THINK THAT THE DEAD live in dreams. Heaven, the afterlife, the next world, whatever you want to call it—it's all in our dreams.

After Rose died, I saw her in my dreams. Not often. Only a few times. But those dreams were so real that I will never forget them. They seemed as real as our wedding day, as real as the day we met, as real as the day she died.

And I still don't know what to make of those dreams— were they just the product of loss and imagination and grief? Or was that really her? They didn't feel like something that I had made up. They felt far more real than most of the waking days of my life.

In the dream that haunts me most of all, she was walking by this playing field called South Green near the streets where she was a little girl. Everything was exactly as I remembered it— Rose, South Green, the little string of quiet shops on one side of the gently sloping field. What was different was this wall of glass between us. It reached to the sky. It didn't bother Rose, this wall of glass—or me—it didn't stop her smiling that same warm, goofy smile. But it kept us apart, that wall of glass, and when I asked her if she could stay, her face crumpled and she started to cry, shaking her head.

She was happy enough. But she couldn't stay. That made her sad.

And that made me believe that the dead live in our dreams.

Take Frank Sinatra. If you want to visit Sinatra's grave, you have to go to Palm Springs in California, then you go to the Desert Memorial Park cemetery, and you will find that Frank is buried in Area B-8, lot 151.

I've never been. I'm not a big cemetery man. I haven't even been to Rose's grave since the funeral. I don't think it would upset me, being at her graveside, in fact I think I would find it quite soothing, a trip out to that small church on a hill above the suburban neighborhood where she grew up. The reason I don't go is not that it makes me sad or I can't be bothered, it's just that I don't believe she's really there, just as I don't believe that Sinatra—his essence, his spark, the thing that made him the man he was—is in the Desert Memorial Park cemetery in Palm Springs. Sinatra is somewhere else. And so is Rose.

If you want to remember the dead—or rather if you want to see the dead, if you want to meet them, to see them smile, to reassure yourself that they are at peace now—then you have to look inside yourself. That's where you will find them. That's where the dead live.

My nan has started to see the dead in her dreams. What is a little bit scary is that sometimes she is awake when she has these dreams. She doesn't need to sleep to see her remembered dead. They come to her anyway.

To make using the phone a little easier, I buy her this portable job and tap in all her most used numbers. My mum. My dad. Plum. Me. A few of her old ladies. The doctor's office. And the next day she tells me that her husband has programmed the new phone, and wasn't that good of him? My granddad, who has been dead for twelve years.

I don't know what to do. Should I just humor her? Or gently remind her that her husband is long gone? I can't let it go. I am afraid that she will slip away into madness if she can't tell the difference between my grandfather and me.

"Nan," I say. "Do you remember? It was me who put your numbers into the new phone. It wasn't Granddad, was it?"

She stares at me for a long time. Then a dim light seems to switch on somewhere inside her brain and she shakes her head angrily. But I don't know if she thinks that it's her who has got it wrong. Or me.

It is becoming hard for Plum to be around her. My nan chats about brothers who died long ago, she talks about her husband coming to see her, she goes back even further—to her own mother and father, to the daughter who died as a tiny child, my dad's sister, pneumonia, happened all the time back then, a death that gave a lot of emotional clout to the first chapter of *Oranges for Christmas*.

My nan talks about the dead as if they are living, as if they are all still around, and Plum is not quite thirteen, her life has just begun, she has no experience of death, and she doesn't know what to think, what to do. I don't feel so very different from Plum.

"It freaks me out, Alfie. She talks about them as if they're real."

"Maybe they are, Plum. To her. I don't know."

So Plum goes off to catch the last train back to the suburbs, back to Bansted, and I sit with my nan, holding her hand until she falls asleep, although by now sleep can come in the middle of the day or not at all, day and night mean less and less.

We play the old songs on the stereo, Sinatra and Dino and little Sammy in all their pomp and glory, so full of life and love those anthems from the fifties, so full of hope and joy, and the ghosts softly gather around my grandmother's bed, the brothers lost, the husband gone, the dead child, the friends of long ago, her mother and her father, all of them slowly becoming more real than the living.

To my surprise, I find that I am dreading the day when Jackie sits her exam. At first I think it is because she has awakened some long-dormant passion for teaching. But it's far more than that. What she has awakened in me is the quiet pleasure you feel in the company of someone you know and like and enjoy being around.

We sit there with our books, sometimes talking, sometimes saying nothing, sometimes arguing as though writing and writers are the most important thing in the world, and I realize that I have come to treasure every second in her presence. I remember how much I used to love it. Being together.

Jackie is the best of my students. Her mind is sharp, curious, challenging. She works hard, in class and on her own, and although her job means that her days often start early and finish late, she always gets her homework and course work delivered on time.

But she is the first student I have had since my years at the Princess Diana Comprehensive School for Boys to turn up for a lesson with a black eye.

"What happened to you?"

"I walked into something hard and thick."

"A door?"

"My ex-husband."

"Jesus Christ, Jackie, you should go to the police."

"For a domestic? You kidding? The police are not interested in a domestic."

"It's not a domestic. How can it be a domestic? You're not even married anymore."

"Jamie hasn't realized that yet. He's always hanging around. Outside the house. Following me."

"Does he see Plum?"

"On and off. He's more interested in who's sleeping with me than my daughter. Our daughter. I've told him that nobody is sleeping with me. He doesn't believe it."

"He gave you a black eye because he thinks you're sleeping with someone?"

She laughs bitterly. "He's the jealous kind, my ex. Always feels sorry afterward. Says he only did it because he loves me. Because he's crazy with jealousy. He thinks I should be flattered, he does. Flattered to be battered."

"Who does he think you're sleeping with?"

"Well . . ."

Someone rings my front door bell.

"Don't answer that," Jackie tells me.

"It's not him, is it? He's followed you here? He's not jealous. He's nuts."

"Really, Alfie." She seems frightened. I have never seen her frightened before. It infuriates me. I feel so angry with this man. "Don't let him up here."

"I'm not letting him up here."

"Thank God. Just ignore him."

"I'm going down to see him."

"Alfie!"

But I am out of my flat and down the flight of stairs where I can see a broad, shadowy figure on the other side of the frosted glass. I throw back the front door and there he is—an athlete who has run to fat, still packing plenty of muscle although it is now larded with the aftereffects of too much junk food and designer beer. He must have been good-looking once—tall, dark, a little dangerous-looking. Handsome if not exactly pretty, back in the days when he was a boy wonder with a ball. But now life has made him bitter and mean. He looks like the worst kind of bouncer, the kind that actually wants you to step out of line.

Jackie's Jamie.

Before I can open my mouth he has wrapped his hairy fingers around my windpipe and swung me into the street, pushing me backward into a little row of trash cans where I fall flat on my ass, getting stuck in this ridiculous sitting position as Jamie proceeds to whack me around the head with a trash can lid.

The Slab, I think to myself. Didn't I see someone attack The Slab with a trash can lid? Didn't No-Neck Toledo assault The Slab with a trash can lid at SuperSlam '98? What would The Slab do in a situation like this? I can't remember, for the life of me. So I just sit there, covering my head with my hands, my bum pulsating with pain.

"Stay away from my wife, you fucking bastard!" Jamie is screaming at me in the kind of London accent that you so rarely hear in London these days. "Stop giving her all these ideas about going back to fucking college! You with your books and stuff! You're giving her all these ideas! And keep your fucking hands off her!"

The trash can lid pounds down on my arms and shoulders with a flat, metallic sound that has my neighbors leaning out of their windows, although they are not so concerned that they do anything more than watch. Jackie is hanging on to Jamie's back, beating the side of his head with her fists, and I reflect that this is probably hurting him more than me. But I am the one who is being publicly shamed.

"You are so stupid!" Jackie shouts at him. "Teachers don't sleep with their students!"

That's not strictly true, of course, but I am touched by her efforts. I don't know when he would ever have stopped if it wasn't for Jackie.

"Just stay away from her," he says, panting for breath. "And stop making her think that she's something she's not."

Then he is gone and Jackie is helping me to my feet, brushing off the bits of pizza and egg fried rice and takeout curry that have somehow attached themselves to my clothes.

"You asked me what my marriage was like," she says, indicating Jamie as he strides off down the street with his what-the-bleeding-hell-you-looking-at swagger. "That's exactly what it was like."

• • •

They talk about people bravely fighting cancer, but in the end the disease inflicts the ultimate cruelty. It doesn't matter how brave you are. Cancer robs you of yourself.

"This is not me," my nan says, as I help her to the bathroom. "This is not me."

She is in pain, terrible pain, and although for so long she has fought this disease with humor and courage, her life is now narrowing down to a sharp edge of unbearable suffering.

She has never been a woman who is prone to self-pity, despair, fear, all the weak, dark thoughts that can make you jump at shadows. But now she clearly feels that it is becoming all too much, that she is fighting a battle that she can only lose, that her humor and bravery and stoicism are all meaningless because there can only be one ending to this thing.

Cancer has kicked the stuffing out of her. Cancer has stolen her sense of self.

I stand outside the bathroom door waiting for her to emerge. There is still so much that my father and I rely on the women to do—my mum, Plum, Joyce, my nan's old female friends. Even at this late hour, my dad and I never go into the bathroom with her, we never wash her. Even in the midst of the ravages of terminal illness, even with cancer staring us in the face, a kind of modesty prevails. For her sake as well as our own.

But tonight is different. Although she has eaten next to nothing for days, doesn't even drink more than a sparrow's sip of the diluted orange cordial that sits on her bedside table, tonight I hear her moaning shortly after I have helped her into bed and turned out the lights and left her. I hear her moaning as though something unthinkable has happened.

She is wailing when I go into the room, really wailing as if she never knew it could be this bad, but it is soon clear from the smell in the little bedroom that it is not the endless pain of the tumor in her side that is causing her distress. The smell in the room is coming from her bed. This has never happened before. How could I not have seen it coming? And how can I deal with it?

There is only one thing to do. I reasure my nan that it doesn't matter, that this is nothing, although when I pull back the sheets and see that the mess is everywhere—on her nightshirt, the bedclothes, her hands—I am deeply shocked and uncertain if I can cope with this moment, this thing I have to do because there's no one else here to do it.

It is her distress that helps me to do what I must do, it is her humiliation that somehow both steels me and softens me— "Oh, Alfie, it just slipped out of me, oh, this is so embarrassing, oh, look at me, Alfie"—and I am filled with such an overwhelming love for her that dealing with this thing becomes natural.

Not easy. Never easy. But natural.

I help her gently from her bed, telling her that this is nothing at all for us, for her and me, that we can get through it together, we will get through it together, and I take her to the bathroom where I help her out of her soiled nightshirt and into the bath, and I run the hot water, as all the time she cries with embarrassment and shame, and I see my grandmother naked for the first time, and I get soap and water on a washcloth and I softly say all the words of reassurance as I clean her up, as gentle as a mother with her child, just as she once cleaned me.

35

ZENG AND YUMI ARE OUTSIDE THE ENTRANCE
to Churchill's, handing out flyers. They both look a little different today. I suppose they are growing up.

Zeng is in a suit, his usually unkempt hair—"like a dog bit
it," the other Chinese students say—now neat and tidy, slicked
down for his interview this morning at a nearby college. Yumi
has stopped bleaching her hair, gradually reverting to her natural color for her return to Japan, and the beautiful, glossy blackness is starting to streak her blond thatch.

"How did the interview go, Zeng?"

"Going to do MBA from October. Very useful for doing
business in China. But offer dependent on exam results. Need
good English to do MBA."

"You'll get a good enough mark to do your MBA." I turn to
Yumi. "And you've got a new look too."

"Going to work in an office," she says. "Big company in
Tokyo. Can't have yellow hair. Not in Tokyo office. Not ever
again. Blond no more forever."

She hands me a leaflet. At first glance it looks exactly like
one of our college flyers. The border is still made up of all the
flags of the world, the centerpiece is still a clumsy silhouette of
Winston Churchill. But in this one Winnie is holding a joint the
size of a Cornetto rather than his usual stogie.

Come to Churchill's Karaoke
End of term sing-song
Say good-bye to all your friends

Up in the staff room Hamish and Lenny are looking at the same flyer.

"Bloody karaoke," Lenny says. "It's the death of the dancing class. There was a time when the end-of-term do was in a disco."

"Nobody under fifty or over ten says disco anymore, Lenny," I tell him.

"Bit of dirty dancing under the strobe lights," he reminisces, ignoring me. "Up close and personal for the slow numbers. Is that an Evian bottle in your pocket or are you just glad to see me? Lovely, mate. Now it's all karaoke. Standing there like a jerk croaking along to Abba numbers. Following the bouncy ball on the teleprompter. Always some dippy couple tripping along the beach on the little film. Where's the fun in that, mate?"

"The interesting thing about karaoke is that it's popular in countries where expression of emotion is frowned upon," Hamish says. "China. Japan. All of East Asia, really. Social convention means that they can't express themselves openly in everyday life. But they can do it in song at karaoke."

"Whereas if we want to express ourselves in this country," Lenny says, "we can just go into a public toilet and pull our trousers down."

"You going to this, Alfie?" Hamish says.

"I'm not sure."

"Are you kidding?" Lenny says. "This man is legendary among the student body. They all admire his technique with a hand-held."

I think I will pass on Churchill's karaoke, but not for the reasons that Lenny the Lech wants to avoid it. I spent enough time in Hong Kong to have purged myself of the embarrassment factor that makes most of my countrymen squirm in a karaoke bar.

But I suspect that the night will feel like one long good-bye, that it will be an out-of-tune wake for youth and freedom, that we will soon all be blond no more forever.

I watch my class working on all the tenses that can be used to refer to the future. Present simple, future perfect, present continuous, future perfect continuous. Yumi and Zeng. *You go, you meet.* Hiroko and Gen. *You will have traveled, you will have met.* Vanessa and Witold. *I am starting. She is going.* But not Olga, she has gone, dropped out, disappeared into the city with her boyfriend. *Where are you going to go? What are you going to do?*

I realize how much I will miss my students. How much I will miss them all.

They are still coming to my lessons, I still see them every day; in fact with the exam coming up fast, they are attending classes more regularly than they ever have, and if they cut back on anything then it is nights at General Lee's Tasty Tennessee Kitchen or the Eamon de Valera or the Pampas Steak Bar, but already their talk is turning to their new lives. Their time at Churchill's International Language School is almost over. Soon they will go and I will stay. I miss them already.

And I wonder if it will always be this way—another year, another set of faces, on and on forever, a series of hellos and good-byes without end.

You will go, you will meet.

My students are happy. They are talking of going home, of taking degrees here in London, of traveling to faraway lands. They are young and everything is before them, everything is exciting—study and travel and work, nothing is less than a great adventure. But a weight seems to be pushing down on me when I hear them talking about their new lives.

You just get used to someone, and then they leave you.

• • •

"What will it be like?" I ask Jackie. "Your life as a student, I mean. When you're taking your BA, going to the University of Greenwich, all of that. How do you imagine it?"

She is sitting by the window in my flat, packing up her books to leave. The lesson is over. The exam is not far away. Her books are no longer new. The days are getting longer.

"Well, I don't know if I'm going to be a student yet, do I? My place at Greenwich depends on my English result."

"Are you kidding? I never saw anyone work as hard as you do. You'll get your grade. Come on—tell me about life as a student. You must have thought about it."

She laughs.

"Only for the last twelve years or so. I don't know what it will be like. I'll be a lot older than the other students. I've been married, I've got a kid. Most of them probably still get their washing done by their mums. And when they go off to their wild parties, I'll be working. I'll still have to work, you know."

"But you think you'll be happier?"

"I know I'll be happier. I'll be doing what I want to do. I'll be making something of my life. For myself and for my daughter. And it will be interesting. Great writers, great writing, talking about ideas, being around people who care about books, who don't worry about getting above themselves. I can't wait."

I can see her there. I can see her growing into the person she has always wanted to be. I can see her realizing that it's not too late, that she is young enough and smart enough to have another go, another try at getting it right. And she will be good. It's true she will be ten years older than the other students, but she is more than smart enough to stand out in any company; there will be no cheap jibes about Mrs. Mop or cleaning floors, because the rest of them will know all about low-paid casual work, and I can imagine her shining there, really shining, asking good questions, not afraid to put her hand up, waking up the tired teachers, inspiring the good ones, having an essay about Carson McCullers read out in class as all the young boys melt and watch the way her body moves inside her tight clothes. Or perhaps her clothes will be different too.

"I don't want to lose touch," I say, my face burning.

"What?"

"I don't want you to just drift out of my life."

"Drift out of your life?"

"I want to keep in contact. That's all. That's what I'm saying. I don't see why we can't stay in touch."

She places her hand on my arm, and it almost feels like a gesture of pity.

"We'll always be friends," she tells me, and I know that I have lost her before we have even begun.

My grandmother is too sick to stay in the little white flat. Her home just doesn't work anymore. Not for her. The stairs, the bath, the isolation from the rest of us—it is a home for someone who is old, but not for someone who is dying.

If my family were the Changs, this would be easier. Without talking about it, we would move her into a bedroom above the Shanghai Dragon and there we would care for her. But my little family is scattered all over the city, not really a family at all, my father and my mother and myself, all of us living alone, and there is no obvious place for my grandmother to go. There are too many stairs in my mum's house, and not enough space in the rented flats where my dad and I live.

We want to be a family. We really do. But we have left it too late, we have been too distracted by other things. We will never be the Changs now.

"In China big children take care of old parents," I hear Joyce telling my mother. "Here, other way round. Old parents still worry about big children. Everything front to back in this country."

We discuss other options. A home—but my nan is already too ill for a home. A hospice—but we can't bear to take her to some strange place to die. Not yet. Not if there is some other way.

There is always the hospital, but my nan fears that place more than she fears death, or at least she sees them as interchangeable, so for as long as we have other options she will be spared the hospital bed. Although she seems to eat and drink nothing and although she needs twenty-four-hour care, her doctor is happy to keep her out of the hospital, even now, even this late. But I don't know if that reflects his compassion for a dying woman's wishes, or just a lack of hospital beds. It is probably a bit of both.

In the end my mother takes charge, calling a stair-lift company and telling them that they have a job if they can do it immediately.

The stair-lift company must be used to these kinds of desperate calls—for who has a stair lift installed unless they are desperate?—and soon a young workman is laying what looks like railway tracks on the staircase of my mother's home. On top of the railway tracks he fits what looks like an ejector seat, stirring childhood memories of James Bond and pilots bailing out over enemy territory. It seems to be a thing of immense violence, this stair lift, but when the young workman sits in the chair and turns it on, it whirrs into sedate action like the most gentle machine in the world.

And later, when my nan arrives, dressed in her favorite white Marks & Spencer nightdress, the one with tiny red roses all over it, her face pale from all the weeks inside her flat and from the sickness, her body so frail that I fear to touch her, for I am actually afraid that I may break her, we excitedly show her the stair lift, explaining how it will make living here easy, as if she was a child on Christmas Day being given a gift that she is too small to truly appreciate.

My father and I gently help her into the stair lift's chair and suddenly she seems to pitch forward, weak from the tumor and the lack of food and the weeks without moving, and we both spring forward to catch her. This had never crossed our minds, that she might be too ill to use a stair lift.

Then my mum explains how the stair lift works, how you have to move a little lever to make it go and how it stops as soon as you take your hand off the lever, making it impossible to hurt yourself, at least that's the theory, and how there's a little wooden landing newly built at the top of the stairs so that there is not one step to climb, not even one. I do not know how much of this my grandmother takes in. She doesn't look like one of those happy old women that you see in advertisements for stair lifts, all twinkling eyes and sensible cardigans and false teeth gleaming. My nan looks as though she never guessed that her life could be filled with so much pain, so much discomfort, so much of what she would call *aggravation*.

But she smiles for our sakes, even now trying to please us, trying to be a good guest, trying not to make a fuss.

"Lovely," she says. Her ultimate compliment.

Lovely.

Then she tentatively pushes the lever of the stair lift and we all laugh out loud, including my nan, laugh out loud with shock and delight as the gentle machine whirrs into life, slowly lifting my nan up the stairs.

There she goes now, looking like a little old angel ascending to heaven in her white Marks & Spencer nightdress, smiling down on us because this is fun, it really is, and most of all because she doesn't want us to worry about her, and she really doesn't want to make a fuss.

36

This is not me, my nan tells me, again and again. Although I know exactly what she means, I still feel that my grandmother is truly herself in these final hours.

Brave. Selfless. Funny. Concerned about everyone except herself. The old lady I love with all my heart.

"What happened to that girl?"

"What girl, Nan?"

"That nice girl."

She makes me smile. "Oh, *that* nice girl." I think she means Rose. "Rose—she passed away, remember?"

She shakes her head impatiently. "Not Rose. I know about Rose. And not the Japanese one. I know she gave you the elbow. I mean the one with the daughter. The daughter with lovely eyes."

"Jackie?"

"Jackie. You want to hold on to her. She's a good one."

"You're right, Nan. She's a good one."

"I want to see you settled, Alfie. I want to see you settled."

You think that you will watch someone die with something like horror, then you watch them die with nothing but love. Because somehow the horror passes, all the black feelings caused by the thousand unspeakable indignities of cancer, or at least you learn to exist with it all. But the love remains, and it overwhelms the fear and sadness and loss, that terrible sense of loss that is worse than everything.

Day and night mean nothing now so we take shifts. I take over from my father around two in the morning. It must be like this when you have a baby—blinking back the sleep in the middle of the night, struggling to stay awake as you perform your various duties. It would have been something like this for Rose and me, if we had been lucky enough to have our baby son or daughter. Except this is the other end of the story.

I do not believe that my nan is going to die tonight. It's too soon. It will surely go on for a while yet. She doesn't seem to be in enough pain. The pain in her side, that unimaginable pain from the tumor, appears to be easing. She is taking no medication. Her mind is clear. She looks peaceful.

Her hair on the pillow is silver streaked with gold, the result of a quick dye job that my mother gave her to lift her spirits. Her eyebrows are not crooked because my mum has drawn them on. She breathes out, closes her eyes.

I sit in a chair by the side of her bed, dozing off although I am trying not to, slipping in and out of an exhausted sleep.

And then her voice pulls me back.

"Mum and Dad," she says.

"You want—should I get them?"

"My mum and dad."

"Nan?"

"They're here."

"Are you okay? Do you want—"

"Alfie?"

"Here I am."

"Hold my hand, Alfie."

"I've got it."

"You're a good boy." Her chest lifts and she slowly exhales, seeming to let go of the fear, the pain, the longing to stay. "You're trying your best, aren't you? I can see that."

"Nan? Can I get you anything?"

"I don't need anything. But thank you, love."

I can't tell if she is sleeping or not. A light seems to be creeping into the room. It's not night any more. The impenetrable blackness is fading away. But how can it be over so soon?

"I love you, Nan," I say, my voice choking up, my eyes suddenly filling. "I love you so much."

Why didn't I say this to her earlier? Why did I leave it so long? Why haven't I been telling her this all my life?

All those days when I had other things to do. All those times when I had somewhere else to go. And I could have been with her.

Thanking her for loving me.

"It doesn't hurt now," she says, her voice soft and calm.

"That's good."

"Just stay with me."

"I'm here, Nan."

"Stay with me, love."

The school is not so different from the one where I taught, the packs of boys pouring out of the gates instantly identifiable as the toughs or their natural prey, with the great mass in between acting harder than they really are, laughing and taking swipes at each other with their battered backpacks, swaggering with a cockiness that begs to be seen as confidence.

What makes this school different from the Princess Diana is that there are girls here. Their presence changes the atmosphere, charges the air. Some of the girls look like children still, but others are more like grown women, women who are young enough to get away with long hair and short skirts, women who are aware of their power over the roaring, unformed boys who swarm around them. They pass me by at the gates, these girls, some of them raising an eyebrow and smirking, evaluating me and dismissing me in an instant. Then I see her. She is not part of any pack.

"Plum?"

Her face reddens.

"What are you doing here?"

"I've got my car. I'll drive you home."

She walks with me to my car, ignoring the jeers of who's-your-boyfriend, Plumpster? and I-don't-fancy-your-one-much, Plumpster. When we get in the car, I make no move to turn on the ignition.

"Why are you here?"

"I wanted to tell you in person."

"Tell me what?"

"My nan died."

"She died?"

"Early this morning. I didn't want to tell you on the phone. I know she meant a lot to you. And you meant a lot to her."

Plum stares straight ahead, saying nothing. I grope for all the usual consolations.

"She was in a lot of pain toward the end. So we can be glad she doesn't have to suffer anymore. She's at peace now."

Plum says nothing.

"And it was a long life, Plum. One day we will learn to be grateful for her life. Not sad about her death."

"She was the one person . . ."

"Plum? Are you—"

"The one person who I could be myself with. I know my mum wants me to be prettier. Lose weight. Do something about my hair. All that. And my dad wants me to be stronger. Tougher. Harder. Not get pushed around. Stand up for myself. All that." She shakes her head. "And the kids at school all want me to just crawl away and die. Just crawl away and die, Plumpster. But she was the one person who just accepted me. Who didn't care." She laughs. "Who actually seemed to quite like me."

"Your mother loves you. Come on, Plum. You know she does."

"But loving someone's not the same as *liking* them, is it? It's not the same as just accepting them for what they are. Love's all right, I guess. I don't know too much about all that. I'll settle for just being liked."

There's a lot to do.

It's good that there is a lot to do.

Because my grandmother died at home, the police had to come to the house. They were there after the ambulance men, who were not needed because it was too late, and the doctor, who officially confirmed that she was dead, but they came before the undertaker and his assistant, who gently invited us to wait in the living room while they wrapped my grandmother's body and removed it from the house. It seems strange that my nan, after spending so many years living alone in her little white flat, should suddenly provoke this house full of people.

My father and I are spending more time together than we have for years. We register the death together, sitting silently in a waiting room full of happy couples there to register the birth of their babies. Then we go to the undertakers, or the funeral directors as they call themselves these days, and choose the coffin, decide on the number of cars, make arrangements for the funeral.

It's still not done. We go to a florist and order our wreath, choosing a big one from my parents and me rather than three little ones—red roses, my nan's favorite. Then we have to talk to the vicar who will conduct the funeral service and he is cold and sniffy because my nan only went to church for weddings, because she was an old girl who didn't see much point in the church unless it was for a celebration, unless it offered a chance to look and marvel at some young bride in her white dress.

Finally we go to her little white flat. And although we have been gently led through the bureaucracy of death—everyone, apart from the vicar, kind and understanding, taking our credit cards with what looks like a genuinely sympathetic expression, telling us where we need to go next, pointing us to the next stop along the chain—there are no guidelines for what we should do in my grandmother's home.

Within these white walls there is the evidence of a lifetime. Clothes, photographs, records, souvenirs brought back for her from Spain and Greece and Ireland and Hong Kong. My father and I stare at it all helplessly, unable to decide if these things are treasure to be cherished forever or rubbish to be left out for the trashmen.

Her things.

I want to keep them all, but I know that's absurd, impossible. The clothes can go to Oxfam. Perhaps some of the furniture. We decide that I will keep the records, my father can have the photographs, but even that is not simple.

My dad opens an album of ancient black-and-white photographs from before he was born, and although he sees the faces of his mother and his father and his aunts and uncles, their grown-up faces shining through the smiles of when they were children, many of the people in the album are complete strangers to him, people he never met, with names he will never know. Not now.

My grandmother's memories. Nobody else's.

It's too soon to think about Oxfam, too soon to think about throwing anything away. Some other day, perhaps.

For now, I choose one thing to remind me of my nan. It sums her up for me.

It is a bottle of lurid red nail polish called Temptation. On the bottle there is an admonition, a piece of advice, a philosophy. *Nail him,* it says. I think of my nan painting on her Temptation nail polish well into her eighties, and I smile for the first time all day.

Lovely. She was lovely.

Despite the unknown faces, my father seems haunted by the

photographs. And there are many. Albums featuring cartoons of seventies' platform-booted babes on the cover. Shoe boxes full of fading color pictures. Photo books with sleepy English fishing villages on the cover and black-and-white pictures from the forties and fifties inside. Ancient black-and-white photographs, yellow with age, behind heavy slabs of glass, and what seems like chain mail on the back for hanging them up. Countless photos still in the envelopes they were in when they came back from the drugstore.

All those weddings, Bank Holidays, Christmases, birthdays, Sunday afternoons. All those lives.

My father finds a scrapbook. It's a scrapbook about him and his career, his success. It begins with his early stories as a young sportswriter and goes all the way up to *Oranges for Christmas,* when he became the story.

My father looks touched, humbled. No, he looks lost. It is clear he never knew this scrapbook existed, never knew that his mother was so proud of him. He seems—I don't know what it is. Ashamed, perhaps. Or alone. Yes, that's it. My father seems alone.

And I can see that you are never truly alone in this world until both of your parents are dead.

37

WHEN I GET BACK from my grandmother's cremation, there's a message from Jackie on my mobile, telling me to call her urgently. It's examination day. For my students at Churchill's and for Jackie too. She sounds excited, and I guess it means that she feels a step closer to all of her dreams coming true.

But I am wrong.

"Alfie?"

"You okay? Ready for the exam?"

"I'm not going to take the exam."

"What? Why not?"

"It's Plum."

"What's wrong with her?"

"She's run away from home."

The examination hall for A Level English is in a college near King's Cross.

The place is full of students—nervous students, confident students, students who have already abandoned all hope. And there's Jackie, older than the rest, frightened for different reasons, for grown-up reasons that have nothing to do with getting qualifications or getting ahead, dressed far too formally for someone who is scheduled to take an A Level this afternoon, waiting for me outside the examination room.

Her paper starts at three. She has just under five minutes. But she is not even thinking about that.

"The school called me. They wanted to know where she was. Then I found the message from her on my mobile. She said she had to get away. She's gone, Alfie."

"What about her dad? Friends?"

"She's not with her dad. And there are no friends. Not now your nan's gone."

"I'll find her, okay?" I look up at the clock. It's nearly three. "You have to go inside now. You really do. If you don't, you lose your chance."

"How can I? How can I think about all of that stupid stuff when my daughter's missing?"

"She'll be back. You can't throw it all away."

"I don't care about any of that. The degree, Carson McCullers, poems by sad old men who wouldn't know love if it took a chunk out of their codpiece. This is all my fault. I don't know what I've been thinking about. I don't know what I've been doing with you. Studying emotions in a dramatic extract and all the rest of that old . . . what a pathetic waste of time. I should have been thinking about my girl."

"You do think about your girl. You think about her all the time."

"What's wrong with the life we've got? What's wrong with it? That's what I'd like to know."

"Stop it, will you? Talking like that doesn't help her and it doesn't help you. Go on. Get in there and do your best. I'll find her. She'll be fine. I promise."

"I just want my girl back."

"You'll get her back. Just get in there."

She puts her hands on her hips. "Is there a dog in here? Who do you think you are? Who do you think you're talking to? You're not my husband."

"Go on, Jackie."

She stares at me as if this is somehow all my fault. Me and my books and my cynical friends. Her eyes are shining and her bottom lip is clenched to stop it trembling. But she starts drifting toward the examination room with all the other students, still watching me with a kind of weepy hostility until the door closes behind her.

Then I walk out into the city, looking for Plum, still dressed for a funeral.

I go to Leicester Square, the gaudy, rancid heart of the West End, and wander around looking at the faces of the children huddling in doorways, hanging out in the park, squatting on the street. Plum's not there.

So I walk down Charing Cross Road to the Strand, for some reason a favorite area for homeless kids, and cover its length from the railway station to the Savoy. Lots of teenagers with their sleeping bags in doorways. But no Plum.

I head north, up into Covent Garden. Plenty of young kids on the street, but for some reason only a few obviously homeless, dragging their sleeping bags across the piazza, ignoring the jugglers and the streetbands and the mime artists who wow the tourists and make everybody else feel like slitting their wrists. And I stare at some dopey git whose big selling point is that he doesn't move, he never moves an inch, and I realize that Plum could be anywhere. She doesn't even have to be in London.

My mobile rings. It's Jackie. I tell her there's no news, please don't worry, go back to Bansted and wait for my call.

She wants to help me look for Plum but I persuade her that one of us should be at home, waiting by the phone, in case there's a call. Reluctantly, she agrees.

Naturally—at least it seems natural to me—I want to know how the exam went. Jackie refuses to talk about it. She gets angry when I press her for information, acting as if all that side of her life—wanting to go back to college, caring about books, wanting a degree, thinking about poems and plays and *The Heart Is a Lonely Hunter* as though they were the most important things in the world—is the root of all her problems.

As though you can be punished for your dreams.

When the sun goes down, the city changes.

The office workers go home and the party people pour into the streets of Soho, Covent Garden, Oxford Street. And I can't imagine Plum here, among the designer coffee and the loud laughter and the empty chatter. It's not her.

So I go to the stations, starting off in the east at Liverpool Street, where the trains from Bansted come in, and gradually move across town. London Bridge, King's Cross, Euston. All the big mainline stations. Then out west. Paddington, Victoria. There are pitiful little groups of children with their backpacks and their sleeping bags in every nook and cranny of these giant stations, but I can't tell who is homeless and who is waiting to go home. Later, nearing midnight, it becomes more obvious. The ones who are going home watch the notice board for departures, the ones who are not going home stare at nothing, or warily watch the men in the shadows who eye them up, waiting to make their move. But there is no sign of Plum at the stations.

I am about to call Jackie when I realize that I have missed Saint Pancras, that Victorian Christmas cake of a station next to Euston.

There's no real reason why she should be at Saint Pancras, apart from the fact that its spires and turrets and lancet windows make it look like something out of a fairy tale, a place where everything works out all right in the end. There's no real reason why she should be at Saint Pancras apart from the fact that it's so different from all the rest.

Just like Plum.

Saint Pancras is smaller than the other stations, less inhuman and modern, more the size of a railway station out in the far-flung suburbs in places like Bansted than those soulless, secular cathedrals you get in the city. But she's not here, of course. It's getting very late now and people are running for the last trains. I am about to call it a day, phone Jackie, tell her to call the police, when I see the photo booth.

Next to a filthy pair of sneakers, there's a book. It's the book I gave Plum. *Smell the Fear, He-Bitch* by The Slab. I knock on the side of the photo booth and pull back the curtain. There she is, sound asleep, her hair falling in her face. I say her name and she wakes up.

"Why are you dressed like that?"

"Because of my nan."

"Oh."

"Your mum's really worried about you."

"I couldn't stand it anymore. It was too much. It would be too much for anyone."

"Sadie and Mick. And their little gang."

"It got worse after you came to the school."

"I'm sorry, Plum."

"They kept going on at me. About my old boyfriend. My old, old boyfriend. They said: *'Where did you meet him, Plumpster? Meals on wheels?'* I told them you're a teacher and they had a right old laugh about that. Mick said you looked like a teacher who had lost all his faculties."

"That bastard Mick. I'm not so old."

"I know. You're only middle-aged."

"Thanks, Plum. Thanks a million."

"You're welcome."

"I'm sorry if I made it harder for you. I never meant to."

"I know that. You just wanted to tell me about your nan. I'm glad you did. It's not your fault. If it hadn't been you, it would have been something else. Any excuse. There's always some excuse for that lot."

"So where are you going?"

She shrugs, pushes the hair from her face, and peers out at the departures board as though she actually has a ticket in her pocket.

"I don't know. Anywhere's better than Bansted."

"I'm not so sure about that, you know. You're loved out there. It's your home. And it's not so easy to find another one. Take it from me. Shall we go home? Back to your mum?"

She shrugs, pouts, pushes her fringe in front of her face.

"I like it here."

"You like this photo booth?"

"Yeah."

"It's a comfortable photo booth, is it?"

"It's all right."

"Really?"

"As photo booths go. Nothing special. Stop going on at me."

I pick up her book. "Still a fan of The Slab, are you?"

" 'Course."

"I'm starting to warm to him myself. He's not such a bad role model for a growing girl." I flick through *Smell the Fear, He-Bitch,* nodding sagely. "Do you like what The Slab has to say about doing the human thing?"

"It's okay, I guess. But I'm more of a fan of the way he elbow-smashes bad people in the cake hole."

"Right, right. Well, what would The Slab do at a time like this?"

"How do you mean?"

"If he was getting picked on. What would the old Slab do? Would he run away and sleep in a photo booth? Or would he stand and face the creeps who are bullying him?"

"Come on. I'm not The Slab, am I? I'm just a fat loser. He's more like a superman. That's what makes him special."

"I think you're tougher than he is, myself. I think you are stronger, better, braver."

"You're crazy."

"You've put up with a lot of crap in your life. Your parents breaking up. All the trouble between them after the split. Your mum working so hard to support the pair of you. Mick and Sadie and the little creeps who follow them around. You couldn't have gotten through all that if you were a coward. And I think you've got more guts than Mick and Sadie put together. All bullies are cowards. I reckon you're a lot nicer too."

"Nice doesn't get you very far. Nice gets walked all over. Nice gets you a smack in the chops."

"I don't know. Look at my grandmother. We didn't love her because she could beat up all the other pensioners, did we? Because she could elbow-smash her way to the front at the bus stop? That wasn't why we loved her, was it?"

"I guess not. So how was the—what do you call it?—burial?"

"Cremation. It was okay. As good as it could be. Lots of people. Faces I hadn't seen for years. Like a dream, really, all those faces I remembered gathered in one place. And people I didn't know. Neighbors, friends. So many friends, she had, Plum. There was so much real affection for her. Love, even. She inspired a lot of love. And there were flowers everywhere. And 'Abide with Me.' Her favorite hymn. And 'One for My Baby.' By Sinatra."

"It's so depressing, all that old music."

"What do you expect at a funeral? *I'm horny, horny, horny tonight?* It worked. You should have been there. You would have seen."

"I don't like funerals."

"It's a way of saying good-bye."

"I don't like good-byes."

"Nobody does. But that's life. A series of hellos and good-byes." I think of pushing hands in the park with George Chang, of learning to move with the changes that are heading your way, like them or not, of finding the courage to become what you need to become. "Look, Plum, you think you're the only person who ever felt the way you're feeling now. But plenty of people do. It's much more normal to be afraid and lonely and sad than it is to be like Mick or Sadie. Or The Slab. You're not the freak. They are. I know it seems like these days are never going to end. But they will." I brush her hair back from her face and see the tears. "What's wrong, Plum? What is it?"

"I miss her. I miss your nan."

"I miss her too. And you were great with her. You really made her life better. The way you took care of her—not many people of your age could have done that. Not many people of my age. You can be proud of that."

"I only did it because I liked her. She was funny." Plum smiles for the first time. "This little old lady who liked sports-entertainment wrestling. She was cool."

"She liked you too. She saw you in a way that Mick and Sadie and these other creeps never will. She saw you the way you really are."

"Is that really what you think? Or are you just trying to get me out of this photo booth?"

"That's really what I think. Listen, shall we go home to your mum?"

"Can we sit here for just a little bit? Just sit here quietly?"

"As long as you like, Plum."

38

THIS NEW ZEALAND GARDENER seems to have taken a shine to my mother. Between you and me, I wonder what Julian—what kind of name is that for a Kiwi who is certainly no fruit?—really has on his mind when he talks to her about bird control and forking borders.

Bird control and forking borders, I think, watching the pair of them out back.

I've got your number, mate.

As late spring slowly gives way to summer, Julian is always complimenting my mum on her knowledge of the garden, her expertise in mulching, her way with the tasks of the season.

It's true that she does know a lot about plants, flowers and all that stuff. And Julian is very respectful. I'll give that to him. If my mum is sitting in the kitchen, drinking tea with Joyce or me, Julian will not come into the room without knocking first. We will be sitting at the kitchen table and there will be this shy little knock on a door that's already open. And then there's Julian standing in the doorway, his suntanned body bulging out of his black rugby shirt and a dopey expression on his face, staring at my mum.

"Is this guy coming on to you?" I demand one day when my mother and I are alone. "This guy Julian?"

My mother laughs like a teenager.

"Julian? Coming on to me? What does that mean? Is it the same as making eyes at someone?"

"You know exactly what it means, Mum. You know more teen lingo than I ever will. Thanks to Nelson Mandela. And your kids."

"Of course he's not coming on to me. I talk to him for hours. About the garden."

"He looks at you."

"What?" She's enjoying this.

"As if he *fancies* you or something."

And I am both happy and appalled. I am glad that my mother has not shut herself away from the world. But I can't pretend that I relish the idea of her going out on dates, or of some rugged old Kiwi roughly sinking his fingers into her top soil.

"Has he asked you out or anything?"

"Asked me out? You mean, to dinner or the cinema or something like that?"

"Yes."

"Not yet."

"Not yet? But you think he might? You think he might get around to it?"

"Well, I don't know."

"But if you say *not yet,* that implies that it's going to happen, doesn't it?"

"I suppose so, darling."

"I've seen him looking at you, Mum. Jesus Christ." Is that a hoe in his combat trousers or is he just glad to see her? "I think he's definitely going to get around to it."

My mother reaches across the table and touches my hand. She is not laughing at me anymore. She is sort of smiling, very gently.

"Don't worry, darling," she says. "I'm over all that."

She doesn't mean that she's over going out to dinner or going to the cinema. She means she's over sex, romance, relationships and all that. I'm not so sure.

The older I get, and the more I think about it, the more I realize that we are never over all that.

My father's little rented flat feels like a place where a man lives alone. There's no sense of two lives mixed and shared. There are no traces left of Lena.

I go around to see him once a week these days. The flat is a bit small to hang out in, so we usually go around the corner to a little Chinese restaurant where they really know how to cook Peking duck and where the waiters all have these strong London accents.

I look at these kids with their faces from China and their voices from Finchley, and it feels to me that these days the world is just one place.

My father's flat is not so sad now. I asked him once what had finally gone wrong with him and Lena. He said that she wanted to go out dancing and he wanted to watch the golf on Sky. Now nobody can stop him watching the golf on Sky. It's not much, being able to watch the golf on Sky, perhaps not what he was hoping, but it must count for something.

He can play his music as loud as he likes. Marvin Gaye and Tammi Terrell. Smokey Robinson and the Miracles. Diana Ross and the Supremes. There's nobody left to tell him that he's out of time. "Baby, baby, baby—where did our love go?" He still loves all of that. ·

And he spends hours sorting through the boxes of photographs that we found at my grandmother's flat.

All those shoe boxes, those cracked and torn photo albums from the forties and fifties with English fishing villages on the front, the ones from the sixties and seventies with drawings of platform-booted babes on the cover.

Some of the faces in these photographs are still a mystery. Some of them are as familiar as his own face. But those familiar faces have their own special mystery. And he stares at them for a long time, wondering about them, and wondering how he got from those crowded streets in the East End to this quiet place on a green hill in north London. Quiet apart from Smokey Robinson and the Supremes.

He is not writing. He still hasn't got around to that. But as I watch him surrounded by all those memories of his parents and the house where he grew up, all the bits and pieces of a life that is long gone but somehow sticks with him, a life that will never really leave him, I think that perhaps he will start writing again very soon.

Because my father has realized that if he is going to carry on, then he is going to have to go right back to the very beginning.

As soon as I get to the edge of the park, I see George.

He is completely alone. There are no posers from the great financial houses of the city rambling on about reducing stress and thinking outside the box. No hippies with tofu for brains in bicycle clips and sandals who think they can learn the Tao in two easy lessons. And no me. We have all deserted him. All the big-nosed pinkies with good intentions. He is as alone as the day I first saw him.

In his hand is a double-edged sword, red and white ribbons trailing from its hilt. I stand and watch George Chang practice his weapons form.

He suddenly stands on one leg, passes the sword from one hand to the other behind his back, spins around with impossible speed and grace, brings the sword sweeping down over his head, the red and white ribbons wrapping around his neck for just a second, then drops to his knees, stands again with the sword poised at the throat of an imaginary enemy, and it's as if his movements are all blurring into one fluid movement and the sword is spinning silver in his hands.

And I wish that Plum could see this. I feel that, in some way I don't quite understand, George Chang is what she has been looking for all her life.

The Slab made glorious flesh and blood.

When he has finished I approach him. I feel guilty. Perhaps the rest of them can let their Tai Chi lessons fizzle out with a clear conscience, but I feel bad about it.

"Sorry I haven't seen you for a while, George. I've been so busy. What with the exams and everything."

He nods curtly, but there is no accusation or resentment in the gesture. It's as if my disappearance from the park is only what is to be expected from a big-nosed pinky.

And as I watch him putting his sword in its long leather carry-case, because you can't walk through the streets of north London toting a double-edged sword, I suddenly realize why I wanted to learn Tai Chi from this man. It had little to do with stress management or losing weight or learning to breathe properly. And despite the sense that the act of pushing hands made of my world, my life, my future, it didn't even have much to do with learning to accept change.

I wanted to be like him.

It was as pure as that.

Calm without being passive. Strong without being aggressive. A family man without being a couch potato. A decent heart in a healthy body. Those were the lessons that I wanted George Chang to teach me, because I knew I would never learn them from my real father.

"Busy time for me too," he says, as if reading my mind. "My son and his wife moving out. Many arrangements to make."

I can't believe what I am hearing. If there was one thing I never doubted about the Changs, it was that their little family was unbreakable. And more than anything, I wanted a family just like that. Unbreakable.

"Harold and Doris are leaving the Shanghai Dragon?"

George nods. "My son's wife think too rough around here. Lots of drunks. Making pee-pee in doorways and fighting. Lots of lovely houses, big money, but also some rubbish people. Not a good place to raise children, thinks my son's wife." He nods in the vague direction of suburbia. "Wants to move out to maybe Muswell Hill or Cricklewood. Open their own restaurant. Nice new schools for Diana and William. Nobody making pee-pee in doorways or threatening to punch you in the cake hole."

I am stunned. "And Harold is going along with all this, is he? Muswell Hill and new schools for the kids? Leaving the Shanghai Dragon? He just agrees to the lot of it, does he?"

"What can he do? She's his wife. Has to listen to her. Not in China anymore."

"But this is so hard for you, George. You and Joyce. Not just because of all the extra work. Not just because you'll miss the children. It's your family that's being broken up."

"Families change. My wife and I, we have to understand. My son, his wife, their children—that's a new family. A family comes apart and then comes together as something else. Muswell Hill—I don't know. Never been. Hear it's nice place. I like it here just fine. But maybe it's a good idea for them. And their family."

George Chang stares beyond the trees, as if thinking about the clean streets of Muswell Hill and Chinese restaurants where no drunk ever threatens to punch you in the cake hole. A future he can't quite imagine. Then he turns back to me and smiles.

"That's the funny thing about family," he says. "Even the best family is not set in stone."

Churchill's karaoke is in a small rented room in the back of a Japanese restaurant in Soho.

My students all pile into this tiny box with no windows as the man who runs the restaurant, who is not Japanese but Cantonese, hooks up the karaoke machine. The Chinese and Japanese students devour the song menus, Yumi and Hiroko and Gen and Zeng, looking for the songs they want to sing, while the rest of us, Witold and Vanessa and Astrud and Imran, Hamish and Lenny and myself, order drinks and wonder how we can get through this thing as painlessly as possible. We glance at the song menu. We are in a universe where Take That are considered golden oldies.

Yumi and Hiroko and Gen are delighted with the menu, because it is full of Japanese favorites, but Zeng is bitterly disappointed that there are no Chinese standards, even though the owner is Cantonese. He sees this as a national humiliation, on a par with the Opium War, but cheers up after a while and sings a spirited version of "Do It to Me One More Time," which we all agree is better than Britney's original.

The Japanese, that exquisitely reserved tribe, sing without any shyness at all, and I see that Hamish is right: karaoke is an outlet for emotion in a society where emotions are not encouraged to spill out all over the place, a society on the other side of the planet where they still expect their people to maintain a stiff upper lip.

Yumi has a sweet strong voice, and although Hiroko doesn't sing so well, she puts a lot of emotion into it and is reluctant to relinquish the microphone. In the end it has to be pried out of her hands. Yumi and Hiroko both sing the same sweet song, "Can You Celebrate?" by Namie Amuro.

"Japanese Madonna," Yumi tells me.

"Very popular for wedding," says Hiroko.

Those of us who are not Japanese or Chinese can't match that East Asian total lack of inhibition at the mike, but after an ensemble version of Abba's "Knowing Me, Knowing You" we loosen up a little. Lenny does a spirited if grotesque version of Rod Stewart's "Do Ya Think I'm Sexy?" and Hamish performs such a moving version of Bronski Beat's "Small-town Boy" that even Lenny the Lech listens in respectful silence. Then it is my turn.

I usually stick to Elvis at the karaoke. With Elvis, you can sink into this mock-trembling baritone and warble your way through "Can't Help Falling in Love" or "Always on My Mind" or "Love Me Tender" without feeling like a complete idiot. Elvis is easy.

But today I go for a touch of Sinatra, the one where the guy is in a bar that is just about to close, and he has a story that he desperately needs to share. "One for My Baby."

> *You'd never know it*
> *But, buddy, I'm a kind of poet.*

It's a line that always reminds me of my dream, that dream I had in some other lifetime to try to make my small mark upon this world. To do what my father had done before me. To be a writer. Long ago and far away, that was my dream.

No, I think to myself, looking at all the shining faces of my students. That wasn't a dream.

That was a plan.

Jackie sails through her exam. Grade A. She has her place at a university. And I am proud of her and sad all at the same time. She doesn't need me anymore.

She wants to take me out to dinner to celebrate, and I tell her that I'll buy her dinner at the Shanghai Dragon. But she says that this one is on her and she wants to go somewhere in the center of town, this little Italian restaurant in Covent Garden, where she has heard they have live music. When we get there the live music turns out to be a problem. There's only an accordion, two guitars and a middle-aged singer, but they perform with the volume turned up to eleven.

The band wanders among the red-and-white-check tablecloths belting out "Volare," "In Napoli" and "That's Amore," and you can hardly hear yourself think. But it's one of those nights when the niggling little details can't spoil it for you.

Jackie has gotten her exam. Her dream is intact.

"What happens now?" I say. Shout, really.

"I'm winding up Dream Machine," she shouts back. "I figure I've spent enough time on my knees. When term starts I'll find some part-time job that doesn't get in the way of my studies. Then I'll get my degree." She raises her glass of red wine. "And then I'll live happily ever after."

"When will I see you again?"

She shakes her head, and at first I think she hasn't heard me. But she has heard me all right.

The band approaches our table, bows and immediately starts banging out an old Dean Martin number, "Return to Me," although the singer is singing *"Ritorna-me."* Jackie and I just stare at each other. It's too loud to talk anymore. Then she starts to laugh, just throws back her lovely head and laughs in that way she has, and soon I'm laughing too, but I still want the band to stop.

"Please, boys," I say. "She's my student. I'm her teacher. Please respect the sanctity of the student-teacher relationship. Knock it off, okay? Boys?"

But they don't care. They keep on playing "Return to Me" as if we were lovers. No, not lovers.

It's more than that. As if we were together.

"WHEN WILL I SEE YOU AGAIN?" I bellow.

But the band has suddenly stopped playing.

And I find I am shouting my head off in a restaurant that is completely silent.

39

"WINE, WOMEN AND WEED," Josh sighs, as we wait for our flight to Amsterdam to start boarding. "Hash cafés. Red lights. Blue movies. One last adventure before I settle down with my beautiful new wife."

For Josh's stag party in Amsterdam, we meet at the British Airways check-in desk late on Friday afternoon, Josh and me and around a dozen of his friends from work, all of them still in their suits from a day in the office and jabbering with nervous excitement about spending a night in old Amsterdam.

It is only a forty-minute flight from London to Schiphol Airport and soon we are checked into our hotel and wandering the tree-lined canals with tall town houses reflected in the water, the compact streets full of bicycles, the sickly sweet smell of hashish and marijuana drifting from the coffee shops.

At first it is all quite sedate. Josh has booked a big table at a good Indonesian restaurant and we eat dinner there. His friends are loud but friendly, not the drooling go-getting morons that I was fearing, and the mood as we head into the night is almost what the Dutch call *gezellig*. Cosy.

But after dinner it starts to go downhill, and it's not cosy at all.

"Wait until you see this place, Alfie," Josh tells me as we flag down a few taxis. "Tonight you are going to be fucked blind, old sport."

"That's a good thing, is it? Where exactly are we going?" I am starting to get a bad feeling about all this.

"You'll see," he laughs.

Our destination is a gabled town house in a quiet street lined with elm trees. Large houseboats are moored on the canal. The only sounds are the bells of distant bicycles. We are a long way from the noise and the girls in windows and the drunken crowds of the red-light district. But the two burly men in black tie outside the door of the town house suggest we are not so far away after all.

"Gentlemen," they say, seeming to take it all in at once—our clothes, our degree of inebriation, our credit card limits. "Welcome."

We pay 150 guilders just to get through the door. Around fifty quid. The place is enormous. This must have been a family home at one time. Now it is something else. Not a family home at all.

A smooth middle-aged man, also in black tie, gives us a little pep talk about what it will cost us to take one of the girls up to one of the rooms.

"Josh," I say, tugging at his sleeve. "This isn't a bar. It's a knocking shop."

"Oh, don't be such a prude," he tells me. "Don't worry, Alfie. I'll pay your way."

"But I don't want—"

"Just shut up and enjoy yourself, will you? For my sake if not your own. Give me a break, Alfie. I'm getting married next week. Be happy for me, will you? It's the most important day of any young man's life. My stag night."

We go into what looks like a Victorian drawing room. Lots of chintz. Big drapes over the shuttered windows. Plenty of large, soft sofas where businessmen are talking to young women with extremely short dresses, lots of makeup and faces that look as though they have been carved out of granite.

What makes the room seem slightly less like a Victorian drawing room is that there is a bar at one end where a large black man with a shaven head regards us without emotion. During our pep talk at the door we were told that we were entitled to a few free drinks. The drinks are now lined up before us while the young women with faces carved out of granite smile at our little drunken group, casting their bait.

We grin back, sheepish and flattered, as if it's our personal charm that has gotten us in with these young women, and soon they are all over us like a skin allergy, most of them bottle blond but with the occasional Indian or East Asian or black girl in with the mix. They all order champagne. It is overpriced and cold. Just like the women.

I see from the menu that a bottle of champagne and an hour upstairs with one of the girls is exactly the same price. Five hundred and fifty guilders. More than £200. The friends of Josh start waving around their credit cards.

There's a tall young black woman sitting next to me, her long legs crossed, blowing cigarette smoke into my face and making labored small talk.

"What hotel you stay at?" she says, the whore's equivalent of *what's your star sign?*

I smile politely, and turn to Josh.

"I don't want to spoil the party," I say.

"Then don't."

"This is really not for me."

"Forget about your pathetic teacher's salary tonight, Alfie," Josh says and sighs, lighting up a cigar, the stone-faced blonde on his arm staring blankly at me. "This one's on me." He leans across me, addresses my companion. "You'll give my friend a good time tonight, won't you, sweetheart?"

The black girl smiles without humor or warmth, as if she could eat Josh for breakfast, chopped up and sprinkled over her muesli. He doesn't notice. Or he doesn't care. He clamps his cigar between his teeth and wraps one arm around me and another round his tombstone-faced tart.

"How can you tell if your wife is dead, Alfie?"

"I don't know."

"The sex is the same but the dishes pile up. How's Mrs. Mop?"

"You know what? You really are a funny guy."

"Is she—you know—still spending a lot of time down on all fours? Getting her fingers dirty? Going where no normal woman dares go?"

"I wonder why you hate her so much."

"I don't hate her, old sport. I don't even know her." He puffs expansively on his cigar. "Can't honestly say I want to. You're not really bringing her to the wedding, are you?"

"But she's just like you, Josh."

"I don't think so."

"All she wants is to change her life. All she wants is to end up somewhere better than where she started out from." I raise my beer in salute. "The same as you, old sport."

Even under the dim lighting of the Victorian drawing room, his face seems to darken. "What do you mean, old fucking sport?"

"You changed your life, didn't you? You put yourself through charm school. You put on airs and graces that you never had. You come on as though you're Prince Charles. And not just another kid with no dad from some little suburb."

He looks as though he could hit me or burst into tears. Or perhaps both.

"Why don't you get out of my life, Alfie? I don't even know why I invited you here. God knows, I knew I'd have to pay for you."

"You've got nothing to be ashamed of, Josh. There's nothing wrong with what you did." And I really mean it. The thing I like most about Josh is the thing that he despises about himself. "You wanted to better yourself. To change your life. Just like Jackie."

"You know I fucked her, don't you?"

This makes me laugh out loud. "I don't think so, Josh. When did that happen? When I went to the bathroom at your engagement party? I know you're a bit quick, but this is ridiculous."

He shakes his head impatiently. Our two hardened prostitutes are looking at each other, starting to get a little concerned.

"Not Jackie," he says. "Rose."

For a moment I can't think. And the moment seems to drag on. I still can't think. What is he telling me?

"My Rose?"

"Your Rose," he snorts. "She wasn't always your Rose, you fucking peasant."

"Don't joke about her. I mean it, Josh."

"I'm not joking, old sport. I'm telling you that I fucked her. Quite a few times. Not that she was very good. Always a bit too keen on the hearts and moonlight, our Rose. Just before you came along with the fucking goo-goo eyes and bunches of flowers and romantic rides on the bloody Star Ferry."

"You're a liar."

"I even fucked her on the day you met her. My flat. Mid-Levels. About six o'clock. Then we caught a cab down to Central for a few drinks at the Mandarin. You didn't know that, did you? Never got around to telling you, did she?" He puffs away at his cigar, its tip flaring red in the gloaming of the knocking shop. "Yeah, we were having a little office fling until you arrived. Didn't last long. A month or so. You did me a favor really, taking her off my hands."

I am off my bar stool and have my hands wrapped around his throat before he can remove the cigar from his mouth.

Then I am shouting at him that he is a liar, even though I know that he is not, and his face is turning red, his eyes burning up at me like the end of his expensive cigar.

Then the large black guy from behind the bar wraps his arms

around me and drags me away, expertly lifting me right off the
ground, pulling me past the stunned faces of the friends of Josh
and the granite-faced girls and the businessmen making small
talk with women who have seen thousands exactly like them.

My feet don't touch the ground until the large black guy
dumps me back on the quiet cobbled street outside the tall town
house.

I walk back to the hotel and check out, catching a cab to the
deserted airport to wait for the first flight home in the morning,
knowing that I will never see Josh again, and that he will always
be wrong about me.

I don't hate it that he slept with her.

I hate it that he didn't love her.

Jackie looks different.

It's more than the way that Zeng and Yumi looked different.
It's more than growing up. It's to do with becoming the someone you always planned to be.

No makeup. That's new. Her hair worn longer, pulled back
in a ponytail, the highlights being allowed to grow out. And she
is dressed in jeans and a short T-shirt. She looks younger, more
casual, less concerned with the image she presents to the world.
But still the same woman. I recognize her in an instant. She
couldn't be anyone else.

I am sitting on a wooden bench facing the college. She is one
of a crowd of students who come down the stone steps of the
building, laughing and talking and toting their books, not a care
to call their own, and then Jackie and some thin young guy with
long hair peel away from the rest of the pack.

My heart seems to fall away as he puts his arm around her
shoulders, as if he has been doing it forever. Then she sees me.

She comes over, the thin young guy with long hair still with
his arm around her, looking uncertainly at her face and then at
me. Maybe his heart is falling away a little bit too.

"How's it going?" I ask her.

"It's going good," she says. We look at each other for a while, neither of us knowing what to say, and then she turns to the guy. *"J'arriverai plus tard,"* she tells him.

"D'accord, j'y serai," says the guy, reluctant to go. Then she smiles at him and he steps back, knowing that whatever my presence means, nothing between them has changed.

"New boyfriend?" I ask her, trying to keep the bad stuff out of my voice.

"Just a friend."

"French guy?"

"Can't keep anything from you, can we? He's in my class. I didn't tell you that I switched courses, did I?"

"No, you didn't tell me anything."

"I meant to phone. Sorry, Alfie. I've been so, so busy."

"I understand."

"I'm not doing English anymore. I've switched to European Studies. It felt right. You know what I mean? It's a different country. Almost a different century. The world's getting smaller all the time."

"How's Plum?"

"She's well. Enjoying school more."

"Still in love with The Slab?"

"I think she's starting to grow out of all that. They change so fast at that age. I think The Slab might one day go the way of Ken and Barbie. How are things at your end?"

"Pretty good, pretty good. Churchill's is just the same. I've got a whole new crowd of students. Nice kids. And I haven't even slept with any of them yet."

"Are you planning to?"

I shake my head. "That's gone the way of Ken and Barbie too. It turned out to be a bit of a dead end, all of that. Always seemed to end in the same place."

"Where was that?"

"Heathrow Airport. But things are good."

"I'm glad."

"Well, that's not strictly true. To be honest, it's a bit lonely at my end."

"Lonely?"

"Yeah. I sort of miss you. And Plum. And just the way we were when we saw each other all the time."

"Oh, Alfie."

"That's why I'm here. I don't want things to change. I know some things have to change. But I don't want to lose any of that. I don't want to lose us."

"You can't stop life happening to you."

"I realize that now. I really do. But shouldn't you hold on to the good things? For as long as you can?"

"Isn't it a little late for you and me? You can't ask me to give this up. Not now that I've gotten this far. I wouldn't be happy. And neither would you."

"I'm not asking you to give anything up. I just want one last chance, Jackie. One last chance to get it right. And I want a family. Some kind of family. It doesn't have to be the old kind of family, okay? It can be the new kind of family. It can be any kind of family. But I want to try for a family of my own. I think it's pretty sad if everyone in the world ends up living alone. It's just too sad."

"What about Rose? You suddenly forget about her?"

"I'll never forget her. And I'll never stop loving her. I've learned that you can honor the past and you can remember the past. You can even love it. But you can't live in it."

"So you're here to claim your future?"

"That's right."

"But it doesn't work like that."

"It doesn't?"

"No. You might be ready to get serious, but I'm not. If you really care about someone, you let them follow their dreams.

And then maybe one day they come back to you. If it's real. If it means anything."

"So you think you might come back to me?"

"We were never really together, were we?"

"Do you think—when you've got your degree and you've met lots of interesting people and you've made friends with some hot young French guys—that you might miss me a little bit?"

"I miss you already."

"Then what's the problem?"

"I don't know. Bad timing."

"That's it? Just bad timing?"

"I've got to go, Alfie."

And she does. I watch her disappear into the crowd of students, all those shining young faces looking forward to the future as though it is their personal property.

She doesn't even look back.

But I don't feel bad. It's strange. My heart seems to weigh nothing at all. I feel something like my old self.

Because I know that even if I never see her again in my life, Jackie has returned to me something that I believed was lost forever.

She has given me back my faith.

And you've got to have a little faith, haven't you?

40

Just over a year later I drop a couple of Hong Kong dollars in a scarred metal slot and pass through the turnstile, joining the crowds waiting for the Star Ferry.

The original cast are all present, if slightly altered in ways that I can't quite define. There are the young Chinese businessmen of Central in their white shirts and dark ties, speaking Cantonese into tiny mobile phones. The office girls with their shining black hair and miniskirts and Prada bags. The old men with their racing papers, frowning as they check the form at Sha Tin and Happy Valley. And me.

Hong Kong has changed too. Not the way it looks, although the way Hong Kong looks is forever changing as land is reclaimed and buildings are demolished and new skyscrapers are raised. It's something in the tropical air. This place just doesn't feel British any more. Hong Kong is a Chinese city now. Brash, confident, unsentimental about the past. It's not my inheritance any longer. If it ever really was.

Yet I love it still. Even if it is not mine to love, I love it. I can't help it.

I go upstairs to the cavernous waiting area and watch the old green-and-white Star Ferry that I am about to catch chunking into the harbor at Tsim Sha Tsui, and I see the soaring steel-and-glass skyline of Central in the distance, the green hills beyond and Victoria Peak looming above it all.

As I walk onto the Star Ferry I get that old feeling—the excitement and sadness mixed. That old feeling of belonging and knowing in your heart that you will never belong.

Soon they are about to pull up the gangway, and I get a feeling of mild panic. I know it's stupid but I wait to see if Rose will make it to the Star Ferry just in time, if she will come running up the gangway just before they raise it, and I know that she will be breathless and beautiful, carrying her large box of legal documents to an office somewhere in Alexandra House.

But of course Rose doesn't appear at the last minute. That's not going to happen. They pull up the gangway without Rose appearing, and I know—know with total certainty for the first time—that I must make the rest of my journey without her.

And then I see her. The young woman in her two-piece business suit. She is just about holding on to a large cardboard box, desperately balancing it on one thigh, trying not to drop it in the middle of the crowded Star Ferry. She is bending forward slightly as she wrestles with the box, her black hair tumbling over her face. I stand up, and for just a moment, it feels like I am addressing a ghost.

"Excuse me? Miss?"

It is only when she looks up at me that I see she is Chinese. And very real. Young, around twenty-five or so, although by now I have known enough Asian women to be aware that their ages are often impossible to guess.

"Do you want to sit down?"

For a second or two she stares at me through her gold-rimmed glasses and then she suddenly smiles, concluding that I am quite harmless.

"Thank you," she says, the accent West Coast American. Educated in the States? Possibly. Although she could have gotten that accent without ever going farther west than Kowloon.

She sits beside me. There's room for both of us if I shuffle up a bit and she perches right on the edge of the aisle seat with the big cardboard box resting across our knees. It is full of documents, files, ledgers.

"You a lawyer?"

"No," she says, still smiling. "I'm an accountant. Well—training. How about you? Tourist?"

"No. I'm a writer."

"Really?"

"Well—trying."

"Trying?"

"I want to write a story about this place. Sell it—I don't know—somewhere. But I know this is the place I want to write about."

She smiles with what looks more like civic pride than politeness.

"So you like Hong Kong?"

"There's nowhere like it in the world. There's never been anywhere like it. There never will be again. It's where all the world meets, isn't it? This is where it all gets mixed up."

"Your first time here?"

"Oh, I've been here before. But it feels like a long time ago now."

Two old Cantonese sailors, stick-thin and impassive, unchanging through the ages, untie the ropes holding us to Kowloon, the tip of the Chinese mainland, and the Star Ferry pulls out into the harbor.

Seven minutes. That's all it takes to get from Kowloon to Hong Kong Island on the Star Ferry. Seven minutes. It always makes me feel a little anxious, that perfect ride, because it is over so quickly. Just seven minutes. There's hardly time to take it all in.

I suppose you just have to make the most of it. Enjoy it while you can.

"Who do you usually write for?" the girl asks me.

"Me? Nobody. Well, myself, I guess. I haven't sold anything yet. And nobody's asked me to write about Hong Kong. It's just something I feel I have to do. You ever get that feeling?"

She laughs. "All the time."

"You've got to have a little faith, haven't you?"

"Oh yes. You've got to have a little faith."

We fall silent and I turn my face to the open window, the fierce tropical heat cooled by the breeze of open water, and I watch the traffic in Hong Kong harbor. The old Chinese junks with their barefoot sailors. A cruise ship as big as a small town. Tugs, dredgers, the police in their motor launches, the newer ferries, painted in louder colors than the low-key white-and-green livery of the Star Ferries.

The Star Ferries feel as though they are part of old Hong Kong, like statues of Queen Victoria and expatriates drinking cocktails on the roof of the China Club and Sunday afternoons spent cruising on the company junk. That lost place, my old Hong Kong, that's where the Star Ferry seems to belong.

But maybe that's wrong, because you can still see them shuttling between Kowloon and Hong Kong, bustling between rest and work, between the past and the future; they are still out there, all the green-and-white sister ships of this one, *Day Star* and *Morning Star* and *Shining Star* and all the rest of them, all the dancing stars of Hong Kong. Still out there.

And I think of my nan, and the souvenirs she kept of other people's holidays, and George Chang, moving by himself on the other side of the world to the silent song inside his head, and my father living alone in his rented flat, going right back to the start. And I think of my mother with the new man in her life, the Kiwi who is definitely no fruit, and Jackie and the French boy who wanted to marry her, and I think of Plum learning to be happy inside her own skin, that lesson we all spend a lifetime learning.

And as I watch that heartbreaking Hong Kong skyline of

glass, silver and gold, I think of my lost wife and the time that will never come again, and that's when I have to turn away from the girl beside me, so that she will not see what is written all over my face.

It's funny. You love something and then one day it's suddenly gone or changed or lost forever. But somehow that doesn't stop your love. Maybe that's how you know it's the real thing. When it doesn't come with conditions and get-out clauses, when it doesn't have a best-by date. When you just give your love and never stop giving it and know that you never will. That's when it is real. That's when they can never touch it or spoil it or take it away from you.

All too soon we are at the other side. It goes so fast, this brief ride. A short, sweet journey that is always over too soon. The girl gets up to leave. We smile at each other and I wonder what she is doing tonight. I know that there will be some handsome young man waiting for her somewhere in this town, and I am happy for her.

"Good luck with the writing," she says. "I'll keep my fingers crossed for you."

"I'd appreciate it."

The girl hefts her big cardboard box in her thin arms, gives me one final smile, and soon she is lost among the impatient throng.

I turn my face to the open window once more. And suddenly I see the two of them moving through the lunchtime crowds of Central. Jackie and Plum.

They are loaded down with their shopping bags, cameras swinging around their necks, laughing together about something.

I smile to myself. When you see them at moments like this, unaware that they are being watched, they always look closer than sisters, and more than mother and daughter. They look like best friends.

There they are now, Jackie and Plum, making their way to meet me where the Star Ferry docks on the other side. They haven't seen me yet. But they will soon. And as I watch their faces move through that great lonely crowd of people who I will never know, as I watch Jackie and Plum until they disappear into the ferry terminal where we have arranged to meet, I wonder how I ever believed that you can have too much love in your life.

Then the Star Ferry is rolling beneath my feet as it is secured to Hong Kong Island, so I join the crowds waiting for the gangway to be lowered, all of us eager to be on our way now, and I can feel a sense of silent anticipation in the air, like someone finally turning for home, or a baby waiting to be born.